BY LIBERTY STOWE

The Vogel Springs Collection

Steady Now
Bottled Up

The Holiday Collection

The Holiday Mixtape
The Holiday Headline

The Holiday Mixtape

LIBERTY STOWE

Dedication

For those who feel like polka dots
in an Ivy League world—
and for the ones who love them exactly
as they are.
Merry Christmas!

Content Warning/Glossary

Hallmark plus spice. Unprotected Sex by two consenting adults. A man so unhinged he may appear possessive at some point, then putty in her hands. Small-town diversity striving to do better. Sarcasm and sometimes sardonic humor not meant to offend, but establish a character's dry wit and cynical or mocking attitude toward a subject. Explicit language at times, and sexually explicit content suitable only for 18 + readers.

Auntie Mame: (film) (1958) Musical Comedy, Starring Rosalind Russell as Mame Dennis, a colorful, eccentric, progressive and independent woman left to care for her nephew when his wealthy father dies. Mame's unconventional way of larger than life living and raising her nephew makes for major life faux pas, incredible adventure, true blue friends and a comedy of errors that lead to perfection in the motion picture as well as a Broadway musical based off everyone's favorite outlandish aunt that launched the iconic Christmas song: "We Need a Little Christmas."

"Tracklist"

1. IT'S BEGINING TO LOOK A LOT LIKE CHRIST-MAS *Bing Crosby*

2. THE CHRISTMAS SONG (MERRY CHRISTMAS TO YOU) *Nat King Cole*

3. WHITE CHRISTMAS – 1947 VERSION *Bing Crosby*

4. HAVE YOURSELF A MERRY LITTLE CHRISTMAS *Judy Garland*

5. WE NEED A LITTLE CHRISTMAS *Angela Lansbury*

6. SILVER BELLS *Dean Martin*

7. O HOLLY NIGHT *Nat King Cole*

8. DANCE OF THE SUGAR PLUM FAIRY *London Philharmonic Orchestra*

9. LAST CHRISTMAS *Wham!*

10. IT'S THE MOST WONDERFUL TIME OF THE YEAR *Andy Williams*

11. CELEBRATE ME HOME *Kenny Loggins*

ONE

Erika w/ a "K"

"Ow! *Fuc*—fish sticks! Archer, that hurt!"

Hopping past my open laptop, nursing my newly stubbed toe, I try not to slip again in my pantyhose.

"Would you calm down and let me see the outfit?"

My work bestie—and only best friend's—sardonic voice grumbles through my laptop speaker. "And it's not 'fish sticks' for the love of God, it's fiddle sticks if you're from 1950. And 'fuck' if you're a normal person."

"I'm policing myself. I don't want to get nervous in the room and cuss like a sailor."

"It's been years, and I can't recall a single time you've delivered a proper F-bomb. I don't think you're capable."

"People do insane things when they get nervous. Okay. Not *people*, but yours truly. You're distracting me and I'm already late."

"I'm waiting to see the second choice, because the first one makes you look like a Sunday School teacher. And you're not late. You can't possibly be. Hell, you got me up at five-thirty to sign off on your wardrobe, when you know—undoubtedly, you'll wear what you planned when you prepped this pitch five months ago."

"I want to look different. This one has to go differently. Better. I want them to see me as an equal and in a new light. This is the one. I can feel it," I yell from my bedroom toward our ongoing Zoom, anchored on the living room coffee table that may have just broken my middle toe.

"Erika. Although I'm known for my patience, there's no commuter in the surrounding Chicago metroplex on their first sip of coffee yet. Now let me see the damn skirt already."

Having raced around my love seat to dodge the first two legs of my coffee table, I sink down past my laptop, bringing my middle finger into a close-up on my camera's view.

"Ah. There she is. She can't say it, but... hey, if actions speak louder than words—"

"Archer." I stand in full view in front of my laptop, staring at my true-blue, who's still in his boxers. "You're not known for your patience. You're known for your persistence. There's a very big difference. How's this one?"

I roll my shoulders back, suck in and stand up straight.

"Hmmm..." The highlights of his frosted, dark brown tips spike downward as his brows knit together, and he tilts his chin lower, motioning for me to turn around.

"What's wrong?"

"I don't know yet. Turn around."

I reluctantly do an about-face, giving my back to our Zoom session. An absurdly long pause goes by.

"Archer?"

"Nope. There's nothing wrong with that. Might not be appropriate for the office, but I wouldn't look away. Is that baby blue or turquoise? No. No, it's peeking through the sheer black netting of your hosiery. That's got to be a vibrant aqua lace. Wow. I always had you pegged as a pink cotton bikini brief girl. At least that's what you had on the last time I saw—"

Twisting my head around, I glance down to my ass where my new skirt choice is tucked in my black panty hose, exposing both butt cheeks to Chicago's biggest womanizing cad.

"Astounding."

I untuck my skirt and turn to face him. "And you said you didn't look that night."

"No. The morning you woke neatly tucked under your covers, fully attired in your cozy pajamas after three Moscow mules and more Dirty Shirley's than an empty stomach could handle, I said 'it was like looking at my sister.' Although I did look, so let's say stepsister. No. That, in combination with the lace I just saw, is giving me half a chub. Cousin. I retract to cousin."

Archer reaches for his French press to pour more coffee. "Now we could say third cousin to keep it—"

"Okay. I'm hanging up now."

"Don't..." He holds up his index finger. "Count to five. Remember... you, me, the world's longest Zoom meeting on the company dime. You can't break our two-and-half-year streak over your surprise choice in underwear, which I must say is a much better choice than either of these outfits."

"You're right. It would be your only hope of a long-term relationship with anything."

"Now I'm hanging up."

"Wait, before you do, may I explain how to do so properly?" Crouching into frame, I raise both eyebrows at Archer. "This is a friendly reminder when you go off-book, or I should say on-book for you, and have a last-minute bootie call that wasn't on the table—"

"Who says it wasn't on the table?"

"Gross. And thus... 'About last night'..."

"Who? Tamera? Yeah. No. I'm not seeing her again. We've already been out twice. She clawed the hell out of my back, and she wasn't hot enough for me to find that enjoyable. That, and she was *really* loud."

"No kidding, Arch! Shutting your laptop doesn't kill the audio! You know the rules. "Muting is our hanging up. You have to mute! I heard everything!"

"Forgive me. I'm just so used to such quiet nights on your end—"

"That's because I mute!"

"That is *not* because you mute. In fact, don't you think a bigger problem in your work life balance is that you haven't had one hiccup of a night where you had to apologize to your best friend for not muting."

"Just for that, I'm leaving my laptop by the TV speaker on the holiday channel's countdown to Christmas, where every night I'll purposely forget to mute and leave you falling asleep to holiday platonic cheer from the world's favorite forgotten TV stars of the late 90s."

"A rundown of your actual bedtime ritual is not an insult or a threat. It's literally what you've been doing since November first. Erika, you've dated one guy in the last three years, and the minute you slept with him you called it quits."

"That's not true. I've been working on my pitch every single night since they offered me the floor, and now I'm going to be late."

"Relax. You'll be fine. You spent all of Thanksgiving break on it. By the time you finished going over and over your mock proposal to the board, we arrived to Friendsgiving just in time for me to savor a dirty martini and half a turkey leg. All the sides were gone."

"That's just it, Archer. It's the holidays. With Christmas around the corner and everyone focused on their break or going home for the holidays, that's all they'll be thinking about."

"Thank God we don't have to."

"What?"

"Home. For the holidays. Thank God it's not our thing."

My gaze drifts for a moment, hearing Archer's words. I'm very aware it's not his thing. I'd never expect anything remotely associated with a family gathering to be in his arsenal. He's never taken a single woman he's dated to meet his parents, or anyone related to him.

Come to think of it... I've never met his parents. Still, I've been so dead set on the winning pitch for this Harmon account that I forgot all about December approaching. And I *love* Christmas. Maybe I should hang up before I turn into Archer.

"Hey, I gotta go. I'm going to go do my hair—"

"With your Power Point presentation playing on your bedroom wall while you mock click the changing slides with your curling iron?"

Archer's voice trails off as I trudge to my bedroom with lead feet. Suddenly the light, nervous energy tingling through me has been replaced with a heavy heart. It's December. It's coming on Christmas...

"Wear the red! It's a power color!" Archer's voice, shouting from my living room coffee table, brings back all the focus I need.

I've got this. I know I do.

"I don't have it. I don't think I can do this."

Archer hands me coffee with a lid from the break room as we walk shoulder to shoulder down the corridor toward the executive offices.

"You changed again."

"Yes. The red had a weird pocket poking out of my hip."

"I should've let you raid my closet. Hot girl in a man's suit—you could say anything in there and they'd nod and smile if you dressed like that." Archer's lips quirk halfway up to one side.

"I don't get it."

"Kim Basinger. *9 1/2 Weeks*? The movie? That scene?"

I blink up at him rapidly.

"Right. Well, it wasn't PG, so. The point is executives love an androgynous look. It's a favorite, spanning multiple generations."

Shaking my head at Archer, I turn from his antics to look toward my destination. The sound of my heels clicking on tile matches my heartrate when I see Sloan and Swartz crowning the opposite end of the hall.

A young man in a suit trails behind them.

"Great. The new sidekick's here for this one." Archer tilts his head toward the eager beaver, making our duo of bosses a trio.

"Have you met him yet?"

"Once, and I'm not a fan of the dangled carrot gunning for my job. This is where I leave you."

"Wait. Do I have anything between my teeth?"

Archer inspects me thoroughly.

"Unfortunately, for the greater male population, no. You do not. What a waste." He pushes me forward as he peels off down a side hallway.

"Go get 'em, tiger. I'll see you in there," Archer calls over his shoulder.

"Erika! Big day today. Was that Archer I saw running for cover? Sloan, let's make a note not to judge her by the company she keeps."

A hand extends in front of me, and another anchors on my back in a patronizing pat. "We can't wait to hear your Harmon proposal." Swartz forces the largest smile his recent Botox injection will allow. His shiny face nods between me and Sloan.

"That a girl. She's going to blow us away there and give her buddy a run for his money," Swartz beams. The sixty-five-year-old's hand is still on the back of my waist.

"There you go, Tom. We might finally get to replace Archer. Kidding..."

I swear to God if this man, who smells like peppermint after scotch for breakfast, expensive shoe leather and some girl's shampoo, pinches my cheek, I'm going to quit on the spot.

"We love the little bastard. Just excited to get some fresh blood on the account with your pitch."

Little bastard. Nice vocabulary Tom Sloan and Erving Swartz. I can't help but wonder how they describe me when I'm not in the room.

I also can't help but melt a little inside. Archer has been so supportive of me getting the floor on this one. I hadn't stopped to think about this being his account. At least, he's the main point on the Harmon account, under the executives.

If I'm successful today... when I nail this pitch, I'm taking on my first account at his level. He never even winced. He just dove in and helped me. When I consider ninety percent of our communication exists through sarcasm—and he left this off the docket? *Awe. My bestie is a good friend.*

"Speaking of fresh blood. Erika, we'd love for you to meet Tate. He's a Princeton man. We snagged him from his program, and we're lucky to have him."

Swartz pushes the distinguished assistant in front of himself. The young grad is handsome, with dark skin, a perfect complexion, and a suit that cost more than my wardrobe. His smile is a dashing display that reaches the twinkle in his dazzling eyes as he firmly shakes my hand.

Do they teach that at Ivy League schools? I can't help but wonder.

That and, if I'd gone there, would I be labeled as a 'Princeton woman'? Maybe these two would've said, 'Princeton gal.' I wouldn't know, as I'm not, in fact, an Ivy Leaguer.

Arch was right. Mr. Princeton is the last thing I need before walking into my proposal.

Go ahead. Say it. Say how you already got your doctorate in the master's program before you finished your bachelor's. This company is so ridiculously competitive.

I tune him out entirely as I smile at the higher ups.

Bells jingle on the conference room door behind Swartz and Sloan.

Christmas bells.

The office doesn't decorate much, not on the executive floor anyway, and it makes me smile to hear them. A warm, serene feeling drapes over me, and I swear, if I wasn't certain the overhead speaker was playing its standard classical music fare, I could almost make out the tune to "It's Beginning to Look a Lot Like Christmas."

One by one, suits file into the conference room prepping for my proposal—and still nothing from my end. I watch as Archer trails behind someone, then looks at me, does a double take, and looks at me again. He waves and points to the men beside me trying to get my attention, his eyes bugging out until I snap back.

"Erika?" Swartz hums my way, one brow cocked higher than the other.

"Yes." *Shit.* I zoned out.

"Anyway, we thought we'd put him straight to work. Tate's got all of your briefs printed for the room, so you should be set."

Tate hands me a thick file folder.

I look down, in what feels like slow motion from a high school 80s movie where someone's lunch tray is about to fall on someone else's head.

Then I see it: My title. My pitch. My handouts for the entire account team, and my name... Erica Amherst. Erica—spelled with a "C"—only my name is Erika with a "K."

Don't ask me why, but it's perhaps one of the most important things in the world to me. And this *fu*—fish sticker misspelled it.

My name!

Four years with a company and they don't even have the common courtesy to spell my name correctly on the biggest pitch of my career?

This is not good. Not good.

It's a sign.

"They didn't mean a permanent break. They just meant... not the Harmon account, and enjoy your holidays."

Archer leans back on my desk and straightens his tear-stained tie. It's practically soaked from me crying into his chest for the last forty-five minutes, which says a lot. Archer doesn't do tears. "I don't understand what happened. I even semi-warned you about the new guy."

"Yes, Archer, as you ducked and ran. You left me there."

"It was your big pitch. You needed—"

"To be able to stand on my own. Well, I did Arch, and just like Hector the Collector in our favorite Shel Silverstein poem... I opened up my trunk, and the people came, they saw... and called it junk."

Hot tears stream down my face, and I begin heaving like a child to catch my breath.

"Time out. This can't be where your *Sidewalk Ends.*"

Oh, but it is.

So much so, I can't even laugh at Archer's Shel Silverstein joke.

"What's the matter with me? How could I fall apart like this?"

"It wasn't that bad. It wasn't good, but it wasn't *that* bad. Okay, it was awful. Like watching a train wreck where only bear cubs survive, and they have nowhere to go once they roll out the windows of the crashed train, and realize they're in some strange, faraway land. Erika with a "K." If you said that once in your intro, you said it seventeen times before everyone got their handout."

"And that's the hill I chose to die on. They misspelled my name."

I drop my head into my hands. "And did you see Swartz step out to take a call? That left two executives instead of my lucky number three."

"I just don't understand how you let them all get to you." Archer shakes his head and stands as if he's finally had enough and agrees that I'm a lost cause.

"Look at me, Archer. You said it yourself... they're Ivy League and I'm... polka dots."

We both look around my colorfully decorated office.

My cheesy artwork of framed city and street signs hanging on the wall. The antique desk toy of an old man smoking a cigar and thinking on a suitcase, that serves as a candy dish. When you raise him up, he blows out a puff of smoke. My light pink office chair and matching keyboard and mouse. The snow globes that line the back shelf behind my desk, and not just at Christmas, but year-round.

Archer gets stuck there, staring at the shelf where my coworkers have books. With his hands in his pockets, he zeros in on the snow globes, almost perplexed.

"They were gifts from Great Aunt Josie. They're all the places she's been, that she'd like for me to go someday."

I look at Archer's troubled face.

He presses his lips together and I sink back into the chair opposite my desk, just really taking in what I must look like to everyone else.

Archer smiles. To his credit, it takes a real friend not to kick you while you're down. "Hey. Speaking of Great Aunt Josie. Did you ever open the package she sent?"

"Over there. It's underneath the box of office Christmas decorations I haven't gotten to yet—or won't, now."

"Let's open it. On to new horizons."

Archer starts to pull the tape off the priority mailer box.

"Sure, we can use the box to pack up my desk," I offer.

"Who's Helen Choi?" Archer squints to read the return address on the box.

"I don't know. My great aunt's attorney or best friend or something."

"Right. Could be either, with her. Just like this could be a leaky snow globe, or a bat, or both. Here. You open it."

Out of complete loss and emotional dread of walking out of my office with my tail between my legs for a mandatory extended holiday break, I oblige.

The box turns out to be quite large for only a Christmas card and a set of keys.

Merry Christmas, Darling. You're up!

5706 Demitasse Drive

Blitzen, Kentucky

"What is this?" Archer inspects the keys and takes the card out of my hand to read it.

"I guess she left me her place in Kentucky."

"Is she dead?"

"Probably not."

"That's right. She's moved onto her next 'patch of the world.' She's not dead. She's just... crazy."

"I was going to say, eccentric."

I look around my office again, from the guest chair I'm seated in, and wonder if I didn't get my quirks honestly—from her. My grandfather's sister is a bit of an *Auntie Mame*. I traveled with her often as a child and throughout my formative adolescence.

I never thought I was anything like her. She's so carefree and uninhibited. There's not a second-guessing, buttoned-up bone in her body, but maybe I got the rest from her... My wild ideas. Could it be in my genes? The big dreamer personality that often puts me on an entire other planet than everyone else's way of thinking.

Funny.

I thought that's what an advertising firm was attracted to.

I guess I'm more off-brand than I knew.

I rise, and shove past Archer, who's still inspecting my great Aunt Josie's card, as if to find a sign of life or another clue in her handwriting.

My hands fall to the snow globe in the middle of the shelf—the most recent one she sent me, when she must have first arrived there.

Blitzen, Kentucky.

I trace my hand along the printed words on its base. This one is Christmasy... I shake the snow as a family of reindeer stare back at me beneath it.

TWO

Blitzen, Kentucky

"Hello? *Helloooo*?" A muffled male's voice infiltrates the space.

Archer?

I race to my talking laptop and open the screen. I haven't realized the time, with switching over to a new internet, and unpacking.

"Where are you? This isn't funny, Erika. I got up super early and did a walk of shame from a woman's arms, of whose company I was enjoying very much, all because my best friend is having a crisis. I missed a morning round of potentially exceptional sex to get you coffee—and you're not home."

I watch Archer yelling and smile inside at the two cups of coffee I see on his bar, while I resist the urge to click on my video settings for just a moment longer.

"Let me guess. You've forgotten all about your misadventures at work, foregone being sad, and you're off buying a Christmas tree for your too-small apartment."

Keeping my screen black, I look around at the massive amount of space that surrounds me.

"Guess again. I'll give you a hint. You know Dasher and Dancer and Donner and..."

"I'll be damned. *You went?* How'd you get to the airport? Why didn't you tell me? Wait a minute—you're *gone?* You just left? What about Christmas?"

Archer is spinning.

Clicking on my video, I smile reassuringly into it. "You can come here."

"To Blitzen, Kentucky. No thank you, Erika with a K."

I slide my laptop forward to Zoom back and show some of the house that surrounds me.

"Oh. Is that a first-class lounge at the airport or is that your crazy aunt's home?"

"My home now," I say proudly with a newfound smile I can't hide.

"That place is sick. Leave it to Josie the insane to find luxury in the middle of Nowhere-ville, Hicktown, Kentucky. It is Hicktown, isn't it? Tell me you've seen it and you're miserable, so I don't have to be jealous. What is that—custom built?"

I pan my laptop over the balcony that looks down onto an indoor fire pit in the largest great room I've ever seen. "I should take the opportunity to explain. It's not some tucked away mountain cabin, but it is a very old, very large Tudor-style, almost mini mansion. Josie's clearly had select parts remodeled, whereas other elements—"

I pan the laptop over the 1950s style mint green Formica countertop. "Not so much."

"Please. That's not old. That's your great aunt. Josie probably chose that chartreuse shit show of a countertop for her color pop."

"Hey. There are fourteen-karat gold swan faucets in all kitchen and bathroom fixtures."

"Alright, I guess I could plan to come for actual Christmas. I've got to see this place. And I'd hate for you to spend it alone." Archer feigns being tortured and I can't help but grin back at him, proud as punch. "Way to bounce back kid."

I'm going to miss him.

Every year, we prep for all holidays together. Or, between his noncommittal dating, he does the holidays big for me.

"Hey, it's either the stupidest thing I've ever done, as it's one more bad idea, or it's the only thing I can do."

Archer's expression turns serious. "You do know they didn't fire you, right?"

"Arch. Anybody who would turn me down or let me go like that... Maybe deep down inside I'm as vain as you are, but I truly feel let down by a firm I gave my all to. It was a good pitch, Archer."

"Erika, wait—"

A knock at the door interrupts Archer.

"I gotta go. That must be Helen. She's old. I can't have her waiting out in the cold."

"And this key is for the storage house in the back." Helen chirps in a pristine voice as she hands the newly marked key ring back to me. I know I'm staring at her perfect pixie haircut, and flawless make up, but I'm in awe. Her sophisticated skirt suit is one thousand percent designer, and what I should've worn the day of my pitch.

The *young* woman screams perfection and, "I'm so sorry, I don't mean to be rude, but I totally thought you were—"

"Approaching eighty?"

"Yes. I thought you were Great Aunt Josie's best friend, and maybe trusted attorney?"

"Guilty."

"Wait. You and my great aunt—"

"Are very dear friends, and I handle her estate as well. Come on. It's not that hard to factor. When I left the city to come back here, she was the most exciting thing we all had going. Let's just say she keeps everyone's spirits high when they're feeling low, and that goes double for this fish out of water."

"I thought you grew up here?"

"I did. But that doesn't mean I fit."

"Say no more. I know plenty about being a fish out of water. I don't think I'm yet to fit in anywhere."

"Nonsense. I think you'll be a perfect fit here. Selfishly anyway, I'm so glad you took Josie up on her offer. I've been bored to tears since she left."

"Where did she—"

Helen rises onto four-inch Prada pumps from the counter where we sit. She heads to the door and grabs both our coats. "I haven't shown you what the last key is for. Come now, as Josie would say, there's always more to see." Her red lipstick smile flashes back at me, and I follow with no further questions.

This is unreal to me. This place, the town we're driving into. Blitzen. It's tucked away perfection. A wince of delight sparks across my face as I blink then blink again at the snow-covered mountains that landscape the picturesque highway we sputter down.

Sputter, roll, skid and occasionally slide into oncoming traffic.

From what I can tell so far, the people of Blitzen are genuinely nice, and quite patient with me attempting to drive the standard shift 1980s Volkswagen Beetle that the final key starts up.

Helen pulls her gloves out of a gorgeous briefcase that most likely costs more than this car, which is older than both of us. "Goodness, I don't remember it taking this long to heat up last winter."

"You rode around in this thing with Aunt Josie?"

"Sure, anywhere but where and when it snows. No four-wheel drive. Just keep that in mind when on your Blitzen escapades. Oh, oh— turn here!" Helen's arm sweeps across my face as she points to a dirt road. "Right here! You love Christmas, right? That's what Josie said."

Barely making the turn, I process her words as I pull up to the cutest pasture of vendors I've ever seen.

I do love Christmas.

That warm feeling I felt back at the firm, when I zoned out to the sound of Christmas bells on the conference room door, is back. Red, green, and all things Christmas fill an entire field under cozy red tents spread out in rows before us.

"It's the Christmas flea market. They start in November and have it every Thursday leading up to Christmas."

"It's part of Blitzen?"

"Well, it's on the way into Blitzen. Surrounding towns participate, so the booths are made up of a mix of vendors from different towns and nearby communities. Come on, we can pop by a few booths, and I'll introduce you to anyone I know from Blitzen. Then we can head into downtown for that coffee."

My eyes swell with excitement. I could spend all day at a place like this. So far, the house, the car, okay... not so much the car, it's a bit of a shit show, but it's my shit show, and I'm loving it.

"Mr. Hawkins, this is Erika. We're just taking a peek."

Helen looks like a Hollywood producer or an actress playing the part of a high-powered attorney next to the humble booth she beelined us toward. It's full of Christmas antiques, like toys and vintage ornaments.

"Ah, Josephine Amherst's niece. We've been looking forward to your arrival, young lady."

The older man smiles brightly, and I eat up the sheer feeling of stepping inside a TV Christmas movie. My eyes drift to his sign: *Hawkins Antiques Booth 3.*

Booth 3. Three's my number.

Looking down at the table in front of me, my eyes land on a cassette tape. It's missing a case and has a small piece of tape where "Holiday Mixtape" is written across the top in permanent marker.

"Oh my gosh! How much?"

"For the tape? Awe, honey, I'm sorry. That just got dropped off half an hour ago, and it came in one of those tape recorders with the handle. Some young 'un came by and wanted that recorder but didn't care about the tape. I'm afraid I don't have anything for you to play it on."

Helen cocks her head toward me, the way Archer would in this moment. She already knows me well.

"I do." After tossing the bit of cash I have respectfully towards Mr. Hawkins, I'm forcing Helen to race back to my Beetle to see if it has a cassette player.

I just know it does, and it's a sign. The right kind of sign.

I've believed in fate and destiny my entire life. Quite possibly another Great Aunt Josie trait.

Lately, at the firm, I lost that.

I thought I believed in myself as much as true destiny or the fate of our stars. I don't know if I let myself down on this pitch or I let the firm let me down. Either way, it feels good to have a gut feeling back.

"Want me to drive while you fuss with the forty-some-odd-year-old tape deck?"

"Are you kidding? I have to practice."

"I wouldn't have it any other way." Helen's seat belt clicks louder for emphasis, again, in true Archer fashion.

And I always thought he was one of a kind.

"Don't you think it's a bit fun that we have no idea what the tracks are? Even after we play the first song, the next one and the next after that are an absolute mystery." I look over and smile brightly at Helen as the tape deck swallows the cassette.

Her lips press tightly together as she holds in a thought.

"What?"

"I'm sorry, I can't. It's just you're so very enthusiastic, but it has to be said. Not to take away the mystery, however, I do think it's a safe bet it will be Christmas music." Helen raises a pointed eyebrow and we both burst out laughing as she ushers me in the direction toward town.

"It's beginning to look a lot like Christmas..." The lyrics ring as the first song on the mixtape fills the vintage Beetle.

Perfect. My soul expands a little from somewhere deep, and I have the feeling I'm in the exact right place in time. *Maybe this...* Maybe this Christmas is what I lost sight of at work. I can't help but rubberneck at the quaint shops that line Main Street, and the colorful coats that cover friendly townspeople, walking about their daily business. It's a busy little town for one I heard was so small.

"Okay, so just pull in that next drive. Careful it's..." Helen stutters as my Beetle stalls in the middle of the main road for me to adjust and turn. "A bit of a hill there."

I turn successfully, sputtering up the steep hill with the coffee shop in sight... but also a person. A man carrying a large box appears out of nowhere.

"Stop! Erika, stop the car!"

I do, but it doesn't.

I hear brakes squealing as I feel a significant bump.

Cans roll from the box I hit—knocked four feet in front of my car—and a very tall, attractive man lies on his back.

"Oh God! Oh no!"

My car door swings open off my sheer will to fly out of it, as I run to the human being I've just taken out. Various cans roll past me, down the coffee shop drive, as an extremely handsome man with sandy brown hair and warm hazel eyes leans up casually on one elbow.

Is he posing? Did I just literally kill someone and their ghost is mocking me?

He stares at me as I approach him. I'm immediately self-conscious. The cans keep coming and I hesitate, not knowing if I should run to catch his cans or to his side.

Oh my God Erika... his side. The human! You run to the human first.

I swoop down onto my knees in front of him, to get a good look at the man's face whose eyes have not left mine.

He continues to stare up at me. His brows shift as he moves his glance up and down me, then warm hazels are back on my face as a humorous grin toys across his substantial lips. "Nice hit."

I don't move. I just sit there and stare at the ghost in front of me. A man was walking, and I ran him down like a complete lunatic criminal. His voice is deep, but his tone is jovial. What did I just do?

"I'd say it was a strike, but I believe you missed one." He tosses a can of creamed corn to me, and I blink as it hits the ground beside me and rolls down with the others. He tilts his head and smiles into my eyes, then sheepishly looks around as if to see if he's on camera or being punked.

Still on my knees, I follow his eyes as he stands up.

That's right. The man I just hit and almost killed is standing up and looking down at me while I sit on my knees in front of him, like I'm about to do yoga or pray to him.

"Are you okay?" There they are. *Words.* The thing you're supposed to say when you run over a pedestrian.

"I'm intact, but I'm afraid the town can drive isn't. You may have ruined Christmas, Miss or Mrs. ??"

"Erika, with a K. No. Sorry. Just Erika, I meant." *Like a normal person.*

"So, Erika without a "K" then?"

"Oh, God. I'm getting your cans." *Could he please stop looking at me like that?* It's only fair. I almost killed him, but he's looking at me like he knows what I look like naked.

And stop smiling at me. I can't help but smile back. *I just hit you.* You can't smile at people you just ran over. Or... one shouldn't smile at people who just ran over them.

Bells jingle a few feet away as the coffee shop door opens for an exiting customer. "Soon the bells will start. And the thing that'll make 'em ring is the carol that you sing right within your heart."

That song again... It must've also been playing from the coffee shop he came out of. Stunned, I look back toward my Beetle to see if it's still playing on my mixtape—and the vintage VW Bug is moving—as in no one's in the driver side—my door is open, and the car is rolling backwards. "Helen!"

I race down the hill, but the man I hit strides faster. He's already got one leg in my car and the other on the ground stopping the second potential nightmare of the day.

"Next time I am, in fact, driving. Just until you get the hang of a stick shift. Better yet— we'll take my car."

Helen is marching up the hill from the passenger side.

"I would've stopped it sooner, but I couldn't get the seatbelt unclicked. I tried to get everyone's attention, but I'm afraid you were both occupied with the first car accident." Helen delivers a fake smile with wide sarcastic eyes.

I don't blame her.

I'm not equipped for a lot of things, apparently. But I'm clearly under-equipped for how to deal with the fact I very nearly took out two people to a Bing Crosby classic Christmas song. I walk back up the hill to join Helen and the perfect stranger who's been run down, then forced to save my car.

He's secured my emergency break and made it back up the hill before I can wipe the shock off my face.

"Please. I'm so sorry. Let me get your information. Insurance. *Um…* Pedestrian right away coverage, I don't… know… where I can send replacement canned goods?" I bend down and rip the label off a can of green beans near my feet and look from Helen to my victim.

"Right. Of course." He hands me a pen from his pocket with the most wicked smile. There it is again. *Stop that.* I can feel my cheeks warming. I'm so embarrassed that I hit him, and almost killed my only friend in Kentucky, and he's making it way worse with his good humor.

Is he enjoying this?

"Okay. So, your name is?" I press the thin shred of paper to my palm and pray that's enough of a hard surface to make the pen write.

"Court." He watches me attempt to write on the can label like he's got a front row seat to the next shit show. I feel Helen peek over my shoulder at my efforts. Her finger points down to where I wrote his name as she corrects my spelling.

"K." It's Kourt with a "K."

THREE

Kourt with a "K"

Her reaction makes me laugh. The woman's blue eyes flare wide with surprise, almost like a cartoon character's. Amusing, that's what she is.

Maybe it's the shock of being run over out of the blue by a miniature vehicle, but I can't help but be a little mesmerized watching her glance over her shoulder at Helen and turn to face me, stuttering, *"Kuh... Kourt?* With a K? Like I'm Erika with a K?"

Blink, blink, blink.

I give her a thumbs up with a grin I can't quash. "Exactly. Kourt with a K."

She's trying to write my name on the back of a thin paper label she peeled from a can, cradling it in the palm of her trembling hand. Her lashes keep fluttering as she bites her lower lip, staring at the pen in her hand, mumbling, almost to herself, something about, "Sign."

She's a deer in headlights.

"Sign?" I dip my chin, locking my gaze on her, to help her focus.

She peers up at me then looks left and right, maybe for a place to run.

Blink, blink.

"Uh, I didn't see a street sign. Sorry. I need your name and the street where it happened."

"Kourt McClain. Third Street."

She freezes and squints up at me in disbelief, then nods and goes back to scribbling. Fixating on her face, I zero in on those lashes. The longest fucking eyelashes I've ever seen… they're paired with long, wild, wavy, almost-black hair that falls past her shoulders.

Long, luscious lashes.

"Are those things fake?" Dammit. It just tumbles out of my mouth like the cans rolling down the hill.

She cuts her gaze from the label in her hand to meet my eyes, then tucks her chin to peer at her chest—and her face comes back to mine with a look of horror.

It hits me—*She thinks I was talking about her tits.*

Her cheeks flame crimson. "I beg your pardon?"

You'd think I kicked a kitten.

"The lashes. You have the longest eyelashes I've ever seen." *And those might be the bluest eyes I've ever seen.* "Are you wearing contacts?"

She blows a disgusted sharp breath. "Of course not. Do they look like I glued them on my face? Really? And I assure you I don't need contacts. I just don't know how to drive a stick."

Before I can pull my foot out of my mouth, Helen intervenes. "Kourt, Erika is Josephine's great-niece."

"Ahh." I tilt my head back. I should've known. Quirky begets quirky. "Blitzen's very own eccentric's phantom great-niece does exist." I offer my hand. "Heard about you. An ad executive from Chicago, right? Nice to meet you, Erika with a K."

She studies my hand as if I'm offering her a bottle of strychnine—and for the umpteenth time since our untimely meeting minutes earlier, her over-reaction pulls a smile from me. I can't help it.

Nothing half-assed about this one. Her every emotion is on her sleeve for the world to see. Animated and unvarnished.

"I don't bite, Erika." *Although given a chance, I might...*

Her lips twist as she stares down at my hand and mutters, "That's the biggest hand I've ever seen." She tilts her chin haughtily to meet my gaze. "Guess I should ask if it's fake."

"Every inch is real."

Helen harrumphs, "Okay, and because this just keeps getting weirder—he's a basketball player. Or was. Kourt's our basketball coach."

"At the high school?" Erika asks. "As in Basketball *Kourt*." She laughs wickedly at her own joke. "Get it?" She smiles at Helen before returning to me.

"Got it."

Since I was ten.

"I also teach history and driver's ed. I'd be glad to give you a lesson in driving a stick shift." Among other things.

Helen clears her throat. "The Blitzers are state champions."

For whatever reason, neither one of us can tear our eyes away from the other.

Poor Helen's trying to figure out what the hell's going on. So am I.

I glance at my watch. "I'm late. I've got to round up these cans and get to practice. Nice to meet you, Erika. Helen, later."

"Well, look at you." Kelsey Waverly smiles at me when I walk into the cafeteria, carting the recovered box of canned goods from the coffee shop's donation drop. She tilts her head at a table in the corner. "You can set it over there."

"Got some scratch and dents in this batch," I announce as I lug the box that's damn near as big as Kelsey.

She jumped at the chance to chair our Christmas food drive. Lucky me. The food drive has always been my thing. Means a lot to me, my students and the town. Most people have no idea how much that food is needed this time of year. They'd be surprised what neighbors of theirs are on the list for it.

Kelsey's made the most of making me her collection pack mule. Any excuse to throw us together.

"That's okay," she chirps. "The food bank accepts scratch and dents."

I neglect to tell our single librarian and Chairwoman of the Canned Food Drive how they got scratched and dented. Not going into that story.

She hit me with her frigging car. Had it been anything but an old Beetle, had she not been stalled heading uphill, I might be in the hospital.

The box lands on the table with a thud.

Kelsey glances up from her clipboard with a needy look in her eyes. She's been trying to get me to notice her for years. Trouble is, I have noticed her. Ash blonde, bouncy and cute, if not hot in her own way, but... I don't know. Not interested? It could be because I'd have to see her every day at work.

"That's from the coffee shop, right?"

"Yep."

Kelsey scribbles a check mark on the sign in sheet and cuts her eyes to me with her neck craned back so far, it has to hurt.

I hit six foot two when I was in the tenth grade and kept growing. Me dating Kelsey would be like Paul Bunyan going out with a platinum blonde garden gnome in navy blue eyeliner. Kelsey's hot in the, *I was a Blitzen cheerleader* kind of way. The problem is... she still looks like one. She's in her early thirties but looks and behaves freakishly like a student.

Okay. It's not the height thing. She's five-foot-two—I'm certain we could make that work. It's just... this woman's entire vibe suggests she fled Kentucky for Bama Rush last week, as opposed to having been our high school librarian for the last six years.

That's not me sorority shaming. She just reads nightmarishly young. And nothing I do seems to detour her.

"Thanks for helping, Coach. It means a lot." Her grey eyes roam my face. "I don't know what I would've done if you hadn't stepped up to help me."

Umm... what we did last year when I helped before you were chairperson. This is becoming uncomfortable as hell.

"No problem. The boys look forward to it every year. We've got football, basketball, and track involved. If they're in athletics, they're helping feed those with hardships. 'Tis the season, and we're aiming to break last year's record."

As I head for the gym, Kelsey calls out to my back. "Speaking of breaking last year's record... getting down to the qualifying games."

I turn to see her brows shifted high with anticipation.

"We lost three good seniors last year. It's still early. We'll see."

"Well, good luck next Friday night. Will I see you at the town meeting next week?"

I moan. "I forgot." Yeah, it's definitely not the height thing. It's this. Pretending to be interested in basketball... memorizing my schedule.

"You better not forget. We've got lots riding on that meeting." She twists her vintage Tiffany charm necklace at me.

Yes, Kelsey. Got it. You see me every day at school, more than the norm for the food drive, and you are guaranteeing you will see me at my upcoming basketball game and the town hall meeting. This is precisely why we do not date. She's good people and I would never hurt her feelings, but—*goddamn.*

I leave the cafeteria and head for practice with my thoughts ripped from my brush with death and Kelsey's death grip, to the bigger problem at hand. If our volunteer fire department doesn't get a new truck by the end of the first quarter, we'll lose our accreditation. If we lose our state accreditation, everyone's property insurance will be unaffordable.

Not a popular position to be in as assistant chief.

But fire trucks cost money. Lots of money. The town meeting next week is to brainstorm ideas for a fund-raising drive.

A shrill whistle brings me to reality as I step into the gym.

Never do I tire of that sound. This place is more home to me than my house. I played my first game on this court when I was fifteen. I went from Blitzen to the University of Tennessee on a basketball scholarship.

Thinking about what brought me back here, all the reasons that don't matter anymore, I still don't seem to want to get away from it.

The smell of leather, the echoes of basketballs bouncing off hardwood, the sound of players running bleachers, their shoes squeaking across the gym... the crowds, the buzzers—*this* is where I live.

"Defense!" my assistant coach, Trent Holcomb, claps his hands at the players. "Huddle up. We're working on zone defense today! Teams of three—"

I'm tired of fighting him on this. "Why are you wasting time practicing zone?" I'm keeping my voice down. The players don't need to hear us disagree.

He replies in an equally hushed tone. "To throw Willow Creek off. If we start with zone, they'll relax."

Not happening.

My heart takes it up a notch, along with my volume. "If we play zone while Willow Creek runs man, they'll run up the score so fast we can't recover." *He knows that.*

Trent shrugs. "Just thought it wouldn't hurt for our boys to be able to play both."

We share an extended stare. "Start with defensive slides then mirror drills. I'll be in my office."

I don't know why that crawls up my ass, but it does.

'Hey Trent... meet Kelsey the librarian.' They seem like a great fucking fit.

This is a sport. If it's not broken... why change it? We won State last year and went to State the year before. What we do works.

But he's right. It won't hurt the team to know how to play zone. "Trent!" I poke my head out of the office.

"Yessir." He jogs to me.

"After the mirror drills, you have time to work on some zone. You're right. Doesn't hurt to know it... even if it's just to guard against it."

"Thanks, Coach."

In my office, the phone rings. "Coach McClain."

"Kourt?"

Shit.

"Hey, Quinn." The woman I *have* been seeing off and on the past few months—more off than on lately, hum-haws on the other end of the line. Everyone seems to have something on their mind today. It's been obvious the last couple of weeks she wants more, and I'm not looking for someone who wants more than we agreed on.

She pauses another second. "I just wondered, why I hadn't heard from you, Kourt. I thought..."

"Just been busy, Quinn. I've got the can drive and the fire department fund raising thing and a game on Friday, not to mention I teach history and driver's ed. Got a lot going on."

"You're not avoiding me?"

Shit. I hope we didn't get our wires crossed. She knows this is casual. She's the one who led with that.

I rest my head in my hand. "Why would I avoid you?"

I hate this. I hate hurting anyone. Fucking cad.

"So, we're on for Saturday?"

That's hope I hear in her voice. I flip through my coach's book to see if I marked a date. *Did I promise something on Saturday?*

Nothing. There's nothing marked. This is her way of telling me she wants more than casual. A reminder that Saturday night is when I take *her* out.

"About Saturday..."

We suffer through a long, crippling silence.... and Quinn whispers, "Never mind, Kourt. Everybody told me not to waste my time. I'm sorry I bothered you."

Click.

She hangs up before I can get a word out. *Everybody? She lives two towns over.*

I stare at my desk phone. I could call her back. But why? I'm not pursuing that.

Leave it alone, man, for her sake. A waste of time? Only if she was in it for different results.

I decide to leave it. I'd rather look like the bad guy than call and give her false hope that my apology saddles me into another month of Saturday nights.

My cell phone *pings*, and I pull it out of my pocket to see a text.

> **Georgia:** Can you stop by on your way home? Need a hand.

I text her back a thumbs up.

"Saw you at Georgia's after school." Helen likes playing nosey neighbor. It's part of her slumming it with me in the small town we grew up in. FaceTime with my best friend most evenings is the only female obligation I look forward to. She is my person.

"I'm going to help them put up their Christmas lights this weekend. She wanted me to drag them out of the attic for her."

"Always the dutiful—"

"It's the least I can do. Bob was at work. And besides, he doesn't need to be climbing that ladder at his age, anyway."

"How are you, after what happened this afternoon? Our Erika's a mess, isn't she." Helen crinkles her nose at the tip in that look. It's a look that lets me know she's enticed and on to something, and she just can't wait to see if I'm aboard.

A hot mess. "The apple doesn't fall far from the aunt, I gather." My air fryer dings with my supper as I slide a plate across the counter.

"Great-aunt," Helen corrects.

"What was that about, anyway?"

"You know Josephine." Helen's noisy ice machine plops cubes into a shaker. "She got a wild hair and took off, sent Erika the keys to her house and car all cryptic, like some estate she just inherited. Erika has time off from work with the holidays, so she showed up yesterday."

Helen throws her head back and giggle-groans. "She wanted to drive the Beetle. I should've known better. Chicago girl takes the L. Sorry about that."

"How long's she here?" I set the phone down to take the pot pie out of the air fryer, giving Helen a close-up of my elbow. *"Shit, that's hot."*

"No idea," Helen says. "What'd you do?"

"Burned my hand. It's fine."

"Do you care?"

"That I burned my hand? Yeah." I wag it to cool it off, muttering to myself.

"No, dummy. Do you care if she stays or not?"

"Why would I?" I grab a potholder to safely move the steaming pot pie to a plate. "I've got two things on my mind right now: the game with Willow Creek—which we really need to win. And this fundraising drive for a fire truck."

"Before we move on to discuss your top priorities that seem quite sad, really, may I at least ask, what possessed you to ask Erika if she had fake eyelashes?" Helen's head tilts back as she lets out a loud laugh. "What was *that* about?"

"Fuck, I don't know. It just came out. I can't get this damn pie out of its holder. The crust stuck to the tin pan."

"Last time I checked you weren't a complete and total brute. You don't ask women if they have fake *anything*."

A smile hijacks my face, thinking about what an ass I was, blurting that out. "Did you see how she looked down at her chest, like I was asking if she had fake tits?" I can't stop this grin, thinking about my stupidity and her reaction.

Helen shrieks, "What if she did?"

"Did what?"

"Have fake tits."

"Anything more than a handful is wasteful. But then, as she said, I have big hands."

"Stop it!" Helen chokes on her cocktail.

"Just saying." I wiggle my hand in front of the phone camera.

"I hate to tell you, McShotty, *no one* has a handful—for you."

"True. A mouthful will do. She's got that."

"*Ahhh!*" Helen screams. "She's my client—well, so to speak. And I assure you, they are real. I don't think there's a fake bone in her body. Odd really."

"How do you mean?"

"I don't know. She's just so real. What you see is what you get, but it's a lot—and so genuine."

"Wait. Hold on a minute. I've got to get this damn pie out of its holder before I starve to death. It's stuck." I set down the phone long enough to get the pliers out of the drawer.

Seeing them, Helen erupts. "This is why I get takeout."

"I'm using the pliers to grip the hot-ass pie tin so I can turn it upside down and dump it on my plate. Watch carefully in case it happens to you."

"I've never met a pot pie I wanted that badly."

"So wait, I don't follow. She's an honest, naïve, but practical version of the eccentric Josephine?"

"No. She's not naïve at all—or practical for that matter. She's... *hopeful.* It's different. Kind of nice."

"Are you suggesting we're jaded?" I attempt my first bite of dinner. "Fuck! Shit that's hot. It's the sauce. Every time."

I drop the bite of pot pie to lick burning hot cream sauce off my finger and wince again.

"I could call us a lot of things after that display." Helen takes a sip of her martini. "We're not quite jaded... more on the road to complacent."

"Nice one, Helen. Just use all your big words tonight for your best friend who got mowed down while volunteering for a can drive by your—what was that again? Hopeful client? And I just burned the hell out of my tongue on top of it."

"That's exactly what I'm talking about, Kourt. It's Friday night and what did you just burn your tongue on? A hot pocket?"

"It's a pot pie. And you're home alone on your second dirty martini. I heard the ice machine again." My words cut through my home sharper than I meant them to, as I walk backwards, reaching for a napkin before stalking to the living room with my dinner.

"That is precisely my point." Helen's head bobs as I pick my phone back up. "Wait. Kourt—is that a *Christmas tree* behind you? Did you actually put up a Christmas tree this year?"

I glance over my shoulder. "It's one of those old, vintage metal trees. Aluminum, I think, like from the 1950s. I saw it at the flea market. You know I like old stuff, so I bought it to satisfy my nagging friend who's been on my ass for three years to buy a fucking tree. Got sick of hearing about it. Are you satisfied now? Do you stand corrected over that complacent comment?"

"You just said it, Kourt. Three years, buddy. It took three years, but you finally have a tree up again. I think I stand more than corrected. I think I might be—*hopeful*."

FOUR

Help to Make the Season Bright

I'm on my ninth row of boxes in my great aunt's attic when I think I hear pounding on the front door. It's faint, intermittent beneath "Chestnuts Roasting on an Open Fire" wafting from the record player in the loft, but someone's definitely trying to get my attention.

I rise from a pool of Christmas tree garland coiled around me like a beaded snake made of tinsel, red ribbons, glitter sprayed wooden cranberries and snow-dusted pinecones.

"Coming!" I scream in vain from above the top story of the house, trying not to trip over piles of ornaments I've categorized.

A sleek black glove drops a set of keys onto the kitchen counter as I tumble down the spiral staircase to come face to face with Helen.

"Woah!" We both practically shout in unison.

She takes a step toward the great room dodging newly labeled boxes and a set of large toy soldier statues almost as tall as she is.

"You look incredible. Do you wake up like that?" I have to ask.

She looks like an Yves Saint Laurent winter ad out of a page in Vogue. Just add a fur muff and a three-stringed leash of little black Scottie dogs with charcoal, red and grey plaid ascots around their necks. I envision them hopping around the hem of her black pencil skirt as she stares at a blow mold of a waving Santa. Maybe that's more of a vintage Ralph Lauren look. I'd have to ask Archer. He surpasses my fashion knowledge in both men's and women's clothing.

"What?" Helen screams, her hands still covering her ears.

"I said you look great! Sorry. It's Nat King Cole."

"Yeah. Is he here? Like upstairs singing with a full band?"

I purse my lips together and race back up to the loft to turn down the music. "Sorry. I found a record player," I call from the loft, as I head back down.

"Of course you did. Did the thing have 'before-it's-time' Bose speakers attached to the needle?" Helen's face settles into a smile, and she slips off her long black gloves revealing short, immaculately painted red nails.

"I guess I got a little excited. You see, it's also track two on the mix tape and totally a sign."

"Wait. Back up. I just came by thinking you might want a coffee, and after yesterday's ordeal, might need a ride to the coffee shop where our near-death incident took place. Or I don't know—moral support walking in to order."

"Handled. I've been up since five a.m. Or maybe I didn't go to bed, apart from a nap at four-thirty. Who cares. I've already apologized to the coffee shop owner for my runaway Beetle and I have our coffee." I reach in the massive stainless-steel fridge and pull out Helen's iced cold brew.

Her jaw drops and she gives me a concerned side eye as she removes the paper from the straw for a taste. "How did you know?"

"You may be the only person in town who drinks cold brew in winter. Your local barista was happy to send me away with your dose they apparently make just for you."

"I'm impressed. I misjudged you for one of those holiday hot chocolate freaks."

"It's Christmas. I'm sure I'll consume my fair share, but nothing replaces the amount of caffeine I require from my iced triple espresso."

"Ah ha. *That's* how you found me out."

"Takes a cold coffee drinker to know one. Anyway, as I pulled away from the coffee shop, track two just automatically started playing on my way back home. It was the Christmas song, you know "Chestnuts Roasting"... Nat King Cole. Then I find this record player in the middle of all this stuff. I plug it in, and simply drop the needle on the record that's already on it—and guess what's playing?"

"Right. I got it. Loud and clear." Helen points to her ears.

"It's a sign. Don't you think? Kismet or something? Just like the first track on the tape was playing when I bumped into your friend."

"Kourt." Helen offers.

"I truly am sorry, by the way. I can't apologize enough, but even with that unfortunate mistake, I think it was fate. When I hit... *Kourt's* box of cans for the Christmas food drive, *It's Beginning to Look a Lot Like Christmas* was playing on my tape. It was also playing in the coffee shop he just stepped out of, with the box of donated cans."

"So, you're saying, no good deed goes unpunished. Not even at Christmas." Helen's eyes drift to the Christmas explosion that surrounds us. "Let's go back to 'all this stuff' you mentioned. Did you buy all of this? This morning? And, why?"

"Oh, gosh no. I... um. Well, I found the attic, and you know... It's Josie. I full-on expected mannequins with one arm, a dusty Italian vase from Florence or a painting of Lake Como from a century that makes it worth more than this house. Or a headless horseman statue she bought from the real-life village of Sleepy Hollow after an impromptu visit to Westchester or Tarrytown." I watch Helen zone out as her gaze lands on the Christmas tree in the corner.

"Last night and this morning, to answer your question. I opened one box and the addiction began. There's still more upstairs."

"All of this, and you had time to put up a Christmas tree?" Helen carves a path through the Christmas decor and looks over my large silver tinsel tree.

"Not my real tree. I'll have to go chop or buy one. That's yet to come. I was just so taken by this one when I found it standing alone and shining upstairs. It's from the sixties, I think."

"Yeah. It is. It's a popular vintage thing." She twists a branch of silver foiled glitter through her fingers. "Wow. In the town that Christmas forgot, I now know two people who already have their trees up."

"That right there. That's what I'm getting at with all this stuff. This place is named Blitzen. Yet, there are no holiday decorations lining the streets or the courthouse. I kind of drove around on the way to coffee. Apart from the Christmas flea market on the outskirts of town, and your friend—"

"Kourt." She says his name with a dynamic intensity. The same intensity as the space he takes up when he speaks or looks at me. He looked at me like I was lost.

"Other than *Kourt*, and his Christmas can drive, I don't see much Christmas spirit."

"It's barely December 1st..."

"Look. I'm not one of those freaks who decorates before Halloween or anything, I... Well, I took a leap of faith to come here, and it just seems like the obvious place for—"

"A Christmas miracle? A Hallmark Christmas movie? A Christmas romance..."

I feel my smile fade as I look down sheepishly. Maybe it's the lack of sleep and the mountain altitude, but with Helen's familiar voice of reason seemingly matching Archer's general logic, I'm starting to feel the way I felt at the office.

My eyes drift to the red and green explosion taking over the trendy contemporary home. Maybe it's all too much. I'm beginning to think I'm too much.

"Okay. Erika. I'm not going to lie to you. It *is* a town named Blitzen. Of course we had a big to-do about Christmas. The town was known for it when Kourt and I were kids. But, things change, stuff happens, people get old, tired and disillusioned."

"Should I get out a walker for you, Helen? I think I saw one in the attic."

"You know what I mean. Right now, it's that damn fire truck and the property insurance fiasco. It's all they can focus on. And it is important. It's potentially debilitating to our town. I don't do that kind of law, but I've looked into it, and I know enough to understand it's paramount for the town's economic livelihood for them to settle on a plan."

"So, it's not me. It's them..." I quirk a half-hearted smile her direction to let her know I get it. On to something else.

"No. If you tell me all this shit you drug out is to decorate this insanely gorgeous home you're already lucky to inherit, then it is you... but if you're thinking bigger, and you stayed up all night digging through boxes for—"

"*Yessss.* Exactly. I mean, these people don't know me from Adam, but enough of them participate in the flea market, and look at your buddy—"

"Kourt."

Would she please stop saying his name that way?

"Right. He cares enough to do the can drive."

"Hmmm. Yes. I suppose Kourt does care enough." Helen's eyes widen and she looks at me suspiciously.

"I'm just saying. I have all these decorations of Josie's. I can't imagine she'd want them to go to waste, tucked away in boxes in the attic. I guess I feel like it's all part of either her grand scheme or some master plan that I'm here and I found them... So in lieu of sounding like a TV movie—let's decorate the town?"

A toothy, but reluctant smile attacks my cheeks.

"Come on, Helen. I'm your client by default. You have to entertain this. If you don't, I'm back to feeling like a screw-up who flew the office coup after being kicked out of my firm."

"You were kicked off a pitch, not out of your firm. Speaking of which, I have to go. I've got an in-person this morning. Hence the digs. No. You were right the first time. I do wake up like this."

"You have to work on a Saturday?"

"I'm an exceptional attorney, with very wealthy, eccentric clients, who hide out in a small town. Of course I work on Saturday."

I give her a pressing look as she grabs her keys off the counter to head out.

"Hey, do I get that copy of keys you have to this place or—"

"Nope. They're mine. I've had my own set of keys to this place since Josie moved in. One of my best friends in the world gave them to me. Tough luck getting them back." Helen winks over her shoulder as she moves to the door with her briefcase and cold brew. "Plus, you'll want me to have them in case I'm the one that has to find you buried under all this Christmas décor."

"I'll let it slide in exchange for where I can get a million extension cords?"

"Blitzen Hardware. It's on Main Street."

FIVE

"If The Fates Allow"

I still can't get over this quaint Christmas town... well, soon-to-be back to its Christmas roots Christmas town when Josie's decorations get done with it. It's beyond picturesque. There's something in the air here that's whimsical. It's peaceful, but with a vibrant current of anticipation.

Maybe it's the smell of those evergreens, or the mountain roads, so secluded until they unwind into a neighbor's drive, or—perfect for me, the much-needed hardware store.

No wonder Helen didn't have more explicit instructions. It's right here, the first store on Main Street. My cassette tape comes on out of the blue, switching to track three.

I know it's the faulty, 1980s tape deck causing it to glitch, jam, or just play the tape whenever it feels like it. But I'm totally subscribing to the fate thing.

In true Great Aunt Josie fashion, and just because it's Christmas, I believe this holiday mixtape was made for me. "Have yourself a Merry little Christmas" begins to play, and my holiday senses perk up.

A sweet hum vibrates from deep within my throat as it pushes its way out of my smiling face by the second verse. Judy Garland's version from *Meet Me in St. Louis*—this is my favorite of the classics. It's wild to me, it's been so long since I really listened, much less sang it.

My hand rests on the door handle, and I hesitate before popping out of the Beetle. It's as if I don't want to leave the vicinity of the song playing. What if the cassette doesn't play when I start it up again?

I roll my eyes at myself and shrug, choosing to be sane and exit the vehicle. Only after applying the emergency brake, of course. *Check.*

Bells jingle in the hardware store, announcing my entry. It's not busy at all for a Saturday. I might be the only customer so far. Familiar holiday music segues to a chorus as I get my bearings and determine which aisle to peruse.

"Hi, there." A male's voice calls out warmly from the front. He lifts up one of those wooden partitions separating the counter from the customer and greets me.

"Hi. I'm looking for—" I stall, my head lifting up to the overhead music playing the chorus of "Have Yourself a Merry Little Christmas."

"I'm so sorry, but that's the same song playing on my tape. The tape in my car. When I got out, it was playing in almost the same spot."

"Ah." His eyes smile at me. He's my mom's age, give or take, and seems very patient and kind. He must be the owner. He tilts his head to the side and takes a few slow steps closer to me, studying my face.

"I sure sound nutty. I just... It's a favorite of mine."

"Mine too. It's a favorite in my family. Brings back a lot of memories. Forgive me—but you... you're... something about you reminds me of someone."

A long moment passes, and my eyes remain transfixed on those of the kind man still studying me as the shop bell jingles again.

The shop owner continues to stare at me, almost in a daze. "You're not from around here, are you?" He almost seems disappointed as he says it. Then his eyes rise much higher, above my head, and I feel a hand press against my upper back.

"No, Bob. She's not from around here." It's Kourt standing beside me, joining my almost ethereal moment with the man keeping the hardware store. His hand is warm on my back, and he doesn't move away.

I turn to see Kourt look up toward the speaker on the ceiling where the music is coming from, as if he, too, has some connection to my favorite Christmas song. Although, as the man said, I suppose it's most everyone's favorite.

"Erika." Kourt looks down at me, forcing me to crane my neck to look up at him. His eyes are pleading with mine in a way I'm not sure I understand, but I can tell they're asking me to try.

"This is Bob. He owns this fine establishment." Kourt is speaking curiously slow as if he's trying to calm a stray animal. "And, Bob, this is Erika, Josephine Amherst's great niece."

We stay standing this way, side by side, facing Bob.

Kourt is seemingly waiting for Bob's reply. His palm slides toward my shoulder blade on one side, as if to make me more comfortable or let me know this awkward moment will soon end.

Goose bumps trickle down that side of my body and I shift my stance involuntarily to compensate.

"Josephine! Well, why the heck didn't you say so? Hot dog." Bob snaps out of his Christmas song-induced trance and claps his hands in excitement. His solemn face and glossy eyes have changed back into the store owner who originally greeted me.

"Yeah. Just arrived yesterday or so. Helen's got her all settled." Kourt's speech has sped back up, and his expression has also returned to what I can assume is normal for him. All things have returned to normal when I feel his large heavy hand lift from my back. Funny, I almost feel more uncomfortable with his hand gone than I did when it was on me.

"We've been looking forward to your arrival, Erika. Now what had you pop in?"

"Extension cords. Very long. Three prongs."

"Aisle two. Go ahead and take a look, and holler if you need me. And Kourt. What brought you in here on your day off?"

"Your wife."

I hear Kourt's response from down the aisle where I hover over brown, black, and orange extension cords that won't match what I'm trying to hide them behind.

"And your canned goods. Georgia sent me for more hooks for the side of the house. I think we're good on the light strands. They all seem to work so far. I can see your donation box is already full. You guys are toppling over." Kourt continues his conversation.

"You're not kidding. We've got another full box in the back."

"I'll take 'em."

"Excuse me, Bob? Do you know if there are any white, red or green extension cords available?"

"I was afraid of that. My new order hasn't come in yet, and the town over cleaned me out of white ones last week. I've got no red, but Fisher's might."

"Fisher's? In what town exactly?" I pull out my phone to plop this place in my maps.

"No, ma'am. Not in your car." Kourt scolds me as if he's the old timer behind the register.

"Oh. She's in Josie's Bug, I take." Bob shakes his head knowingly.

"You guessed it." Kourt reassures him.

"Yeah, they've got snow-covered hills up that way, even though nothing's hit here yet. That's not for your Beetle, I assure you.

Kourt? Why don't you drive Erika here to Fisher's? She can help you with the second box of cans."

"Oh, I think she's helped plenty with the can drive."

"Nonsense. Georgia won't mind. I'll call her and tell her you had to run an errand for me. I actually do need you to pick up her clips for me. Out of those, too, until the shipment comes in. Just give me a sec, and I'll grab that other box of cans from the back." Bob trots off, and I feel the annoyed energy between us as Kourt and I stare straight ahead.

After a beat he huffs, but I open my mouth to speak first. "Look, you don't have to take me. Helen can drive me some other time or something I—"

"I have to. Bob's making me." Kourt bites out without looking at me.

"Making you? What are you—five?" I turn toward him, truly curious.

"No. Just afraid Santa will put me on the naughty list if I pout and refuse." Kourt brings a fake, almost sardonic smile to life as he turns his head to look at me. "That, and we've got to keep you off the roads as much as possible. Can't have you taking out the town before our big vote."

Kourt slams his tailgate shut after the last box of cans slides onto the truck bed. I almost encounter PTSD from the multiple cans of cream corn staring up at me in the box I carted. I look back as Bob waves us off with a bright smile. Mine fades, and my lips press together in wicked curiosity as I watch Kourt saunter to the driver's side of his truck.

What? Am I just supposed to get in?

A key fob clicks and the doors unlock with a beep.

"Get in."

Reaching for the passenger side, I catch him pausing to look over at me from outside the truck cab. He's tall enough to stare over his truck bed right through me.

I stall before opening the door. "Look, I mean it. You don't have to do this if you don't want to. I'm sure you've got better things to do than chauffer your attempted murderer."

"I do. Starting with hanging Georgia's Christmas lights, and Pops says he's out of hooks so—"

"Who?" I shout back at him, confused from across the truck and freezing my rear off.

"Bob. I mean Bob. It's his lights I'm hanging, too. He and Georgia's house." Kourt looks down and away from me a moment. As if we should go no further than we already have in this conversation. As if he's contemplating whether to let me in his truck or not. "Bob's as good as gold. If it felt odd back there...with the song... it wasn't you, it—"

"Oh. I wasn't—going to ask." I shake my head with a slight, reassuring smile. "It's an iconic song." I say it loud and firm, my voice carrying across the large truck. "It's significant to a number of people, if not everyone's favorite, a close second." I nod again like I'm in some western movie.

Kourt nods back. A twinkle in his eye inspects my face. *So curious.*

"It's settled then. You'll get your pink and purple extension cords, and I'll get their clips."

"Red. I need red and green."

"Right. Two birds with one stone, see?"

He slides into the driver's side with ease as I open my door, mumbling back, "Like the way I nearly took you and the food drive both out with my Beetle."

I'm not positive, but I think I catch the remnants of a chuckle on his end as I climb into the passenger seat.

"I'm pretty sure that was more like—one fell swoop. At least, you're more of one anyway. You nearly took me and the town's Christmas can drive out in 'one fell swoop'." The corners of his lips rise into a smile as the ignition starts.

Kourt reverses out of his parking space as he fiddles with the heat. I blow on my hands, rubbing them together as I reach for my gloves in my purse and force my stiff fingers through them.

We pull up to the bottom of the drive. His turn signal ticking makes the sounds of the truck and everyday errands the most natural thing on the planet between two strangers, only I feel his eyes back on me while we're stopped.

I refuse to entertain looking in his direction, but I can guarantee it's a stare in combination with a sly smile.

I don't even know him—but I know that look of his already. And why does it send a cascade of heat erupting in my belly and shivers down my spine?

Does he make me nervous? Well sure. Almost kill someone with your car and then have *them* offer to drive *you* somewhere... I suppose that would make anyone a little on edge.

"Seat belt."

"Huh?" I turn toward Kourt, my eyes wide with question over what he just said, when a large chest bulldozes my face. My senses fill with cedar, nutmeg and—stone? What earthy embodiment other than the cool rocks that line the ocean shore or cover the bottom of a riverbed smell like that? Fresh, natural, clean, and solid. I duck my head away and toward the large arm crossing my body until I hear a loud click.

Kourt's hand is an inch from my hip when I look back up to his face that's now an inch away from mine. I was right about "the look" of his. Honey-colored eyes, with a slight green hue stare into my blinking lashes, complete with his sly devilish grin.

"Seat belt."

The accelerator brings the truck to life once more as he turns onto Main Street, heading away from Blitzen.

SIX

Cords and Clips

"It's *so* mountainous. I mean, I know we're in the mountains—but seeing up close..." Erika presses her fingertips to her lips as my truck begins the steep climb toward Black Mountain. "It's... insanely beautiful up here."

I point to the east, at the massive mountain that disappears into snow-laden clouds. "That's Kentucky's highest peak. Black Mountain."

My chest tightens.

Something inside me goes as cold as the snow that blankets the roadside, as the words come out. "People die on these roads up here all the time, Erika." I cut my eyes at her. My best friend's client sits in my truck in awe of the scenery. My warning appears to fall on deaf ears. I've known her Aunt Josephine for years, but still—she's as much a stranger to these mountains as she is to me. She has no idea how dangerous they can be.

"That's why I couldn't let you come up here in that Beetle. Josie's car's fine for summer driving, but not in winter, not here anyway." The idea that she would have popped Fisher's in her navigator and headed to the next town on the highest point. Clueless.

"Is this coal mine country?" she asks, still wide-eyed, her gaze flicking back and forth from me to the countryside. She's from Chicago—she's eating up the rugged, forested Cumberland Mountains.

"It *was*, back in the day—long before our time. In the 1940s, the coal mines employed thousands of men. All the other businesses supported their families and the mines. But now, fewer than a thousand people work the mines."

She turns toward me. "So, what keeps people here now?"

The answer comes out without thinking. "A sense of place. Belonging. Roots. These are the Cumberland Mountains, home to Daniel Boone National Forest. You're in one of the most storied... historic parts of America. People who are born here end up staying here."

Erika's face lights up. She's peering at the winding highway ahead, but soon her eyes are back on me, almost sparkling in the morning sun. And this time, unexpectedly, I'm struck by the light freckles that dot her nose and cheeks, the faint scent of gingerbread wafting between us as she all but whispers, "I'm not sure why, but I was meant to come here, I think. *This* is where I'm meant to be—at least right now. I feel it."

"You're in good company. This is the birthplace of Loretta Lynn and Dwight Yokum and Blue Grass music."

"Tell me something—"

"If you don't know who those icons are, I can't help you."

She rolls her eyes only to have them meet mine again.

Our gazes join as I wait for what's coming.

"You said something earlier about the town meeting and a vote. What were you talking about?"

"There's a town meeting next week to decide how we're going to pay for a new fire truck."

"Oh."

"Disappointed?"

"No. I just—I guess I hoped it was for something else." Her chin lifts in contemplation. "Doesn't the county or city take care of firetrucks? Through taxes?"

Watching her pretty face change with each thought, consequently I'm focused on her, not the wheel, and I make an effort to pull my gaze back to the road. "Not here. All we have is a *volunteer* fire department. It's not supported by taxes."

"Let me guess. You're part of it?"

"Everyone is one way or another. Anyway, some jackass state inspector comes in from Frankfort earlier this year and decides we've got to have a larger capacity firetruck, or we lose our rating."

Her brows pinch tight. "What rating?"

I feel a growl coming from my chest. "It's about property insurance. Bottom line is, if we can't buy a bigger fire truck by the end of January, everyone's property insurance is going through the roof."

A confidence leaks from her voice as she stares out her passenger window. "It sounds like you need a fundraiser."

A chuckle bubbles free. "You could say that."

"Damn." I let out a whistle as we pull up to Fisher's Freight, seeing the ocean of vehicles in the parking lot. It looks like a convention.

Erika's eyes scan the packed two-acre parking lot. "It's bigger than I expected."

"And crowded. But then again, it's Saturday. In December." A twinge of guilt hits me that this place is so packed with business. I'm proud Blitzen isn't massive parking lots and corporate franchises, but it sucks for Bob that his weekend customers are probably all shopping here instead of at home.

"Where are we going to park?" She's peering from one side of the truck to the other.

"You can walk, right?" I look over my shoulder, backing my truck into a space about as far from the building as we can get. What the fuck? Am I going to drive around for thirty minutes, like a vulture, trying to steal a parking space from some old couple?

"Where do all these people come from?" Erika asks.

"From all over this part of the state and western West Virginia."

She lifts a brow curious for more information. "Have you ever heard of Harbor Freight?"

She shakes her head.

"Sam's Club? Walmart? Costco—Bass Pro Shop?"

"Of course. I grew up in a suburb not Mars. They were just called one of the above names, not Fisher's." She shakes her head at the sound of the foreign franchise.

"Think of Fisher's as the answer to all of those in this part of rural southeastern Kentucky. If your town doesn't have it, Fisher's does. Whatever it is. From a rifle to scotch tape to a five-gallon jar of pickles. Or a flannel jacket."

With the truck stopped, Erika grabs her door handle and tosses a look over her shoulder encouraging me to come on.

"Is this excitement?" I have to ask.

Long, dark—almost black locks of hair flip behind her as she jumps from my truck and moves to walk ahead. "Of course it's exciting. Everything new always is." That coil of confidence winds from her throat through a devilish grin she pauses to throw my way.

A thump or two knocks at my chest as I race to catch up to her.

"I mean, I can't commit to the five-gallon jar of pickles, but who's to say it won't be an impulse buy. That, and my wardrobe's low on flannel."

Isn't she proving to be the eager little beaver who's game for anything. *Right this way.* I gesture forward behind her, shaking my head at the acres of cars before us. *She's funny.* It takes me by surprise. And for a second, I'm not sure who's in charge between the two of us.

The thought is fleeting when we enter every grown man's nightmare—shopping through a crowded store on their day off.

"Kourt. Fancy running into you here." I don't get a smile with the greeting as we walk into Fisher's.

Apparently, being taken by surprise is the order of the day. *Great.*

"Morning, Quinn." I muster a mannerly nod.

Standing right in the entry, her eyes drag over Erika. "It's just a great day, I'm sure."

What do you want me to say, Quinn?

"Heard your girls played a hell of a game last night. Surprised… to see you here."

"Mamma dragged me with her. She wants one of those blow-up snowmen for the yard." And, she keeps glaring at Erika.

Cutting my eyes at the innocent Chicagoan at my side, I make the introduction. "Erika, this is Quinn Greely. Quinn, Erika Amherst."

Erika nods, smiling politely at the woman who's glowering at her. "It's very nice to meet you, Quinn." There's that genuine thing Helen mentioned. Erika means it.

She's classy.

Quinn shifts a little and darts her eyes back up to mine in an accusing glare.

Jesus.

"Quinn coaches girls' basketball and track at Willow Creek."

"How exciting." Erika says with more sincerity, then tilts her head back to meet my eyes. "I'll leave you two to it. I'm going to find the extension cords."

She grabs a shopping cart and rolls away, leaving me alone with Quinn.

"So, *she's* why…"

"No. She's just a friend. Not even that. An acquaintance."

"I know about you and friends."

Is there a fire retardant anywhere nearby? "Quinn, listen… I'm not—"

She shows me her palm to dismiss me, and I notice her long, fake fingernails. Something I never liked. It's not the fake thing, it's basketball. How could you legit play or coach with those things? It's painful to think of.

She snaps, "I don't want to hear it. I was just one of the trophies you collect." She nods in the direction Erika went. "Guess she's next." Quinn storms away.

I let her go.

What. The. Fuck. I'm not about to settle down with anyone. Quinn Greely's the perfect example: you see a woman for a few months, and she can't wait to change your bachelor status—as if it's a crime for a man to live alone and date. I just broke it off with her and she's still calling herself part of my collection. Oddly, that's exactly what she wants to be.

I didn't *use* her. We had a good time. If I used her, she used me. I always made sure… fuck. She was a consenting adult who told me she didn't have time for a relationship either.

"Got 'em!" Erika surprises me with a basket full of extension cords in every possible Christmas color combo and length. "Did you find your clips?" Something shiny catches her attention and she looks away from me. "Have you seen all these decorations?"

She's a kid in a candy store.

"Not yet."

Erika's gaze catches Quinn, who's easy to see, a head taller than any other woman in the place, pushing her shopping cart briskly away. "Was that your girlfriend?"

"No."

Erika dips her head. "Oh, sorry. Guess I mis-read."

"Clips, this way." I turn us away from Quinn and down a random aisle. Any aisle.

"Kourt!" The second most patronizing voice I could hear today calls out across the store. This one is a baritone, and a bastard.

What the fuck?

Is it old home week at Fisher's? Half of Blitzen and then some are here.

I look over my shoulder to the voice, seeing Ellis Andrews striding my way. *Christ.*

"Who you got here, McShotty?" our head football coach asks, his eyes about to pop out of his skull as he drinks in the woman at my side.

None of your fucking business.

I look at the classy girl who is most out of place in this neck of the woods and back at Ellis, who, I have to admit, is the winningest football coach in eastern Kentucky. *Fucker.*

"Ellis, this is Erika Amherst, Josephine's great-niece. Ellis Andrews is our football coach."

That smile on Ellis's face makes me want to punch it off. The piece of shit is salivating, his gaze dragging from the top of Erika's head to her furry snow boots and back up, lingering on her pretty pink lips. Her cheeks are the color of cherries from the cold.

Sucker's not even trying to be subtle.

Erika doesn't seem to notice.

"Erika, nice to meet you." Ellis tips his head, indicating me. "Heard you almost took out our basketball coach the other day."

Her pink cheeks flush crimson as she cuts her eyes up at me with shock. "You told everyone?"

"Not me." I didn't tell a soul.

Ellis, who likes to consider himself a ladies' man, smiles smugly, showing off a big dimple in his cheek—which Erika *does* seem to notice. Her eyes sparkle back at him.

I guess the fucker is a ladies' man.

Ellis keeps drinking her up with his eyes. "Nothing's secret in Blitzen. Everyone in the coffee shop got a front row seat to you bowling him over in the little Volkswagen. They've all been buzzing about what a knockout you are." He winks. "No pun intended."

She doesn't know what to say. After a couple of eyelid flutters, she's staring wide-eyed at Ellis with her mouth slightly open and mutters, "I apologized for what happened..."

Ellis and I lock eyes. Son of a bitch wants to get in her pants. Not happening.

He wants to drive a wedge between me and her—but he can't. There is no me and her. Still, I don't want her to think I've gone around town badmouthing her.

"Ellis, don't you have some shopping to do?" I take Erika by the elbow, guiding her away from the football coach who likes to score.

Erika's pushing the basket quietly, as I turn us down the actual aisle for clips.

"You know, I didn't tell anyone," I volunteer.

Erika shrugs and answers, not meeting my gaze. "You only get one chance to make a first impression. I guess I blew mine with Blitzen, if everyone's buzzing about my faux pas, like he said."

Can't say you haven't made one hell of an impression on me.

Pulling out of the parking lot—having dumped enough extension cords to light up half of America in the bed of my truck with Georgia's clips secured in the back seat, my stomach grumbles audibly.

An eyebrow rises from the passenger side, and I can't help releasing a smile.

"Are you *hungry*?"

"Yeah, I'm as hungry as a buzzard at a barbecue."

"I'm sorry?" She turns back to me slowly, squinting those beautiful blues and biting her bottom lip, which gives me license to go on.

"A mosquito at a picnic? A jackrabbit in a carrot patch? Is that small town Blitzen enough for ya?"

She's trying to press her mouth closed, but I like her laughter unrestrained. I like hearing her voice.

"How about as hungry as a basketball coach who hasn't eaten all day?" I look both ways as we pull out.

"Speaking of basketball, do you still play?"

"Some of the guys and I play when we can."

"Don't be modest. Helen told me you went to college on a basketball scholarship." Her big baby blues take me in, evoking the kind of energy that comes over me before a big game. A rush of adrenaline. *What the fuck?*

"Helen's a blabbermouth." I counter to shake the feeling.

"So, I have a thought." Erika shifts and positions herself toward me in her seat.

"Over somewhere we can eat?"

Her train of thought is interrupted by my proposal of food, and I swear when I drop my eyes I see her cheeks flush. She rolls her eyes as I return mine to the road. Cautiously, I wait for the idea to manifest, finally prompting. "Shoot. No pun intended."

"None here either. What about a charity basketball game? You get some of your college basketball buddies to come play against you and the volunteer fire department—people pay God-knows-what to watch—plus, the ladies auxiliary or Lion's Club, or any other organization vying for proceeds for the truck can do the concession stand and make a ton of additional money for your cause. What do you think?" She asks cooly, like she just proposed a dare.

"I think it's a hell of an idea—if anyone on the volunteer fire department could dribble a basketball and if any of my old buddies still played. Most went into coaching, like me, or teaching or accounting." *And the rest—are in the NBA, but who's counting.*

"It's not about how good you are—what is that everyone calls you, McShotty? It's for charity. The point is *you* entertain them on the basketball court, and they pay to watch. You get your college buddies or a good enough group that has a competitive following and you'll have more outsiders than you think. That's key. Bringing in more than Blitzen."

Smart. I'll give her that. She's smart.

"Maybe. It's not a bad idea."

She claps her hands again and wags her shoulders with pride. "Good. Then it's settled."

"I'm afraid I can't settle anything until my stomach is settled. You hungry? We can hit up a place on the way back."

"Okay. Since you drove me, I'll buy. I mean, if you hadn't had to drive me up here, you'd already have eaten, probably."

She pauses and almost pales, fumbling the words. "I mean, if you want to. You don't have to... if you're ready to get back. If there's someone or some reason you need to get back."

Nope, not letting her back out of this, but no way is she paying.

"The only thing I have to do when I get back is put up Georgia's lights. And you, Erika with a K, ad executive from Chicago, apparently, have to iron out some details of a charity basketball game."

SEVEN

Like Christmas Morning

Still out of breath from racing to meet Helen for breakfast, I trace my hand along the diner's glass tabletop after blurting out my order. My mind's tracing the red and white checkered cloth at the lunch spot Kourt drove me to the day before.

A quaint hole in the wall just outside of Blitzen that only locals know. I smile replaying the look on his face—like he was excited to take me there. Even though we stopped out of necessity, it was the same as riding in his truck. I never felt like I was riding with a stranger.

Intimate. The charming little place was *intimate.* Not us. Obviously. The cave man simply had to eat.

"Could I have fruit instead of home fries with my egg white omelet, please?" Helen's voice snaps me back to the bustling Blitzen diner.

"Already had the fruit cup down." Our waitress winks at Helen.

"Thanks, Dawnie." Helen's smile stretches across her tiny angular face. She chirps effervescently like a bird when she speaks and apparently eats like one too. I puff air into my cheeks in total recall of the sheer volume of breakfast fare I just ordered.

"So, you're sticking with the eggs benedict, extra hollandaise, a side of hash browns, and the gingerbread waffle with extra whipped cream?" The waitress also reminds me.

I nod as I zero in on her name tag. *Dawnie.* She seems nice enough. Nothing wrong with a sense of humor, and everyone in this town seems to have one. Her maroon apron spins away from our table and toward the onlooking breakfast goers.

I'm guessing that football coach wasn't far off. I'm still the talk of the town. My eyes graze across the town's faces. I assume it's the entire town. The diner is full, and the population in Blitzen is not that large.

"Ignore them. You're fresh meat. At least this is only a quarter of them, and the tame quarter at that. We've dodged the church goers. The real vultures won't be let out again until noon." Helen waves at what looks like three generations coming through the door as an older man and his son follow what must be the grandson to his favorite booth. The family resemblance is uncanny.

"They're sweet." I nod at the three ball caps staring our way as they settle into their booth.

"Don't stare back too long. This is a small town in Kentucky. Ever seen *Deliverance*?"

"Helen!"

"I'm *joking*. They've all been looking forward to you coming and now that you're here they—well, they're staring. That's all there is to it. I don't have a valid excuse or an antidote, other than you'll get used to it."

"It's fine. Aunt Josie's a tough act to follow. I'm sure they're wondering where my top hat is or when I'm going to leap out of our booth and ask the line cook to dance to the first song that comes on the juke box."

"Speaking of songs on the juke box... anything new with your mysterious tape?"

"Nope. It didn't play for me this morning on my way here. I hope that's not all she's got. But hey, it's inspired me already, so let's just skip the jokes about how Aunt Josie's place currently looks like the North Pole after a few too many, and that I literally just caught you—"

Several large plates are dropped in front of us, and Helen squints at me above the egg white omelet.

"You have to work for it, you little devil. No one over the age of twenty-three has a metabolism that produces a statue in heels such as yourself, and you my little pixie, bird-like, Vogue model attorney friend, don't either."

"F— you, Erika with a K. I happen to love egg whites and fresh fruit cups."

"Fish sticks. You can say 'fish sticks' when you have the urge to say—"

"Do you mean, *fiddle sticks*?"

"Never mind. So. I've made a chart." Brushing my hair behind both ears, I fan my hands out in excitement. Our table is full of piping hot holiday deliciousness, but I'm suddenly not hungry anymore as I lean down toward my large red velvet tote with the braided white handle. It has an applique of a ice skate on the front of it. A fun find from Josie's attic. It's vintage and I'm obsessed.

With my extended three-ring binder in hand I scan the plates below looking for more room, only to find a massive bite torn from my waffle. Helen blinks fake interest my way, trying to divert me from her full cheeks as she chews with her mouth closed.

"Really?"

"It's gingerbread and it's December. It would be a crime not to taste it while it's hot."

"Okay, fine. Your lack of any real restraint when it comes to holiday breakfast items suggest we actually may become good friends. Now, swallow that, and tell me about Walter Miller and his trees."

Helen takes a large gulp of her coffee and tilts her head feigning confusion. "Well. Mr. Miller used to have a tree lot, but he hasn't in years. Not since Kourt and I were kids, and not since I came back into town. Who told you about him?"

Opening my notebook to the first page, I check off the box by tree lot. "So, it was a bona fide tree lot? And he still produces trees? He just doesn't sell them anymore?"

"I mean there's talk of the demented old buzzard still out there every two weeks with garden sheers or whatever you shape Douglas

Firs with, but no, he doesn't run a tree farm anymore. And he never sold them. That was the main issue."

"What do you mean he didn't sell them?"

"When we were kids, he had just retired. His wife passed long before that, and they had planted those initial trees together for something fun to do in our Christmas-themed town after retirement." She eyes my gingerbread waffle.

"No. Not until you finish. Keep going."

"Anyway, he didn't have the heart to charge the people of Blitzen, so in honor of his wife, he opened the lot and let each household come pick out and chop down their own Christmas tree."

"That may be the most endearing thing I've ever heard."

"Wait for it. People are picky, especially in a town named after an iconic Christmas character. Every year more people came to the lot and every year more trees were wasted. The boyfriend would chop one down and girlfriend thought it wasn't full enough after all, so they tossed it aside. Mom would point and dad would run over with the ax, then when mom got there with the kids, she'd say, 'No! It was the taller one two rows over.' And so on. You get the point. Each year, until Kourt and I turned about thirteen, it was a Christmas tree massacre. At one point surrounding towns were coming over and taking advantage of the free hayride Mr. Miller offered—"

"Hayride?"

"Yes. You need transportation through the acreage of evergreens. How else would you pick out your tree and cart it back?"

"Okay. The fact that you know this, and don't insist it keeps happening every Christmas, is stunning to me. That, and does this story get better?"

"Unfortunately, no. Mr. Miller created the Christmas chain saw massacre of Blitzen in the mid 2000's. Fed up with wasted trees and greedy towns folk, he locked the gate."

I look at her, appalled at her hometown's behavior. "I don't blame him."

"Well—he blamed us. Still does. Mr. Miller became a recluse, showing up for the town meetings only to taunt us with his scowl and never vote for or against anything, and he makes Dawnie here deliver his Salisbury steak every Thursday night after her dinner shift."

Dawnie rolls her eyes toward me as she refills my coffee. "Yup. He refuses to come in and associate with the likes of us anymore. But he'll eat our food. Lord knows we can't let the salty bastard go hungry."

"This is the *worst* story I've ever heard."

"Not really. Who else you got in that notebook of yours to ask about? I'm here all day." Helen reaches for more of my gingerbread waffle, and I'm too dumbstruck to spat her hand.

"Okay. But not all day. I actually have a two o' clock." She speaks blatantly with her mouth full.

"On a Sunday?"

I can't imagine what in this tiny town has her working on the weekends.

"Don't ask. Don't tell."

"Gross." I look up at Dawnie for confirmation, but she's already walked away laughing.

"Hey, how do you know I'm not getting right with our maker. It is Sunday after all." Helen throws her crumpled napkin in her half-eaten plate of egg whites as she dives into my cold benedict.

"Oh, don't worry. I've got your number. Let's just say you remind me very much of someone else I know."

I try to smile, but I can't. All the holiday banter aside, my heart is broken over Mr. Miller.

"Speaking of someone you know. Who the heck told you about Mr. Miller and—" Helen's pristine red nails trace down the names of townspeople in my color-coated notebook. "And everybody else—*Dang*. Am I on there?"

Helen's pointer finger pauses by Bob and the hardware store. Her tiny red nail taps on my scribbled in excerpt by his name as her face slowly changes and tilts to mine. "Kourt. Kourt told you about all of these people." Her face is strange.

"Wow. You're good. See, I went to the hardware store, like you said, and I bumped into your friend."

"Kourt."

"Would you stop saying his name like that?"

"Could you start saying it? I mean, you clearly know him now." Helen makes a face I don't recognize. It's a knowing look that suggests she knows something I don't.

"Anyway. Go back to the hardware store where you bumped into my best friend."

"Okay. Bob was out of everything I needed and your—" *Fine. I'll play.* "*Kourt* needed clips for Bob's wife's Christmas lights.

Something about hanging them on the outside of the house under the gutters. And Bob was out of those too. He suggested we go to Fisher's to get everything we needed."

"Who suggested? Bob? Or Kourt?"

"Bob. Bob recommended Fisher's."

"Ah. Now we're getting somewhere." Helen's demeanor completely relaxes, and she goes in for another bite off one of my neglected plates. "I'm sorry, I just had to understand how the contents of that three-ring binder came about. There is no way Kourt volunteered all that information."

"He didn't. In fairness to him, I ask a lot of questions. Actually, that may have been unfair to him, seeing as how I developed his answers into a complete town overhaul of a Christmas agenda over lunch."

"Wait a minute—You two had lunch together?" Helen's red stained lips paint a wide smile, and she waves Dawnie over to refill her coffee and probably eavesdrop. "Do tell."

Starving from the big breakfast I never achieved and skipping lunch, I search through Josie's cabinet for anything that resembles a can opener to make my tuna fish. I've got to get to a grocery store. I'm afraid Great Aunt Josie having a cherry pitter and a crème brûlée torch in the drawer that should house a can opener solidifies that.

I slam the drawer shut and reach toward her gold swan faucet to wash my hands, wishing I could hold the can of tuna under hot enough water until it popped open. My mind flashes to the lunch I had the day before where I felt quite satiated.

Damn it all. Why does she say his name that way, and why do I keep replaying it?

After brunch with Helen, I went through the rest of the boxes in the attic.

My hunches were all confirmed as the last row of boxes revealed enough Christmas decor to, in fact, decorate a small town.

That, and the wine cellar I found in the back of the attic, God love Aunt Josie, instead of in the basement... *Wait. Is there a basement? Hmmm.* I'll save that one for another day when I'm not two over-poured glasses of Chablis-in on an empty stomach.

Kourt-schmourt. He's just a boy man in a great big, small town. What does he know about anybody or anything? He did buy me lunch though. A red and white checkered tablecloth and his smell-good smile.

I made this binder on my own off information he volunteered and I'm proud of it. He didn't show me the ropes. He drove me to Fisher's. *Possibly for rope as they would have that there. They have everything. Even hot basketball coach chauffeurs and hand-some football coach gossips and all of their floozy Archer-style lady friends.*

Hungry, and with heavy feet, I slump my way to Aunt Josie's absurd sectional. It looks like it belongs in a speakeasy.

I can't be certain of the time that passed. After all, I'm on moun-tain time. Wait, am I Central time, but just in the mountains or is this Eastern? "Alexa! Who is Kentucky's time zone? And, why is there a can of tuna fish in my hand?"

My stomach growls again. *Or wait. That's not my belly.*

"So when am I picking you up?" The sound of my best friend's voice is so faint it's almost like a dream or early stages of schizophrenia as I'm hearing him in the walls.

"Oh!" I dig through the garland-covered coffee table and lift an array of Christmas tree skirts from where they're draped across my laptop. "Hey." I've been riding such a high since breakfast turned brunch with Helen—turned fasting for me slash wine for dinner, that I forgot who I am. "Jesus. Archer!"

"How very Catholic of you on a Sunday."

I toss my monstrosity of a notebook aside so I can take its seat in front of my laptop to see my best friend. "Pick me up?"

"From the airport. You've got to be bored to tears by now. There are some situations, Erika with a "K" not even you can make the best of."

"Actually, it's not that bad."

I lean into frame with a wide-eyed grin I can't salvage, as I toss my can of unopened tuna fish onto the discarded Christmas tree skirts. "Arch. It's really amazing. I think my great aunt sent me here for a reason."

"Is she dead? Did you find out yet?"

"I don't think so. There would have been a lot more paper-work."

"So, Egypt or some trip to a nudist colony with bored Midwest-erners, then? What's the deal? She's going to leave you the last place she inhabits every time she moves onto greener pastures? I can't believe she wouldn't just tell you where she is."

"Hey. I know somebody else who exists relying on greener pastures. Her philosophy has always been freedom and anonymity are the key to knowledge and adventure. If anyone can identify with that sentiment, it's you, dear heart. Honestly, I think this is a one-time place. It's like she handpicked it for me. You said yourself when we opened the envelope, it couldn't have come at a better time."

"Yeah, it's a nice break after a pitch that went south, but you don't have to stay. What am I'm going to do for the holidays?"

"You said you would come here."

"I was pretending to be supportive."

"Archer. I'll say what you won't say for fear of hurting my feelings. You'll be stuck in town inundated with the Harmon account I was dropped from."

"Not the entire time. What about the rest of the holiday break, and the employee Christmas party? You know I can't bring a date. They'll think it's serious."

"That fruitcake is a package I have no interest in unwrapping."

"Which part?"

"Not your love life, we both know that has no resolve. Me. Office. Christmas Party. Not this year, buddy."

"Fine. But what about the rest? We spend every Christmas together. We decorate every year."

"No, Archer. We don't. Chicago decorates for Christmas and we sneak a peek on the way to meetings until they let us off for a few days, of which you and I get together between your failed second dates and share a Merry Christmas toast at our favorite bar with the fireplace, clear white lights, and one perfectly tasteful wreath hung with the red velvet bow. All the while I walk home alone in the cold, wishing I'd gotten a Christmas tree after all."

"But I thought—"

"This place is different, Archer. I don't know... I feel it's—like I'm supposed to be here right now. Hey. Knock Great Aunt Josie all you wish, but in true *Auntie Mame* fashion, these people *need a little Christmas*... and so do I."

Loud claps sound from my laptop, and I peek back at my screen to see Archer slow clapping. "You really drank the Kool-Aid, or I guess Eggnog is more appropriate."

"*Woo!* Good idea." I jump away from the couch to grab my grocery list on the kitchen island.

"What? It doesn't pour from their faucets?" Archer's sardonic mumble is barely audible.

"What?"

"Nothing. It's just been a tough week at work on the Harmon case. Talk to me later."

I step back toward the frozen black screen where Archer has muted his mic and closed his video feed.

EIGHT

Out to Lunch

"What the fuck, Kourt?" Helen's glare feels like a slap.

She never glares at me.

"What are you talking about?" I'm shouting into my phone. At a time like this, Helen's 'Everything we say, we say to each other's face' rule—aka we don't call, we Facetime—is less than ideal.

Helen's delicately arched brows pull together, which makes that normally beautiful face a lot less beautiful as she throws a snarky accusation at me through the screen. "You spent Saturday with Erika?"

"No."

Shit.

She chunks an imaginary something at me, then opens an overhead cabinet door. "Yes, you did. If you took her to Fisher's *and* ate lunch, you spent most of the day together."

Christ.

I'm stretched out, comfortable on the couch, with my eyes on Monday Night Football. Now, I have to sit up straight to defend myself. "Look, I had to go to Bob's to get clips for Georgia's outside lights, and when I walk in, Bob's sending Erika off to Fisher's in that Beetle of Josie's. The one she doesn't know how to drive. I couldn't let her get—"

"Don't say it."

"Bob brought it up." I flail my arm. I still don't know why brown or black cords wouldn't do but they wouldn't. "He didn't have what she was after, so he told her I'd take her to Fisher's. What was I supposed to do? Say 'fuck, no, I'm not taking you,' and let her wreck on her way up the mountain? That'd be a little rude, wouldn't you say?"

"I said don't go there." Now *her* voice is ice.

"Shit! Fuck! What a stupid play."

"Are you talking to me?"

She knows better. "The game."

"What game?"

"Bengals. They're getting their asses handed to them."

It's a train wreck on TV and I can't pull my eyes off of it.

"Should've known you'd be watching football on Monday night." Helen takes a deep breath and twists her neck. She's studying me like I'm a crook and she's a cop, as my attention pegs between her and this massacre of my favorite team.

She pours herself a glass of red wine, standing at her bar. "You ate lunch?" Sounds like another accusation.

"I was hungry by the time we left. What's with the Inquisition? I'm watching the game. Burrows just got sacked again."

"Screw Burrows."

"Steelers just did that." *Shit, that hurt.* "They blindsided him."

"Pay attention!" Helen's yelling at me again. She never yells at me. "I never knew you to spend a whole day with anyone, McShotty. Not since—"

Okay. That does it.

"It wasn't the whole day and like I said, I got railroaded."

"You're saying you don't like her?"

"I'm saying I did your quasi-client a favor. I thought it was the right thing to do on your behalf."

My attention swings back to the game with a raucous roar of the crowd that fills The Jungle. Can't help it.

"Dammit, guys, give him some fucking protection. Who's coaching the offensive line?"

Helen's got a one-track mind. "Let's get together and have a drink, you, me, and—"

"Nip it, Choi. I mean drop it. Fuck. Enough. You're not setting me up with anyone. How many times have I got to tell you?"

"So, I take it you don't want to have a drink with—"

"Bye. I'm going back to my game."

Why does everyone want to set me up with someone? What's wrong with my life like it is? I'm good. I'm grounded. Leave me the fuck alone.

"Are we ready for the meeting tomorrow night?" Randy Jones, our fire chief pleads for our attention. He's a big guy. I mean he's as tall as I am, which makes him one of the two tallest men in town, but Randy outweighs me by at least a hundred pounds.

He retired in Blitzen from the Knoxville Fire Department five years ago and slid right into the position of Chief of our volunteer fire department. He was a natural fit. He brought so much knowledge and professionalism that none of us had.

He's put us through all kinds of training that's given us a better rating than we had before he arrived. That alone lowered property rates. Now, this edict from the state to get a bigger, fancier fire truck has probably worried him more than anyone. He feels responsible.

The truth is the guy's as good as gold. His grandfather was the first black fire chief in Knoxville, so Randy started an after-school program for all ethnicities represented in professional positions and acts of service to give back and let the youth see their faces making a difference in the community. He started it in Knoxville and brought it to Blitzen when he and his wife moved here.

"Any ideas on how we're going to raise the money for this truck?" Chief asks our monthly meeting of volunteers gathered in the high school cafeteria.

It's not the first time he's asked it, and once again, not one of us has an answer.

I have a flash memory of what Erika said the other day. "Can we raise money through taxes? Can't we create a fire district that collects taxes?"

Randy's grin is laden with snide. "Sure. Absolutely. If the deadline wasn't next month."

We all look at each other, helpless.

"Grants?" someone asks.

"Again. Deadline looming." Randy sighs. "Okay. The town meeting's tomorrow night at city hall. Everyone, go home and pray for a Christmas miracle. Pray someone comes forward with an idea that will save us. Dismissed."

As I stand to leave, I hear, "Kourt."

I didn't escape fast enough.

"Ellis?" I turn to face him.

He saunters up to me in his Burbury sweater. Ellis spends more money on clothes than I do on my truck. Surprised he didn't leave the price tag on.

He eyes me up and down. "So... you and the chick at Fisher's..."

"Erika. What about her?"

He shrugs. "Are you a... *thing*?"

Ellis is maybe four years older than me. Never married. Having played college football, he's tall, but not as tall as me, thick through the shoulders, getting a little gray around the ears as he ages. But he's almost always got a girl salivating on his arm.

I knew at Fisher's he had a hard-on for her.

"I drove Erika to Fisher's to get extension cords for her Christmas decorations. She's got a shitload that belong to Josie. That's all. Why?"

"That means she's fair game."

That's a statement, not a question, that for some reason, makes my hackles rise. The odd sensation makes me bite back. "She's not a fucking white-tailed deer."

"You know what I mean. If you don't have a claim—"

Why do I want to reach out and throttle him? "I don't have a claim, but she's not your type."

He grins like a barn cat about to pounce on a baby chick. "She'll say yes if I ask. And just to be clear—*what's my type, McShotty?*"

Ellis is bowed up.

So am I. Feels like we're circling for a throwdown. "Your kind? The kind you can fuck and forget."

That's not Erika. If you went there, you wouldn't want to leave. You won't be able to forget. Like I said, not his type. Or mine.

Ellis scoffs. "Fuck 'em and forget 'em? Sounds more like your angle lately."

I'm going to wipe that sneer off his face.

"Coach Greely didn't seem too happy to see you at Fisher's with your new friend. Can't say I'd kick Quinn off rotation, but for Erika, I might."

I may go ahead and throttle him.

"Kourt! Ellis! I need you two!"

Saved by the Chief's bark. *Ellis* is saved by the Chief. I was about to grab his thick neck and lift him off the ground. I've got him by half a foot, and my hands are big enough to reach around his stovepipe neck. I guarantee I can...

"My wife has an idea." Chief waves us over.

His wife is at his side with short gray hair, bright eyes, and a knowing smile. They're a matched pair. Randy has his arm wrapped around her shoulder.

"You two look like you're... competitive." Sharletta Jones says, looking from me to Ellis.

Guess we had an audience.

"What would you two think about a friendly competition between the basketball team and the football team? Let's channel that energy in a positive way."

Ellis cuts his eyes at me and scrubs his hand over his chin. I know him. He wants to blindside me. He'll find any way he can to do it. Shithead.

"What kind of game?" he asks, peering at Sharletta. "You mean football or basketball?"

"Neither." The chief grins and his eyes glimmer as he and his wife exchange looks, both of them smiling. "To make it fair, Sharletta and I challenge you two to a fund-raising competition. Which of your teams can raise the most money for the fire department?"

They cut their eyes between me and Ellis. It's like they expect us to go ahead and start throwing punches any second.

I might.

"Any way we want?" I ask.

Sharletta smiles up at Randy to confirm, but this is her idea. Randy nods at his wife, giving her back the floor.

"All's fair in love, war and fund-raising, gentlemen." Sharletta winks as Randy helps her into her jacket.

Ellis and I glare at each other for a long beat. Fucker.

"I'm in."

I feel my smile growing. It's a little smug. Someone gave me one hell of an idea the other day.

Ellis offers his hand. "You're on, McShotty."

NINE

Pitching Blitzen

Make an S, or was it an H? H. Yes— 'H,' like Helen, the one who taught me.

I make my best H motion with the stick shift, hitting what feels like reverse, and roll down the drive. I'm hoping my leg is shaking because it's freezing cold in this short sweater dress.

I can't be nervous. *Can I?*

And is a short—let's say shorter than I'd normally wear—sweaterdress the best choice for today?

Yes. I stand by that choice.

Archer always says if you want to get noticed, you have to get seen first.

Here's looking at you, kid.

I peek down at my bare thighs and knees. That's a lot of skin exposed.

To be fair, my boots are tall, and the leg warmers come up four inches above them. Still. A pair of tights wouldn't have done any harm. However, I am Josie's great niece, and I'd like them to recognize me at the meeting.

Who am I to let anyone down.

I pucker my raspberry lip stain in the rear-view mirror. Jeepers, my eyelashes do look fake with this new mascara. Shockingly I'm the poster child for a product that works. Deal with it, Kourt.

Still shivering from the waist down, I reach to turn the heat all the way up and the tape deck clicks on instead. A smile spreads wide across my face as I coast down Main Street beaming like a lunatic toward town hall, to children singing, *"Roll Out the Holly!"*

I laugh out loud.

It's from the Rosalind Russell movie *Auntie Mame*. Or—the Broadway show first, then there was also the Lucille Ball version, but who cares? Despite her Easter egg-dyed red hair color, Great Aunt Josie actually looks more like the Rosaland Russel version.

Wow. Yes. *Yes, we do need a little Christmas, Blitzen.* Perfect timing.

"Wowsers! Look at you, Erika." Helen turns to eye me up and down as I approach the small group she and Kourt are huddled in. She steps toward me with wide, sparkling eyes.

And damn it if she isn't dressed down for this. For the first time, she's in sleek dark denim jeans and a navy-blue turtleneck. Great. *This* is when she wears her weekend clothes, on a Tuesday night among all the other town folk ironclad in their flannel shirt jackets.

I look like a cupcake in snow boots next to all the denim and plaid.

A pair of slacks turn front and center and beeline a few steps to land by Helen. I feel eyes on me as I raise mine from his charcoal-colored, neatly-pressed pants legs to a nice black belt and perfectly fitted dark teal sweater.

My heart skips a beat before I realize who's looking at me.

"And here I thought you'd have found one of Josephine's ugly Christmas sweaters and sported that for affect."

Kourt's eyes find mine and I watch them trace up and down my outfit. He pauses when they reach my eyes again, and I squirm a little in my boots like a child who has to go to the bathroom. At least he dressed up for the meeting. Maybe that's what he wears when he teaches... when he's not coaching.

I smile toward Helen to get my head in the game.

"You do look great!" Helen insists, and with that, something comes over me.

"Well, I would have gone for the ugly Christmas sweater... 'tis the season, and to fit in and all..." My eyes flash back up at Kourt's face and land on his gaze. "Sorry to disappoint."

I flash my lashes at him, then roll my eyes back to Helen. "You'll never guess what song came on in the car on the drive here." I squeeze Helen's boney arm with excitement. "We Need A Little Christmas!"

"'Right this very minute'?" she recites part of the chorus with a cunning smile.

"Sarcasm will get you everywhere with me," I all but squeal, thinking of the meeting and the pitch I prepped for the town. "It's a sign, don't you think?"

Kourt leans in with his hands in his pockets. "That happens to you a lot, doesn't it?" He squints down at me with a wicked smile, as a gavel sounds within the double doors behind us. The crowd begins shuffling inside.

How are there so many people?

"I thought this town was small."

"*Everyone* comes to the meetings. It's their thing." Helen answers over her shoulder as she ushers us in through the packed doorway. An accidental shove pushes me to the side as someone worms their way through, and I see a hand reach back for mine.

I grab it, thinking it's Helen's, only it's way too big to be Helen's delicate hand, and it's attached to something much taller.

An electric charge shoots through my arm like I stuck my finger in a light socket, and I freeze as Kourt's eyes blink back at mine in shock as he pauses through the crowd passing around us.

I pull my hand away and search for Helen. I'm sure that's whose hand he thought he was reaching for anyway. *Although sufficiently awkward, nonetheless.*

This place is packed. Why would so many people show up for a town hall? I'm amazed at how quickly people filter into place. Someone calls Kourt's name across the room and I see him lace through the crowd to take a seat next to several high school kids in team jerseys in the rows of chairs on the opposite side of the room.

"Erika!" Helen shouts from a few rows in front of where I'm standing. She pats the chair next to her and motions for me to hurry. The gavel sounds again and I'm staring at a row of very serious-looking town officials. They sit facing the crowd. There's nine of them staring right at me.

"Relax. You've been deer in the headlights since the first knock of the gavel. It's only a tiny wooden hammer, tapped by a tiny bald man who has nothing better to do than run this meeting. This is a cake walk compared to what you're used to in Chicago."

"I'm fine. I'm relaxed." I pull my hand away from where Helen pats it. It's the same hand Kourt held and I'm back to squirming like a child. "I just don't get it." I whisper-shout into her ear. "All these people. They all turn up for this, yet not one Christmas decoration? What's their motivation for this, above the Christmases they're used to?"

"Money. Honey. Seriously, if they don't solve this issue, the insurance premiums and taxes could end small business, home and property owners, and that's what this town is made of. I'm afraid they're null and void of the Christmas spirit, worrying about their own futures in Blitzen instead."

The gavel knocks faster and angrier this time. Whispers cease, as all eyes turn to our mini meeting.

"Mrs. Choi. I've been calling this meeting to order for the last five minutes. Your guest apparently has a lot to say. Should we have her take the floor first? I see you've penciled her onto my list." The tiny bald man with the tiny wooden hammer looks above his glasses at me. He looks like an elf, or a misfit toy at the very least. If Archer were here, a joke of him running a meeting in a town called Blitzen would not be lost on this moment.

Helen pushes me out of my seat, and I'm on my feet pulling down my absurdly short sweaterdress to make sure it covers my butt.

"She's ready, Mayor Harris." Judas hands me my heavy three ring binder.

I don't remember setting it down or even walking in with it. I've got this. I really do. Selfishly, I adore Christmas and coming to a small town to experience it in true great Aunt Josephine style should be motivation enough to nail this pitch.

"That's right, Mayor Harris. I'm excited to be here and for the warm welcome everyone I've met has given me. Blitzen is just a wonderful place. I'm sure all of you fine people are responsible for that."

I smile and look at the long table stretched in front of me.

There's no warm reception, so I drop my eyes and turn to the crowd surrounding me. Again, crickets.

Helen clears her throat beside me. I don't have to look down at her to know she's urging me to get on with it.

"As most of you know, I'm Josephine Amherst's great niece. Apart from being delighted to be here through the holidays with you all, I found I couldn't wait to experience a touch of the magic that is Blitzen during Christmas. Upon arrival, I noticed it's fallen short of that magic this year."

I pause, as the silence behind me is deafening.

There's an additional throat clearing somewhere near where Kourt sits, and then what feels like a concert of whispers conducts its way through the crowd.

"Aunt Josie has a tone of decorations in her attic. Enough to decorate the entire town."

Oh. My. God. Why am I talking so fast?

I blurt that out like Ralphie from *The Christmas Story,* "And I know you have plenty from yesteryear, probably stored in this building. Aren't there some tinsel-covered candle sticks from the 1960s the size of a large awning to hang on the streetlamps? Or a gigantic wreath or two for the courthouse and post office? Come on now. We're batting for zero here in a town named after Christmas that apparently was once famous for its holiday magic. Ergo, I propose we give it a go again this Christmas."

Wow. I just used 'ergo' and 'give it a go' in the same sentence. I sound like a real fish-sticking wordsmith. "And I was hoping I could help."

I step forward and look around the crowd. And now I sound like a complete jack ass.

"Mr. Miller? You and I have a tree lot to discuss, and where's June? June, I heard you're in charge of the town lights and decorating the courthouse and town square every year. Don't people come from miles away to drive through and see the lights? Or *didn't they,* once upon a time?"

A silver-haired, attractive women with a weathered face and a nasty scowl peeks up at me from her buttoned-down flannel. A wisp of white hair drops across her face from her low ponytail as her eyebrows pinch together. June, I presume. She looks to be in her seventies and not very happy about it.

The gavel sounds again, and my heart starts a slow, timed out thump.

Yet I persevere.

"First Baptist. You're the church with the Charles Dicken's choir costumes for caroling, I heard. We just need to schedule you on the evening along with hot chocolate and hot apple cider venders while the people are driving through town square. They could get out and walk the grounds and shop venders. There's enough of our people that participate in the Christmas Flea market to put their booths between here and the courthouse."

Raising up on my tip toes I search for my antique dealer-friend who sold me the mixtape. "Where are you Mr. Hawkins?" However, I quickly pipe down when I feel my sweater-dress riding up.

"You guys could have a bona fide Christmas on the square again."

"Miss Amherst, I presume. Do you have any idea what this meeting was called for tonight? Blitzen's in real trouble. And I'm afraid our Christmas décor is the last thing on the list."

If I wasn't getting reprimanded in front of an entire small town, I would've laughed out loud. Mayor Harris literally sounds like he's delivering a line from a classic Claymation Christmas cartoon.

"Exactly, Harris. Erika knows *exactly* what this meeting is for. That's why she's here." Helen stands beside me and grabs the notebook from my side. "This notebook of hers is full of ideas. Huge ideas that are bigger and better than any fundraiser we've dreamed up yet."

"It is?" I whisper to Helen, and she elbows my side as she continues.

Helen scans the town officials in front of us and lands on a more reasonable-looking, middle-aged man. "Now Tom, you know yourself, you've only got bake sales and Christmas car washes on the list, and that's small potatoes compared to what this town has to draw in. We all know what a fire truck costs. If you hear her out, you'll see that bringing back Christmas to the town of Blitzen doesn't just benefit us by way of holiday spirit and boosting morale, but we'll charge folks from surrounding towns a reasonable amount to come enjoy. You don't need a bunch of small fundraisers. This—*she* is your fundraiser. Erika's got enough in that notebook, that the fee to park for out-of-town visitors will make thousands."

A mumble snakes its way around the crowd, and I hear people whispering behind me.

"Go ahead Erika. Tell them."

Ten

Great Idea

Helen leans in to whisper in my ear, "Dollar signs, honey. It's all in your big black book. Just add dollar signs. Money talks, and they're desperate for some."

She sits and gives me back the floor.

"She's not wrong, we could charge for all of this. It could be free to all residents of Blitzen, and a fee for those coming in from surrounding towns, with discounts for kids and students and seniors, of course. We keep it affordable, friendly and welcoming. But if we draw in the numbers, we'll make the money you need off of hot chocolate sales a heck of a lot faster than any car wash."

Pride consumes me as I get exactly why Helen and Aunt Josie made a great team. She's a genius, and at this juncture, I'm not sure who's crazier.

"Okay. As Helen said, we start with the already scheduled activities, we just charge and make it part of the Old-Fashioned Blitzen Christmas of yesteryear. Once we decorate, surrounding towns will catch on. There will be press and articles that suggest Blitzen is back and at it again, 'just in time for Christmas'."

"Give *her* the key to the storage with the lights, if she's begging for it. Hell, let her do it if she wants to this bad. No skin off my back." June rustles in her seat as her raspy voice declares me officiant of the Christmas lights.

"That's absolutely not the spirit, June." I try not to make eye contact with my new frenemy.

"Just remember, kid, what goes up, must come down. I assume you'll be gracing us with your presence long enough to clean up— or will you be back in your windy city while we're left taking the holiday shit show down?"

June's a real peach apparently.

More rogue shouts produce from the crowd.

"Yeah. If she wants Christmas here again, let her do it! Let her put forth all the work and effort it cost us in the past."

"But it's your ultimate fundraiser, as Helen said. It would be earning you the firetruck," I defend. My heart grows heavier in my chest, and I feel like I'm about to break out in a cold sweat.

"Tom, how do we even know if she could make us money like this?" A random man shouts from deep within the crowd and several other men and women second his emotion in rapid fire.

"Heck, we've already missed the first week of December by the time we end this meeting and get started. That's more than behind. We've never pulled it off so quickly in the past, and that's before we charged folks." Another naysayer gets theirs in.

My head is spinning.

I feel like I'm back in the office at my ad firm—that Ivy league assistant who spelled my name wrong, staring me down and Archer hanging his head embarrassed for me.

"Wait a minute. You didn't even hear her out. You all should be ashamed of yourselves."

A voice I recognize all too well, given that he's a practical stranger, silences the crowd.

Kourt stands and all eyes flock to him.

"No one else has come up with anything better. Ellis and I have been solicited for a fundraiser in a little friendly competition between the football team and my basketball players, but apart from that, I didn't see anyone else signing up for this proverbial bake sale being tossed around. And Helen's right. It won't be enough. Erika knows what she's doing. These are time-tested traditions the town has pulled off before, but this time they'll achieve our fire truck. It's brilliant. Trust her. It's what she does. She already gave my team our idea for our fundraiser. We're going to have a play-off game that brings in more than just our town to enjoy."

Heat fills my chest and stomach as I hear Kourt, of all people, singing my praises.

I can't even look his way as I stand staring at the Mayor and who-ever Tom is, and a beautiful black woman in her forties wearing a blue velvet blazer at the end of the official's table. Kourt must really want this truck to put his faith in me. I can barely drive a stick shift.

"That's the ticket right there. It's what Helen was trying to tell you. You can't have a fundraiser that bleeds the town dry. If we all had the money, we would've donated it for the truck already. We need some serious dough to pull this off by the new year, and Blitzen being the Christmas town it once was under Erika's plan of outsiders coming in and paying affordably for their holiday enjoyment—you can't get a surer bet than that."

Kourt's basketball team stands and claps behind him.

More from the crowd begin a slow clap, and Helen winks beside me. The gavel goes off as Kourt takes his seat. It takes me a moment to realize I'm still standing like some sacrificial lamb. Was this Helen's idea or Kourt's? Or was it all in my black binder from the start, I just didn't realize how bad or soon they needed a fire truck.

This time Tom bypasses Mayor Harris' gavel and stands. "Erika, I think you've got yourself an Old-Fashioned Blitzen Christmas, and we're delighted to have you here working on our behalf. But—" Tom zeroes in on June and the rest of the crowd. "You can't do it all by yourself. Folks, she's going to need each and every one of you to make this happen in time. We're already behind on decorating, much less pulling off the events and recreation for people to come and enjoy."

"That's right Tom, how will we bring people in? How will they know?" The lady I thought I liked in the fabulous blue blazer throws the town another wrench.

"You leave that to me, Tom. I'm in advertising, that's one attribute I can absolutely bring to the table. There'll be a campaign launched at Fishers before noon tomorrow." My voice rings of confidence as I look the blue blazer lady in the eye.

"That's even better Erika, but you still can't do this alone. Even if everyone in your notebook cooperates, you don't know anyone or how to go about soliciting their help."

"Tom, she's got to have a right-hand person to show her the ropes and tell her who to call on for what. Hell, somebody to drive her around and keep that pour excuse of a Volkswagen off our highways." Mayor Harris ignites in laughter and so does the crowd.

"He'll do it!" Helen's scream funnels through my right ear as her arm points across my face like an arrow shooting straight at Kourt. "I nominate Kourt. He's already making weekly stops to every business for the can drive. He can take Erika along, and to whomever or wherever else she needs to get to."

The Mayor scans the rows of chairs and dips below his glasses to confirm. "Kourt?"

This has to work. I stare down at the phone tree chart from past Christmases the mayor gave me. He might as well have directed me to the Blitzen phone book if there is such a thing. I make a gallant effort not to sigh in defeat as I tuck the twenty-page list in my notebook and search for Helen in the exiting crowd.

Careful what you wish for. I *have* to do this now, and I know I can. Since leaving Chicago, the office... Archer, I haven't looked back, and it's served me. I've found a friend in Helen who makes me feel closer to Great Aunt Josie, wherever she may be.

God rest or fuel her antics.

I found a town that didn't quite embrace me, but now they're counting on me, just like I'm oddly counting on Christmas like it's my damn job. And if I can't do my job at work, I'm going to make this the most successful Christmas break ever.

I need this.

However, I don't need to be a burden on anyone. I search through the filtering crowd. Some make their way to the exit while most hang around visiting, as if these town folk are friendly. You could've fooled me. A young couple turns to stare at me as I pass. They must be on this list. Dreading my call or upcoming visit. *They seem happy and bright.*

Great. I'm already on track to becoming the most annoying person in town, meanwhile with a little effort on their part, my plan could save them. Well, partly Helen's plan. She added the dollar signs.

The look on Kourt's face when she solicited him—*Ugh.* Talk about a holiday buzz kill. He was like a completely different person. Magically repelled by me and all the Christmas I bring. I don't know much about Kourt, but signing him up to do a favor he doesn't want to do feels akin to asking Archer to watch someone's baby when he has a hot date, or just... ever.

Or asking Helen to volunteer at an old folks' home in her best suit skirt and four-inch pumps. I can see her helping with crafts in a memory care unit while she's trying to check her email and send briefs from her phone. It would be like finger painting with puppies next to a white sofa.

Speak of the devil. Devil number one and devil number two. These two are worse than me and Archer. Are they attached at the hip? I need to inform Helen, although grateful for our fast friendship, I don't do threesomes. Not when it puts someone out or makes them feel obligated to me—

"Speak of the devil." Kourt shoves his hands in his pants pockets and darts his eyes from Helen's to mine as I approach.

"I couldn't have said it better myself." *I did say it to myself.*

I raise my arms to put my jacket on and Kourt's eyes drift down my waist to my bare legs where my sweater dress must be riding up to show the better part of my thigh and hip-ass. *Awesome.* Now he thinks I'm too stupid to dress myself for winter.

"So?" Kourt's voice is curt and forced. This is not the man who just stood up for me.

"So..." I repeat with bug eyes.

Helen steps between us. "Oh my God, you big babies. You both fought for this in there. Why are you suddenly acting like you lost the chance to go first on the playground?"

"What time tomorrow?" Kourt gets to the point.

"Umm. Tomorrow?" I'm shocked he wants to start so soon.

"If you don't count the week of Christmas, we barely have three full weeks to pull this off, and each of those weekends our town should be open for business. So, we have less than a week if you look at it that way." Kourt searches my face. He's serious. Maybe he wants this fire truck as much as I want an old-fashioned Blitzen Christmas.

"Okay. What time is good for you?"

"I work, Erika. I'm not on Christmas break yet, and after teaching, I coach so—"

"Just let me know what time, Kourt. Yes, I do understand the concept of working, and I worked so hard, I'm on a much-needed break. A break I'm spending for your cause ultimately. So, you just tell me what time is best for you. What—do you need me to get down on my knees and beg?"

"I'd like to see you try in that dress."

"Kourt!" Helen interrupts our shouting match.

"What did you say?" I heard him, but I need him to repeat it.

"I said, nice dress. I'll pick you up at four thirty, and I'd wear something warmer than that if I were you."

"Noted. I'll be sure and wear my fake eyelashes as well."

ELEVEN

Naughty or Nice

Unbelievable. Un-fucking-believable. I slam my truck door shut when Helen raps on my window.

I roll it down and glare at my pint-sized, life-long friend who just crossed a line, volunteering me for this—in front of the whole frigging town. I was too stunned to protest.

Bet my chin's bruised from hitting the fucking floor.

What was I supposed to do after I stood up and defended her in front of everyone? I had to. They ate her up in there. Blitzen never used to be this inhospitable. She was about to shatter with all the grumbling opposition she was getting from all sides. And I don't blame her.

"You were the only choice." Helen defends her actions before I can open my mouth.

"Do you realize how much time you just obligated me to? I've got a basketball team, Helen. I teach for Christ's sake. Fuck. The food drive isn't enough? Now this?"

"Come on, McShotty." She reaches up and grips my forearm, which is resting on the window.

My heart's thumping hard. "Why'd you do this? Last night you were trying to get me to go have drinks with her and now this?"

Helen cocks her head and raises a brow. She can do that—raise one brow. "Do you want a new fire truck or not?"

"You know I do."

She sneers. "Well, then you have to sacrifice."

"Why am I the only one who has to sacrifice? Why don't you drive her all over kingdom come to help?"

"Because one, I don't own a pickup truck big enough to haul Santa's sleigh—and you do. And two, because you know everybody and everybody likes you better. I'm still the little half Korean chick the old timers refer to as that *part oriental girl.*"

"Bullshit. Apart from a misguided boomer when we were eleven, you were practically Blitzen's homecoming queen."

"Football Sweetheart." Helen bats her eyes proudly, and I move to roll my window up.

"Fine. Come on Kourt, my family built a dynasty from practicing both sides of corporate law. The shoes in my closet combined cost as much as the fire truck we're striving for. It's awkward, and then I have to explain to them all that I can't contribute because my dad already gave me my charity share and I sunk it into that new children's hospital wing. Then they'll want to ask why the going back and forth in and out of town and why I'm still here—"

"Why are you still here Helen?"

"Do you really want to have this conversation tonight?"

"I'd rather inject Herpes into my right eye."

"Good. Then it's settled."

"And all this time I thought Chicago just wasn't your kind of town."

"Hey. You drive the five hour and fifty-nine-minute commute twice a week and tell me how you like it."

"Please. As if you have to drive it."

"And that's another thing—I won't be here to be at her beck and call every day or night of the week. This wasn't a Machiavellian plot to make a match between you and Erika. I did it because you're truly the best person to help her pull this off. Now, will you please put a smile on your face? Those eleven lines are vicious."

I growl.

She backs away from my window and breaks out into song. "He's making a list, checking it twice, gonna find out who's naughty or nice."

Christ.

I shove a hand through my hair. "Get in your car before you freeze."

Her teeth are chattering, and I'm cold as fuck with my window down. The temperature plummeted since midday.

Speaking of which, what was with the bare legs? It's freaking December in the Appalachians. The girl's got a lot to learn about this town and culture. It's all things wool and flannel in the winter.

Driving away, the visual of her sweater hiking so far up her thigh I could make out the side of her hip where it must round into her perfect ass, I realize—I don't even have her phone number.

I call Helen on Bluetooth. "Text me Erika's phone number, will you?"

"Okay. Hey." She's back to her normal Helen voice. "Thank you. I think together, you two can save Blitzen."

I groan. "You sound like a B version one of those TV Christmas movies. The chances of us pulling this off at this late date are—*shit*. The odds are, we'll go down in flames. You know that, right?"

I get nothing back.

"Right? Helen? You do realize, if Erika pulls this off, she'll have done something unheard of. She landed here the first week of December and she's going to save the town in one month? That's not a Christmas miracle. It's a fairytale."

"Well..." Helen begins and stops.

"Well?" I finally prompt, sick of the pregnant silence.

There's defiance in the voice that answers. "If anyone can do it, Erika can. I mean, she's unicorns and stardust. A dreamer when we need one the most. She's a believer, Kourt. So let her believe and support her, and the whole town will be better for it."

"Let's just start with her phone number."

"How are we gonna do this?" I call Erika on my lunch break.

"You said you'd pick me up at four-thirty." Her voice is energetic and chirpy, but she cuts it with a matter-of-fact edge.

I can't help but smile a little knowing she's making that effort just for me. "Are you good with that?"

"Sure. Hold on. No! Not there—there. Sorry. We're getting organized."

I hear a lot of background noise, drills and hammers. "Sounds like you already have a lot going on."

"Oh, we do."

"Where are you?"

"Town Hall, of course. We're working on street decorations."

"Do you know what you need me to do tonight?" Mentally, my fingers are crossed. *Come on. Say, 'Oh, I don't need you tonight.'*

"Well..."

Shit. Another Helen kind of pause.

"Well? What?"

She clears her throat. "Would you mind taking me to meet Mr. Miller?"

"Christmas tree Miller?"

"Yeah."

I roll my eyes. "He might shoot us. I mean, it's dark by five o'clock. You better tell him you're coming, so he won't unload a shotgun on my truck."

Silence.

"Hello?"

I can feel the grimace on her face as she sputters. "I thought... may... maybe you'd do that. I mean, you knowing him and all..."

Of course, you want me to call the most stubborn man on the planet.

This is going to be the longest December on record.

"Okay. Four-thirty Josie's house?"

"Oh, no. I'm sure I'll still be here. We have so much to do."

The courthouse square is the heart of this town, figuratively and physically. Town Hall sits directly across from the courthouse—and I'll be damned if my jaw doesn't sag a little, seeing multi-colored lights all over the courthouse square and the block that surrounds it.

It's a beehive of activity. She's already got lights covering the building and the bushes that line the front lawn.

In one day.

She's taken charge of this. I have to give it to her: Her excitement is infectious. Everyone here seems as eager about this as Erika is.

Everyone but June. She looks like her hair's about to catch on fire. That's June for you. Grumpy as hell to hide her heart of gold.

Pulling up and parking, I've got my eyes on Erika. She's talking with her hands to June and a circle of helpers. She's almost child-like in her enthusiasm.

The thing is—she looks anything but childlike in that soft cotton candy pink sweater, as it hugs her shape just enough for me to know she's got a mouthful plus some.

Shit. Fine. She's sexy as hell, not that I gave her credit for it. Oddly enough, watching her with the group she kindly commands, I don't think she gives herself credit for that either.

The evening sun casts a ray across the courthouse lawn and parking lot as it threatens to disappear behind the mountain. The side of Erika's face brightens from the warmth, and the texture of her sweater is illuminated where it clings to her chest. I catch myself staring at the anomaly next to the people I've known my whole life... wondering if the most annoying woman on the planet—okay, to be fair, the current thorn in my side—knows she's hot.

Helen's right. She's a unicorn. To her, this place is her own holiday wonderland full of possibilities. Maybe because she's a stranger in town. Maybe Blitzen is more special than we realize. I mean, it's all we know, but she's seeing our town with fresh eyes. Maybe we should appreciate what we have more.

Erika beams proudly, seeing me approach. "What do you think?" She spreads her arms and twirls in a slow circle.

She pulls another grin from me. "I think you scored three points."

"Huh?"

"Sank it from the cheap seats."

Blink, blink.

"Have you ever been to a basketball game?"

"Not really. I mean, in high school but I was nerdy. Not an athlete. So, well..." She draws her gaze up to meet mine sheepishly.

"No." She hangs her head apologetically. "I mean, on TV with Archer—"

"Archer?"

"My friend back home."

I squint at her. "What kind of friend?"

Her mouth opens wide enough to swallow a baby hawk, and those blue eyes are roiling. "I beg your pardon?"

I show my hands defensively and snicker, "Just wondered if I was going to have some jealous boyfriend after me, hauling you all over Kentucky in my truck every night."

"If you don't want to do it, just man up and say it."

Is she mad? Like, actually mad?

"If I didn't want to do it, I wouldn't do it."

Our gazes are latched like bull horns.

"You certainly act like you don't want to do it."

"By asking if you had a psycho stalker boyfriend? Seemed innocent enough to me. Did you ever watch *Sleeping with the Enemy?* You saw what happened to the nice neighbor."

She snips, "What is with men and movie references? *The Godfather, Scarface, Fight Club, Anchorman, The Dark Knight* and now apparently, *John Wick.* I get it. It's like you're pre-requisite to masculine comradery—"

"You forgot *No Country for Old Men.*"

"May I remind you, I'm not the one bumping into fresh break-ups every time I turn around."

Quinn. "Right."

"It was obvious." She turns her back to me and crosses to a group separating lights by a step ladder. "June?"

June glares up from the tangle of lights she's messing with.

"Can you tell me how to get to Mr. Miller's house? I need to see him."

"Get in my truck before I pick you up and put you in it." I nod and smile at June as Erika and I step aside. June enthusiastically waves us off.

"You're being a dick."

"You're being a brat. Get in the fucking truck."

"I will not." She strides briskly away from me.

"I've got one step to your three." I halt in front of her. "I called Miller—like you wanted me to do. He's waiting. If you dilly dally too long, he'll be in bed before we can get there."

She glares.

"Are we doing this or not?"

Her gaze narrows.

"Great. Get in."

"Do you think you can refrain from snide remarks about my friends or lack thereof?"

"Didn't know you had a lack thereof. But I'm hungry. Can we go through the Dairy Maid on our way?" I nip her comeback in the bud. First because I am so hungry my stomach's going to start growling, and second because I am being a dick.

What can I say? Her smart ass mouth paired with innocent eyes brings it out in me.

"I thought we were on a time crunch to get to Mr. Miller."

"It's a drive through."

She peers up defiantly. And thus begins the whiplash. She and I apparently have a knack for going from all grins to disdain in zero to sixty. "Fine. I'll buy since you're spending your gas, and you wouldn't let me pay the other day."

Good luck with that.

TWELVE

Calling of the Bears

Erika gives me a long side-eye with a half grin as I unwrap my burger.

"What?"

She shifts in her seat to turn and face me. "That's your second burger."

I wipe the crumbs off my chin with a paper napkin, eating and driving. "Sometimes I eat three." My mouth isn't totally full as I respond and take a gander of what's in her lap. "Is that all you're going to eat? A baby burger?"

"I didn't just escape from Alcatraz, so I'm probably good with just this."

"I didn't have time for lunch. Picking up donation boxes for the food drive."

"Oh, that's right. You do that, too." She starts sarcastic, but the inflection in her voice trails out softer.

"Yeah, I do that, too."

"Okay. Well... again, I'm sorry you keep getting—"

"Just drop it, will you?" I swallow a long drink of soda, cutting my eyes at her. "We're in this together. Now moving on, some things you need to know about old man Miller."

"That's kind of disrespectful, don't you think?"

"Fuck." I turn my head to stare into the darkness out my driver's window. Shit. Nothing but black once we left the town lights behind. No moon. No stars. No houses on this stretch of road.

"What?" she demands.

I shove what remains of my second burger into my mouth. "Let me rephrase. Some things you need to know about Mr. Walter Miller. That's his English name. He's Cherokee. His given name is Waya, which means wolf. And he is. Strong, solitary. A lone wolf since his wife died."

"I didn't know."

"So, when we get there, show respect by not looking him directly in the eyes and don't speak first. Let him speak first."

"You've got to be kidding me."

"I wouldn't. Not on this. As a matter of fact, if you want to wow him, offer him a gift."

She tilts her head. "Well, it would've been helpful to know that earlier."

I shrug. "Just came to mind."

"Empty handed as I am, what do you propose I give him."

My eyes unwittingly drift from the steering wheel to her pink sweater. I'm certain she didn't mean that as clever and sexual as it sounded, but I had to take a beat to check.

"Pull over." She cracks the words out like a whip.

"Where?"

"At the Dollar General. Let me run in and get him something."

"Look around. We're fifteen minutes out of town. Besides, you wouldn't know what to get."

She peers at me like I'm some devil Grinch whose sole purpose is to fuck with her. "I'm sure I can find something in the vein of candy canes or Christmas cookies."

"If you want Christmas cookies, there's a country store about a mile up the road that sells homemade cookies." I glance at the clock on the dash. "If we can get there before they close."

Walter lives on the back side of Whispering Bear Mountain. Erika's VW Beetle couldn't make it here even in the summer. The road's too rutted.

He's waiting outside for us, sitting on a big log in his front yard with a roaring campfire in front of him, bundled up warm with a blanket around him. His hands grip a steaming mug.

Getting out of the truck, I look at the sky. I almost can't see it for the low cloud cover. Looks like it could snow any minute now.

"Remember. Let him talk first. It's his home and time we're intruding on," I whisper, my hand on Erika's back, guiding her to Walter.

He watches our approach. If you look at him from the front, you won't know that his hair hangs below his shoulder blades. He pulls it back tight and wears it braided, usually with a battered sun hat or ball cap.

I'd guess Walter's late seventies give or take. His hair is mostly silver now. I remember when it was black.

His kids moved off to the cities, leaving him here with his wife, who died a slow, painful death of cancer. Watching her die did something to him.

No. Closing down the tree farm did more to him.

"Mr. Miller, I'm so glad to meet you," Erika hurries his way.

Dammit. She not only speaks first—she's looking him dead in the eyes when she does. Does she not listen?

I try to intercede, "I'm sorry, Walter—"

He holds up his hand, cutting me off. His eyes pierce Erika. "What is it you want, young lady?"

Her gaze flickers from Walter to me, and I see the fear on her face, illuminated by the fire blazing beside us. But I've got to give it to her... she grinds on. "I want you to re-open your Christmas tree farm. But this time, not for free. Make people pay."

"And why would I do that?" Walter sips his hot drink from the Thermos mug, watching her over his cup.

"To help Blitzen get a new firetruck."

He nods gently. His gaze narrows, zipping from her to me... back to her. "I'll think about it."

"But you don't have time to think."

Jeez.

I groan, "Walter, we can come back."

"What's your urgency, young lady?"

"I'm sorry. I didn't introduce myself. I'm Erika Amherst. You may know my great aunt—"

Again, he stops her with his hand. His voice is like gravel. I happen to know Walter smokes like a chimney. "You wouldn't be here if I didn't know who you are. Saw you last night. I know Josephine."

This isn't going well.

Erika makes her peace offering. "I brought you these." She holds out her box, which Walter eyes but doesn't reach for.

His gaze cuts into her. "Did you make them or buy them?"

Her gaze falls to the campfire as she answers apologetically, "I bought them."

"Because Kourt here told you to. Right?"

She nods.

Walter looks at me. "She's honest. I like that. Come back tomorrow and I'll give you my answer." He sets down his mug and pulls a pack of cigarettes from his shirt pocket, digs into his pants for a lighter, and lights it.

He takes a deep draw and blows out smoke. "In the meantime, young lady—"

"Erika," she interrupts. "Please."

"Erika. Now that I think about it, there's something I'd like to ask of you. Will you incorporate the Cherokee tradition of the Calling of the Bears into this winter festival? My wish is for our town's Christmas celebration to recognize my people's traditions, honoring the winter solstice as part of Blitzen's heritage." He looks directly at me. "I think my wife would like that, Kourt. You?"

We share a long stare-off as chills crawl up my spine. "Yeah."

"I'll consider re-opening the Christmas tree farm, and you can set the price for the trees. All proceeds will go for the Blitzen Volunteer Fire Department." He holds up his hand again, showing his wide palm.

Erika beams, peering from Walter to me, and claps her hands silently. "I can't imagine a better idea. Thank you, Walter. I'm grateful to learn more about the Calling of the Bears."

She's so effusive, she reaches over and grabs Walter's hands, squeezing them. "I'll see you tomorrow? After settling everything with town hall?" She glances at me. "Could we Kourt?"

I nod. *Jesus.*

"Same time. Same place tomorrow," Walter says. "I'll have some warm cider for you."

Erika turns to leave.

"You can leave those cookies." Walter points at the log beside him.

I've got Walter, sitting by the campfire, in my rearview mirror when Erika shifts in her seat to face me. "How do we make the Calling of the Bears part of the festival? We have to get it right for him."

Watching Walter sit alone as we drive away, my gut's back at that campfire.

"Kourt?"

"Yeah."

"Where were you? What's wrong?" Her brows are knitted tight.

"Nothing. Calling of the Bears. First, it's on the winter solstice so you'll have to do that on December 21st. They do a ceremony at dusk at the mouth of a cave, because they believe it's the womb of Mother Earth."

"That's beautiful."

"Yeah. Anyway, the Cherokee believe the Bear People transcend this world and the next. They're believed to rest and dream in the cave during the winter. On the winter solstice, the Cherokee people light a beacon fire to show the Bear People the way to the cave, and they leave offerings. Berries, honey, fish."

She tweaks her mouth to the side, "'To rest and dream in a cave.' Wow. The imagery is magical. Like the idea of snow at night."

"What?"

"You know. It's one thing to dream of a white Christmas, but those rare moments when it snows during the night... when you step outside at just the right moment to see a pitch-black night sky and all around you is blanketed in glittering white snow. There's an almost eerie peace about it. It looks like heaven on earth. Surely that happens here in Kentucky." She opts for sarcasm in the absence of my response.

"Almost every night in the winter." I say it dryly as I look over at her.

Blue eyes pierce mine.

"I live higher up on the mountain than you do."

A pause infiltrates the inside of my truck along with that vanilla cinnamon scent when she turns away from me first. The air grows thicker as if the heater's gotten too hot.

I glance at her across the console, bundled in her white down coat and red scarf. At least this time she dressed for the weather. "So anyway, good luck finding a cave close enough to town. But, hey, you're the creative one."

"Well, you could help."

That was a little snippy.

"I am helping. By the way, speaking of helping, why in the name of all things holy did you do the exact opposite of what I told you to do? You spoke first, looked him in the eye—Jesus."

"I thought it went well."

"You were going down in flames until you pulled out those cookies."

"Looking people directly in the eye when you speak to them builds trust. Everyone knows this." She shifts her shoulders away from me. "I was showing him respect."

"Cherokee's a different culture. To him, it was rude. And for Pete's sake, the next time you see him, let him speak first. It's their way."

"Aren't you critical and archaic."

"I'm honest. That's what I am. And you're deaf, apparently."

And dammit to hell, you smell like those fucking Christmas cookies. Warm vanilla and cinnamon. Did she move closer to me?

"Wow, Kourt."

My ticker's beating double time. "Why didn't you listen to me? You want me to take you to these places, get you in to see these people to make your festival come true—and you don't listen to my advice."

She turns her head, peering out her window, her chin tilted high, muttering under her breath.

"What?"

She faces me with fire in her eyes. "You're rude, Kourt Mc-Clain. You don't know *everything*."

I tilt my head and let out a good laugh. "Rude?" I shake my head. "Unbelievable. Un-fucking-believable. I know my friends and the people of this town."

We ride in silence the rest of the way to the courthouse parking lot.

Her Beetle is parked right in front. The entire car is iced over. It must have sleeted over downtown while we were gone. The temperature is probably in the teens. She'd have hell getting her car door open, much less getting the engine to turn over.

I roll past the Beetle.

"Where are you going?" She all but shrieks, looking in the back window.

"Dropping you off at your house."

"My car's back there."

I stop at the stop sign and square off with the little hellcat. "Your car won't make it home. I have four-wheel drive. The roads are black ice. Listen to me, like you didn't before. That Beetle won't get you back to Josie's house on this ice. You live in Chicago. You comprehend ice, right?"

"How will I get around? Tomorrow?" Panic is written on her face.

I make the turn, headed to Josie's big house on the hill. Hell of a hilly town to be stranded on foot. In ice.

A heavy sigh dissolves in the passenger seat. "This won't work."

"Yeah, I know."

She whips her head to glare at me. "What do you mean?"

"I mean, you can't walk all over town and your car won't navigate icy roads."

"Well, Josie drove it, right?"

"Yeah, in the summer. She also had a four-wheel drive Range Rover with chains on the tires for winter."

Her jaw drops as her gaze flicks left and right. "Where's the Range Rover?"

"Your guess is as good as mine. I'll swing by and pick you up in the morning on my way to work—drop you at your car at City Hall. The temps rising tomorrow morning so the next few days should warm up enough for you to drive your Beetle downtown and on the main roads in the daylight."

"And every other time?" Erika looks at me appalled.

I toss a hand off the steering wheel, then take a fake bow.

I can't be certain, but between my breaks squealing to a stop and her slamming the passenger door shut, I think we both muttered, "*Great,*" under our breaths.

THIRTEEN

Killing it w/ Christmas Kindness

Rushing through the kitchen to stop the noise, I almost forget I have Helen on speaker phone. My ears are ringing from the alarms I set this morning and the kitchen timer going off on Aunt Josie's commercial kitchen oven.

"What time did you say?" Helen's voice yells above the incessant beeping, as I slide the cookie sheet out and search for any open space on the counter. "Hang on. Let me get this oven timer to stop."

"Oh God. Don't tell me. Please. I can't. I'm not ready for this from either of you." Helen persists even though I can barely hear a word she's shouting.

"Finally. I got it to stop. That was the last batch, so we're good." I stare at six dozen cherry icebox cookies lining the green Formica countertop and shake my head.

I don't know what's more of the conundrum.

Aunt Josie's half-vintage to falling apart relic of a home with select modern features, or the fact that my go-to Christmas cookie is called an "ice box cookie" but still required me to wake up at four-thirty this morning to bake them in the oven. Who cares. Every morsel of them is worth it, and if these folks don't do it for me, they'll do it for my cookies.

"He stayed over and you've cooked him breakfast?" Helen doesn't sound like Helen anymore. I drop my oven mitts and grab my phone to bring it closer.

"What? Who? No! And, absolutely not. Are you insane? I learned my lesson from Walter. Never empty-handed and never store bought no matter how gourmet and delish. Kourt dropped me home last night insisting my Bug stay in the courthouse parking lot. Something about the temperature dropping and black ice or whatever."

"Oh." Helen sounds like herself again.

"Yeah, when are you two going to acknowledge I'm from the Windy City? Our temps drop just as low if not lower—"

"It's different in the mountains."

"And I've been in weather so bone-chilling your hands turn blue if you forget your gloves."

"Yeah... still not the same as driving in it, especially with no four-wheel drive, which brings me back to—what time today?"

"Speaking of four-wheel drive, did Josie have a Range Rover? Kourt said something about a Range Rover."

"Were there keys to said Range Rover in your envelope? Or was there one parked out front?" Her voice sounds as annoyed as it can get, realizing I know about it.

"No," I half whisper like a defeated child.

"Right. So, what time today?"

"I'll get to my car and run my downtown errands if you could just be available to drive me to Fisher's on your lunch break or whenever your meeting breaks? I've got to handle the rest of the promotional tools with them, and they're this close to not only donating that massive sleigh but delivering it to us."

"Wow. Nice work, city slicker. I'd ask what's in it for them, but from one ice coffee drinker to another, I'll respect a girl's got to have her secrets." Helen's voice is high-pitched and ringing through my kitchen, until her previous words hit my ears on replay.

"What would make you ask if Kourt stayed over? Why would you even think it? I mean, I get that he's your friend, which at some point you must delve into explaining those details so that I have a better understanding of how you tolerate him—the man's infuriating."

"Glad to know I still have that effect on you from over five hours away." A male's voice only I would recognize calls to me from my laptop on the breakfast nook.

"I gotta go. See you just after noon or so." I slide my thumb toward the end call button.

"Who's that?" Helen's shock is disconnected prematurely by my thumb tap as I race to open my zoom screen.

"Not you Arch, darling." I smile widely upon seeing the snarky, but friendly face I've missed. "You're a lamb in wolves clothing compared to this local."

"It's just shy of a week and you're already in good with the natives?"

"I'm not sure I would say 'in or good.' The man's a six-three-plus educator responsible for coaching young minds, and he all but pitches a tantrum, spouting some crap about how I can't just come into town and run things and turn his life upside down. And over something that was partially his idea to hear him stand up for me in the meeting the way he did."

"Wait, which of the townsfolk is this? Who stood up for you?"

"It doesn't matter. By his overreaction to me, you'd think I surprise decorated the guy's house."

"Wait. Have you been to his house?"

A loud honk followed by two more honks echo through the carport and pierce my sanity.

Of course he's a honker.

"Gotta go, Arch. Have a great day!" I catch Archer's face drop as I close my laptop already one foot toward the door. *Damn it.* I rush back, stealing the time to open my screen and click my camera back on. "Hey. Chin up. We'll catch up tonight. I promise. I miss you, Arch."

The horn blows again, as I grab everything I prepped for the day and race out the door. Kourt sits in the driver's seat with the truck running and the largest grin on his face I've ever seen. His hand is braced on the horn as if ready to go again when he rolls the passenger side window down. "Just wanted you to know I'm here." He cocks an eyebrow, waiting to get a rise out of me.

Oh. I know you're here. He's not a honker. He's fucking with me.

I let one of the boxes I'm balancing slide a little too far forward. His gloating is short-lived when he notices all I'm carrying so unsuccessfully.

I almost smile inside at how fast he flies out of the truck to come and help.

He lifts the bakery boxes from my hands and slides the large tote bags off my shoulders, opens the door for me and places them gently in the back seat of the truck. The smell of butter and sweet sugared cherries engulfs us like flames as he rises from the back.

My foot is propped on the step to push up into the truck when I pause and turn to meet him on his way from the back seat. My lips unintentionally graze his ear as I whisper, "Bet you feel bad for honking now."

Kourt goes stiff, freezing where he stands, partially leaning down from rising out of the back seat. And my lips, still touching his ear.

Heat from embarrassment swells through me, and I slowly turn my head away from him, then vault myself into the passenger seat at record speed.

Ugh. I was trying to give it back to him, but I wasn't trying to give *that* off.

I whispered into his ear like I had a sweet nothing to say... I wouldn't do that to anyone intentionally, not even if I were drunk or high. It's just after six a.m. *What is wrong with me?*

It wasn't what I said, it was the logistics. I didn't realize we'd be that close when he rose up or—my voice would come out so taunting. I face front with my hands clasped in my lap like a good little girl who has no intention of misbehaving again. As if that will play it off. *Nice one.*

Kourt didn't say much on the ride to my VW earlier this morning. I take it he's not a morning person. That, or he's highly confused by the baker of Christmas cookie madness who practically kissed his ear. Which is exactly why he shouldn't have offered to drive me in the first place. Are we certain Blitzen doesn't have Uber or Lyft?

Maybe I should implement that into the Old-Fashioned Christmas. Some sort of "Sleigh- Ride share app."

Attempting to warm my mittens by what little heat my Bug gives off, I shake my head discouraged. He wasn't wrong judging by the amount of ice I scraped off the windshield at seven a.m. while he drove away smirking.

Still, only a complete fool would volunteer themselves for something they one thousand percent don't want to do.

On that note, I see June's tiny Toyota pickup drive in beside me at the courthouse. That thing's got to be as legendary as my Bug. I think they stopped making those small pickup trucks before I was born. Ha. This town is like a *Tuck Everlasting* for old vehicles. Wonder what gas station they get their "special oil" from.

I laugh at myself as June huffs out of her car. Wonder what her motivation is? She clearly isn't excited about helping me. Yet here she is again.

My car door creaks open as I step out to greet her. *Kill them with Christmas kindness.*

"June. So great to see you again." I hand her a white pastry box with a bright red ribbon I tied into a homemade bow at about 4:55 this morning.

"You just saw me yesterday. What's this?" She inspects the box.

"They're Cherry Icebox Cookies."

"What?"

"They're like the ultimate Christmas sugar cookie, only full of Maraschino cherry flavor and super soft in the middle."

"If you give away all the cookies you make, you won't have any to sell for the festival."

"Oh. Well, these are just for you, because..."

"I'm a type two diabetic, so thanks. I guess." June pitches my little box into her truck and produces a large ring of keys, motioning me to follow her up the side steps of the courthouse.

"I really appreciate you letting me in to get the info. If Blitzen Manor works out, we can put all the vendors on the grounds like they did back in the day."

"Yeah, well good luck getting ahold of the grandson. If he does answer, I wouldn't be surprised if he wants to charge for using the place."

"I thought it might save you from having to rope town square off for me and figure out parking," I say as I look down. "I know I've already put you out by asking for so much."

June focuses on the key to the storage and doesn't say anything.

I'm truly batting zero with this woman.

Her silver strands shine where they tuck back into her low ponytail, and her jewelry clad fingers are outlined with potting soil, as if she's been working in a flower bed. She smells like a plant lady. Fresh, earthy, and her attractive face is covered in those deeply embedded wrinkles that only come from years of summers in the sun. You can tell she was once beautiful.

She would be now, if she wasn't so salty and mean.

"June, I almost forgot to ask. Do you know of any caves around Blitzen?" I regret asking the moment I hear it roll of my tongue.

"A Christmas cave? Look honey, I know you've got big ideas from Chicago and your marketing firm, but I draw the line at talking toy soldiers, and life-size gingerbread men-lined walkways. I don't do caves for Christmas."

"It's for Walter Miller. The Calling of the Bears ceremony."

A knowing smirk escapes her crooked smile. "*Ahh,*" she nods. "Everybody has an agenda."

"What's that mean?"

"Everybody always wants something. Blitzen is never enough. You'll see." She reaches above my head and pulls the huge frame out. "Here. The estate's information is taped to the back. You'll find Gregg's number listed."

She hands me the large black and white photo of a 1930s Blitzen Christmas at the manor. I'd seen it when we pulled the lights and the town's decorations, and I couldn't get it out of my head.

"He's the overseer now. Careful, he's a bit of a miser." She stands above me glowering over the picture.

"That's okay. I'm used to difficult people." I smile up at her as genuinely as I can. Her expression doesn't falter as she takes the hit, and I grab my phone to snap a picture of the info. I can't be sure what she meant about Blitzen not being enough and people always wanting more.

Reluctant, and busy with their own lives, sure, but for the most part I've been blown away with everyone's willingness to help. Including June's.

I wave goodbye to my newfound frenemy as we both start our engines. There's no response from her, but my tape deck clicks on after lying dormant all night. I smile as I pull out to rush and meet Helen on her lunch break, curious what song will fill my VW. I recognize *Silver Bells* right away and my heart swells a little, pulling away from the town square when I hear the line, "It's Christmas time in the city."

Maybe I miss Archer and Chicago more than I thought.

The heater in Kourt's truck blasts through the front cab putting the Bug I sputter around downtown in to shame. I have to admit, knowing it will get dark, and the temperature will decrease significantly while running errands this evening, I'm grateful. For the heater, that is.

"Where to, Your Highness?" His deep voice rolls out begrudgingly.

"Fantastic. His mood has vastly improved since this morning." I flip my head away from him toward the passenger side window.

"I'm sorry I had to honk this morning." Kourt's voice is calm, matter of fact, and holds a hint of amusement.

"I don't think anyone *has* to honk. It was certainly a choice." I don't turn to him to look, but I can sense his infamous smirk developing.

"So, Fisher's or..."

"No, that's already handled," I announce proudly.

"You didn't drive there, did you?" Kourt's brows flinch inward, and he grips the steering wheel.

"Oh, no. Helen. She picked me up on her lunch break."

"I see. I'm not your only chauffeur." He relaxes with a smile.

"It takes a village..." I look over to the driver's side. Some part of me is curious and I have an urge to study his face. *Him.*

He keeps his eyes on the road as I take in his tall frame, the large masculine hands that steer the winding roads out of town so effortlessly. The evergreens stand in all their glory past the cab windows and in the fading sun, the darkened hue of his honey-colored hazel eyes almost matches the green of their foliage.

I one thousand percent planned to look away after catching my glimpse, but the air is thick with him. The smell of his truck, the clothes he coached in today... I inhale slowly and a certain warmth invades my senses.

"Where—" We both move our mouths to speak. I clear my throat. "I was going to ask, where you prefer to go first. I have two big boxes to check off. I need to see a man about a cave, and probably timelier, I need to go check out Blitzen Manor."

A loud beeping and vibration comes from Kourt's phone. It's extra loud, akin to an Amber alert, but my phone isn't going off.

He grabs his and answers. "Got it. I'm on my way."

Brakes come to a screeching halt. Kourt U-turns in the middle of the highway, and a siren comes out of nowhere as he rolls down his window and places the flashing bulb on the top of his truck.

I shiver at the gust of cold wind rushing in.

"Duty calls." Kourt winks as he rolls the window back up.

"Is there a fire?"

"God, I hope not, given where we're going. Looks like I'm taking you on an adventure instead."

FOURTEEN

Grilled Cheese and Tomato Soup

Kourt flies back up and through the rolling streets we just steadied down. My mouth falls agape as I grip the 'Oh shit' handle. It remains open until he parks in front of a modest brick home that sits what feels like a mile past its own mailbox and the main road.

"Wait here." Kourt leaves the truck running and grabs a first aid bag from the back. I sit, still a little stunned, and then I process the order he barked.

Absolutely not. I don't see any smoke so...

I kill the truck's ignition and climb out. I walk carefully up the front porch. A rocking bench built for two sits below the front window and several potted plants that appear neglected either from lack of care or the harsh winter season line the porch steps. A small ramp that looks like it was added on the side of the porch, for bypassing steps. I pause when my boots hit the worn-out old mat with *Welcome to Our Home* written across it.

I press my ear to the door.

"Mrs. Phillips, you're just going to have to trust me. I'm going to step in and get behind you ..." Kourt's voice is firm but has alarm to it. I can't quite make out the rest of what he's saying. It's muffled behind the thick wooden door, and it sounds like water is running. I look behind me, wondering if back up or more of Blitzen's volunteer fire department isn't barreling down the drive.

"G.W.! Bring me a towel or a blanket, for God's sake!" Kourt's demand is loud and clear, and I can't ignore the concern in his voice.

I push the front door open and barge in. An old man greets me with a kind expression and dancing eyes. He's wearing overalls and slippers, and he seems as if he doesn't know what's going on back there.

"Hello, Miss." He smiles up at me from the kitchen bar where he fiddles with a can opener. "Are you here for my buddy Kourt? Sit down if you like. Carol will be glad to have you two stay for dinner when she gets out of the shower." He tries again at the can opener.

"G.W.! Get a blanket!" The urgency in Kourt's voice rings through me like a bell, and I try to pull my knitted brows apart and wipe the confusion off my face. I nod at the old man and muster a genuine smile to leave him with as I race down the hallway of a home I've never been in. I see a throw folded on a day bed in a middle bedroom and grab it on impulse as I continue toward the sound of a shower that's been running way too long.

"Erika?" Kourt has a foot, leg and a shoulder lodged in the bathroom doorway. His neck is strained, and he's holding as tight as he can while I hear a woman behind the door crying hysterically, "Don't look at me. Don't look at me. Please! You can't come in!"

I lean through the door past Kourt to see an elderly woman half sitting, half lying on the tile, clutching Kourt's arm to a debilitating extreme. The shower curtain is askew, and water is pouring from both the shower head and the bathtub while she faces opposite the door and cries in terror.

"Get G.W.! Please. Get him to lift me, then you can help me out. Please! I'm unclothed."

"Hello? Mrs. Phillips?" My voice is strong, and I cringe at my adrenaline burst that could prove nothing more than over-confidence.

Kourt's red, stressed face searches mine as he waits to hear her response.

His shoulder is jammed if not trapped inside the door she's pressing her back to with all her might. Kourt could obviously push it open with his strength, but out of respect for her privacy, or maybe to avoid hurting her, he's allowed himself to be harmed.

I peek through again to see if she's hearing me, and I see where Kourt's arm is supporting her upper back by hooking under her shoulder.

"It's Erika, Mrs. Phillips. You don't know me, but I'm sure you knew my Great Aunt Josephine. I'm here in Blitzen staying at her place for the holidays."

"Josephine Amherst's girl?" Mrs. Phillips' voice trembles from the other side of the door.

I step closer to Kourt and the gap in the doorway. He's so tall he's looking down on me. His ear pressed to the door, his chin almost touching the top of my head from leaning in to sacrifice his arm where it's pinched. I can feel his fast breath on my cheek as I press my face to the door to hear her better.

I take a half step closer to Kourt. My body presses against his and my face is directly in line with his as I look up at him, craning my own arm through the door with the throw I found. Kourt's eyes dilate as he stares down into mine and I know he's about to inch his brows together in complete horror and confusion as he asks me what the hell I'm doing.

My breath hitches as I feel the blanket reach what must be the top of her shoulder. This could go completely wrong. If I scare her, she could buck back on the door, slamming both our arms and hitting her head on the tile in the process.

Please let this work.

My eyes lock on Kourt's. "G.W. gave me this blanket to give you, Mrs. Phillips."

We stare through each other waiting for her response.

"He did?" Mrs. Phillip's voice is slower, lower.

"Yes, ma'am. He said I should get that flannel blanket you like and wrap it around your shoulders to cover you. You've got your bath towel covering the front of you, and if you can lean forward to let me in, I'll have your throw he gave me wrapped completely around you before anyone can see in."

My breath ticks up and my heart beats wildly at the lies I told her, assuming the soft man in the kitchen with the can opener is G.W.

"It's just you then?"

"Yes, Mrs. Phillips. Kourt has his back to you and the door. I'm watching him as we speak, and G.W. is here waiting to see if I can get your blanket to you. May I slide in behind you?"

She takes a deep breath and sighs. "Well, G.W. knows best. Kourt, you can let that Amherst girl in."

Kourt cringes, and I see how red his forearm, wrist and hand are from holding her up. I squeeze through the door, adding more pressure on him for a split second before I slide my open palm down her back and prop her shoulder with my other to replace his.

The door closes behind us.

I work quickly with the throw to cover her.

The floor is slick and a spongey bathmat is soaked through with water.

Careful not to slip myself, I sit behind her so I don't move her. I'm clearly not the paramedic here and I'm acutely aware of how delicate and brittle her bones and skin feel under my touch.

"All covered now Mrs. Phillips. Can Kourt come in and turn the shower off and get us off the floor?" I lean our bodies away from the door so Kourt can get through.

"Oh, yes, of course. Kourt, I'm so sorry you've had to come after me. And with me not decent."

Kourt's hands replace mine behind her back and I move in front of Mrs. Philips so she can see me.

"Nonsense, Carol. I'm happy to stop by any time." Kourt's voice is soothing, and a smile of relief twinkles up to his eyes as he goes to work to get her stable enough to lift. "It's always good to see you, regardless of the circumstances."

I watch Mrs. Phillips gush as I kneel in front of her.

"Oh my. Aren't you a pretty little thing. Look at those lashes—"

I can't stifle my burst of laughter.

"And those blue, blue eyes."

Kourt clears his throat. Flattering and embarrassing as this is on my end, he's working to save her, and I'm keeping her mind off one of the most embarrassing moments of her life.

"You're too kind, and I'm happy to meet you, Mrs. Phillips."

"You call me Carol. Kourt knows he's supposed to. I just hate we had to meet with me so exposed," she starts again.

"There's no such thing as modesty where your safety is concerned, and besides that, Kourt here is supposedly quite the gentlemen." I lean toward her with a smile.

She matches me, leaning in, and whispers, "I'm certain a moment alone with you will fix that."

"Carol." My eyes widen at my new friend as I hear commotion outside the bathroom door.

"They're in the back bathroom." A male's voice shouts toward us. "Kourt, you got her?" A man I recognize as the fire chief from the town meeting appears with two younger men behind him.

"Carol, I'm going to let them through to help you up, and I'll go let G.W. know we got you all covered up and settled." I try to keep my voice strong and confident, so she doesn't go back to the fear and embarrassment that made her panic before.

"Oh, yes. Please let G.W. know I'm in good hands."

I slip past Kourt and out of the team's way in search of the lost old man who greeted me. Before we can get reacquainted, a stretcher rolls past, and Carol is sitting up, wearing a robe and strapped onto the gurney.

"Alright, Kourt. We're gonna go ahead and take her in for X-rays, to make sure nothing's broken. Thanks for getting here so fast." The chief nods at Kourt over the heads of the others making their way out with Carol.

"I'm going to stay and get this cleaned up." Kourt motions to the flooded bathroom with a thumb but shoots an additional nod and silent glance toward the old man standing next to me in the kitchen.

The chief nods back and mouths thank you as he turns to leave. "Don't forget to add your girl here to the incident report tomorrow. Thanks for your help young lady."

"It's Erika." I smile back at the chief.

A younger, shorter version of Kourt turns to look at us from where he rolls the stretcher. "Did you, ah, need a ride back into town with us, Erika?" he asks, like a hopeful puppy.

Kourt's eyes cut through the small crowd to him, and he gives him a lasting glare.

I look to Kourt, genuinely not knowing what I'm supposed to do, and since I give up my power, Kourt takes it back and smiles cockily in my direction.

"Erika?" His eyebrows rise, as if he's suggesting I should answer his colleague's question.

"Oh, no young man," a small voice calls from behind the kitchen counter, answering for me. G.W. stands, still holding a can opener. "The young lady and Kourt have been invited to stay to dinner." G.W. smiles at me as if it is settled.

Kourt's lips purse together, and he blinks at me, watching my face as I try to hide the fact that the old man made me blush.

The rest of the volunteer fire crew chuckle as they slide out the door and Kourt and I both land on G.W. as we watch him hold the can opener upside down.

My eyes drift back down the hallway thinking of the two of them here and how they manage. For the first time, I catch a walker at the end of the hallway. It has a pink purse pouch and seat attached. It must belong to Carol.

It's clear that, left to his own devices, G.W. cannot open a can of tomato soup and it's difficult for me to imagine Carol holding down the fort and cooking their meals from her walker.

My heart sinks. For them.

"Let me grab that, G.W.—Tomato soup and grilled cheese? Is that what we're aiming for?" Kourt pats G.W. on the back, man to man, as he slides the can from the wrinkled, stiff hands that have failed G.W. as much as his mind.

"Carol's favorite. She's a dunker. It's a soggy half she takes, and I take a whole sandwich, but my soup, separate. I was trying to fix some supper for us while she took her bath. But I don't know where to get the cheese. She likes the white kind in her grilled sandwich, but I don't see any bread and I'm not sure that soup's hot." G.W. looks up at Kourt to see what he thinks about the situation.

Kourt pulls a package of fresh mozzarella and a stick of butter out of their fridge. I watch him open the soup and pour it into a pan to simmer. He plucks a leaf of fresh basil from the small potted plant in Carol's kitchen sink window and winks at me.

"Not yet, G.W., but it'll be hot and ready in two shakes."

FIFTEEN

Christmas Time in The City

The drive home is long, and after the wild night of rescuing Carol and laughing over an impromptu dinner with G.W., I'm not sure what to say.

"Thank you," Kourt says it first. "Mr. Phillips is a little—well I guess he's gone down faster than anyone knew. Carol has taken care of him since his stroke, but they're both getting older, and now his mind wanders." Kourt's words are slow to come to him.

I can tell it troubles him to see them like that.

"It's okay. I enjoyed them very much. I mean, not the circumstances of her falling—"

Fish sticks. Now my words are slow.

"They're lovely. I'm glad we were there. I mean that you—were there. To help them." I take a deep breath and try speaking again like it's not a foreign concept. "You must know them well."

"My whole life. The way we all know everyone in this town. My mother-in—I mean Georgia. Bob from the hardware store's wife, Georgia—" Kourt's the one tongue-tied now.

I look over at him trying to understand.

"She checks in on them periodically, but we've all been so busy—"

"With an Old-Fashioned Blitzen Christmas I forced on you, I suppose."

"No. I didn't mean that at all. It's the holidays. All businesses are in their busy season regardless. That's all I meant." Kourt glances from the road to me as he over corrects.

"Oh," my voice softer than I intended. I look straight ahead to see the lights of town glowing from a distance.

"You were great by the way," he says firmly.

"No. You were their hero. You're very great with them."

Very great? What?

"Except for the getting out of the car when I told you to stay put part." Kourt sounds as if he's scolding me and not in a joking way.

"Well, that was your first mistake. Telling me to stay put."

"Noted, Erika. Next time I'll waste precious minutes to drop you off before I get to a victim because you can't follow simple instructions." His voice has a bite and there's no question this conversation has taken a serious turn.

"Look, I'm sorry but it—"

"What if there had been a fire inside or something much worse? Just forget it. There won't be a next time."

I freeze in silence and stare out my passenger side window, unable to come up with a retort. I'm not sure I have one for that.

Did he just revoke his duty to drive me around and help with a Blitzen Christmas?

The long pause between us continues, until it terminates with his voice. "I just meant, it's not likely for there to be a next time, that's all. The odds of me getting a call again while we're out working on Christmas stuff. That's all I mean."

We ride in more silence as my eyes lift to watch the lights of Blitzen dazzle upon approaching downtown.

Kourt awkwardly fumbles with the heater, checking to see if it's on full blast, meanwhile it is perfectly warm in here, if not getting too hot due to his lingering tone. He turns another dial, again, as if he doesn't know his own truck that well, and he accidentally knocks the radio on. The all-too-familiar melody of *Silver Bells* is playing. I watch his hand go back to the steering wheel then reach again for the knob to cut it off.

"Oh, please don't. Let it play." I nod toward the dash for him to acknowledge the Christmas lights of Blitzen coming into focus as the music plays. "This exact song was playing in my Bug today as I drove away from town."

"I'm pretty sure they play Christmas classics on a loop on all the surrounding stations." He says like a jackass.

"No, but it was on my—ah, never mind—but it played at just the right moment, and I haven't seen it all lit up at night like this yet." Our eyes glow at the Christmas town before us. It's magical. "I guess I just…"

The song hits its line, "It's Christmas time in the city…" as we drive under a lit archway meant to represent a covered bridge. I almost think I see Kourt smile out his window, until he turns to me, ignoring all the impressive hard work.

Now I feel I have to say something to fill the space before he makes fun of me. "Anyway. It's—"

"Beautiful."

I turn to see Kourt looking right at me while we wait at the decorated stop light on Main Street.

"Does it look like it did when you and Helen were kids?" I just want to know if I did it right.

"Better." Kourt's voice catches in his throat and his eyes don't leave mine to look back at the spectacularly lit downtown, nor do they when the light turns green. Brows pinch and he starts to speak just as our green light turns back to red, but I don't let him.

"Hey, it's a sign," I say, beaming as bright as the Christmas lights. I feel my cheeks swell from smiling, and God if I can help it. "May I show you something? Just pull over and hop out. It won't take much longer than the red light, and I think it'll be worth it to you."

Kourt's face shifts from contemplation to curiosity. He slides into a parallel parking spot in front of a deserted downtown shop and kills the ignition.

The whole area is deserted apart from all the town lights and Josie's decorations. I run across the vacant street to the courthouse without bothering to look both ways.

"Come on! Kind of exhilarating, isn't it? Like roaming the halls of your high school on a Saturday with no teacher in sight or hanging out in a bank while it's closed." I walk backwards coercing him to catch up.

"I'm not sure if you just made a *Breakfast Club* reference, to insult me as I do roam the halls of my former high school daily, but I'm definitely not robbing the Blitzen bank with you."

"Careful, don't speak too soon. You really need that firetruck." I smile as he catches up to me and we see our breath in the cold as we laugh. "Keep walking. Okay... it's just behind...Wait—do it right. Close your eyes."

"Hell no."

"Come on, it's Christmas."

"Not yet it isn't." Kourt reluctantly closes his eyes, squinting a peek down at me as I take his hand and lead him behind the courthouse.

"It is now—Open."

Kourt opens to see a massive lump covered by a big blue tarp. "What's this?"

"Sorry. Brilliant unveiling fail on my part. I kind of need you to help with the tarp. And you can't make fun. You and your basketball team inspired this."

He looks down at me confused, then takes a step or two forward. There's a hint of excitement or curiosity at the very least in his eyes, when he takes the bottom of the tarp in both hands. Racing to the other side, I grab my end. "Okay, lift on three, but try and close your eyes again."

He's done with the anticipation. "One. Two—" He stops counting and the tarp flies behind him, no help on my part. A massive, shiny red sleigh full of toys is revealed.

"What is all this? How did you get all this?"

"You said Fisher's had everything, and I saw this massive red sleigh outside in their lawn and garden department when I veered off for extension cords. They were the first call I made when I got the idea to bring back Christmas in Blitzen. The day after the meeting I solidified everything, and they delivered it this morning."

Kourt steps up to a royal blue BMX bike and trails his hand down the handlebars to a Barbie pool party set, and a massive stuffed Koala bear wearing a T-shirt inside a box. There's a magnificent amount of toys. "And me and my basketball players gave you the idea?"

"Well, you and the Josie's tape deck in the Beetle. I swear that car's possessed in a Christmas magic kind of way. See, the people from your can drive who need food probably need toys for their kids."

"Ha! How did you get all of this?" Our eyes trail down the sleigh to the eight not so tiny reindeer tied in front of it.

"Fisher's donated a lot of it. The rest is from Blitzen. The volunteer workers from the last two days brought toys—there's more to come. And the decorations are from Josie's attic." I watch Kourt zero in on the only reindeer with a collar that has BLITZEN monogramed around his neck.

Kourt takes a step back to look again and take it all in. "But why did you hide it in the back?"

"Can you imagine their little faces when they turn the corner and see all of this? They'll look like you do right now. Last time I checked, Santa's pretty discrete in where he parks his sleigh. I couldn't have it in front of the courthouse for the taking. That, and Walter doesn't know it yet, but his twenty-footer town tree has to be the focal point for the Christmas Eve Tree lighting."

I stifle a chuckle when I realize Kourt is silent.

Giddy with Christmas and the insanity I pulled off through Fisher's, I may not be aware of how ridiculous this all seems. I clear my throat.

"Anyway, every family on your can drive list has free admission to Blitzen Christmas and their children will receive a ticket to come back to the sleigh for a toy. No charity here. All this came from Santa." I take a deep breath and move to drape the tarp back across it.

"You really do think of everything, don't you? And everyone."

"It's Christmas. That's when you're supposed to. So that's that. Fisher's really came through. Now it's just figuring out the vendors and parking."

Kourt follows my lead and secures the tarp on his end. The look on his face when he glances back at me, I can't figure out.

"Why Christmas? Why here—I know there was a work thing or whatever Helen mentioned, but why Christmas? Why all this?" Kourt looks at me in earnest. "I mean, I've never seen someone care so much who's not from Blitzen."

Guess he's trying to figure *me* out.

I start my walk back toward his truck. "Don't make me do it. Any conversation that begins with, 'When I was a kid...' is cliché. Even at Christmas."

"Fine. Then don't start it that way. I challenge you to not say—"

"Okay. Once when I was several feet shorter than I am now, and unemployed?"

"Nice."

"I think I must have been nine—"

"Foul ball."

"Saying my age at the time doesn't count."

"Fine. When you were nine." Kourt purses his smile, encouraging me to continue with doughy, exaggerated eyes.

"I spent the night with my cousins and our family took us to this random amusement park in their town. But it was December, and it wasn't about the rides. They had turned this theme park into a Christmas of every kid's dreams. There were hot chocolate and old-fashioned Wassail stands. Like, they actually had people dressed up in Charles Dicken's style fashion relaying the history of mulled cider as they poured you a cup. There were Christmas cookies, and a breadmaking shop, an ice skating rink, and old-fashioned carolers. It was like what it would be at say, Disneyland or Six Flags today, only not so commercial. This was truly special. It was real, and I loved it. I thought they made it just for us."

Kourt strides slowly next to me with his hands in his pockets. "Did you ever get to go back?"

"Oh, I looked for it for years after that, but they stopped doing it. Someone sold the theme park, and it's a parking lot for some convention center now. Anyway, I guess that ideal Christmas has always meant something to me. But then I grew up and went to Chicago, met Archer, and learned that ideals truly vary from one person to another. Decorations go up and come down. If you're too busy to notice them, you simply work through the holiday and it's over. Little by little it means less to you each year."

"Then why here? Why Blitzen. It can't just be because of your great aunt."

"When you and Helen mentioned Blitzen had this when you were kids—"

"How incredibly cliché of us." Kourt interrupts with a dashing smile I almost can't look away from.

"It reminded me of that time, and thinking about what matters most to different people. I don't know. It struck a chord with me. My mother used to always talk about this merry-go-round she had when they were kids. They didn't have a lot of money at the time, but her grandfather was so proud to have them around that he made them a merry-go-round. Like, literally built this huge merry-go-round by hand for his grandkids. She used to smile fondly and say, "We didn't have much at home or at school, but we had a merry-go-round that was just ours.""

Kourt stops and looks at me funny.

"I guess it comes down to that universal thing that makes a kid feel special, and for adults, giving it is the magic. So, I thought having a Blitzen Christmas again went along those lines for all parties. It belongs to Blitzen."

"What? Christmas?"

"Well, yeah. And this entity, this festival, the people coming together to pull it off and the ones coming to celebrate and enjoy it. It's just like Walter and his Calling of the Bears. He can do that every December 21st, but if people come together and do that with him, then it's his special thing he gave, and you get to come appreciate. It's all the same idea, you see." I stop talking. I've said more than enough, and I have no idea what he's thinking with his head dropped to his feet as we shuffle slowly through town square toward the truck.

"Hey." I finally break the silence.

Kourt looks up at me, his honey green eyes shining.

"Now that it's clear that I do love Christmas... It's fucking freezing out here!" I take off toward his truck and don't stop until I get there. Kourt picks up his pace behind me, and we drive the rest of the way home in silence.

SIXTEEN

Blitzen Manor/Manners

His massive truck's engine is so loud I don't know why I bother screaming above it with my passenger door open. Maybe I'm hoping he'll only half hear the additional favor I'm asking.

"Can we make a stop before Blitzen Manor, or maybe you could just drop something by for me when you stop to check on the Phillips?" I slide the large, insulated tote tucked under my arm toward the middle of Kourt's truck as I hoist myself up and he looks inside.

I watch him scan the easy-open, self-heating trays of mashed sweet potatoes, green beans, and mac & cheese for two labeled "Heat me."

"There are soup containers in there too. They can freeze them until they want to use them. The bag will keep everything the right temp until you get it in their fridge."

Kourt looks up from the insulated storage bag and glares at me. It's not a glare as much as wide eyes that question... everything about me.

My stomach flips as he looks through me. I hope he doesn't think I've offended them. I shift uncomfortably and quirk a smile to lighten the mood. "No can opener required." I wink up at him.

"You did all of this? You cooked it for Carol and G.W.?"

"Easier than several dozen unwanted Cherry Ice Box cookies."

Kourt narrows his eyes at me. "You do know that Carol and G.W. have nothing to do with Blitzen's Christmas festival. I mean, there's nothing they can help you with or offer." His eyes remain two hazel slits zeroing in on mine.

That stung.

But I'm used to being misunderstood. I don't have to defend myself all the time. Frankly, with Kourt, I don't feel like I have to at all. Who cares what he thinks?

I move on. "Yes, they can. Carol already told me she'll let me come get them and take them to the festivities on one of the warmer nights. They're very excited about Christmas coming back to Blitzen. G.W. is really looking forward to it."

Kourt pauses, his hands tapping on the stirring wheel. "What makes you think I'm going to check on them anytime soon?"

"Umm. Well, I don't know you that well, but I know you enough to know it's a safe bet you were planning on heading there after you drop me off tonight. Am I wrong?"

Kourt moves my bag of prepared food to the back seat. "Blitzen Manor it is."

"So, you'll drop it off tonight when you visit them?"

"Yes, Erika. Obviously. Only... are the mashed potatoes home-made or instant? Because these people are friends of mine."

"Homemade. Obviously." I roll my eyes as Kourt pulls onto the highway with a smile threatening his face. He chuckles to himself and his smile sticks.

"What?" I can't imagine what he's thinking right now.

"Nothing." He plays coy.

"Oh, you're such a coward."

"Me? You, Erika with a K, are calling me the coward? I'll remember this. Payback's a bitch." Kourt puts his blinker on.

What he could possibly have in store for me, I don't know, but I can't say I'm not intrigued.

"Okay, so help me out here. I've slept and coached and—"

"Saved lives?" I can't help but interject and call out the town hero.

"Shut up. I'm just saying I recognize last night knocked us off track, so let me help you prioritize. Apart from the why on Earth Blitzen Manor, tell me the overall plan here. What's the official start date? Because when we used to do this, Blitzen was open all through December. This late in the game, I'm not positive we can draw the vendors or the crowd." Kourt stops talking as if he worries he stumped me.

I smile in my seat. This is too easy.

"What?" Kourt peeks over.

"Nothing," I shrug.

"If you don't start talking, I'm turning the truck around and you know I'll do it. You don't have that kind of time to waste." Kourt's voice is firm and bossy in a good way. A way that makes my blood rush and my heart race a little.

My eyes widen at the prospect of just where the hell he thinks he would take me if he turned the truck around, like I was some child who misbehaved.

"Fine. This week everything gets locked down. It's our only buffer week to prep and solidify all locations, and schedule people, and festivities. The lights alone ordaining all of downtown are almost a call to Christmas announcement, seeing as how Blitzen hasn't had it in several years."

"It's been a good decade," Kourt informs me.

"Then, the ad at Fisher's will be at the store and in this week's sales flyer, and every week in December after that. It's mailed to everyone in three counties. So, we kick things off this weekend, and I've been careful to log each vendor as they sign up that can set up every day up until Christmas, as opposed to just the remaining weekends. That brings us to Blitzen Manor—"

A large thud in the back of the truck interrupts my speech.

"What the hell was that?" Kourt scans his rearview mirror trying to see into the bed of the truck.

"Uh, well, it's a statue, I think. But don't worry, it's wrapped really well so it won't scrape your truck bed."

"Scrape my truck bed? You would've been better off telling me you think we hit a deer. What exactly is back there?"

"Does it matter? It's for the auction. The coaches' fundraisers. By the way, you two have to schedule your dates with me so I can put them on the official Blitzen Christmas calendar that goes out tomorrow. Ellis already claimed his night for the auction. Do you want to do the big game back-to-back or on the weekend?"

"Ellis' auction?"

"Yes."

"You put something in my truck to serve his cause while I'm driving you all over town?"

"Our cause. All of your causes. Both fundraiser's serve *the* cause you're driving me around for."

"Unbelievable." Kourt shakes his head, and he doesn't appear to be joking. "The game, *my* charity basketball game was your idea. How could you contribute to my competitor?"

"I didn't contribute to his idea, only a piece for him to auction off, which the entire town was asked to do. It's like a great big ole' white elephant gift you bring to bid on. Get it? You're supposed to bring something too, Scrooge."

"Okay. Now I'm offended. All the work I've aided and abetted you in, and you call me a Scrooge?"

"Get over yourself, Jack Frost. What are you going to do this time, really turn the car around or start charging me for gas? Just don't forget I already offered."

"You're a real piece of work, Erika with a K. How long does that monstrosity stay back there?"

"So competitive. Maybe more Christmas competitions are what Blitzen needs to make money. Who knew? We're dropping it by on the way back when we're done. I already confirmed when he called."

"He called you?"

I look away from Kourt's antics when the most gorgeous venue I've ever seen surfaces on the hilltop. "This must be Blitzen Manor."

"In the flesh—well, brick and mortar and obnoxious columns." Kourt smirks at himself. "Why are we here again?"

"Let me find the picture." I reach for my phone to show him.

"Not that picture. Don't tell me we've wasted another precious evening."

"What are you talking about? I made arrangements with the grandson to walk the grounds. They've left me a key."

"Let me guess, Chicago. Some idiot showed you Blitzen's proverbial Old-Fashioned Christmas claim to fame spelled out in black and white with young couples ice skating on a frozen golden pond with children sledding down the hill of the Blitzen Manor in the background, and you thought that would get you an ice skating rink."

"No. I'm not that stupid. I know you can't count on the weather or the lake freezing over."

"Well, they certainly could that one day circa 1937." Kourt continues to mock me.

"Look. It's a beautiful venue, ice skating or not. It's only half a mile from town, there are acres for parking on one side, and the vendors' booths could surround the lake. Select activities will be so picturesque out here."

"What's wrong with town square, where we held it for decades after that photo?"

"June."

He takes a deep breath. "Ah. I see. She said, 'No'?"

"Not in so many words, but I felt compelled to find an alternative. She acted like parking would be a nightmare."

"And it will be. But it was every year. This year we'll get paid for the headache of orchestrating it. June may give you a hard time up front, but she'll be the first one there when you need her. Just ask her for what you need."

"Yeah, but look at this place. You don't think it will draw in a crowd?" I climb out of his truck and take it all in. Kourt slaps his door shut with one hand and squints up at the vintage mansion. "It'll bring something in."

I grab the set of keys left in the coded box and open the gate to the grounds. I only got permission to tour outside.

"The thing is—" Kourt extends his hand pushing open the gate I unlocked. "This place isn't really Blitzen."

"Are you telling me Blitzen Manor isn't Blitzen?"

Kourt struggles with his response. He sounds oddly sincere. Maybe that's his real struggle. "The original owners were obviously named Blitzen and that's how we got our start, but they weren't what made the town. They were more than well-off and represented old money that wasn't easily shared. Let's just say they weren't very generous being on the *have* end of the haves and have-nots."

"Oh." I try not to gasp as we step out onto the grounds that open their arms to the most beautiful private lake I've ever seen.

"Look, I know you may have been met with some disillusionment and a few disgruntled old folks—"

"Old?" I raise an eyebrow at Kourt, suggesting he's included in that bunch.

"Fair enough, but in Blitzen we take care of each other. What matters to us tends to matter a lot, and it's not over-priced venues that no one in town's allowed in. I'm guessing Gregg didn't offer to let you tour the inside."

"Well, I got the impression there would be a fee to rent or secure it so..." I trip over my own foot as I step down looking up at him. I'm trying to listen to him, but he's being genuine and I'm not sure how to read his face. Apparently, my solution is to fall down in front of his feet.

"You alright there?" There's a flirtatious glint in his eye that suggests he's enjoying this. His, 'I'm better at being an ass' charm is back as he plows on. "Like I said, *they* aren't exactly our Blitzen."

Kourt takes my elbow and leads me down the hill I was so desperate to see. I feel his fingertips press gently on my funny bone and I almost giggle as goose bumps trail up that arm and I shiver.

"You cold already?" He looks down as he surveys me, stepping away and toward the walkway that encircles the lake.

"Yeah. What—did the temperature already drop ten degrees?"

"It does tend to do that here, but not enough to freeze your lake for skating."

"Are you ever going to acknowledge that I didn't, for one second, think we could rely on that? I didn't know it wouldn't be an option at all, but I absolutely did not intend to count on a frozen lake through December for an Old-Fashioned Christmas."

We walk closer to said lake, and it looks like we're standing where the picture was taken.

"Yes, you did." Kourt beams at me patronizingly. "It's okay. It's cute, until someone falls in. Look around Erika. Don't you think having vendors and holiday festivities set up here is a huge liability for Blitzen?"

"I told you. I don't intend for anyone to try and skate, not even if it does freeze solid."

God he's irritating. He goes from sincere to the most shamefully infuriating person I've ever met in seconds. That's saying a lot, considering I'm best friends with the most trying person in Chicago.

Dogs bark in the distance somewhere behind us, but we're apparently too busy facing off to care what they may be after.

Kourt takes a step closer to me as if he's intentionally trying to get in my face to prove his point. "What's worse than a lake that's not frozen in winter, Erika?"

"I don't know, *Kourt*? What does that have to do with anything when we're not using the lake?"

And why am I yelling at this man?

"A lake that's half frozen." Now Kourt's yelling back. "That's what's worse, and that will happen at some point this December. *That* you can count on. All the little sleds you have dreams of kids renting to slide down the hill—what happens when a mom turns her head to dig in her purse for change for hot chocolate, and little

Cameron decides to slide his or her sled across what they think is a frozen half of the lake?"

Dogs are barking to a deafening degree in the background.

I yell back even louder, to be heard over their approaching barks. "Little Cameron? Who the hell is Cameron?" I'm standing on my tiptoes to get back in his face. "I told you Kourt, no one is skating or sledding across this pond, so no one is falling in the lake!"

A gunshot fires in the background and three bluetick hounds halt a hair away from us. I step back, not thinking, and my foot leaves solid ground. I feel Kourt's arm around the back of my waist as I'm jolted forward.

"Care to repeat that?" Kourt raises his eyebrows as I wiggle out of his grasp and take two steps toward the dogs, and away from the lake I nearly fell into. More barking issues from the grounds of the home next door, as the owner of the shotgun emerges about a hundred yards away from us. She's carrying the large gun and wearing a familiar velvet blazer, only this time it's red.

I recognize the beautiful black woman from the town meeting. She sat on the right, and I thought she was on my side until she snubbed me. *Awesome.*

"Is that you Kourt?" The woman's voice carries across both massive yards.

"Yes, Angelina." Kourt waves at her. "I was just showing Erika Blitzen Manor."

"Showing *me*? I'm the one who organized this." I whisper-shout up to him.

Kourt doesn't even flinch, still smiling and waving like he's on a parade float. *The jackass.*

"Sorry about that! Guess they thought they saw a duck." The attractive woman with the demanding presence, who hates my ideas, waves at us and heads back inside with her red blazer and shotgun.

"Judge Angelina Pritchard. She lives next door and raises—"

"Hounds?" I interject staring at the two wagging their tales in front of us.

"And, pointers, and setters, but who's counting."

"She looks like she's ready to go on a fox hunt herself."

"That's only on the weekend." Kourt chuckles and I roll my eyes, continuing my walk around the lake. He takes a half stride to catch up to me. "I'm not trying to say I told you so or get you to admit you wasted our time—"

"Wasted our time?" I pivot to him with fire in my eyes.

"Yeah. Absolutely," he snaps back.

"And I suppose your whole angle is 'let her see for herself or dig her own grave or—"

Barking ensues behind us again. It's louder and sounds like there are more dogs, but no gunshot this time, so we don't bother looking up. Kourt doesn't move from his glare he's locked down onto me.

I go to open my mouth and he opens his first. "Erika. I'm not trying to make this harder for you. I want you to get to do it your way. I want you to have your ideal Christmas you told me about. Hell, I carted you down here when you asked because I thought you might know something I don't. You're so fucking smart and it's damn impressive what you've done in less than three days."

The barking becomes a cacophony of ten or fifteen dogs now. "I just think you're also so fucking stubborn, and you won't let anyone help you or tell you anything, and it's not even your town." Kourt screams his hurtful comment over the barking.

His face is so close to mine I have the urge to reach up and bite him.

"I listen to *everything* you say, and I heard the part about this not being my town loud and clear." My voice comes out strained, I'm yelling so loud.

"Of course, you only heard that part, and if you truly listen to everything I say, then why do you do the damn opposite every time?" Kourt grabs the bottom of my chin tightly and something rises fiercely inside me.

My heart pounds and my cheeks burn.

The barking is so loud beside us I almost turn to look, but then I hear the duck.

We both must, as Kourt and I lift our eyes from our second face-off of the evening to see a mallard flying across the lake.

Our next look in unison is toward the dogs approaching us at record speed as they tackle, trample and knock us off the path into the deepest, coldest part of the unfrozen lake.

A massive splash, tangled legs in the water, and gasping for air ensues as Kourt hoists me up onto the path with him. The howl from a coonhound or two later... we are teeth chattering, locking the gate and dripping back to the truck.

No one says I told you so because our lips are blue and frozen to our trembling teeth. Kourt reaches in to start the engine and turn the heat on, then moves to the cab of his truck bed and pulls out an old camping blanket.

I shake so hard at the door handle I fear my hand is frozen to it. I try to unlock it when I see Kourt shake his frozen head at me in a death glare.

"Uh-uh. Take off your clothes."

"Don't be ridiculous." My voice cracks as the words shake out of my shivering body.

"There's no point in a blanket if it's as soaked from our clothes as we are. You want to get warm? You'll shed the clothes before you get in the truck. Shoes and socks too."

Okay. He's not wrong. Driving back to Josie's in clothes as wet and cold as that lake isn't ideal, and assuming he's gentlemen enough to give me the blanket...

Fish sticks-my life, The Blitzen-fucking manor.

I don't respond with words, only shivers as I stare back at him from over the truck bed wondering if my face is as purple as it feels. I shuck off my jacket, sweater and pants like a good girl, eyes still locked on him with savage anger, but confident as my body is covered by the truck.

Kourt removes his shirt and, my God, if he doesn't have bronzed skin in the winter, and not in the creepy tanning bed, body builder way. In the... 'my skin just does this to highlight my natural six pack' kind of way. He leans forward to pull his jeans off, but changes his mind, and for a split second I forget I'm standing in front of Blitzen Manor in my bra and panties.

"I don't know why you're staring at me like *you're* mad, or I got *you* into this." Kourt barks as he rebuttons his jeans.

"I wasn't staring. I just froze to death for a second."

Kourt's eyes haven't left mine, and I watch him stifle his amusement. Then his dark hazels drift down my neck to my shoulders, darting between my baby blue bra straps.

"I'd shed it all if I were you. At this point, being dry is more important than getting under the heater."

"I'm not getting naked under a blanket with you for any length of a car ride," I announce through trembles I no longer feel, as my body has gone numb. If the lights hadn't gone out at the house next door, I'd have no qualms about racing over to the judge's house in my matching bra and panty set, bare feet, and blue lips.

What have I got to lose? The judge already expresses disdain for me. Can't be worse than getting naked with Kourt.

"What was that you told Carol—there's nothing to be modest about when it comes to your safety."

"Then give me the blanket."

Kourt throws the blanket across the truck at me. I take a half step back as the heavy, full-size blanket hits me like a fluffy brick. "I'm not modest. I just have a preference in who I get naked next to."

"I typically find I'm preferable to most women I encounter."

"Lucky for us both you have not encountered me."

"Is that an invitation?" Kourt renders under his breath, almost inaudible.

"What did you say?"

"I meant there's a joke in there somewhere, but the reality of it while I'm literally watching you peel your wet clothes off in front of me is—"

"Stop watching, Kourt!" I tighten the blanket I hold with one hand around my neck and shoulders as I peel my wet underwear off, and maneuver to unhook my bra with one hand.

"Right." He doesn't even pretend to look away.

"I'll keep my pants on, but you're sharing one side of the blanket until the truck warms. I do have to coach tomorrow as opposed to die of pneumonia."

"You don't catch pneumonia from being cold."

"I'm sorry, I didn't hear you through your teeth chattering."

"Hypothermia is the best you could count on, and the heater in your truck should solve that one." My teeth keep chattering uncontrollably and I'm shaking.

Kourt crooks an eyebrow up. "How's that heater in my truck working out for you right now?"

"Noted. At least the most we'll lose with hypothermia from here back into town is an appendage."

"I happen to be very fond of all my appendages."

"I'm sure the entire town is."

"Get in."

"Turn around."

"No."

"Fine." I peel my door open with frozen hands and crawl into the truck, keeping the blanket intact as much as possible. In fairness it *is* a large blanket. However, there's no blanket large enough for me to share with him this naked.

Kourt waits outside his window until I'm settled. His door flies open, and he leaps in rubbing his hands together and blowing on them as he adjusts the vents of his heater towards us.

"Wouldn't that Judge lady have let us in to change and warm by her fireplace?"

"Angelina? Absolutely not. She would've called us in for trespassing or upsetting one of her precious hounds."

"Liar. You're enjoying this."

"There are many things I enjoy with a naked woman right beside me, but being this cold is definitely not one of them. Now give me some of my blanket." Kourt pulls the middle console up and pats the seat next to him.

Wrapped tightly, and snug as a bug in a rug in his large flannel blanket, I shoot daggers back at him.

He raises an eyebrow and motions toward turning the ignition off.

"Fine. Don't move." I turn completely away from him to face my passenger side window, where I inch down to one side of the blanket, keeping just enough to cover the front of my body. Then I take the rest and slide over to Kourt, fully covered in my one side like a cocoon.

Kourt shifts to raise his arm and allow me to nestle closer.

"I said don't move." He puts his arm back down to his side, and I scoot as close to him as possible, throwing the other half of the blanket across the front of him. There's blanket covering the front of me and a barrier to the side of me.

"Wow. You just found a whole new way to share a blanket with someone. That's impressive. If I knew you could keep us from sitting skin to skin, I could've taken my pants off."

"Don't you dare."

We coast a few feet down the driveway. "I do have to move my arms to steer." Kourt raises his arms to the stirring wheel, and his part of the blanket drops down to a small strip just covering his torso. I feel him shiver next to me as we head out of the manor's long drive.

"Fine." Keeping the wrapped layer of my blanket tight across my back and front, I relinquish the side barrier between us and slide my blanket-free hip to meet Kourt's. I feel his soaking wet jeans on my bare skin, but he can't feel me. I reach his side of the blanket behind his back and over his shoulders while he drives, wrapping him tightly and pulling my body next to his.

My front is fully covered, save my one arm around him that leans to wrap us both inside the blanket. My bare hip continues to rub against his wet jeans with the motion of the truck as we drive—and my ribs, plus the entire side of my upper body I did not account for in my master plan—press into him.

Literally my side boob is touching his skin.

My eyes widen on contact.

And there it is. That feeling again. We just fell into a freezing lake, yet heat swells in my belly and carves it way through the rest of my body, setting my skin on fire.

Kourt's body stiffens and he doesn't say a word.

We were soaked to the bone, so the only skin felt should be wet, cold and clammy like two fish flopping around on a boat deck, only—my side presses against his shirtless skin. And from my ribs down to that side of my waist, all I feel is his warmth. An exhilarating charge of it.

A beat goes by as we ride in silence.

My arm is awkwardly reaching across the back of his shoulder, holding the blanket around him as he drives. My heart pounds loudly in my chest as some brave part of me I haven't met scoots in a little more to pull the blanket tighter around his shoulder.

"Better?" I ask from some sardonic low tone of my voice that sounds way too confident and sexy to be my own.

Kourt's jaw ticks and his eyes stay glued to the winding roads before us. We continue back toward town, without moving. His skin on mine makes the flannel blanket almost obsolete. I'm not shivering anymore and neither is he. But then he speeds down a turn I don't recognize. We wind up several more hills on a two-lane road when he stops the truck at the edge of a driveway and clears his throat.

"Wait here." Kourt leaves the ignition running and sprints inside a charming log house I've never been to before. Seconds later he comes out wearing a grey sweatshirt and a pair of navy-blue sweatpants.

"Here. Put these on." He tosses a sweatshirt and sweatpants my way and backs out of the drive without looking at me. There are no jokes, pretense or attempts to look my way as I slide all the way over to my side of the truck and jimmy the Blitzen Volunteer Fire Department sweatshirt over my head.

With the blanket all to myself I'm able to slide the top down without exposing any of my chest and I do the same thing to slide into the sweats.

We're silent through town, heading back to my side of the mountain until I let out a sheepish, "Thanks."

"Don't mention it." Kourt's clammed up before, but not over something as uneventful as sweatpants. That, and I can't help but wonder why he didn't invite me in to change. Was it less awkward for me to get dressed in his truck than it would have been to allow me to change in the bathroom at what I assume was his house? Odd.

But, there again, I suppose I did practically get naked in front of him. Maybe he thought slipping into sweats to remedy the situation was child's play after that.

"Oh wait, I think that's the turn to Ellis' place, right? He said he lived off Old Mill Road. I forgot about the statue." I look over at Kourt from my side of the truck that feels strangely far away now and stands as a reminder of an embarrassment I'm not sure we're coming back from.

Kourt slows by the turn to Ellis' Street and looks at me. His soft brown eyes, now darker somehow with an emerald hue I can't escape. They trace up and down his sweats swallowing me, and back up to my wild wet hair.

Then he looks in the rearview mirror clocking the baby blue lace demi bra I hung to dry on his truck coat hanger hook thingy. I squirm a little in the passenger seat as he fixates on it like a mad man, then shifts uncomfortably and looks back to the dash.

Without acknowledging me, Kourt accelerates past the turn to Ellis' house. "You're not dropping anything off to Ellis looking like that. I'll take it to him at work tomorrow myself."

What?

Okay, yeah, I would prefer to pop by Ellis's dry, with a brush run through my hair, maybe a little make up as opposed to mascara streaked down my cheeks from swimming in a lake in below-freezing weather, and maybe even clothes that fit me—but to not drop it off just because I'm in a pair of sweats? I'm so confused. *Oh.*

Oh. I get it. He doesn't want Ellis to assume we... I mean they are his sweats, and Blitzen Volunteer Fire Department written across the front kind of gives that away. My wild wet hair could give the impression of bed head, sex hair, and I'm not wearing any underwear.

For many that's a non-issue in a sweatshirt, but I'm endowed enough to let not walking in a convenience store in a tank top without a bra be my gauge of appropriate in public. I do have more than enough to require a strapless in a sundress.

I see. He doesn't want to ruin his reputation by Ellis thinking we got together or something equally ridiculous. Because, in that regard, I guess I would look insane knocking on Ellis' door like this and pulling that crazy statue out of Kourt's truck. Wow.

Okay. Well, that's just fine and dandy, Kourt, because I don't want Ellis getting the wrong idea and thinking you and I got together, either!

I sigh out the window at my new revelation, and pulling up to my driveway couldn't come sooner.

"I promise. I'll give it to him," Kourt encourages as he pulls up and slows to let me out. I hop out of the truck prepared to take off without a word but damn the good Samaritan in me that sees the bag of food I packed for the Phillips.

"Oh, I'm so sorry, but please don't forget the food for Carol and G.W. Or I can totally drop it by tomorrow, no problem." I move to grab the bag handle, and Kourt's hand catches mine.

"I said I've got it. I'll take it to them. It's fine. Your car won't make it to their place, and I don't want you going over there without me. It's too far up Grinder's Bend. Those hills are too steep for your Bug." He looks down at my hand he's still holding, and a physical current, similar to the one I felt when I pressed against his side, pulses through me.

"When you want to visit them. I'll take you."

Heat fills my stomach again, and I pull my hand away abruptly to leave. "Great. Thanks. Get home safe," I say over my shoulder with a flippant wave.

Great. Thanks???? Awesome. I have no idea what's happening.

When he's not behaving like a neanderthal or some curious version of a twenty-first century, overly protective, almost possessive male lead from a romance novel you'd like to fuck or drown, I'm behaving like a sixteen-year-old waiting for her first kiss.

That, or I fling my naked body at him under a blanket and make the most confident, arrogant man on the planet, other than Archer, as uncomfortable as he can possibly be. And somewhere in the middle of all that, I'm supposed to pull off a Blitzen Christmas that saves the town. The town I don't belong to, as Kourt so graciously pointed out.

Aunt Josie, you better be dead, or you'll have hell to pay for leaving me to this.

SEVENTEEN

Baby Blues and Lace

S hit. Dammit. Hell. I groan and shake my head. I'm two minutes from school and what do I spot in my rearview mirror? A lacy blue bra dangling in the side window. Fuck me.

I make a quick turn on a side street, hop out of the truck, and snatch the bra off the backseat hook. *Jesus.* Her panties are wadded on the seat. My head tilts and I pause before retrieving the crumpled blue lace attached to a tiny taunting bow. I have to squash a million filthy thoughts courtesy of every ounce of blood rushing to my cock before I lay a hand on them.

It couldn't have been more innocent, but pulling up to school with a bra hanging in my backseat window...

I let out a loud laugh. Hell, some of them would expect it from me.

But not her bra, obviously.

I'm lucky she didn't realize the hard-on she gave me when the truck heated up. I didn't know I had it in me. I was so frozen from the lake, I never dreamed I'd get a boner like that. I felt like I was fifteen with her bare skin touching mine. She made me fucking hot all over.

I let out another groan and tap the back of my head against the seat.

What am I doing spending this much time with her?

You're playing with fire, I tell myself. But I'm locked into this. *Keep your head in the game.* How many times have I heard that in my life? How many times have I *said* that in my life to a player—never dreamed I'd be saying it about... her.

"Coach!" Trent jogs toward me as I get out of my truck. "You won't believe who I just took a call from!" He's out of breath.

"Calm down, buddy. Who?"

He may be an assistant coach but he's jumping up and down like a grade school kid.

"Jet Holloway! You know him?" His smile is as wide as his eyes. "Why's Jet Holloway calling you?"

"We played college ball together. What'd he say?"

"I answered your desk phone. Said to tell you he's in."

I blow a sigh of relief. "Great."

"What's it about?" Trent's not giving up until he has his answers. Jet—Jamarcus Holloway—is one of the biggest names in the NBA.

"It's a fundraiser for the fire department. We're going to throw a charity basketball game. I called him the other day. He said he's in? Hot damn."

Man, that's good news.

"You played with Jet Holloway? Really? I didn't realize."

No wonder. "Jamarcus went onto the NBA. I went into coaching. Don't put us on the same level. Just college friends." I open the door to the gym to let him walk in first.

"Impressive. When?"

"When did we play together?" How many years has it been?

"No, when's the charity game? If Jet Holloway's playing, we can get a shit ton of people here."

"That's the point, Trent."

"Well, fuck, coach. When. Is. It?"

She asked me that last night. "The day after the auction."

"What auction?"

"The one Ellis is having. It's a competition to see which coach can raise the most money for the fire department." One I plan on winning. I don't like losing. Especially not to Ellis.

Which reminds me. "I forgot something. Go ahead and get the scrimmage started. I'll be right back."

What did she put in the back of my truck for that fucker? I told her I'd give it to him.

Fishing around, I find something wrapped in a packing blanket. Long, kind of cylindrical. She said it was a statue or something.

Reaching over, I grab it. Part of me wants to accidentally drop it so the fucker breaks.

"Kourt?"

Fuck. She's got such a soft voice when she wants it to be.

"Yes, I delivered your food to G.W. and Carol. That was nice of you, making them meals like that."

"Thank you. I knew you would deliver the food—"

"And I got your bra out of the window. And your panties. They're in a bag."

She groans into a low laugh. "A bag?"

Why does she make me smile? Even over the phone? "No worries. I'll give it to you when I see you tonight."

"About *that.*"

Long pause. That's never good.

"Just say it, Erika with a K."

She clears her throat. "Would you mind terribly, horribly... I need to go back to see Walter. He's waiting on my answer."

"Which is?"

"Ugh, Kourt," she groans. "We've got to move it into, or closer to town, if we're going to make The Calling of the Bears part of the festival. Everyone at town hall agrees, and honestly it's the only way to get traffic there. Walter wants people to come. That's the point."

"I didn't think of that." Walter Miller's about as unmovable as Black Mountain. I hear a sigh of frustration from her end of the phone.

"How are you by the way? No bad cold from our evening swim?" I wondered about her last night. *All night.*

"Nah, I'm tough."

"Listen, we had morning practice, so I'll cut out early and let Trent handle the afternoon. I can pick you up a little before three. Does that work?"

"I'll be ready."

"Hey, Jamarcus Holloway said he's in for the charity game. Said he'll get more NBA volunteers, to be named. Now I've got to throw together a team to play the stars. I've got some other buddies I'm calling. But everyone's asking when."

"Who's Jamarcus Holloway?"

"Ja-mar-cus Holloway."

No response. How does anyone go through life and know *nothing* about basketball?

"Jet Holloway. Think, Erika. You've seen him in the razor commercials on TV. The—"

"Oooh!" There's the recognition. "*That* guy! He's famous."

Jeez-us. I want to bang my head on the desk.

"Trust me. He's an even bigger draw for basketball fans. As soon as I have the other names, I'll let you know, but the charity game is a go. We just need a date. The location will be our gym. I cleared it with the principal."

"Sorry. I just choked a little on my coffee—not over your celebrity buddy crush, but your willingness to follow through with my idea. I think I'm stunned."

"You're certainly not stunned silent. Whatever. It's a good idea. What's that they say about a broken clock being right at least twice a day—"

"Funny. I was thinking more along the lines of you potentially pulling this off and beating Ellis. I mean, every dog has its day."

"Wow." Shaking the smile off my face, I take a moment, uncertain if there's something else to say. Maybe I'm just not ready to hang up. How does she not know a damn thing about basketball and why does it amuse me more than turn me off.

Helen was right, she's something different. Quick as hell. Resourceful and caring the way she handled Carol and G.W.

Damn it.

"Gotta go." I click the phone off as abruptly as I answered her call.

Keep your head in the game.

Sliding into my truck in front of city hall, Erika finds my face with determined eyes. "You don't have to worry. I promise, I've got Walter. All jokes aside, I truly appreciate what you've done for me, introducing me to him, and I have no intention of letting him down."

"Just do what you do, Erika. It seems to be working." *Like that red sweater's working on you right now.*

She looks at me as if uncertain. "Where's the catch?"

"No catch. Just when I drop you off, don't forget your—" I couldn't help but notice the lacy bra was a C cup. Perfect.

"Of course. I didn't plan on hanging it off your side mirror this time. Did you remember to give Ellis the statue?"

Fuck. "Sorry. I got it to my office, but I never ran into him."

She cocks her head to the side. "That's what he said."

"You talked to Ellis?"

"He called me about the auction."

I feel a growl rumble deep in my chest and she turns to face me. "What is it with you and Ellis, anyway?" She's glowering at me. Why is it I can go from hero to zero faster than anyone on the planet? "Nothing."

"Something."

"It's nothing, Erika. I've got a lot going on. I didn't think about Ellis or his damn auction." I can fix this right now. I punch Bluetooth. "Call Trent."

Bluetooth responds, "Calling Trent."

Erika stares at me. "What are you doing?" she mouths.

I hold up my index finger to stall her while Trent answers his cell. "Yeah, Coach."

"Trent, remember that tube thing I brought in this morning, wrapped in a packing quilt? It's behind my desk."

"Looking at it."

"Will you take that down to Ellis?"

"On it."

Erika straightens and relaxes in her seat.

"Tell him it's from Erika Amherst for his auction. Then tell him, 'Coach said to shove it up his ass.'"

Trent lets out one hell of a laugh. "Will do, Coach."

I cut my eyes at her. "At least he'll have it."

What's fucking Ellis done for her besides try to get in her pants? I'm the one who's carted her all over the Appalachians, rescued her from a frozen pond—and she's bending over backwards to help Ellis the ass wipe.

"That was some exemplary sportsmanship." Her cheeks are as red as the fuzzy sweater she's wearing. The very one hugging her curves. "Guess that makes me even more excited to see you in action on the court, McShotty." Her voice is rich with sarcasm as she cuts her eyes away from me to her side of the truck.

"Are you hungry?"

She's staring a hole through the windshield now. "After that, I couldn't eat a crumb."

"I could eat a horse." I swing through the drive-through at Dairy Maid.

"Do you ever eat anything besides hamburgers?"

"You seemed to enjoy yours the last time."

"I'm just wondering if we should have your cholesterol checked before we head too far up the mountain."

"Can I take your order?" the attendant crackles through the speaker.

I turn to Erika, who's sitting stiffly in her seat. "I take it you don't want a burger?"

Twisting her lips to one side she turns to look at me. Blue eyes dripping with remorse at the smell of hot grease wafting from the Dairy Maid.

"Two Big boys and one Junior Burger."

The Dairy Maid's been here since before I was born. It's the only privately-owned fast-food joint for miles. A real mom and pop that made it through three generations. The burgers are a rare anomaly of fast and homemade.

They make sausage biscuits for breakfast on hand-rolled biscuits, and their soft serve ice cream is famously poured over a Styrofoam bowl hosting a slab of homemade cherry cobbler. Only a devout vegan could resist this place. I'm not arrogant, but she's never met a food truck in Chicago like it.

The young girl at the drive-through window is a sophomore history student of mine. She smiles brightly at Erika as she passes me the bag. "Coach McLain? Do you and the Chicago Christmas lady want ketchup, salt and pepper? I put a large fry in for y'all to share, so you might need some."

A dimple flashes toward Erika as my student ogles her through the truck.

"Thank you—" Erika looks at my student's name tag. "Brittany. I love the fries here. I think Coach McLain hogged them all the last time. I will take extra ketchup, salt and pepper, thanks."

"I like your sweater." My student is relentless. Apparently, the town also goes from zero to sixty where Erika is concerned.

"Thank you, Brittany. Make good money tonight. We'll see you at the festivities on your nights off, yes?"

"Oh, yes, Miss Amherst. My church is helping with the live nativity. I'm signed up for costume changes. And my dad is supplying the sheep." Brittany, from second period history, hands me a heaping hand full of salt. Pepper. Ketchup.

"Amazing. I can't wait to see you guys there. Merry Christmas." Erika's genuine smile flashes and I have to remind my dick she's the enemy.

"Merry Christmas, Miss Amherst!"

I drive away as my student waves at her girl crush in my passenger seat. Guess she wants to grow up and be just like her.

Yes, dear Brittany, you too can relocate to a small tucked away town and rearrange the people's lives and plans at your every holiday whim. 'Merry Christmas Miss Amherst—'

Please.

I'm into my second burger before Erika says, with an almost-full mouth. "Thank you."

"Welcome."

She bats those baby blues at me and something in me just has to relieve the tension. And, maybe I need to give her credit where it's due.

"Look, I meant what I said. Do what you do, with Walter or anyone. It's working. You've got the whole town excited about your Christmas festival. Hell, even June was pleasant this afternoon and she's never pleasant to anyone but me. You've got an NBA player bringing his teammates to town for a charity game. Do you have any idea how much Jamarcus gets paid for one commercial? And he's coming and bringing teammates. We should pack the house."

"I didn't do that, Kourt. You did. I looked him up, by the way. He *is* huge."

I can't stop this grin. "You actually took the time to look up something about basketball?"

"Yes. I'm excited to come to your game Friday."

"Nice."

"Ellis asked me." I choke on my last swallow. The hairs on the back of neck prickle to life. What can I say? Not a damned thing.

As Walter's place comes into view, Erika breaks the silence. "You've been quiet."

"Got nothing to say."

It's been a long twenty minutes.

To her credit, she doesn't push it. "We're here." She jumps out. Before I can get the truck turned off, she's in the back seat, fishing out a box of homemade cookies, no doubt.

As we walk to Walter's front door, it hits me. She's seeing this place for the first time in daylight. His house is surrounded by his trees. Fraser firs to the left, Eastern white pines on the right. God knows how many acres he still keeps, and it looks like, all this time, even though he hasn't been selling trees, he's been keeping them trimmed.

He's also kept the house up. Keeping busy since his wife died. That's what widowers and widows do. They've got to go on living, so they stay busy.

Walter walks onto the porch before we reach it, watching us. Unlike the first night, Erika says nothing.

"I expected you yesterday," Walter calls, a little too gruff.

"That was my fault. I had an emergency. Sorry."

"Carol?"

He's heard.

"She alright?" he asks.

"Yeah, she's okay. Didn't break anything." I tilt my head at Erika. "She saved the day."

"That's what I hear." Walter keeps an eagle eye on the woman at my side.

Erika hasn't said a word.

"Whatcha' got there?" he asks, and this time he's smiling.

"I brought you a real present this time." She holds out her box.

"Homemade?"

She smiles back at him with a smile that would thaw anyone's heart. "Absolutely. My favorites, just for you, Mr. Miller."

"Walter." He tilts his head. "Come on in." He holds the door open for her and points in the direction. "Put 'em on the table over there. I thank you."

The house smells like fifty years of secondhand smoke. But it's as clean inside as it is outside. A board and batten house with cedar shakes in the gables. A deep porch across the front.

"Well?" Walter never was one for small talk. He cuts right to it without offering us a seat.

Erika hangs her head a moment, staring at the plank floor, then brings her eyes to meet his. "I understand you normally do the

Calling of the Bears out here. On Whispering Bear Mountain." I don't hear fear in her voice.

"Yes, the cave on the backside of the mountain."

She clears her throat, cuts her eyes up at me, and back to Walter. "Would it be possible, this one year, to do it in a cave in town? Or nearer to town?" She glances up at me. "Much nearer town?"

Walter's mouth tweaks to the side as he stares a hole into her. His gaze shifts to meet mine, and I give him a nod.

Before he can answer, she pleads, "It would mean so much for the town to get to commemorate The Calling of The Bears this winter solstice with you, this special holiday season where Blitzen found its way back to Christmas."

He coughs into his hand, and I swear I see tears in his eyes. *Jeez-us*. She's good. And I think, no... I know she means it.

"There's a cave on the outskirts of Blitzen," Walter offers.

Oh, shit.

"You mean Devil's Lantern Cavern?" They both hear my surprise and snap to me.

Walter rubs his hand over his chin. "Only one I know of, in Blitzen."

It's supposed to be haunted.

"Devil's Lantern?" Erika looks and sounds like he just invited her to a séance. "That doesn't sound..." She hesitates, looking back and forth between me and Walter. "Christmasy. Or Calling of the Bears-y." She punctuates it with a big, defeated sigh.

"Some people call it Angel's Hollow," Walter offers.

Her face lights up.

I've never heard it called that.

"Are you sure?" she asks with a big smile.

"Yeah." Walter saunters over to the box and opens it, peering in. A second later, he's stuffing a big green Christmas cookie into his mouth. "That's good." He's still chewing.

Erika's smile spreads across her face. "Pistachio." She claps her hands together, like in a prayer. "Does that mean we can do the Calling of the Bears ceremony at Angel's Hollow?"

She and Walter have officially renamed Devil's Lantern Cavern to Angel's Hollow.

"I guess. For this special occasion."

Erika looks up at me with so much hope in her eyes, she makes me think of a kid looking up at Santa Claus. Or the Tooth Fairy. The Easter Bunny. Whoever will make her dream come true.

She's full of bite and wit one minute, then—irresistible. "Do you mind taking me to see it? To figure out how we get people up there?"

I grumble. It's hard not to think of her fucking fondness for the football coach right now. It's on the tip of my tongue to ask why she doesn't ask him—

"Come on, Kourt." She smiles up at me like she thinks I'm going to refuse her. As if I ever have.

I wink at Walter, where she can't see. *Screw it.* "Sure you don't want to ask Ellis?"

Her mouth falls open.

I glance outside. "The ceremony's at dusk. Let's go if you want to see what it'll look like for the ceremony."

"I'll be right behind you." Walter shoves another cookie in his mouth and grabs his truck keys. "I need to get gas. Don't go in without me."

EIGHTEEN

Caving In

My eyes dart from the clock to the sky as the sun begins to sink between the peaks. It's like the mountain is swallowing it with its gaping mouth. I'm racing to beat it. The winter solstice is around the corner. The days are short enough, but between these peaks and valleys, they're even shorter.

Erika leans over the console, peering at the speedometer. "You're driving faster than normal."

"Gotta get you there before it gets dark."

She draws back, studying me. "Are you pissed at me, Kourt?"

I take my eyes off the road to answer, and I'll be damned if I don't see a little hurt looking back at me. "Why would I be mad at you?"

Those eyes search my face for a long beat before she shrugs. "I don't know. I'm sure having to chauffer me everywhere gets old." She glances out the window. "I hope you feel you have the freedom to say no regardless of Blitzen or Helen. I could always ask someone else, to lessen the burden.

"Go right ahead." I punch Bluetooth. "Call Ellis Andrews."

"Kourt!" she shrieks. "What are you doing?"

Bluetooth croons, "Calling Ellis Andrews."

"Hang up!" She looks like she's about to bail out of the moving truck.

Naw, I'm driving too fast.

The phone's ringing as our gazes lock and latch, and Ellis picks up. "McClain, shove that statue up your own ass."

"Figured it was a good fit for yours."

"Eat me."

"You're a fucker, you know that Ellis?"

"Just described yourself, McShotty."

I cut my eyes at Erika, who's every bit as red as her sweater. "Just wanted to make sure you got it."

"I got it. I'll be sure to thank Erika next time I talk to her."

"Go ahead. She's right here."

I'm not sure she's *not* going to bail out the truck, even at this speed.

Erika yells, "Ellis, I'm so sorry, he's being—"

"I know what he's being. He's a natural born dick. Thanks for the statue. It'll do good at—"

Click.

"You hung up on him!"

She. Is. Mad.

Good. So am I.

"I placed the call. I can end it when I want."

She turns in the seat to face me, square on. "You didn't let me ask him to take me to Angel's Hollow."

"Erika, there's no fucking Angel's Hollow. It's Devil's Lantern Cavern, unless you and Walter can get everyone in the state of Kentucky to agree to rename the damned place. And I guarantee Ellis wouldn't know how to find it—and if he could, he wouldn't scuff up his fancy shoes hiking up the mountain. He's a golf course guy. Probably too big a coward to go into Devil's Lantern, anyway. He'd shit his pants."

Now that's a look I haven't seen on her. Something between shock and rage.

"Wow. That's the most words I've ever heard you string together without a pause or a grunt."

I heave a sigh. "Talking to you is over-rated."

"Let's just forget it. I'll get someone else to take me another day."

"Walter's already on his way to meet us there."

If the twenty minutes of silence driving to Walter's felt uncomfortable, the drive to Devil's Cavern is like fingernails on a chalkboard. She's sitting over there stewing.

This silence isn't all that golden.

Does she really want Ellis Andrews? Can she not see through him? I thought she was smarter than that. Is she doing it to get under my skin?

"What do you see in him?"

What does anyone see in him?

Nothing. No answer. She doesn't even look my way.

Screw it. Maybe I will hand this festival shit off to someone else. Let Ellis have her.

"He's nice to me." She's talking to the windshield.

And I'm not?

"It wasn't a big deal. He asked me if I wanted to go to a basketball game." She turns to face me with so much hurt in those eyes. "A ballgame you'd be coaching. I wanted to see you in action in your environment."

Well, fuck me. "You could've asked—"

"That's the point, Kourt! *He* asked *me*. I'm your albatross. You have to drive me everywhere because all I have is the Beetle and you refuse to let me drive if it's below freezing—"

Our gazes meet. "You still don't understand how dangerous these roads can be. And you're not my albatross. Just... anyone but Ellis Andrews."

Her eyelids flutter with a million questions as I pull onto the gravel parking lot. "We're here." Thank God.

She stares ahead, her delicate brows shifting high, following the cliff wall as it towers toward the sky. "*Up there?*" The cave is halfway up.

"Yep." I open my truck door. "We need to hurry. The sun's getting low."

Her gaze darts around, surveying the limestone face of the sheer rock wall, looking almost terrified as she stands outside her door. "Will people climb all the way up there?"

My stride slows and I pause to look over at her, watching her take it all in. The way she's always awestruck by what she sees... I don't know why, but it affects me too. She makes me see it all again for the first time.

"The climb to Whispering Bear is steeper and enough people go there every year. So, I'd think so. There's also a trail, with steps. The state's made it easy for tourists. And there's a wide, flat entranceway for the ceremony."

"Oh." Quiet. She's very quiet.

I'm a dick.

"Walter's behind us. He'll show us the ropes." I take a look at her shoes. I hadn't thought about her shoes before. "You wore boots so we're good." Stepping forward I reach my hand back for her.

Hesitantly, she puts her hand in mine. It feels almost fragile next to my massive palms. Warm. "Sorry I was an ass."

"You *are* an ass, Kourt."

"I know. Come on."

It's a five-minute hike zig-zagging uphill. But the view at sunset is worth it. So is her reaction to it. Our anger seems to have dissipated on the way up.

"See the way the sun hits that peak and slices down the mountain? Just before it goes completely down it makes a glint of light in the middle of the cave opening, between the rocks' shadow. That's why they named it Devil's Lantern."

"Too bad. I'm running with the angel schtick. I refuse to call it Devil's Lantern on a Christmas flyer."

Damn. I guess the marketing exec showed back up.

She takes in the view one more time and lets out a chilled breath. I feel her eyes smiling at me before I turn to look at her. "I want to see inside."

"Walter said specifically for us not to go inside—to wait on him." I scan the empty road below. "He'll be here any minute."

"What are you, the cave police? It won't hurt to peek in the entrance. I've never seen a cave."

"Erika, no."

Her lips curl into a smirk. "Are you scared? Like you said *Ellis* would be?"

My heart may thump out of my chest. I can't believe she threw down that gauntlet. "I'm not a caver. Stay in the entry."

"Come on!"

Shit. She's heading in.

"Hold up, dammit. It's a fucking cave!"

Cave... cave... cave... echoes off the cold, damp cavern walls.

Erika turns, eyes wide. She makes a funny, spooky face. "Eerie."

"They say it's haunted."

"Really?" Even in the dim light, I see her wicked grin.

"It's what they say."

She startles and turns. "Did you see that?"

"I can't see much of anything. We need to go back outside."

"Over there." She aims her arm straight ahead. "I saw a flicker."

"No, you didn't. If you did, it was a reflection from the sunset. Let's get back outside. Walter will probably have a flashlight when he gets here."

"You don't have a flashlight?"

Are you shitting me? "Do I look like I have a flashlight?"

"You look like the kind of guy who would have a flashlight."

"I don't."

"Cellphone?" She's hopeful.

"On the charger. Yours?"

Her voice falls. "In my purse."

"Then let's get the fuck out of here."

"Now look who's being scaredy pants." She marches off in the direction she pointed, I guess, looking for some phantom light.

"Goddammit, Erika come back!"

Four long strides—and fuck it—I've lost her. "Where are you?" My bellow echoes off the walls.

Are you... are you... are you....

"Over here," she whispers. No echo.

"Where?"

Where... where... where...

How big is this damn place?

"Kourt?" I turn to the whisper.

"What?"

"I can't see anything."

No fucking shit.

I move toward the voice, arms extended, my voice low. "Stand still, Erika, and talk to me, quiet like that. I can find you." This damned place is infamous for drop-offs. Some a couple of feet, some a couple of hundred feet. I'd think the state would have them roped off but who the hell knows in this blackness.

"I'm sorry." Her voice sounds so small.

"Just stay where you are." I'm moving her way slowly.

She sniffs.

"Are you crying?"

"Absolutely not."

"Yes, you are." I heard it. Her voice broke.

"I am not!" she yells angrily.

Not... not... not...

I turn in a circle. The sound bounces around. It's impossible to get your bearings in this blackness. "Erika, sing something. Just... sing. Softly."

"What?"

"I don't know. Anything. A fucking Christmas song."

She huffs—I feel the heat of her breath—she's right here. Turning, I grab her and tug her to me. She smells like Christmas cookies.

"Kourt," she whimpers into my chest.

"It's alright. Walter can't be far. The sun set before we were counting on it." I wrap my arms around her, and an intense warmth invades the cold space around us.

"I can't see my hand in front of my face." Her mouth moves against my chest.

"Then don't put your hand in front of your face."

She nudges my chest with her head. "You're impossible."

"I've been told." I blink. I can't see. Not a frigging thing. Not even her, nestled in my arms. I can feel her. Smell her. Hear the rhythm of her heart beating against my chest, or is it mine? "Listen.

I don't want to move around, because there could be a drop off. So, we're just going to sit down, right here, and wait. Okay?"

She nods against me. I hold her shoulders. "Let's sit, together."

"Okay."

I turn her as I squat and sit, and she moves with me. "Rest here, against me." Nothing to rest my back on, so I spread my legs wide, knees bent. I pin her between them. "This way I won't lose you again."

"I'm not going anywhere."

Damn right you're not.

Silence. And pitch darkness. An occasional *drip... drip... drip...* as time creeps by.

No Walter.

I hear her breathing. A louder drip bounces off the cave bottom somewhere near us.

"It's colder here than out there."

"Yeah." I snug her against me. Her hair tickles my neck. *Shit.*

"We should talk so Walter can follow our voices. Where are you from? Originally?"

"I grew up in Willow Meade. It's about thirty minutes outside Chicago. You?"

"Right. Here. College?"

"Northwestern. You?"

"University of Tennessee."

"On a great big basketball scholarship." She remembered.

Helen's a blabbermouth.

Silence.

Drip... drip... drip.

"Brothers and sisters?" she asks.

"Both."

"Do they live here?" The surprise in her voice hits me, as if she feels like she should have met them by now.

"No. They're in Florida, where my parents moved, when I went to college. Dad relocated. You?"

"Only child."

"That explains a lot."

She elbows me.

"Hey, lucky you. My brother and sister were pain in the asses. Lovable pains in the asses."

Silence.

That last wiggle when she elbowed me stroked my fucking cock. Dammit. What was I thinking nestling her ass in between my legs? Where the hell is Walter?

Exhaling a long breath, I try to relax, but my hand slides down her ribs to her waist only to land on bare skin where her sweater has ridden up from her jeans.

Goose bumps lace above her hip bone as my hand flattens across the bare flesh of her side, and my fingers press into her, against my will. "You should button your coat all the way down around you, to keep you warmer." There's a silence insistent on lasting as the palm of my hand stays against her flesh, covering the side of her waist.

We both know there's nothing warmer than the way we're sitting right now, and the moment we're pretending not to be caught in. My dick twitches and fuck if it hasn't sprung to life. There's no way she can't feel how hard I just got. She's leaning against me.

"Wh—"

"I for—" We both speak at the same time. Our voices anxious to make nervous chatter, but our bodies have not deviated from their position. My head drops down to hers and I slowly turn my lips to her ear. "Why did you come here? Why not home to Willow Meade for Christmas?"

She shivers against me, acknowledging my breath in her ear. I feel her turn toward my face, testing how close we are. "My mother." She mutters carefully as if she realizes her lips could be close enough to touch any part of my face. They are. I can feel it.

My heart thuds so loud in my chest I know she feels that.

She turns her head back to face away from me.

"It's just she and I for a while now. She's got a cruise with her book club she's been paying out and saving up for. It's a two-week holiday at sea over Christmas with her good friends, and she's really been looking forward to it. I didn't have the heart to tell her about work, and that I could come home. I wouldn't want her to miss it just to have Christmas with me."

"You're her only daughter. She would want nothing more." My voice is low, and a little saddened by her *Gift of the Magi* sacrifice.

"She came up to Chicago in the beginning. Every Christmas almost, but I think she got bored of just me and Archer. Us working through her visit and all our inside jokes. Couldn't have been a very nice Christmas for her."

Archer again. "The friend?"

"He's my Helen."

My heart thumps triple at the acknowledgement of Helen. She gets it, our friendship. And maybe I just got confirmation that Archer's just a friend.

"You and your buddy Archer never…"

"God no. Archer's a womanizer and not in the redeeming—wait until the right girl changes him kind of way. He's truly arrogant, superficial and the most shallow person you will ever meet."

"This is your best friend?"

"Well, yes, but I mean all this more to suggest that Archer and I would never be each other's physical type. He likes models. He dates girls that look like Helen in a pencil skirt."

"I'm sorry. I'm just curious as to what you think you look like in a pencil skirt."

"You know what I mean."

"No. I'm afraid I don't."

"Regardless, Archer would never look at me like that. And I will forever know he has the emotional attention span of a fruit fly."

She turns her head, and I feel her smile on my chest.

Fuck. She doesn't know she's gorgeous or what she does to men.

She stirs innocently in my lap, as if to dismiss the trance we've physically been in. But then her hand falls softly to my forearm that's holding her. I tense a little at the contact and a spark shoots through me.

You'd think we were fresh out of those, sitting this way in a cold damp cave making idle conversation. She moves her hand away quickly.

She has to know what she does to me. I know she feels it.

My throat clears and I shift a little to relieve the pressure before silence falls on us again and I do something I can't come back from.

"Hey, maybe you could sing like I mentioned before. It won't really help to yell with the echo, but if you sing quietly, it will carry, and Walter might hear us."

She turns her head to face me—I feel it—trying to see me looming over her. She's trying to look into my eyes, in this abyss. "What do you want me to sing, a *'fucking'* Christmas song? That's what you called it earlier."

"You mean when I was hunting you down in a dark cave silently praying neither one of us stepped down a drop off that led to our deaths?"

"Still. It was uncalled for. All Christmas songs are... well... nice by nature of being a Christmas song. They're sacred."

"I'll take your word for it."

How can my dick get this hard when we could both die?

"What's your favorite?" she whispers.

"Don't have one."

It was her ass rubbing my crotch, but now she's facing me. Walter better get here fast.

Turning back to face away from me again, she drops her head back, resting it against my pecs. "Everyone has a favorite Christmas song, Kourt."

"No. I really don't. I like 'em... all. Actually."

"You could've fooled me."

"I know." That truth stings a bit. "Sing, Erika."

"And have you chastise me later?"

"Never. I actually like your voice."

She pauses a moment. Her head laying lethargically back on my chest. And then, out of the dark silence of the cold dripping cave, "O holy night, the stars are brightly shining..."

Her voice is angelic.

I feel criminal holding her so close, my face dropped down smelling the top of her hair. Remnants of the aroma of cinnamon from the cookies. Her shampoo smells like fresh linen and sweet berries. And there's a hint of a perfume I've never been close enough to smell. It's soft, but spicy. Sweet, like orange blossom, but intense with amber.

The tempo of my heartbeat stutters as I indulge a deep inhale of her.

"Fall on your knees... Oh hear the angel voices... O night divine—"

"Kourt! Erika!" *Erika... Erika... Erika*

"Over here!" We yell together.

Here...here... here.

The golden glow of a flashlight sweeps in front of us. No walls in sight.

"Here, Walter!" I'm standing, pulling her up with me. "Hold the light still and we can move to it."

It... It... It...

"How in the Sam Hill did you two end up this far back? I told you not to go inside."

I can't blame him for being cranky.

"Some people are hard of hearing," I say as I usher Erika to him, my hand splayed across her back. I look down. My hand covers her shoulders from arm to arm.

"Oh, Walter. It's my fault." She rushes to him like a long-lost father, wrapping her arms around his neck. "Thank you for rescuing us."

Why does she always accept the blame? For everything?

Walter's eating it up. Just like he did her Christmas cookies. She's killing me. I've got to get the fuck out of here.

"I can't believe neither one of you had a cellphone, to use the light." Walter will be telling this to anyone who'll listen.

"We left them in the car."

"Let's head down."

Outside, a breeze is blowing, and the December temperature up on the cliff's edge has dropped.

I grab Erika's hand. "Watch your step."

Walter guides our way down with his flashlight. I hope I'm as spry and sharp as he is when I get that age.

"Thanks, Walter." I nod behind me as I walk ahead to my truck. Erika's re-engaged in conversation with him about the ceremony.

Opening my truck door, I see half a dozen missed alerts on my phone and snatch it.

"Shit! There's a fire on Sixth Street. Walter?" My eyes snap to his and he nods to me from where he and Erika stand.

"I'll get this girl home. Go on, Kourt." There's a flickering moment in my chest or mind—hell, I don't know. It feels strange to leave her. A beat goes buy as I lean into my truck and I almost stall to look back at her.

"Kourt!" Erika calls after me. She makes me look back. Our gazes catch—Confusion paints her face.

And there it is again. Hurt in her eyes. A half smile hijacks my face to acknowledge her in some way or to give myself permission get in the truck. I can't do this. I can't fucking do this.

NINETEEN

Black Ice

Walter's truck smells of cigarettes, hard work, and home. He has it nice and toasty, but I feel so cold staring out the passenger window as we ride in silence.

What was that back there?

The cave, the closeness. I practically sat in Kourt's lap and sang him a song.

Oh, God. And the look on his face when he got the call. He couldn't wait to get away from me.

"Listen to the wind. It talks. Listen to the silence, it speaks. Listen to your heart, it knows." Walter says it as sage as he looks.

"I'm sorry, Walter. I shouldn't have gone in the cave."

"No, Erika, you shouldn't have. The ceremony will take place outside of it, so it wasn't necessary to put yourself in danger. Your heart however, that is a danger you cannot help."

"Walter, I feel I never truly thanked you for doing this again for Blitzen. I think it will mean a lot to your wife and her memory."

"The tree lot is not for my wife. The ceremony is. The trees are not for Blitzen as much as Kourt. I was talking about Kourt before." Walter cuts his eyes from the road for a fleeting moment to scan mine. "You're good for him, Erika. He needs you."

"Pardon me?" I turn to look at the old man who must have his wires crossed between Christmas and an age-old native American adage, because that's as far-fetched as an assessment can get.

"Listen. And follow what you hear inside. Kourt knows the loss I know. It took him one year to breathe steady again, another year to listen, and year three we got him back. Three years after she died, and now you are here."

I turn in my seat, giving Walter my full attention, shock rocking through me like a tidal wave.

"Died? Oh my God Walter, who? Who died?" I can't grasp what this man is referring to between his metaphors, and my stomach that just swallowed itself. I currently have no trouble listening to my heart per his suggestion. It's beating so loud it's deafening.

"His beloved. Kourt lost his wife as I lost my Sherry."

"Wait. His *wife*? Kourt was married?"

"Young. Right out of college. He came back here with his high school sweetheart to start their life together. He and Angie and young Helen grew up here together, you see. Angie's parents own the hardware store."

"Bob and Georgia." I say robotically.

He clears his throat and nods, confirming.

"No. Walter, I don't see. What on earth happened?"

"Black ice. An unexpected cold evening. The temperature had dropped faster than anyone realized. She left the house for something. Winded down the roads she's driven her entire life, and she hit a patch. You don't see black ice. Especially at night. It blends in with the highway."

I have no idea what else Walter is saying. What could he possibly add to that? I tune out and stare out of the window until I see my familiar surroundings and know the ride will end soon.

The Christmas lights of town square come into view, and I see my car parked where I left it when Kourt picked me up. My stomach sinks again at the thought of Kourt picking me up—who I thought he was versus what I've learned of him. And I'm not sure what to think of him or me.

I wave bye to Walter without saying much more and turn the ignition to the VW that started this all. Pulling out, I forget about Walter, the trees, Christmas in Blitzen…

What an unbelievable fool I've been.

The cassette player clicks on, and I wind through the roads back up to Josie's when I hear 'Oh Holy Night.' The very words I sang to Kourt while nestled in his lap in the pitch-black cave. It felt ethereal singing that song, so connected to him.

How can this keep happening? Impossible.

"*Ugh!* You've got to be kidding me!" I scream out loud and with one click of the eject button I silence the tape myself.

A yawn stretches the back of my throat as I reach for the glass of red I've been twirling under the coffee table. Thank God for a buzz and thank God for Archer.

"Wait. Explain better." Archer requests as I blink at him through my computer's camera.

"I told you when we met, I learned that he was Kourt with a K the same as I'm Erika with a K. At first, I thought that was a sign."

"Uh-huh. A sign of what?" Archer lifts his head, tilting both ways, as if examining me.

"You know, sort of kismet, like a new meant-to-be friend in the town I landed in."

"A *friend*?"

"But I was way off. Maybe my stars just haven't been aligned right since the pitch."

"Yeah, Erika, about that..." Archer rubs his hands over his face and then through his hair.

"You saw me, Arch. You even berated me for it. I waltzed in there like my grand idea would save the account and look at where it got me. Now, I suppose, I'm doing the same thing here in Blitzen. Helen, and my hopes for the holidays, are my enablers. And Kourt is there to remind me I'm out of my league."

I drain another sip of wine from my glass.

"Kourt?"

"But then that damn mixtape rears its next song at just the right moment, as if it's taunting me."

"Wait." Archer reaches for his scotch. "This local yokel made you a mixtape?"

"God, no. The one I bought at the Christmas flea market. At booth *three*. It's broken. Or the tape deck is. It plays randomly and at uncannily significant moments. I almost can't ignore it. Anyway. Sorry. I'm sure you tuned out twenty minutes ago."

Archer coaxes one eyebrow higher than the other and glowers at me. The frosted tips of his dark gelled hair pristinely manicured apart from one piece bouncing down to meet his temple and match his five o'clock shadow. "Do I look like I'm not listening? Actually, I need to know, this came up once or twice this week."

"Yes, Archer. Something about your overall aura generally has anyone participating in conversation with you racing to get their point across before your eyes glaze over and drift down to sift through the latest dating app. So, yeah, before I lose you entirely... what was it you needed to tell me about work?"

A small pit forms in my stomach for the third time today, and I brace myself to hear more about how I embarrassed the team, and I may not, in fact, have a job waiting for me when I return.

Thus, whatever you do, don't screw up drowning in a small Christmas town, because after upsetting widowers, Great Aunt Josie's crazy carved-out pathway of life may be all you've got left.

Archer watches my face on his screen for a moment. It's almost uncomfortable.

He tilts his head and narrows his eyes at me. "Actually, I'd like to go back to this holiday Ouija board of a mixtape. I think I'm far more fascinated by your goings on in Blitzen than relaying the latest from our fickle bosses."

He pours himself another night cap and swirls his peaty scotch in the glass like it's his favorite part of the day.

"Speaking of big ideas on my part. Did I tell you that I got them to decorate the courthouse, and the entire town showed up to do it?"

"Wow. Sounds like Looney Tunes Josie had some pull with these people."

"No. Arch. It was me. It was my plan, and it worked."

"Okay. Calm down, Erika. Relax. Have another drink with me. It worked. Your work there is done and a huge success." Archer facetiously toasts me through the screen.

"Are you kidding me? I haven't even started yet, I have a list a thousand miles long, and there are multiple fundraisers going. This entire project is a fundraiser, and not one cent has changed hands yet. I haven't even begun my work on Blitzen's Christmas festivities and timing is crucial. I just now found the cave, and I've got to get an ice skating rink, a—"

"An ice skating rink?" Archer looks baffled.

"You surprise me. Most people pause at the cave part."

Archer sloshes his drink at me. He's totally buzzed. "It's just funny to me that you would need to find a rink when it's cold as—what would one say in Kentucky? As cold as a well digger's ass down there. Don't ponds freeze or some shit?"

"Yeah. It is that cold, and great minds think alike. But unfortunately, we're wrong. The issue is, they don't always freeze, not solid anyway. Especially in town or down the mountain where the daytime brings more sun. This is what I've been learning."

"Just buy one." Archer's eyes droop a little and he couldn't look more *Archer-esque* if he tried.

"It's a fundraiser, Arch. If they could afford to bring a rink in for a Christmas festival, they could afford to buy their fire truck. And anyway. It doesn't matter now. I've gone and acted like a fool in front of the town's youngest widower. It seems the infuriating Kourt with a K was actually quite nice to me under the circumstances."

I see Archer has already dozed off. I toast him with the last chug of my wine. "Then I go and ruin everything pushing him into a lake and leaving my bra and panties in his truck. How disrespectful of me."

"I'm sorry. What did you just say about Kourt with a K and your bra and panties?" Archer sits at attention and reaches for another scotch. "Are you sleeping with a married man?"

"No. She's dead."

"Great Aunt Josie?"

"No. Well... I'm not entirely sure about that one yet, but I'm talking about the wife. His wife. She had a tragedy." I'm feeling the bottle of wine I've accomplished, and I can barely hold my head up, much less make sense, but Archer is alive and invested.

"How old is he, and what happened to her?"

"Maybe your age or mine, and she was killed in some mountain car crash. Black ice driving is dangerous here, Arch."

"Oh my god. Erika. What's going on with you and the widower, and who's married at our age? Oh, right. It's Kentucky."

"Shut up. He's perfectly capable of having been married at our age. You and I are just hitched to our job."

"Yeah, again. About that—"

"Tomorrow, Arch. I gotta' go bed and get my bra and panties back. I'm sorry I messed up Christmas. There's not going to be a winter wonderland, and trust me, best friend, when I say, baby it's cold outside." My cheek meets the couch, and I fall asleep to the rhythm of Archer's drunk snoring.

Pounding at the door alters my state. I turn my head to put my opposite cheek in a pool of drool while the pounding continues. I can't even sit up straight before Helen barges in with her keys.

"Oh my God, Erika! Are you okay?" Helen races toward me. She's in jeans and a T-shirt but her pixie haircut and makeup are as flawless as when she's dressed in a suit skirt. "Get up. This is all my fault, I never should have forced you two together in the first place."

I feel tugging at my arm pulling me up right.

"Tell me you only had one bottle, and there wasn't a Percocet involved. If there was, I'd like one please. You know, I generally love to rock the boat, but this time I truly thought I was helping. I couldn't have known this would end with you both wasted after only one night together and apparently, he left you in a cave?"

"What? Oh. No. He got a call for that fire—"

"The electrical spark at the machine shop on Sixth Street. Yes, I know. It was out before he got there. Just a spark. No biggie. But I then find him as plastered as you are in his pajamas with a half-eaten Dairy burger on his coffee table, and another warm in the bag."

"No one can eat that many burgers." My head drops back and hits the hard frame of the couch.

"Erika. Focus. Did he leave you at the cave? He kept mumbling on and on in slurred speech that he just left you standing there and couldn't forget it." Helen's face is full of alarm.

I sit up and look around. My head is pounding. "What time is it?"

"A little after midnight. Why, how long did he leave you there?"

"Helen. He didn't leave me anywhere. He left me with Walter so he could go to the fire, and Walter drove me home. What's the matter with you?" I finally make real eye contact. For the first time since she arrived, she's only got one head, not two.

"So what's this about you getting stuck in a cave? I couldn't understand what he was trying to tell me, and don't you dare defend him. One night with him does not justify his behavior."

"What?" Now Helen sounds drunk.

"I'm just saying, I know he's charming and all, but just because you two slept together doesn't mean you have to—"

"Slept together?" Archer's voice chimes in from my laptop as we say it in unison.

"Go back to sleep, Arch" I hiss as I close my laptop. He's like having a gremlin in your purse, and someone's always giving it too much water.

"Who's Archer?" Helen inspects my closed laptop.

"Later." I sit up straight and give Helen my undivided attention. "What, in all of Blitzen, and by the power of an old-fashioned

Christmases invested in me, are you possibly referring to?" My eyes are so big I can feel them about to pop out of my head, and I have never sobered so quickly in my life.

"You don't need to cover for him, Erika. I know him. He's my best friend. That, and I saw your bra and panties."

I look down at my tee shirt as if I forgot it and I'm sitting here in my underwear, and then it hits me. I take a breath to calm my racing heart.

"Erika. I saw the bag on his entry table. It had a light blue bra and underwear set, and when I asked what it was, Kourt slurred out that it was yours."

"First of all, your best friend has been a perfect gentlemen as much as he's been a perfect ass. Apart from me forcing us into a freezing lake and having to get naked under a blanket next to him. He left his jeans on and nearly froze. I got the blanket and left my underwear in his truck. But your best friend did not try anything. Not on me anyway."

God. *Do the hits just keep coming?*

Somehow, it's more humiliating that he *didn't* try anything.

"Ugh. Helen. Why didn't you tell me she died?"

Helen rises off the couch. "She's not dead, and she told me not to tell—"

"Ah ha! I caught you." I jump from the couch with my finger pointing after her. "I wasn't talking about Great Aunt Josie, although now I suppose I know where the Range Rover went. I'm talking about your best friend's *wife*."

Helen ignores my tirade and sinks back down onto the couch, defeated. "I'm sorry, Erika. There was just a lot with your great aunt, and you came fresh off bad luck at work, and then you took to Blitzen and Christmas here so quickly, it never felt like the right time. I had no way of knowing Kourt would become so significant." Helen's eyes plead with mine.

"He's not. There's zero significance, there's just me running about Blitzen making a complete holiday horror show of a total ass of myself because I didn't know!" I scream and drop my head into my hands.

"It all makes sense now. Why you came here. I wondered what a high-powered attorney such as yourself was doing hiding out in small town USA. I thought it was just one of those quirky Aunt Josie things that you two were also best friends, but putting two and two together... you grew up here. You came back for him when she died."

Pain strikes on Helen's face.

"Let me guess. You were the maid of honor at their wedding."

"Best man," Helen corrects.

I throw myself into a mistletoe embroidered couch pillow and wish for a moment I could suffocate.

"Look. All is right as rain. He didn't leave you in a cave. You didn't sleep together, and you just found out, without any other details, as I refuse to let the entire cat out of the bag, that dear Aunt Josie is, in fact, alive."

"Yeah, but Kourt's wife isn't."

"Angie." Helen makes it even more real. "Erika, things happen. Tragedy strikes a lot of people. Don't treat this like one because you just found out about it. This isn't happening to you. It already happened. A while ago now. Kourt and Blitzen have moved on, and we've got an old-fashioned Christmas to plan." Helen's harsh words are true. I recognize it more clearly as her voice returns to its natural chirp.

Maybe I'm overreacting. I took Kourt's distance from me right after the cave and packed this onto it. His abrupt exit tonight had nothing to do with his deceased wife and everything to do with me.

He's not after me in any way other than helping with the festival, and I made things weird and inappropriate in the cave. That's got to be it. My stomach flips remembering how warm it felt when he held me. How his strong arms found me in the dark, wrapping so tightly around me in a way they never had before.

He embraced all of me as if he was lucky to get to. His scent behind me. The relief that washed over me once he found me...

That's it. That's what it was. Relief. That's all. It was the cave and the dark, and now everything is back to normal.

"Hey. Glad you're okay. I've got to go. Got an early morning." Helen grabs her keys.

"Helen?" I call after her. "When you were so convinced we'd slept together—I know you don't know me like you know Kourt, but what made that so believable? What made you even consider it?"

"Easy. You just said it yourself. I know Kourt."

As the door shuts behind Helen, the stark realization hits me that I must not know him at all. That, or I don't know myself very well. He's definitely not made what is obvious about himself to Helen and the rest of town available to me.

TWENTY

A Safe Haven

This has always been my safe haven. The Blitzen High School gym hasn't been upgraded since I played here. I know these hardwood floors like I know the silence before the swoosh—the *thump, thump, thump* of the ball bouncing off waxed floors, the same way I know the weight of the ball in my hands.

The floor's sheen is interrupted only by colorful paint lines and scuff marks. Every one of those scuff marks has a little bit of a kid's soul embedded in it. So many memories right here.

This morning, I'm chasing the good ones.

I pivot, jump—snap my wrist. The ball spins off my fingers and... *Swoosh!* A three-pointer. *Yes.*

As I race to retrieve the ball, I hear, "What are you doing Mc-Shotty!"

Turning to the voice—which I know too well—I see Helen clicking toward me briskly, in shiny black stiletto heels.

"Practicing. What does it look like?"

I turn my back dribbling... racing for a lay-up. "Two!"

Rebounding, snatching the ball in mid-air as it drops through the basket, I turn, smiling back at her. "I still got it."

"Stop avoiding me. We need to talk."

"Not avoiding you." I dribble in place. Love the feel of this leather in my hands.

Helen glowers. She's cute with her pixie hair and almond eyes, wearing a thousand-dollar white wool suit over a blue silk blouse. She's probably headed to court.

She snaps, "Yes. You. Are. Now I want to talk, and I don't have a lot of time."

I tuck the ball underhanded, holding it at my waist, legs braced. "About what?"

She's marched up so close, she's straining her neck back to meet my gaze. "You know what. You being drunk last night."

"Love ya' but fuck off." I spin with a jump shot—*Swoosh.* "Two!"

She glares at me.

"I've got to practice. You realize Jamarcus is coming here and bringing some other NBA guys for the charity game. You don't want me to look like a fool do you?"

"I heard. And you'd never look like a fool." More glaring.

I sigh. "What, Helen?"

"Let's talk in private."

"About what?"

Fuck.

She lifts her brows. "Do you want me to twist your ear?"

That brings a raucous laugh that I can't throttle as my head tilts back. "As if you could reach it."

"Never underestimate me. Now come on. You're here at the ass-crack of dawn. I know, because I'm here, too, trying to hunt you down." She swings her arms as she sashays for the exit.

I'm not moving.

"Why do you feel the need to hunt me down? You should start with that." I yell at her back.

She spins around on those heels that probably cost as much as the suit, with fire shooting from her eyes. "Really? Because I know you."

"Not really."

"Bullshit. Now are you going to have a coffee of not?"

I glance down at my legs and snicker, "I'm in shorts. It's cold outside. I don't want to get re-dressed."

"Then come sit on the bleachers and let's talk. Dammit."

I'm not getting out of this. I follow my favorite person to the bleachers so she can get whatever it is off her chest.

She sits daintily, pulling her pencil skirt to her knees, which she tucks together, while I plunk down a row higher, my legs on the floor. "Shoot."

Our gazes are latched.

"You were drunk last night."

"Not the first time, Helen."

"First in a while. What happened with you and Erika?"

None of your fucking business.

"Nothing." My jaw grinds with a mind of its own.

"When I left you, I went to her."

Ping in the gut. "How was she?"

"Drunk. Like you. What the fuck happened?"

I inhale my lungs full of cold gym air and exhale. "Nothing."

Shit. Dammit. Hell.

I have no idea what I might've done if Walter hadn't walked in when he did—I was seconds from leaning back, pulling her on top of me, and devouring the shit out of her. My dick hadn't been that hard in years.

My hands wanted to be all over her warm body. They were on fire, right under her soft C-cups. It was all I could do not to slide them up and start fondling those perfect tits. *Jeez-us.*

"Kourt?"

"What?"

Her onyx eyes bore into me, the thin black brows drawn tight.

I scrub a hand over my jaw, shaking my head. "Nothing."

Helen stands abruptly, so our eyes are dead even, as she gets loud. "I think you've said 'nothing' one too many times. Now come clean."

A part of me wants to snicker at her acting so threatening with me. As if she thinks she can intimidate me like some idiot on her witness stand. She can't. But I know her as well as she knows me—and that tiny pit bull isn't give up.

I hike a shoulder.

"I don't know, Helen. She's…" My gaze wanders across the gym. I can't bring myself to say it. But I finally do. "Different, I guess." My eyes meet hers. "Nobody's made me feel like that since—"

"Say it. Angie."

I glare back. Jaw clamped tight.

"Kourt. If you two had been together for fifty years that'd be one thing. But you were married two years when she died." She holds up two fingers. "You cannot *not* go on living. You're too young to say never again."

"Life already said it for me." Our gazes are locked tight, and I hear the bite in my voice. "Now fucking let this go."

"The hell I will. I've known you longer than you knew Angie or Erika and I've always had your back. I'm telling you; I see a spark between you and Erika that may be stronger than what I saw between you and Angie, may she rest in peace. You two married because it was expected. It was the natural course of things, being together through high school. You stayed together through college, with an engagement just after. You were almost forced into it. Both of you. But I swear to God, Kourt—I see it. Erika makes you… I don't know— exude happiness in a way you never have before. *With anyone.*"

I open my mouth to speak, but she cuts me off, drilling her manicured fingernail into my chest. "I'm not wrong about this." She stomps off.

Four-inch heels echo off the gym walls, dragging me back to that fucking cave.

I groan. She's right.

My wife. I loved Angie. I'll always love her. Her death knocked me to my fucking knees, and I couldn't get up for a year. How do you comprehend—one minute she was here and the next she was gone?

But the truth was that, after two years of marriage, we were already rocky.

It was her idea to come back here after college, which I did, for her. After a year, she changed her mind. She wanted me to try for an NBA spot, or get a position as a college assistant coach because my high school coach's salary and her teacher's salary weren't enough to keep her in the lifestyle she had in mind.

We argued again and again, me trying to get it through her pretty blonde head that, "I can't take a job and quit after one year." No one would hire me.

Then... she was gone. Ice.

Shake it off.

I go back to the court, dribble, set my feet, and take a shot—and miss.

Crap. The ball bounces off the backboard.

"Rebound, Coach!" Logan Ramsey yells from the sidelines. One of my best seniors. He's got real talent.

"*You* rebound!" I yell back.

"Come on, Coach. Let me see you sink a three-pointer!"

I've been doing it all morning.

I dribble behind the three-point line—jump—spin—and the ball rolls off my fingertips. It cuts through the air. *Swoosh!* The ball kisses net on its way through.

No way I'm even trying to stop this smile.

"I can't wait to see you play, Coach! You and Jamarcus Holloway. Sweet!"

"Hey Logan, no game this Friday."

"Why?"

"Jonesborough cancelled. Said the weather's too risky for this away game for them. They're not chancing getting the bus up here."

"Dang, I was ready to kick their asses." He trudges toward the lockers.

"You will next semester. We'll reschedule."

I dribble —jump—bank shot.

The corners of my mouth rise to gloat. Now Erika doesn't have a date this Friday.

Helen missed our FaceTime tonight. I let her. We talked this morning—more than enough.

I'm lying flat on my back, staring at the ceiling, cutting my eyes at the bedside clock. 11:00 p.m. Erika never reached out, and neither did I. Maybe we both need a break.

I haven't slept since I left that cave. Drawn to her? Fuck, yes. Too much. But I don't understand the rest of it. A kaleidoscope of thoughts, made up of blue eyes, lip curling smirks and long dark waves invade my mind. Over a fire truck and a town Christmas festival? I'm sure that's all this is.

We got too close hanging out every day trying to make the holidays happen in Blitzen. The town absorbs her. I absorbed her. If it wasn't for the fundraisers, she'd just be Josephine's hot niece that came to visit who hit me with her car. We would never have gotten this close. *Are we... close?*

It's her fucking innocence that has me so damn curious. No, hell, no—She's not all *that* innocent. She's a woman who knows exactly what she wants. That's what intrigues me. But still, she's... I don't know. I can't put my finger on it. She's wicked smart, but then so genuine and trusting of other people—strangers even. She's curved like a fucking walking hourglass but makes me wonder if she knows it. She doesn't realize how hot she is. What does that say about her?

She's also climbing the ladder at her ad agency in Chicago, so the appeal of Blitzen, other than a fun escape provided by her great aunt, is beyond me. What she's done here, organizing, pulling this festival together, it's—she's moved mountains.

I'm pretty fucking happy right here. I chose to stay in small town Kentucky, and I had my share of other offers. I don't need to earn three figures a year to be happy. Different strokes for different folks. I'm just not clear on what hers are.

I knew last night—both of us wanted it. She was so warm against me. The dark cold cave had nothing on the heat between us when I wrapped my arms around her. I wanted to rip that coat off of her, get my hands under that sweater—

Stop it, McClain!

If you go there you might not want to come back. And you made up your mind, once was enough.

This will pass.

I roll onto my side. Tomorrow's another day. And I need to be at the gym early. Be damned if I'll make a fool out of myself in front of Jamarcus and the rest of the world.

TWENTY-ONE

Four Wheel Drive

It's after five o'clock on day two. I've heard nothing from Kourt, and I haven't reached out, per our norm, to schedule a ride, either. Coincidentally, my mixtape has also been completely out of commission and refuses to play.

Blitzen's Old-Fashioned Christmas, however, is well underway. Hot chocolate vendors, hand-blown glass ornaments, and gingerbread decorating booths are all arriving at their allotted times. Multiple candy confectioners and Christmas cookie concessions have signed up for both weekends and select weeknights, and all the events are scheduled.

We have enough activities and attractions to draw the crowd the Fisher's brochure promised from now until Christmas. I even have extra Charles Dicken's-style carolers to make multiple sets for switching out, so we always have music. A few local churches have agreed to bake Christmas cookies, supply jams and holiday quilts to set up booths to fill in any gaps. We're really coming along.

What feels the most special? The right here right now of it all. The Christmas I've been missing the past few years. This is what I came here for. This is what I needed.

I look up to the left of my big black notebook and see June orchestrating the orange cones and blockades for setting up parking. She even has a little red ribbon tied around her silver ponytail today.

The young couple who gave me the stink eye at the meeting waves from a distance as they help the Lions Club unload boxes of turkeys for smoking. People will buy those like hot cakes to save for Christmas dinner when they smell them smoking next to the hot chocolate they buy to sip. I even convinced them to sell a few turkey legs as a concession for people to eat as they walk and enjoy.

My heart feels as warm as the patch of sun hitting my face as it threatens to go down the mountain.

A tap on my shoulder has me spinning into a familiar face. This time her blazer is dark hunter green and up close she's more divine than I remember.

"Erika, the young trespasser responsible for all of this—"

I smile at Judge Pritchard. She winks back at me. "I believe this has your name written all over it too, and I've been tasked to determine where to put the monstrosity. Care to help?" Her voice sounds like one of the characters from *Steel Magnolias* as she shoves a telegram-looking purchase order in front of me and reads: "Go big or go home, Erika with a K, everything's a sign. Trust your gut. You got this. Merry Christmas, Arch." The bottom of the invoice is stamped paid next to a City Ice Rental logo.

"Oh my God!" *I can't believe he did this.*

"Yes, darlin' and now that something has frozen over, where the hell are we going to put it?" The judge smiles brightly at me, as if it's a grand problem to have, and I know I've impressed her.

"Umm. Let me go grab June. She'll have an idea."

"You do that, honey. I don't run in heels, not even from something this big."

I turn and face the largest structure I've seen in any Chicago neighborhood. Archer must have rented the biggest one they had available for Blitzen. Tears fill my eyes, and I have to catch my breath to take it all in.

A truck engine pulls by beside me with a sound I'd recognize anywhere. High school basketball players pop out with food drive boxes and run into the local downtown shops behind me.

Kourt rolls his window down. "So, you found a way to ice skate after all." He marvels at the large rink they're unloading in front of town square.

"Something like that." I do good to turn and squint out a half smile.

"I swung by before practice today to check in and see if you needed a ride."

"Oh?"

"Yeah. You weren't there."

"Duty called. Guess I'd already left."

"I can see." Kourt pauses a moment, as if he's not sure what to say. I keep my eyes on the prize ahead. My ice rink.

"I need to return your items to you."

I bite my bottom lip, then turn back around to face him. "Oh, thank God. It's the only bra and pair of panties I own. It's been dreadful going without." I say it loud using the excuse of trying to talk over the running engine.

Kourt looks left and right, then back at me with wild eyes and a crooked smile as if surprised by my wit. It's about to be game on, only I don't give him time to play. I see June coming toward me and I beeline to her without looking back.

"You can just toss 'em," I say over my shoulder as I rush toward June, putting as much space between Kourt and I as possible.

He kills the engine.

Damn.

And his truck door slams behind me.

"Kourt McClain! You two have the nerve to go skinny dipping at Blitzen Manor and don't bother to invite me?" The Judge is loud. Really loud as she sashays over to Kourt, and I tense as all of Blitzen's eyes are on us.

"I'm pretty sure your dogs were invited, Judge." Kourt's voice is much closer to me than I anticipated as he yells behind me across town square.

"They do love a good swim," Judge Prichard shoots back. "Now get over here and help June and your girl with this ice rink. I've got a hunt to get to." She waves in my peripheral vision, and I continue my walk toward June.

"You thought you were off the hook." His hot breath brushes the side of my neck before I realize he's caught up to me.

Chills trail up and down my body and my entire center fills with heat.

"You want me to toss them, eh? Does that mean I get to keep them?"

My lashes shoot up to my eyebrows like rockets.

"Blue's my favorite color." He persists.

"I didn't take you for a lace guy under your basketball jersey, but whatever gets you through the day."

"Walk." He demands as he pokes my lower back with his fingertips, stepping us both toward a smiling June.

I don't think I've ever seen the woman smile this big.

"Isn't it incredible, Kourt?" June beams up at him.

"Just like the old days," he says, as he takes in all the new things added.

"Better. Kourt. It's better than it's ever been." June steps forward and squeezes my hand. "I have a surprise for you, our Erika of Blitzen. It's on my property, and will be requiring an extra pair of hands, and an additional truck." She nods at Kourt as if that signs him up.

"Mine won't make but a small dent of a load. And we've got a trailer and a hitch we can also use. You just let me know if you've got some time tomorrow or the next day to swing by."

"June, you had me at surprise and trailer hitch. I'll call you first thing tomorrow." Shocked as I am, I look her in the eye, acknowledging the feeling is mutual and I'm proud of what we've accomplished together.

"You were right about this one, Kourt. She's magic." June smiles at us before releasing my hand and all but twirling away.

Who was that woman? That is not the same person who reluctantly let me hang Christmas lights that first day.

"Magic, huh?" I look up at Kourt.

"I didn't tell her what kind."

I step away and he follows.

What's happening? I thought I couldn't be mad at the town widower, and I was resolved to make nice and keep my distance.

"Guess you'll be in need of a truck."

"Oh. Absolutely. Look around the parking lot. Everyone and their mother drives a pickup truck. I don't foresee it to be a problem."

"I leave you alone for a day and you've got the entire town eating out of your hand."

"Two days. Is that what you were doing, Kourt? Leaving me alone?" I turn to walk away from him.

"Erika, wait."

My phone rings and I make a show of answering it, so I don't have to look back or even come back to the conversation. It's Helen. She's called multiple times, and I know it's about the thing at Bob and Georgia's tonight. *Or should I say at Kourt's in-laws'?*

My venture into the hardware store this morning opened a can of worms none of us are prepared to hook—a get together at their house.

I look behind me to see if he took the hint and I spot him walking slowly away from me. He hesitates a moment, then continues to stride toward his truck.

Just. Go back to your can drive, Kourt.

How is this happening? On what planet would I be invited to these people's home? "Helen, I think—no, I know this is a horrible idea."

"Oh, for fuck's sake Erika. We're already here. You have to come in, or I won't hear the end of it. They called me twice at work today to make sure I asked you, and again after they saw you at the hardware store."

"Buying a back up generator for the ice rink, not soliciting to impose on your best friend's former in-laws, or the parents of your deceased other best friend."

"Don't put this on me. You walked right into their invitation."

"That's because I had no concept of what they were inviting me to, because you didn't tell me, either."

"Well, I'm telling you now, my plus one, and if you of all people, Miss Christmas, can't stand up straight and walk in for their holiday-themed take-out dinner of a good time, I will never forgive you. I don't pretend to know what's going on with you and

McShotty and I'm not sure I want to know. I left the playground back at Blitzen Elementary, so you guys can have it."

"Thanks, Helen. And I assure you—there's nothing going on."

And I can't imagine there will ever be after this.

I feel like Helen and I are having our first tiff. Or at least we're grating on each other's nerves.

"I didn't ask to be invited anywhere, especially if it feels like I'm going to ambush the very person I'm trying to avoid."

"No. You just asked if you could decorate an entire town for Christmas—" We both look at each other and burst out laughing.

"And rightfully so, my friend. I must say you're doing a stunning job of it." Helen hugs me tightly as if to apologize. Her tiny frame crashing into me with all her might, choking me with her collarbone and perfume.

She doesn't owe me an apology. She's been nothing but good to me.

This has to be hard on her too. She works full-time, back and forth sometimes when she goes into the city. She's kindly become fast friends with me as Josie's ward, but she belongs to Kourt. He's her best friend. And even this bizarre monthly dinner they both attend at his former in-laws' house has got to be hard on her, because it is, yet again, about Kourt and their daughter.

Then here I go with my Blitzen Christmas and not wanting to be awkward around Kourt, making it all about me.

"I'm sorry Helen. I'll be a good sport. They're incredibly sweet people. I hate that I complained."

"Woah. You just graduated to Blitzen Junior High with that attitude adjustment." She winks and rings the doorbell. My eyes drift behind us to Kourt's truck parked in their drive and back to the door as I squeeze the container of cookies I brought.

"They did a lot for Blitzen Christmas back in the day. They may offer some help or sound advice." Helen raises her fist to knock, and the door opens before she can.

Kourt's gaze shuffles between us and lands apologetically on mine.

"Helen? Is that you and the darling that's saving Christmas?" A woman's voice rings out from the kitchen as Helen pushes past Kourt into the living room.

"I'm sorry," he mouths silently to me.

He's sorry? I'm the one who looks like a stalker slash intruder.

I've never laughed so hard in my life at a snack table by the Christmas tree with anyone's parents. These people are top notch and pure Blitzen. Helen and Kourt didn't have to go out of their way to make me feel comfortable here. They have so much fun with Bob and Georgia that it all naturally fell into place. Helen is right. Georgia has a lot to do with committees that can help with the big Christmas Eve tree lighting ceremony. She's volunteered her time as well as outdoor ornaments she had Kourt box up from the attic for the town square tree.

Heading down the attic stairs with the last box of Georgia's ornaments, I make a detour of the formal hallway instead of cutting through the dining room and knocking my hand on the dining table again.

I stop in my tracks when the photograph on the wall stuns me to my core.

It's Angie. Blonde hair, graduation picture. The box in my arms voluntarily rests on the entry table below the portrait as I give the photo more attention.

"They say the hardest thing in the world is for a parent to lose a child." Bob steps quietly behind me. His hands in his pockets and a calm smile secures his face.

"She's beautiful," I say carefully.

He smiles at me. "Things don't seem to mean as much anymore, after that. Kourt means a lot to us, and Helen, too. You seem to matter a great deal to them, and all of Blitzen. Georgia and I will never win the race, but we have small victories here and there. Takeout with this bunch, watching Blitzen reacquainted with all it's Christmas splendor. It's the little things that keep one going. They *do* mean something, and just because this picture means so much to me and Georgia, I would hate to see it haunt you during your time in Blitzen—no matter how long that might be. For what it's worth, Georgia and I hope it's a very long time, and you are always more than welcome in our home, if not expected."

I leap for Bob, embracing him in an overwhelming hug as he catches my ornament box from falling off the table.

Is this hug inappropriate like most everything I do?

Absolutely.

But does he begrudge me? No, he does not. Bob's eyes dance with something like pride and genuine kindness as I pull away from my attack, speechless and teary-eyed.

Anchoring the box in my arms, I step off the porch into their yard. Kourt looks up from closing his tailgate. There's a curious expression I don't recognize in his eyes as his gaze searches mine for answers.

I turn away before I attempt to solve the equation and head to my Bug—grateful. I've had another beautiful day in Blitzen, and strangers who have become friends have given to the cause, and not just Blitzen's—my selfish cause of wanting to have an old-fashioned Christmas here.

That's all I need today.

TWENTY-TWO

Poinsettia Poison

Two loud honks shake me from my sleep. I rise to peek out the window and find Kourt's truck waiting in the carport, followed by a knock at the door. I'm not even dressed. I rush down as decent as possible and open the door.

"What are you doing here?"

"June's orders."

"Oh, bullshit."

"What did you say to me?"

"I said fish sticks," I correct as I shoot him the finger and turn from the door, holding my robe closed.

My satin robe is on the very short side but should conceal that I'm solely sporting panties and a vintage silk camisole I found in Aunt Josie's things. "Don't you coach or teach or something?"

"Faculty day. There's always one the week we get out for the holidays, and this year all of Blitzen faculty has been asked to help with the Christmas festivities on our admin day."

"How lucky for Blitzen." I fake a charming smile.

"I brought breakfast." Kourt sets down a tray of to-go orange juice, cranberry muffins and two hot beverages.

"I see that," I say as I watch him maneuver uninvited in my Aunt Josie's kitchen. "I have to get dressed."

"I see that." He looks me up and down and cocks a crooked smile. "It's cold out, where are your flannels?"

"I don't sleep in pajamas."

Kourt's smile fades. His jaw works, and I turn to ascend the stairs. "I'll be down in a moment. If you can't wait, by all means go without me."

Wow.

What in the hell is the matter with me? I spent a lovely, unexpected day with Bob and Georgia, everything plus some has come together for the festival. Aunt Josie is, in fact, still alive, and Archer rented me an ice rink. How can I possibly have beef with anybody?

Wait. Me? I'm the one minding my own business.

What is he even doing here? No one asked him to be *Mr. Christmas.* His duties have been fulfilled. As I pointed out to him, there are multiple trucks available to me in this town.

Still, why am I so mad at someone whose wife died? Maybe that's it. I'm mad because he's an ass and now I've learned something about him that gives him permission to be?

No. That's not it at all.

Reaching for my warm boots, I slide them on and begin lacing up the side tassels. It's the cave, and the two days after. He's the one who pulled away, leaving me to feel like I did something wrong, or I took advantage of his help.

I'm too busy with what I have to get done to be made to feel that way. I'd never take advantage of a friend.

"Bob and Georgia really enjoyed having you yesterday."

"Helen insisted I go." My voice comes out short. It's like a whip cracking and I can't soften the blow.

The morning view out my passenger side window is breathtaking. Kentucky *is* beautiful. It's hard to be this callus watching snow-covered mountain tops glisten in the early morning sun.

"Look, I—I guess I should've told you. I'm just so used to everyone knowing around here. It's obviously not something that comes up on the daily." Kourt forces it all out.

"I didn't expect you'd have it printed on your T-shirt or blurt it out on the ride to Fisher's. It's fine. You don't owe me any kind of explanation, Kourt Mclain."

"*Kourt Mclain*. Using my full name now are we? So formal."

"Would you prefer I use your nickname, McShotty?" And that came out more playful than I intended. *Damn it.*

"Now that you mention it, I'm not sure what I'd like you to call me just yet. I can think of a few select names off the top of my head that—"

"Oh, look! Oh, June! I can't believe it." I roll down my window at the sight as Kourt pulls into a drive that can only belong to June. Acres of greenhouses stand before me in rows, and she has truck beds full of bright red, pink and white poinsettias.

It's a poinsettia farm. Oh, June.

My heart grows three sizes, and I smile, remembering the potting soil I clocked under her fingernails. I spot June and fly out of the truck as soon as Kourt stops. "June, you did all this for the festival?" I walk toward her with open arms as if she and I always hug each other.

"It's available to you for our Blitzen Christmas, but don't give me that much credit. It's kind of what I do." June smiles sheepishly, and I watch her eyes lift up behind me as I feel Kourt approach and stand so close we're almost touching.

Is the guy trying to get a rise out of me?

"June owns one of the most famous nurseries in Kentucky. She's highly sought after come Christmas," Kourt interjects.

"Poinsettias are kind of my thing." June motions to our surroundings.

I shake my head in awe. "Then how could you guys ever let this *not* be a thing for Blitzen? I just don't get how it could fade out."

"Erika. If you stick around any length of time, I doubt it will again. Come on back, I've got to show you the new gold leaf hybrid

I've been growing." June leads us to a smaller green house in the back. I look up at Kourt and can't hide my smile. This is amazing.

June slides up a table with smaller gold leaf pots growing into their first blooms. They're so tiny, but they look like decorations almost. I've never seen that color on a real plant, only on an artificial gold glitter kind or painted ones in stores.

"For the longest we just had that hybrid color that looked like the inside of a banana to me. This is a true gold leaf," June boasts and swirls one through her fingers.

I touch one delicately as Kourt's arm dives over my head and plucks a gold leaf or two off one of the pots in the middle.

"Are these the ones that taste like basil? Go on Erika, try one. You can eat them like you do mint leaves, but they don't taste like mint." Kourt puts one in his mouth and chomps it between his teeth.

"They're not that poisonous, but I'm pretty sure you're not supposed to consume a poinsettia the way you do basil or mint," I inform him dryly, as he continues to absurdly eat off the plant.

"Well, I hate to break it to you both, but these gold hybrids *are* poisonous and not fit for human consumption at all. I have to keep the barn cats out of here. It'll kill them if they eat the leaves. I'm not sure if you should be eating those even as a joke, Kourt."

June turns to look at Kourt as he lets out a strained hiccup. Unbuttoning his top button very sloppily, he begins to cough it out.

Kourt stumbles back onto the tables of plants behind us, squashing a few as he tries to catch his breath. Now I'm watching him gasp for air.

"Honey that's not poisoning, he's choking on the leaf! He's getting pale as a ghost!" June screams and calls over her shoulder through the greenhouse door, "Harry! Harry! Bring the golf cart!"

Either shame on Kourt for scaring her, or June's a damn good actress. That's the only part I haven't figured out yet.

I look back over at Kourt just in time to see him fall backwards. *Okay. I'll play.*

"Kourt! Kourt!" I hold his face in my lap and slap his cheek. Nothing.

I should slap his cheek again harder.

"Kourt!" I scream again and lean toward him, pressing my face against his lips to feel if he's still breathing. June is behind me. She's giving an Oscar-worthy performance. I can't disappoint her.

"Honey, I'm gonna go ahead and call," June says as frantic as she can muster.

I'm no detective but seeing as how June and Kourt are so close, he may have worked a summer or two here as a kid. I don't think this is their first time to pull the old poinsettia routine.

But again, I'm not a bad actress myself.

"Get up, Kourt. Wake up! June!" I scream as I lay him down flat and put my ear to his lips. "He's not breathing at all!"

I stick my finger in his mouth to try to clear his airway. He almost has me here if this doesn't get him, because I do it realistically, the way you check to see if someone has something lodged in their throat.

He's a fireman. He knows what an airway sweep feels like, and it's not glamorous or sexy.

Okay.

So, on he and June's little stage, he's not breathing at all. Which means it's time for mouth to mouth.

You dick. If I were only the slightest bit braver and not pissed at the guy, I'd slide my tongue down his throat, shock the hell out of him and end this charade, but June's clearly worked as hard on this stunt as she has the poinsettias.

Who am I to disappoint?

And just because it's Christmas time, I squeeze his nose tightly together and try to appear as if I'm counting to remember how many rescue breaths you're supposed to give in so many seconds after you see their chest rise.

And then I start. His nostrils pinched between my two fingers, one hand on his chest to watch it rise, and I place my lips across his mouth and start to breathe.

"If you wanted your mouth on mine Erika, all you had to do was ask."

Bingo.

I lift up a little, my mouth still above his. I feel his chest rise under my hand, and his hot, steady breath hitch as my eyes drift up to his in slow motion.

"Got ya!" His eyes flare wide with excitement.

Okay, again, for June—I rear back on my knees away from his face and chest.

"What are you—twelve? I thought you were about to convulse! I thought your throat clogged up and you stopped breathing! That you choked on a leaf or stem or something."

Kourt laughs hysterically as June chuckles behind us.

A confidence only my best friend Archer could instill in me rises to the occasion. I place my palm back on Kourt's chest. His eyes shift back to mine in confusion when he feels my hand stay firmly pressed on his heart.

And the Oscar goes to...

I pause and stare down into his eyes before leaning intimately into the side of his face, my lips brushing his ear when they move to form words. "If I wanted my mouth on any part of you, Kourt, I wouldn't have to ask," I whisper slowly, enunciating each word, and then I pop to my feet innocently to acknowledge June.

"Sorry Erika, I kind of had to go along with it. House rules and all. Kourt here is Blitzen's biggest prankster." June raises a brow between the two of us.

Kourt doesn't even look at me as he moves to get off the floor. He stands and clears his throat.

"Used to be," he says, annoyed.

"No one else rose to claim the title," June adds.

"Pity," I say with a hint of promise.

And—*Oh. My. God.* The next time I decide to channel Archer to prove a point, could I please not do it while the formerly-crotch-ety-turned-nicest, most generous woman on the planet is gifting me enough poinsettias to make a tree out of them in the middle of our Blitzen Christmas?

I suck in a breath of cold air to keep my cheeks from turning red from the heat that blazed through my body when I whispered those words to him.

Have I lost my mind? Or maybe, don't play with fire if you don't want to get burned, Coach McShotty.

"We can start loading the trailers now if y'all want to. Kourt, why don't you take Erika to the back to show her the stands for the tree. There are several rows of 'em but it will give you both an idea of how to set this thing up. You'll want to use all one color until you get to the bottom row, and I was thinking the tree of poinsettias could go to the left of the ice rink, so it's seen on entry to town square and also as in the backdrop of the ice rink when people take photos. That gives our town's live tree that Walter will supply full focus in the middle of the festivities on Christmas Eve." June bows her head on completion, and I clap.

"Perfect. This is truly first-rate, June."

Kourt takes off behind the greenhouses and starts lifting the layers of the tree racks to load. He doesn't say a word. I step up beside him to help him lift one and he immediately puts it down.

"Over there." He points as he puts gloves on. "Go stand over there."

"I don't understand," I offer staring back at him.

"I'm going to need you to stay about five feet away from me the rest of the time we're here. And after that stunt you pulled, I can't hear your voice until we get back in that truck." Kourt returns to lifting the rack without looking back up at me. "And wipe that satisfied smile off your lips, it's not helping the situation."

TWENTY-THREE

Corkscrewed

I'm in a shit mood. Erika. The little minx turned that around on me. Gave me another fucking hard-on.

My phone rings with Helen, Facetiming. "Hey!" She's chipper. "Are you going to the auction?"

"Ellis's auction? Fuck. No."

It turned wicked cold again this afternoon. I'm on the couch, licking my poinsettia prank wounds with my feet stretched toward the fireplace, thinking about her mouth on mine—what she whispered before she got up—and a football game on TV I haven't been able to focus on.

Erika wants to play games? She doesn't know what she's getting herself into.

"Come back to me, Kourt. What are you watching?"

"Ballgame."

"Are you ready for *your* big game?"

"Ready as I'll ever be. Scares the shit out of me, playing with Jamarcus and those guys. I can't hold a candle to them."

"Actually," she lifts her brows. "You can. You know you could have, if Angie hadn't insisted on dragging your long-legged ass back here. Admit it."

"We don't know that."

"Because you never really tried or even threw your hat in the ring." She waves her arm high. "You *knew* you were coming back to Blitzen."

I rub my hand over my face. I haven't thought about Angie this much since, I don't know when. "Maybe."

"Maybe my ass, Kourt. You didn't even go for it."

"Wasn't any point in trying."

"Do you regret it?"

I stalk to the refrigerator and pull out a cold one on that question. She's always known how to jerk my chain. "Not really." I take a swill.

"Go light on that. I intend to see you at the auction."

"Told you. I'm not going." I turn it up just to get under her skin.

"You have to."

"Why?" *Why am I always expected to do what I don't want to do?*

I aim my beer at the TV monitor on the wall by the fireplace. "I've got a game on and a fire going."

"To support your fire department, dummy. If you don't show up because you don't like Ellis, you're shooting the finger to the whole fundraiser thing. It's poor sportsmanship. You two are competing to see who raises the most money. Now close up your pity party, get out of that sweatshirt—and I'll see you there. You need to bid on something. To contribute."

I choke on the swallow and wipe my mouth with the back of my hand. "As if I haven't spent a couple hundred dollars on diesel since Erika hit town. For the fundraiser, I remind you." I grumble and finish off my cold one.

"No more, Kourt. School gym. One hour. You're not going to turn into a drunk over this Erika shit."

"What do you mean?" My ticker revs. "This has nothing to do with Erika. I can't stand the guy. You think he's going to be at my basketball game?" Okay, I'm a little loud.

She smirks. "I'll bet money on it."

"How much?"

"Fifty."

"You're on."

The high school parking lot is packed. Even my space, with my name on it, is taken. Jerks. I drive around 'til I find a spot a quarter mile from the gym, which is just as packed when I finally reach it.

She's pulling it off. Every dime made here is going to the new fire truck. Erika knows what she's doing.

I stand in the rear of the standing room only crowd—I can see over everyone—as one item after another is brought to center court, where ass wipe Ellis has set up a little stage for himself and his auction items. I hope that son of a bitch doesn't scratch up the floor for tomorrow night's game. He didn't even ask.

"Alright everyone, something special." Ellis is wearing a frigging tuxedo, holding the microphone as he stands beside what I'm guessing, by its size and shape, is Erika's statue. They've got it covered with a cloth, which he swishes off with a flourish.

The crowd mumbles. So do I. *What is it?* A big coil?

"This piece belongs to our own Josephine Amherst—you all know her niece, Erika, who's the mastermind behind this year's Old-Fashioned Blitzen Christmas, which is our primary fundraiser for the new fire truck. Stand up for us, Erika."

I crane my neck, along with everyone else, as Erika stands in the bleachers. She's a damn knockout, dressed for this shit auction. Looks like a million dollars in a fitted black dress she sure as hell didn't buy in Blitzen. She smiles, nodding, and sits back down. I know her. If I were closer, I'd see those cheeks are the color of raspberries.

"Okay, now!" Ellis gestures toward the statue, reading a card. "This piece is called *Time Spirals*. It dates to 1898 by Jebediah Helstrom, a retired locksmith."

The crowd chuckles as Ellis holds up his index finger and keeps reading. "Erika did some research. Helstrom believed the act of uncorking a wine bottle represented the release of time, so I guess this... represents a corkscrew. We'll start the bidding at a very conservative $200. Its value has been placed as high as a thousand. It's actually made out of old keys."

He taps his gavel, opening the bidding.

The audience is quiet. People are looking at each other.

No one alive but Josie Amherst would want that monstrosity in their house.

I know Erika. She's dying up there.

"Do I hear a hundred-fifty?" Ellis bellows, his gaze roaming the crowded gym.

Nothing.

"Two hundred!" I raise my hand. Shit. One more time, Kourt to Erika's rescue. She doesn't know it's me in the back of the crowd. Neither does ass wipe.

"Sold!" Ellis looks in the direction of the voice that bid, but I don't think he can even see me in this jam-packed gym. "Pay the lady at the counter for..." he bends down and looks at the ticket attached. "Item Number 27!"

I back into the hall. She doesn't have to know.

Two hundred dollars lighter and another quarter mile hike to my truck and back—and the auction is, apparently, over. Until dickhead says, "We want to make as much money as possible, so tonight, ladies, we've got another auction. Guys, come forward."

His football team marches onto the little stage, flanking Ellis. All in tuxes.

"You're bidding for a Blitzen Blitzer football player for a date, or a day of honey-dos. We start the bidding at fifty dollars a player, starting with quarterback, Cody Baker."

I groan.

My team surrounds me in less than a minute. "Coach, why didn't we do that?" Logan is at my side, looking back and forth from me to the football players in their tuxes. "We need to contribute, too."

"I've got Jet Holloway here tomorrow. The basketball team is contributing." I'm going to choke Ellis Andrews.

"Come on, Kourt!" Someone in the stands yells through cupped hands, seeing me with my players. "Get those basketball players out here, too!"

"Come on, coach. Let's go." They push me forward and the whole damn gym applauds, interrupting the bidding for Cody, chanting, "Kourt! Kourt! Kourt!"

What can I say, Blitzen's a basketball town.

Shoved by my team to the stage—we line up in our street clothes beside the football players in their tuxedos. About a third of them play basketball, too.

"Bidding for the basketball players starts at sixty dollars!" I yell to the crowd. "My guys are worth it!" I wrap my arms around the shoulders of the two nearest, my star seniors, Logan Ramsey and Asher Reece. "What do you say? Sixty bucks to support the fire department for a day's worth of work from one of my guys."

The two players beam, having a higher price on their head than Ellis put on his.

And... they're off... auctioning one athlete after another as the other coaches and I slip away. Almost every player goes to their parents or grandparents for a hard day's work. A few have girlfriends bidding.

Kind of feels good, I have to admit.

"Now, ladies, I'm offering *my* services for a day or a date." Ellis flexes his bicep, and I almost upchuck on the gym floor. "I can do a lot of mowing and hoeing with these guns." He smiles big and flashes his dimples. "Or dinner buying—for the highest bid."

He had it right at hoeing.

Ellis turns and faces me squarely. "And I challenge Coach McClain and the rest of the coaches to do the same. Assistants, too." The prick summons us with a big wave. We're all huddled under the basket to watch his shit show. "Come on up! Let's raise some money for the fire department!"

The whole damned crowd applauds again.

Bill Ellerby, standing beside me, let's out an F-bomb. "Can you believe this shit?" Bill coaches baseball. He shoves a hand over his crewcut. "Motherfucker." He cuts his eyes up to meet mine. "Payback's gonna be hell."

"Damn right."

Reluctantly, one by one, all the coaches and assistants make our way onto the stage, every one of us grumbling.

"Aw, come on, coaches. Put on a happy face!"

Ellis gets a line of fake smiles.

He turns back to face his audience. "Okay... I'm going to hand the microphone to Erika Amherst. Erika, come on down and run this bid so I can join the other coaches."

Does he know what a jackass he is? First of all, wearing that idiot tuxedo when everyone else is bundled in wool or flannel or down. But dragging Erika into this?

She gracefully makes her way to the stage wearing high heels like Helen. I've never seen her dressed like this. I can't take my eyes off of her. I thought she looked good from across the gym but watching her—she's classy as hell with that long, wavy, almost black hair pulled into some kind of up-do, those big blue eyes and lashes most women would kill for, in a tailored black dress that looks sewn to her curves.

Pillowy pink lips.

Damn.

"Let's start with Coach McClain," Ellis says as he shoves the microphone into Erika's hand.

A half grin hooks me, along with a vision. The expression on her face if I shoved that mic down Ellis's throat. I'd have plenty of help.

Ellis coaxes, "Go ahead, Erika."

Hesitantly, her gaze now locked with his, she takes the microphone. "Hello everyone. I... I didn't plan on this. But, I'd say, if the players went for sixty dollars each... what do you say, we start the bidding for the coach at..." She turns from the crowd to look straight at me, smirks, and turns back to the crowd. "Two hundred dollars?" She taps her gavel. "Do I hear two hundred dollars for a day or a date with Coach Kourt McClain?"

Nightmare. Night-fucking-mare.

"Two hundred!" a woman shouts.

"Two-fifty!" another yells.

How fucking embarrassing.

"Three hundred dollars!"

There's not a hole deep enough to crawl into.

"Three-fifty!"

Okay. Take it easy ladies.

I can't do anything but stand here and take it.

"Can I just donate five hundred dollars?" I whisper out of the side of my mouth to Ted.

Trent, on my right, elbows my arm. "I should've shoved that statue up his ass like you told me to the other day."

Bill's as red as I am. "You think you're embarrassed? My wife didn't come. Nobody's gonna bid on me."

"Five hundred!"

"Sold!" Erika finally chirps. "Coach McClain, your services for a date or a day of chores has been won by—let me see—stand please." She motions toward the crowded bleachers.

Up pops Bama Rush. Kelsey Waverly.

Fuck me.

Kelsey marches to the stand, holds out her hand, and I step down, take it, smile and bow. "At your service, ma'am."

Got to make the best of it.

She holds my hand the whole way as she marches me to the payment table. This is the only way she'd ever get a date out of me, but it's not in me to be rude to her. We'll make the most of it. But Ellis Andrews is going to regret this day.

Kelsey and I take our place in the stands to watch one after another of our coaches get auctioned off... until finally, it's Ellis's turn.

How was he saved for last? I hope some old lady bids for that son of a bitch and works his ass off. I hope he has to scrub her floors on his hands and knees. Instead?

Erika asks the crowd, "Is everyone out of money?" She's comfortable as hell in this new emcee role.

Everyone cheers.

She glances at her watch. "It's getting late. We've had a wonderful success tonight. Thank you so much. What you do for your community is... so meaningful. A new fire truck will save lives and Blitzen's livelihood."

"Hear, hear!" Someone shouts from the stands, exciting the crowd, and Erika garners several whistles.

They're enthralled. She's so... fucking genuine. *That's* what it is about her. She's all in, even when it doesn't belong to her. If it helps someone else, she makes it her cause. Erika Amherst is the real McCoy.

"In the interest of saving time and saving all the rest of you money, how about I match tonight's highest bid for our remaining coach, Coach Ellis? Anyone opposed?"

"No!" The crowd cheers.

"Sold!" Erika turns to smile at the son of a bitch in his tuxedo. "To the highest bidder." She cuts her eyes at me and winks, mouthing, "Gotcha."

TWENTY-FOUR

Dance of the Sugar Plum Fairy

Helen's droning on and on about the auction, and as much as I enjoy her company and am glad we came together, I—something feels empty or as if I left one of my belongings behind. My purse, keys, wallet, or that favorite tube of lipstick deserted on the public restroom sink. There's a small vacancy in my chest that I can't seem to dismiss or get to the bottom of. The auction couldn't have been more successful. I just one upped Kourt a second time, and I'm in great company.

Why is there a small part of me looking back toward that gym wondering where he is right now, if he's already driving home—wanting to be in that truck with him. My stomach sinks a little at the thought and the vacant spot in my chest pulses like a highlighted section on a map, marking the spot.

"I have to admit, the first date I thought you'd go on in Blitzen was not with Ellis Andrews." Helen scrunches her nose up as she turns on the road that leads to my street.

"It's not a date. It's an auction bid for the cause. And just who would you have me go on a date with, in Blitzen?"

"Don't play coy with me, Erika with a K. I'll call your damn aunt! First of all, *this* is a very small town. It is a date, because the head case asked you to one of Kourt's games the first week you got here."

"It was canceled."

She rolls her eyes and turns her brights on as we head further up the dark mountain road. "It was meant to be a date all the same. And you know perfectly well who I thought you'd go out with. It's why you bid for Ellis in the first place. A warning—if you play games with Kourt, you better know what you're getting yourself into. Especially with how invested you two are."

She's right. Only it's not the challenge she's warning me of that scares me... maybe I wish I hadn't won tonight. Maybe I wish...

"Wait. Invested?" I can't help but look sideways at my crazy friend.

"Yes, Erika. Invested. Careful there. Ellis is an ass and Kourt's not a fan. There's history there. He's the last guy your friends would want to see you with."

"Helen. He's the only one in town who has asked me on a date, and again, this is nothing. It's for the auction." I try to use reason to get through to her.

Helen's dark eyes pierce my side of the car. "And just what is it you think you've been doing with my best friend all this time?" She looks at me as if she needs to get something through my head.

However, and on the contrary, Helen—I let it rip. "Your best friend is someone I see almost daily pulling together the town's Christmas festival. And talk about *'all bark and no bite,'*" I force myself not to use air quotes, "On the day you assumed nature took its course and we slept together, the truth is, he was so uncomfortable having my bra and panties in his possession, that he couldn't wait to give them back to me. I sat alone in a dark cave with the man with his hard on pressing against my ass—forgive me, TMI—only to find he couldn't wait to get the hell away from me. He is *clearly* not interested. So no, Helen. I don't know what the fuck you're talking about." I take a deep breath and turn, hoping my house is in view.

Hot tears threaten to spew. The humiliation I didn't know I had bottled up is ready to pour out onto one of the few friends I have. I'm so embarrassed. Damn that vacant spot on the map of my heart, and damn Helen's intuition.

A lengthy pause mirrors my thoughts.

"I don't know whether to be offended you dropped your first F-bomb in Blitzen on me or thankful I didn't have to hear fish sticks out of context again," Helen chirps in her delightfully up-beat voice. "Erika, I would love to get in-depth here and tell you the very obvious that you're missing, but he's my best friend. It's not mine to tell."

Helen pulls up to my carport and puts her Lexus SUV in park. "What I can do is make you aware of your own part in this. It's what you've both been participating in since the day you met—foreplay."

My jaw drops.

"You two aren't just playing games with each other. This is foreplay for something much bigger, and I have a hunch it's not one accidental roll in the hay."

Helen looks down for a second at her leather driving gloves fastened in her lap. "You're a big girl, Erika. You don't need me. Josie said you wouldn't. I just liked you so much I had to meddle. It feels good to have another girl around, especially since Josie left. You don't owe anybody anything, not in this town where you've been so generous. You do, however, owe it to yourself to realize what's right in front of you."

Helen yawns daintily as if she didn't just drop a grenade in my lap. "I've got to go. Early morning again and I've said too much." She pats my arm and unlocks my passenger side. "That, and Kourt's tried to FaceTime me seven times during this car ride. You two are ludicrous."

"Text me when you get home." I grab my purse and close the door.

Baffled. I walk away. Totally baffled.

Tossing my keys on the counter, I bypass my laptop and race up the spiral staircase to my room. I shed my heels and coat, and I dive into my bed to bury my face in pillows.

I'm so exhausted. I can't believe Ellis called me up on stage... Kourt... the look on his face... Everything Helen said. I don't know if she's right, and I'm a fool for not knowing, or if I'm right and I've acted like a fool around someone who has no real interest in me.

My eyes flutter closed and I contemplate forcing them open to talk to Archer about it all, but I can't.

This is Archer 101. He'd be so disappointed in me. *'See, Erika, this is why you don't date well. You show all your colors too fast and right away.'* I can hear him now. Translation, you're misguided enough to think a guy like that would go for you, just like you were ignorant enough to think that pitch was a home run for the Harmon account.

And was I thinking that? Do I want Kourt? Were we playing games, or was it all about the festival the entire time?

I'm half asleep in seconds with my mind racing to the very telling click of the mixtape. I hear it. Or maybe I'm dreaming.

In truth, I think I almost embrace riding with Kourt because the mixtape scares me. Not the fact the cassette deck has a mind of its own, but the songs it plays and what they lead me to... *who*, they led me to every single time...

"Look, I know there was a work thing or whatever Helen hinted at, but why Christmas, why all this?" Kourt looks at me in earnest. "I mean, I've never seen someone care so much who's not from Blitzen." His voice pleads loudly to be heard in my head and I see his face by the sled, marveling at it, marveling at me. It's the same look of pride and anticipation he has when he lifts the heavy boxes of canned goods. Every time, he smiles like he's excited that it's heavy, and it's his pleasure to carry such a gift.

Kourt stops in front of me, his eyes racing back and forth across mine.

"What?" I ask.

"Nothing. I'm just looking at you Erika with a K." He looked at me that night like I was a gift. I dismissed it and ran freezing to the truck. *The tape deck clicks on again and plays Sleigh Ride, and I hear dogs barking in the background. So many dogs. I feel Kourt's hand take my chin. He was so mad at me, but when he lifted my face to meet his... Dark hazel eyes fall to my lips. He was going to kiss me before we fell in that water—*I shake my head so hard it hurts, and I feel smothered in my pillow.

I didn't know.

I toss and turn.

The mixtape clicks again and George Michael's Last Christmas plays. I can hear Archer screaming, "Hello? Hellooooooo?" From my laptop, and we must be late to the firm's holiday party. I've changed my dress three times and Archer tells me to put on something differ-ent.

The music stops. The tape deck clicks. There's a long sad pause, and I feel like crying. Please Celebrate Me Home by Kenny Logins plays, and familiar hazel eyes are back dancing on mine, there's snow somewhere in the distance and I feel so warm inside.

He's holding me so tight, and I don't want him to let go.

The mixtape switches, and the music cuts off entirely. All I can see is a homemade label with 'track 3' written all blurry and flashing at me. Bing Crosby's voice rings through my ears acapella, as he croons 'I'm Dreaming of a White Christmas...' I'm still in Kourt's arms. He hasn't let go, and his eyes plead with mine as they have so many times before.

Kicking my covers off the bed, I roll to the other side, and hear Kourt's voice loud and clear from the banks of Blitzen Manor—*"I want you to get to do this the way you want to."*

My eyes pop open. Fully awake and seated upright in bed, I stare through my dark bedroom. The only light visible is the glow of outside streetlamps streaming through Josie's lavish satin curtains. The ice blue-silvery fabric hangs from ceiling to floor and my weary eyes dart up and down it, establishing where I am.

My heart gallops out of my chest. There are no covers on the bed.

He did this for me.

Not for the town or his firetruck, but because of what I told him about my Christmas memory. But why didn't he say so? He never—I sigh, and I slam back into my pillows.

What if Helen's totally misgauged the situation? I know my gauge can't be trusted when it comes to Kourt.

Or can it? He believes in me. He has from the start. The man stood up for me in the town meeting, and that was before Helen solicited him to help. Even when Kourt disagrees with me—even when we argue and he's mad as hell... *'just do what you do, Erika, it's working.'*

Heat coils through me like an electric blanking warming me from the inside when those words replay in my head. The visual of his face above mine, honey green eyes dancing at me. I roll to a different side of the bed to try and fall back asleep. My lips tremble at the words I say out loud to myself with shaky breaths, *He believes in me.*

Closing my eyes, I drift back to sleep with the click of the cassette player in Aunt Josie's VW haunting me the rest of the night.

TWENTY-FIVE

Playing the Game

At home, getting ready for the big game, I take a hard look at my shaving foam-covered face in the steamy bathroom mirror. My scalp tingles. Reality sets in. This is it.

It's been years since you played with these guys. What the fuck are you doing?

They're on the court, either playing or practicing, every day of the year. You're going to make a royal ass out of yourself tonight.

Dammit.

"Okay, suck it up," I mutter to myself.

It was Jamarcus's only condition: If he plays, I play. No backing out. "They better name the fucking fire truck after me," I tell my reflection in the mirror. "Nobody's given more to this fundraiser than I have."

I groan, dropping my head, hiking my shoulders. *Except Erika.* Screw it.

"You can't afford to think about her today. Mind control." I go back to shaving.

That little stunt she pulled last night—winking at me after she bid on ass wipe? I'll get her. And Ellis is lucky if the whole coaching staff doesn't run him through a woodchipper.

"Hottie McShotty!" Jamarcus' voice booms across the tarmac as he spreads his arms wide and pulls me into a tight backslap. At six-ten, Jay makes me feel petite. He's got a wingspan that makes defenders rethink their career choice.

We were close back in the day. He's getting a little gray, which I don't see on TV.

Greeting him, I ask, "How's Tiana? The kids?" I met him and the team when they landed at the private airstrip outside of town.

"Awesome, man, my youngest will be taller than me. You doing okay?" He grips my shoulder with a hand the size of a baseball glove, studying me while I study him. It's the first time we've seen each other in over three years. The funeral was the last time.

Born and raised in Atlanta. A couple of years ahead of me at Tennessee. One hell of a good guy. Somewhere, he got the nickname Jet Holloway... but his teammates have always shortened Jamarcus to J. Not even Jay.

"I'm good. Thank you for doing this."

"No problem, Bro. Our PR people look for goodwill shit like this for us to do, so they can't say anything when I find one I want to do. We're on our way to Charlotte to play the Hornets tomorrow night. What'd you say, we split into two teams—red jerseys and green jerseys. You're on my team, like old times."

"I'm in." Got no choice.

"You remember the Elevator Doors?"

A slow grin spreads across my face as our gazes join. "Hadn't thought about that in years."

J tilts his head. "We're gonna pull it on 'em tonight for old times' sake. Me and Dante will be your screen."

My brows shift high. "You know how long it's been for me?"

"Like riding a bike, McShotty. But I gotta be honest—it's gonna be odd as hell playing on a high school court again." There's that familiar grin the fans love. "This is gonna be fun."

"No shit." An NBA court is ten feet longer than ours. They'll have to adjust their shots.

"Got TV cameras coming, too."

A moan escapes my throat. "Great, so the whole world can watch me show my ass."

He tilts his head back and guffaws at the sky. "Naw. Just Kentucky. You ought to know, the team does a charity event like this, and management's going to have the news media all over it. Can't get rid of the fuckers. Come on over and meet everyone."

Shit. Dammit. Hell.

The thunder of the crowd vibrates into the small dressing room. We're the red team.

Our opposing team took the girls' lockers, so it's just me, J, and about five other guys in here. Seiger Petrovic is a seven-foot blond Serb with a thick accent. Dante Reed is famous for his trash talk, goading his opponents into fouling damn near every game.

Then we've got Trey Valencia, J.J. Jefferson, and Connor McB-room.

That puts two of us on the bench at all times. Hope no one fouls out, because we need some bench time. Especially me, since I don't play every day like they do.

We're up against Omar Farouk captaining a team. He's known as The Big O. Omar was a higher draft pick than J, and just as famous.

He's gonna be tough to guard.

"This place is packed." Trent had to get a pass to get into the dressing room. "I mean packed with a capital P. Twice as many people as last night. Maybe three times as many."

My ticker's doing double-time. *This* really is it.

"Trent, meet J—Jet, Jamarcus Holloway. J, my assistant Trent Holcomb."

The kid's grin stretches across his freckled face, with a twinkle in his light eyes. He'll tell his grandkids about meeting Jet Holloway someday. "What an honor. Nice to meet you, Mr. Holloway."

"I'm J to my friends. Kourt's told me all about you. Played for West Virginia, right?"

Trent cuts his eyes my way. They're filled with new surprise. The kid doesn't know I brag about him all the time to anyone but him. "Yessir."

J says, "Let me tell you, Trent—I wouldn't be here," he points at the floor, "if I hadn't had a good high school coach who cared about me. You remember that. Good coaches are the foundation of this sport. What you do is important."

It shows in his glow. What J said. Trent is overwhelmed. "Thank you. Well, I'll see y'all out there in a few. Knock 'em dead." He looks at me and nods, "Coach."

"You ready?" J asks.

"As I'll ever be."

The crowd goes wild as we walk on the court, Jet Holloway and Omar Farouk leading the way—TV cameras rolling, fans cheering, and I'm dumbfounded for a second at the size of the crowd.

The fire department gets all of the proceeds from this, plus the NBA team is matching what we draw on the door. I beat Ellis before we even step onto the court. He'll know if he's here.

It was Erika's idea.

Focus. Can't go there.

"You ready?" J asks again.

I nod, since I can't find my voice.

TWENTY-SIX

Game Day

I'm not sure who I dressed to impress or who I'm hoping to turn off. All I know is the original Blitzen meeting sweater dress had to make an appearance, but this time, appropriately, with black tights underneath. I'm wearing the same leg warmers, but they scrunch out of a heeled boot this time. A very high heel. In my defense, Ellis is a tall man, too.

The buzzer dings ending the opposing team's warm up as we step into the gym and the air feels immediately different than the auction. My boot heels click on the glossy, hardwood floor as we glide past the already-crowded bleachers. This does not feel nostalgic of high school game days, oh no... the professional giants passing the ball back and forth and more of Blitzen than I've ever seen before in the stands feels like I'm at a Bulls playoff game.

Maybe because that's not all Blitzen. There are people from towns all over here tonight. There's a news crew. Wow. I look up and around, taking it all in, while Ellis mumbles something beside me. "Total showoff. They don't call him McShotty for nothing."

"What?" I look at Ellis like I've heard him for the first time this evening. He asked to take me to dinner, but I told him I didn't want to be late for the game.

"Nothing. Want a drink or something?" Ellis stands with his hands in his pockets. His shifty eyes roam my body up and down.

"Hey, what is it with you two anyway? Do you guys go way back or have some kind of rivalry? Is there something deeper-rooted than basketball versus football?" My hand lands on Ellis' forearm as I look up at him sincerely asking. I'm making an effort to give him my undivided attention.

Shrugging it off, his eyes roam the gym, and I sense my sincerity is completely lost on him.

"Why? Didn't he tell you?"

My eyes blink wildly up at Ellis, completely dumbfounded.

"It's... whatever, but wow. I can't believe he didn't take the opportunity. Let's just say you're not the first girl we've shared an interest in."

"Excuse me?"

"I know. It's hard to believe that guy and I could have the same taste on anything. But you're undeniably attractive and so was she."

Again. Excuse me?

"Did he tell you about Angie? I mean. It's not my place, but you asked—"

"Yeah, and I think I'm sorry I did. That's absolutely none of my business." Was this amazing asshole about to speak ill of the dead? Or worse... say something about a man who lost his wife?

And I paid money for this.

A voice in the background has me standing up straight, and my eyes leave Ellis in search of what has my heart pumping faster.

"On second thought, I'm parched. Any soda they have is great, thanks." I toss the words over my shoulder as I take a step or two forward. And there he is. A little side room off the court between the restrooms and the concession stand has four or five extremely tall men hanging out before the game.

They're a good ten feet away from me, but the smile on Kourt's face as he high-fives his equally giant friends and spins the ball might as well be at me the way it highjacks my stomach, the rhythm of my heart and the thousand butterflies that awaken and scurry through me. He tilts his head back laughing heartily. I've never seen him so happy. It's almost mesmerizing to me.

Oh my God.

My body is behaving as if I had a sex dream over a boss I loathe or something. I had no such thing. It was a Christmas dream, thank you very much. A holiday mixtape of a nightmare that Kourt starred in without a basketball.

And now he's here, in the flesh, standing next to NBA stars. And he looks like he belongs there every bit as much as they do. It's shocking to see him in a basketball jersey and shorts, as opposed to his normal coaching duds.

"I do love a man in uniform. And lucky us, there will be at least ten out there playing for Blitzen tonight." A hip bumps mine as very expensive perfume invades my senses and a wink launches from below a red spectator hat. Judge Angelina stands beside me, seeing what I see.

"Of course, we both know the others aren't necessary, handsome as they may be." She squints into the room with the door cracked open for our viewing pleasure. "You only have eyes for one."

"Oh—I—"

"It's alright duck, wait until you see him on the court. No pun intended. He used to play ball with my son. I never missed a game. Hell, look around, none of Blitzen does." Angelina looks above me and her enthusiasm fades as her lips pinch to one side and her eyes stretch back down to me.

A wax paper cup adorned with a lid and a straw appears in front of me and I realize my date is behind me.

"Oh my. Don't make me wrong about you, duck." Judge Angelina gives me a poignant look, then floats her eyes up to my auction prize. "Ellis," she says, as she nods at him on exiting, without really meeting his eyes.

I catch Ellis in time to see him rolling his eyes at the Judge.

Good God, has this guy pissed off everyone in town?

"Shall we?" Ellis presses his hand in the small of my back a little too firmly, guiding me toward the bleachers. I peel my eyes away from watching Kourt's smile as he's still enthralled in conversation with his basketball buddies. He's really in his element.

Ellis leads us through the bleachers, looking for room to sit. I spot June grinning at me as we scootch and weave through the stands. She tugs at my jacket on my way past her. "Now you'll see why they call him McShotty," she taps my hand.

Finally, we squeeze into a spot in the bleachers where there's barely enough room for us. I'd say he did it on purpose, so we have to sit this close, but the place really is packed. A lot fuller than it was on auction night. I see Bob and Georgia sitting next to Helen as the three of them make a huge production of waving at me.

Helen puts her dainty fingers to work and whistles like a construction worker across the stands at me and we both laugh out loud.

Once settled, I'm almost positive I catch Walter leaning by the rail on the side of the bleachers waiting for the game to start.

Ellis doesn't seem affected by any of the people I've grown to love. Meanwhile, I feel like Rose DeWitt Bukater at the end of *Titanic*, when the old lady ascends into heaven's version of the ship and is reunited with all the people she knows who helped her along the way as they greet her back onto the ship—the whole reunion thing... not the dying part.

"Ladies and gentlemen, it's December again in Blitzen!" A booming voice comes over the loudspeaker like a colosseum. The announcer's words vibrate across the gym. Everyone whistles and cheers so loud I can't hear the rest of what the announcer says.

"Let's go center court and get ready for the jump ball!!!!" The voice rumbles again and so does the crowd over their applause. They begin cheering wildly and I can't hide my smile.

I even direct it toward Ellis assuming he's just as excited, but I'm met with another eye roll. I shrug and return my focus to the gym floor. Kourt does some special handshake with Jamarcus, then Jamarcus steps out with the ball. I don't know if there's three or four NBA players here tonight, but there are definitely more than Jet.

Jet wins the jump ball for Kourt's team. He turns, dribbling the ball and passes it to Kourt. Whistles blow, the score climbs, and all I can hear between the roar of the crowd and tennis shoes screeching is the rim rattle every time Kourt nails it in the basket.

Ellis is talking to me, and I have no idea what he's saying.

"Go, go, go, go. GIVE 'EM THE BALL!" The buzzer goes off again, and I realize, that's me who screamed at the top of my lungs.

I watch as the players shuffle below, then a whistle blows and Kourt is dribbling down the court with the ball. The opposing team stops him in his tracks, and I fly out of my seat screaming for him to shoot. My soda tips over by the heel of my boot and it spills all over Ellis' shoes.

I look over at him as apologetically as possible, as he shakes the ice and carbonated liquid off. "Did you want another?" He asks as annoyed as he can be.

Normally I would say no and not let anyone make a fuss over me, especially seeing as how this is my fault. However, I look up at Ellis and say, "Yes please, and thank you. That is so generous of you."

It's the least he can do for the money I paid.

The guy stalks through the crowd toward the concession stand. Let's be honest, he's better off. This has to be painful for him to watch.

TWENTY-SEVEN

The Big Win

I've been holding my own. Had several three-pointers, but I can't compete under the basket with these giants. At seven feet tall, Seiger can grab a rebound on his tiptoes. That's why I'm the perimeter shooter, like I've always been. The sniper, they used to call me.

We're deep into the second half, score tied, the crowd deafening, when J mouths. "Ready for the Elevator?"

I nod.

"Time out!" the ref calls and motions with his T hand signal, pointing. "Green team."

Fine with me.

We huddle by the bench as J tells the team, "We used to call this the Elevator Door. O's going to inbound it. McShotty here's gonna steal it. Me and Dante set a screen for him while he spins and shoots. We good?"

Everyone nods.

Then fuck if, when the buzzer sounds, I don't catch a glimpse of the stands. Erika's on her feet with those beautiful blue eyes glued on me. Her hands are over her mouth, like she's on pins and needles.

Our gazes lock for a fleeting second.

I don't need her in my head right now. It hits me—what she said in the truck, about wanting to see me in my element. She's wanted this. She came to see me. My mind goes numb.

"Damn, Kourt!" J's in front of me. "What happened? You're supposed to steal the fucking ball!"

"Sorry, man."

"Get back in the game. We can't lose you, man."

Yeah, you could lose me and still win this game.

But I've already won. She's here. With Ellis—but he doesn't exist. Her eyes are on me. And it's not a pending prank that I see in those baby blues. It's desire.

Big O throws the ball in again—I come from behind, slap it out of Valencia's hands and dribble back—J and Dante close the elevator doors behind me—a second later, "Three!" the announcer yells.

Three baskets later, the announcer roars to the crowd, "*McShot-ty's* on fire, folks!"

Damn right.

I hear the long-forgotten chant, "Mc—*Shotty*! Mc—*Shotty*! Three! Three!"

My heart drums as fast as the basketball. Yes, this is where I live. This is my court.

Dante shoots—it bounces off the rim. J wins the rebound, lobs it high over everyone's head to me, waiting at the sideline, where he knew I'd be.

I jump to catch it, come down, jump again, arms extended overhead, flick my wrist, the ball rolls off my fingertips—silence as the leather ball sails through the air and... *Swoosh!*

"Another three!" the announcer booms. "The red team is up by nine now. McShotty's a flame-thrower, folks."

"Hell of a game!" The guys surround me. Damn, it feels good—not to have made a fool of myself. I don't know if my knees are weak from playing, jumping, or relief. It's over.

"You still got it." J pulls me into an embrace on the crowded floor in front of everyone, his arm around my neck. I smile against this thick chest.

I'm surrounded by giants, backslaps and handshakes, thanking all of them.

It was fun after all.

Sheriff's deputies and city cops hold the crowd back in the mayhem after the final buzzer.

"Gotta run," J says. "Plane's waiting. God, it was good to see you, man." His eyes sparkle.

I think he did have fun.

"I can't thank you enough, Bro. Tell them all how much it means."

"Will do. Come see us soon, Kourt."

Stepping out of the showers, the gym is still alive with people.

"Great game, Coach!" Trent's the first to grab me. "I can't *believe* you can play like that." He pats my back.

"Lucky night. Thanks Trent."

"Great game, Kourt!" I think that was the mayor.

"You were awesome!" There's another back slap from someone's big hand.

"Thanks." I'm surrounded by a mob—old, young, men, women, even school kids—all congratulating me.

It's great. I smile at each one, shake hands—but it's hard to keep up. I'm flattered. They didn't have to wait for me to shower. Truth is, I love the victory and the fans.

But right now, I kind of wish they'd all go away.

My gaze roams the gym—searching. *Did she leave with him?*

"Kourt! Man!" Chief Jones pulls me into him with a bear hug. "You won't *believe* how much money we made tonight." He offers his hand, and I grasp it. "Between this and the festival, we'll get our new firetruck."

"I came through for us. Thanks, Chief."

Where is she?

I'm hugged, backslapped or my arm is squeezed by one person after another and I tell each, "Thanks... Appreciate it... Glad you came," as my gaze keeps roaming the bleachers.

There.

She's standing on the bottom bleacher, staring at me, in her trademark form-fitting sweater dress—that wavy hair falling below her shoulders, those blue eyes locked on me. *That* makes my heart pump triple time.

"Thanks... Excuse me... Sorry..." Sidestepping and pushing through the crowd, I only have eyes for her. The voices fade as my feet find their way across the gym floor with my gaze and Erika's locked together.

"Coach." Someone calls in the distance, but I don't look back. I keep striding toward her. I could say I make a beeline to her, but I'm there in two giant strides. Her blue eyes trace mine and she blinks down at me from the bottom bleacher rail.

I grab her underneath her arms, lift her over the railing, and scoop her into my arms.

"Kourt, what are you doing?"

"We're going to need some bacon and some eggs."

"McClain what do you think you're doing? That's *my* date." Ellis yells across the gym through cupped hands.

Dick can't even say *she.*

"Fuck off, Andrews. Date's over."

TWENTY-EIGHT

Home for Christmas

Kourt carries me to the truck in silence. We leave the stunned Blitzen crowd speechless, back in the gym. He opens the passenger side and puts me in. A few more silent moments later, the ignition starts. "Buckle up."

"No." I reach across, put the truck in park, then slide over the console, crawling into his lap, straddling him. His hand presses against the back of my waist and he pulls me into him, dropping our foreheads together.

"Erika." He breathes me in. A hot tear drops down my cheek, and his thumb moves to wipe it away. "You watched me play. You rooted for me."

"You were the best one out there. It's where you belong, Mc-Clain."

Kourt smiles at me and brushes my hair behind my ear, studying me for a long moment.

"Why did you take me Kourt?"

"You know why."

"Say it."

Kourt grows so hard underneath me, I whimper as I adjust in his lap. He looks deep into my eyes as his large hands trap my cheeks on both sides. His expression is too complicated to read. "I haven't even kissed you yet." His eyes roam my face.

"Tell me, Kourt."

"I can't watch you with anybody else, Erika."

"Why?"

"Because I want you so bad I can't fucking see straight."

He pulls my face to his lips. We come together with a tender kiss, and I pull away from the strong peck it becomes with butterflies unleashing in a frenzy. My eyes wide on his, and then, as natural as if we'd been doing this for years, his hands leave my cheeks, our faces tilt and he opens his mouth on mine so hungrily I almost can't contain it.

A warmth I've never known fills my chest and the pit of my stomach. The moment he pulls slightly back, scraping his teeth on my bottom lip, then licking it until his tongue moves inside to find mine—I'm molded to his lap. I lean in, kissing him back as ferociously, and he groans into my mouth so loudly I feel it in my center.

Strong hands trail through my hair, and it's all I can do not to rock my hips into him.

"Fuck, Erika." He pulls away, looking up at me. His hands squeeze into my hips and ass, holding me in place on his lap as if he can neither handle me leaving it, nor moving in it.

A few key fobs beep, car doors open and shut, ignitions start, and more voices are heard coming out of the gym.

"You better put the gear in drive," I warn as I force myself off of him and slide back to my side. Kourt lifts the middle console in his truck, and with one arm slides me back to him, to his side.

"Trust me. It already is."

He grins, raising an eyebrow, and I roll my eyes and try to keep from smiling like a child. He pulls out of the gym and races up the mountain, faster than he drove when he got the emergency call.

This place... *his* place. It's incredible. I suspected it was a modern log cabin from the outside, but the architecture, and the way it's designed inside—this must have been custom made by someone who knew exactly what they wanted and how they want to live. And the beauty of it is, I can't tell if it was built by some Hemingway-type coal miner way back in the day, or a hippie master craftsmen in the seventies, or a top-notch contemporary designer.

My mind swirls at all the questions I want to ask Kourt as I shake my head and bite my bottom lip, looking it all over. Later, though. I don't have to know it all today, and I would never want to pry too deeply into subjects rooted with his wife.

All I need to know is this is his home, and I'm ashamed to admit to myself how much it feels like one... to me.

Josie's place is incredible and has so much potential to be anything one could want it to be, but this cabin—God, people in Chicago dream of having the wherewithal to create or carve out a home like this, be it in the middle of their high-rise building or in some tucked-away forever home they finally get to migrate to.

It's masculine and screams bachelor in the most delicious way. It's private but inviting. Independent, yet all open concept. Every corner is cozy and warm, with traces of the man who inhabits it. It's charming as much as it's virile and red-blooded, and the smell of him surrounds me. Forcing myself to ignore the heated swell in my lower belly causing my core to ache at the new discovery of him, I turn back toward the living room.

Kourt's aluminum Christmas tree sparkles in front of me. The silver branches are made of tinsel-like threads, exactly like the one I pulled out of the attic and set up at Aunt Josie's. Only, his branches glow in the crackle of the fire he lit for us.

It's beautiful, and of all the Christmases I've been chasing, standing in Kourt's cozy living room by the tree and fireplace with the most incredible mountain view I've ever seen is the closest I've come. The glow of the fire beckons me, and I step closer, tracing the stone mantle, a trophy or two, and a few pictures of the siblings he spoke of.

A gasp flies from my open mouth. To the left of the fireplace behind the tree, stands Great Aunt Josie's statue from the auction.

"What can I say? I'm a corkscrew enthusiast. It wouldn't fit on the mantle... or anywhere, so—"

"Kourt," I whisper almost inaudibly, still facing the statue. *It was him.*

He bought my auction piece.

An arm reaches over my shoulder and he hands me a cup of hot spiced cider. The entire house smells of cinnamon, orange, and clove now. And... *Wow.*

"Spiced rum, brandy or whiskey?" *Or very fragrant gasoline? This is strong.*

Kourt winks. "Whiskey, but all you need to know is go slow on that one. It's my great grandmother's tradition, and it's meant to be sipped."

He stares at me by his fire, then goes back to his blanket sorting.

"Are you making me a fort?" I ask with a small grin. I'm the most comfortable I've ever been in my own skin, but at the same time, everything he says, everything he hasn't said since we got here has me ready to jump out of it. I'm nervous in the best possible way. The anticipation kind. I have no idea what Kourt has in store for me, but I know I want it. Without question.

"You just sip and get warm," he reprimands.

Oh, I'm quite warm already.

Moments later, and lost in the fire, I move to take another sip from my mug, when I feel Kourt on his knees behind me. My sweater dress lifts up to my waist, and I suck in a short, tight breath.

"Is this the outfit from the town meeting?"

"Umm. It... is." I stutter at the surprise of his warm hands on my thighs. His voice so firm and matter of fact. I force mine to match his. "The very sweater dress, yes." It comes out as cool and criminal as I planned.

"You're more covered up this time. You have on tights." He pulls the nylon material away from my thigh between the pads of two fingers and snaps it back in place. A crooked smile he cannot see betrays my face.

Sending goosebumps up my spine, he runs a seam down the center back of my leg—slowly. Tantalizingly, his finger traces back up my leg.

"I didn't want to give Ellis the wrong impression."

"So... you showed up bare-legged for me that day of the meeting. If I were to slide these down now—that would be the impression meant for me?" Kourt slides my tights down my hips, upper thighs, and legs so slowly, electricity tingles through my body.

"That depends on what impression you have." I'm visibly shaking at his touch, but my voice comes out remarkably coy and controlled. It's insane what he conjures out of me—words I'd never say, feelings I've never felt, and judging by how very turned on I am right now... things I'd never normally do.

In one small motion Kourt turns my body to face him. My tights are rolled down to the ankles of my high heeled boots. Kourt's face is eye level with my most intimate parts.

He takes in my red lace panties and licks his lips. "What was that you whispered in my ear at the poinsettia farm, Erika?" He hooks his finger in the crotch of my panties and slides them to the side exposing me to him.

I suck in a shallow breath and cut my eyes down to his.

"You said, Erika, that if you wanted to put your mouth on any part of my body, you wouldn't have to ask. I'm under the impression I'm allowed that same courtesy."

My eyes pop open. My heart thunders and before I can respond, Kourt's mouth is on me. No, his tongue is in me in the most feral way. He went from a calm, strategic criminal to a hungry thief.

"You're so fucking wet it's unreal. Fuck. Is this what it's like to taste you..."

The sensation as his tongue slides deeper inside me is more than I can handle. My legs are already quivering.

He smiles. I feel his lips across my center as he notices. In one balanced motion, he rolls backward onto the blankets. My knees bend and lunge forward to meet him on the floor. His one finger hooked inside me and the other reaching through, cradling my ass, as if he could lift me that way with ease. The way he handles me... In that smooth motion he has me sitting on his face, and I am already trembling again from anticipation.

"Is this what you had in mind when you whispered in my ear?" He looks up at me, from me.

"Please... Kourt." I can barely breathe, much less think of a witty comeback.

"Please, Kourt, what?" He flicks his tongue across me and slides his finger deeper inside.

"Better," I let out a breathy moan as I run my hands through his hair. "It's better." I've never felt so exposed, and I'm still wearing my dress, the sweater is scrunched up above my belly button.

I slide it the rest of the way off, and toss it to the side, leaving me in my bra, panties and the tights I forgot rolled to my boots and stretched to the max between my ankles.

Kourt's tongue stops. His eyes roam up my body. He slides me down his chest and stomach to rest on his erection. I feel how hard he is on my bare skin, the fabric of his jeans pressing into me where my lace panties are still pulled aside.

Kourt sits up with me in his lap, his lips glossy from my arousal as he looks at me with starving eyes. "What did you just do?"

For a moment I don't understand, until he looks down at my bra strap, his eyes primal, and he drops one strap to the side. He kisses my shoulder obscenely, and reaches around to unhook my bra, but surprises me instead when two hands large enough to palm a basketball slide, with ease, up the front of me, through the underwire of my bra, and he palms both my full breasts.

My nipples are painfully erect as he catches them between his fingers, massaging me like my breasts are his new obsession.

"Fuck me," he growls as he discards my bra and replaces one hand with his mouth,

Oh, God...

"What are you doing to me, Erika?" he mutters as his tongue plays with my nipple.

Nothing yet...

Then my hands move down to unbutton his jeans. The fireplace, crackling behind us, illuminates everything we see. I've never had sex with the lights on, not like this.

Kourt looks up from devouring my breasts, and his eyes freeze on mine as I reach my hand back and unzip his jeans to release his more than substantial cock. I nudge myself down over the zipper I undid to view the prize.

A demented smile takes agency across my face as I look up at him, hitch my breath and bite my bottom lip. My core throbs just looking at it.

Only I must have lost my mind as this thing could kill me. *Jesus.*

I want to take him in my hand so badly, but he pulls me back up to him, holding my face above his. My lips can't resist, and I lean in to find his mouth, licking myself off him, letting him know how unbelievably turned on I am.

Kourt takes over the kiss, exchanging my tongue with his over and over until I'm senseless. He drags his lips away panting into mine.

"Fuck it. I want to be inside of you so bad." He opens the end table drawer and pulls out a condom.

Rolling me carefully onto my back, he slides my panties down. A smile negotiates the condom in his mouth when he gets to my tights and heeled boots, still trapping me at the ankles. I see his cock twitch at the realization, and he tilts his head. I can only guess, contemplating whether to leave them on or not. He frees me instead, tossing the boots and peeling the black tights from my feet.

My body is on fire. I want to taste him. I almost came twice moments ago on his face, but I don't want anything else right now but him. Enough foreplay.

Kourt moves between my legs and brings his face to mine, hovering over me. "Spread your legs for me Erika."

Oh... my... God.

Something that would be so foul coming from anyone else's mouth has me salivating and pulsing inside. I do as I'm told, and he whispers in my ear. "Do you want me to fuck you, Erika?"

I buck my hips toward his tip and lean up to his ear. "I need you to, Kourt. I need it."

Kourt fists his cock to line it up to my entrance, and I rise on my elbows to meet his face, whispering in his ear, "Do you want me to take your cock, Kourt?"

He growls and closes the gap between us. His mouth and cock crash into me at the same time and I'm stretched further than I have ever been stretched. He groans into my neck, and my breath catches as I try to adjust. I knew he was big, but this is a whole other level.

He pauses, staring at my blinking eyes as my walls stretch to take him, contracting wildly around his shaft.

"Fucking hell, Erika. You are so... unbelievably... tight."

I wince when his eyes meet mine again, as he stays still inside me, savoring the moment. My heart throbs as fast as my center around his cock. My breath is quick and steady underneath his chiseled, warm chest that smells like *him*.

Is this what it's like for other people? Is this what Archer's been boasting about all along?

Kourt balances with one arm and pulls a stray hair from my face, then looks down at my chest pressed against his. My nipples trace his pecks as my chest rises and falls.

He smiles at me. And then he pulls out and thrusts back inside, the way I begged for him to. It's so rigorous, the friction of our bodies together. I can barely keep up underneath him when I buck my hips forward to meet his cock diving into me.

Thrust after thrust, I roll my hips into him and we keep up the over exhilarating pace of finally being together. It's abrupt, raw, and feels like the most natural thing I've ever done when I look at him watching me the entire time.

His eyes don't shift from mine as my body moves up and down beneath him from the magnitude of him pushing as deep as I can take him.

The urge to lean up and kiss him battles the euphoria of lying underneath him, captivated by the way he looks at me. My fingers press into his upper back and the palm of my other hand presses onto one of his tight pec muscles to brace myself against him. Kourt's brows pinch together and his eyes flicker back at mine as if he's experiencing a conflict of his own as he breathes heavily above me. "Fuck. Erika."

I close my eyes and let my head roll back as my back arches, and I feel like I'm going to come from the stimulation of his cock alone. He pulls my body back to him, with his hand across my lower back, pressing my chest to him again as he fucks me until I *do* come like that.

Kourt lets out a guttural moan and collapses on top of me.

He's so large inside me, I feel his release even with a condom on, and my mouth stands agape.

What just happened here?

I had sex like I just got out of prison.

"No clothes. Not in the living room. That's what the blankets are for." Kourt tosses the bra and sweater dress I reach for to the side. We both must have dozed off for a minute. Whatever it was moments ago, it was so intense, I needed the physical and mental break from it. I'm still catching my breath from being that connected to him. Reaching for my clothes seconds ago was the only nervous distraction I could think to rely on.

Unabashed and naked, he rises and heads to the kitchen, opening the fridge. "You thirsty? Hungry?"

"Oh, am I invited to dinner?"

Good. I still have sarcasm.

"I already told you. You're staying for breakfast."

I wrap a blanket around myself and traipse toward the kitchen to join him. "I wasn't sure I'd ever be invited in after that night you pulled up just to grab the sweats. I guess I thought I wasn't allowed in."

Kourt spits the juice he just swallowed out of his mouth. "You weren't allowed into my house because you made me so hard that night we wouldn't have left for three days if you'd have come in."

"Really? When and what brought that on?"

"Erika, the sound of your voice makes me hard as a fucking rock. All you had to do was start talking. And in all those truck rides—I was set up for the longest night of blue balls in history. Which you can understand how maddening that is when you say asinine shit."

Kourt takes another swig of juice and pours a glass for me.

"What about you?" He sets the glass down where he stands and stalks over to me.

"When did this start happening for me?" Pulling the blanket apart, he slides a hand between my thighs and slips a finger inside me.

I swallow a breath, looking him in the eye. "The first time I rode in your truck with you, when you reached over to buckle my seat belt."

Kourt's eyes darken. The blanket falls behind me on demand of his fingertips. He stands above me, tilts my head back and kisses me without restraint. I feel his length harden against me, and I don't know what it is about this man, but I don't ever want to get dressed again.

Archer wouldn't know me if he saw me right now.

My legs lift when Kourt pulls my thighs to wrap around him. His tongue still feverish, tasting every corner of my mouth as he moves us to a small rolling desk chair, sits, and watches me squirm in his lap.

Losing my mind from the friction as I grind on his erection, gliding my slit back and forth on his shaft—without letting him inside me.

Kourt halts me, his palm pressed and splayed firmly across the middle of my back. He's supporting me and holding me still, while honey green eyes dart back and forth between my longing face and my breasts. He bites down on one nipple, reaching for a condom from his desk drawer with his free hand.

I lick my lips as he tears into it like a mad man.

I'm breathing like I just ran for my life, and I scoot away from him, further down his lap as he lines the rubber to the tip of his hard cock. He looks at me curiously.

"I like to watch you. I mean, I want to watch you put it on." I've never been so open or brazen with a partner in my life, and somehow Kourt brings this wicked curiosity out in me.

He rolls the latex up his shaft slowly to give me what I asked for. "Do you want to watch me put it in?" He studies my face. "That's—my favorite part." Kourt props me up and leans me farther back as he lines up to my entrance, with me craning down to see.

He doesn't watch this time. His eyes search mine as I watch him disappear inside me. I gasp at the sight and the feel of him filling me again.

I'm sore from being stretched the first time. But... oh. My. God. If it's not a good sore.

He glides me slowly back and forth, his cock sliding in and out of me while watching my face as he uses the position of me straddling him on the small chair and him holding me up as leverage.

I lean up to cradle into him and he growls as the angle fills me deeper. I buck my hips toward him. I can't stop. He feels so good. *This* feels so good.

"What—is—this, Kourt?" I whisper almost drunk off him into his ear, my hands latching onto his neck as I clench uncontrollably around his cock.

He kisses my cheek intimately as he thrusts deeper. "It's you and me, Erika."

"Please," I beg as I feel like I might come undone this second. "Don't let it stop."

"I have no intention of letting it stop." Kourt licks my earlobe, and I can't help but moan.

I'm on the verge of panting when his eyes drift behind me for a moment and I catch them dazzling.

"Erika," he says, as he pulls my ear to his mouth by the nape of my neck. "It's snowing." Long arms of steel lift me off him and he turns me in his lap to the open view of the window spanning his living room and kitchen. It's his very own view of nothing but trees, sunsets and sky, as he lives so high in the mountains. With no other houses behind him, there's nothing to block his panoramic view and no one can see in.

My eyes flutter like the flurries falling, as I chase them on their way down to cover the empty branches in front of us. I've never seen anything quite like it.

"Does this happen a lot?" I mutter, sitting in front of him on his lap.

"Only this high up the mountain. Not as often downtown Blitzen or even where you live," he whispers in my ear so slowly, calmly... His voice like his scent—it sooths me when he purposely speaks so tenderly to me.

The pads of his fingers soften and trail down the side of my arm. Shifting from the snow outside the window, my body tingles as goose bumps rise from his touch, reminding me how intimately I'm sitting naked in his lap. A snow flurry has my gaze drift to look directly out in front of me, catching our reflection.

Clear as day, staring out the snow-covered night, I see myself sitting on Kourt's lap. I watch his eyes meet mine in our reflection. His cock swells underneath me and he slips into me from behind, startling me into pure, unadulterated bliss.

I don't pull my eyes from our reflection. I can't. And when he picks up our pace, one hand reaching around and circling me above me taking him inside me—I realize I'm bouncing in his lap. My ample breasts bob up and down in a way I would normally be embarrassed by. I can't think of anytime I've taken it to the point that I'm bouncing like a porn star, but I can't stop myself.

I pick up his rhythm and go faster as the snow falls heavier, surrounding us in the background nature laid out before us. I hear him moan so guttural and loud behind me as we watch each other, and I know he's close. I stare as hard at our reflection as he pushes me down onto his cock and I watch myself come undone in the window.

TWENTY-NINE

Reflections

I'm spent.

The game. Erika. Both of them exceeding any expectations, and the reality of *her*—better than fantasy.

Never have I experienced anything as sensual as us watching ourselves just now.

That was new. And unintended.

We were just watching the snowfall—until she saw our reflection in the glass. Her face when she noticed... eyes raking over our bodies in the window drawing mine in to follow. I've never been so hard in my life.

Looking down at her resting on my chest, I comb her hair with my fingers, sweeping it away from her ear and whisper, "You want to sleep on the mountain of blankets in front of the fire? You might be more comfortable in bed."

Nuzzling deeper into my neck, she responds with her eyes closed. Her voice low and soft like velvet muttering out of her swollen lips. "Here, with the wonderful fire and the tree."

"Done. But, with a bathroom or shower break." I scoop her into my arms, striding for the bedroom. Her smile hikes above my shoulder to peek at the scene behind us and around the hallway as she takes the rest of my place in.

"Oh," Erika gasps as she gawks at my bed. Her eyes drift from the California King to meet my gaze. "You could get lost in that thing. It's the biggest bed I've ever seen."

"Had to have one long enough. It's seven feet." I can't help but smirk as I cut my eyes toward hers.

"Umm hmm." She bites both lips as her eyes twinkle at me.

My head tilts back. God, she makes me laugh.

I set her feet down on the tile bathroom floor and she looks around with slight reservation. "Leave, so I can clean up?"

I nod and head back to the living room to secure the fireplace. After tossing two large oak logs into the fire and covering it with the screen, I head back down the hallway. My heart drums in my chest like thunder as I stride to my bedroom knowing she's in there. *Fuck.* You'd think we hadn't just spent the last several hours doing just that.

The bathroom mirrors are steamed from the hot shower. Erika's inside, standing underneath the strong stream of water. All I see through the glass door and fog is her form. Full breasts, her smooth stomach dipping into the deep curve of her cinched waist and round hips. With her head tilted back, her dark hair falls down to her lower back.

She is a vision.

Already naked, I open the door and join her. Erika blinks her eyes tightly and opens them to look up at me. Water drops from her long lashes onto her cheeks as she shifts a nervous step back, taking me all in. We've been naked all night, but this feels different. The shower beats steadily and loud down her back, my chest and the tiled floor. A tension rod connects my gaze down to hers, and I'm somehow the one feeling exposed.

She sucks in a tight breath and reaches for the shampoo. The water sprays off her shaking arm, as she wraps her fingers around the plastic. My hand closes on top of hers as I pull the bottle slowly from her. For the first time since sliding under the water with her, our eyes break contact, and she turns giving her back to me. Tilting her head back and closing her eyes, she waits.

Pouring shampoo into my hand, I watch the water stream over her shoulders, sliding across her firm, full tits. My gaze follows the water sliding down her body...

Fuck.

My hands thread through her hair creating suds, and I can't keep from pulling her to me. Our wet bodies slide against each other, and she turns to face me.

Erika lathers soap, rubbing it over my chest. I try to swallow a moan when her hands find the small of my back, gently grazing my ass.

Her trailing fingers leave my back, sliding around front. She grabs my already hard cock, rubbing her soapy hand up and down the shaft.

Not hard. Not fast. She keeps her warm hand tight around me, slowly massaging, then begins to stroke back and forth, back and forth...

I may explode.

Bending to her knees—she shocks the shit out of me, taking my cock in her mouth. Fisting. Pumping. Sucking.

I have to brace myself with each hand on a tile wall as I let my head tip back and I moan.

She sucks hard, twirling her tongue, fisting me tight, still stroking me. Then turquoise eyes hit mine, staring up from black lashes—

I grab her, lifting her high enough to slip her legs around my waist. "I have to get a condom."

Carrying her from the steamy shower—the bathroom is nothing but a fog cloud—I grab a towel to cover the cold counter before I put her on it, wipe the mirror with another towel and flip on the exhaust fan.

"I want to watch again," she whispers into my neck.

Pink tints her cheeks as she waits for my reaction. "I'd never done that before... like we did in the window."

Opening a drawer, I grab and sheath a condom, slide her off the counter and turn her to the mirror. Dark blue eyes trace her own body in the glass before us as she tilts forward, and I watch her pert nipples press to the marble counter. Her trepidation over pressing herself all the way down or not to honor keeping her eyes on my reflection is scandalous.

I nod at her as one hand finds her hip pressing her ass to me. My other hand fists my cock and lines my tip up to her entrance. Brows wince together on both our parts as my tip presses through her. She's so unbelievably wet. Holding back to keep from thrusting so deep I get to watch it drip down her thighs in more agony than a man can take, but her face—her fucking face as she bites her bottom lip to no avail and lets out a whimper. I push in as deep as she can take me, letting out a groan that would wake the dead.

It's a damn good thing I don't have neighbors.

Losing my mind, I fuck her with a slow intensity so raw and visceral, I have no idea where it comes from or how I have it left in me.

I'm watching her watch us as we move together.

"Oh, Kourt," her words escape, as her eyes flutter shut.

I pick up speed, driving like a madman. Her eyes come back to meet mine. Her body trembles as her walls throb around me as she cries out again, coming on my cock.

Pulling out, I'm pulsing as I slide the condom off and explode, releasing on her lower back and ass. A small beat infiltrates the impossibly steamy bathroom long enough for us to catch our breath.

"Do you like my hot load dripping off your back?" I lean down and whisper into her ear.

Erika turns to find me. "I want it dripping from everywhere."

Fuck me.

If that doesn't bring us both to our fucking knees on the tile floor. Her lips crash into mine, and there it is... Heat balloons inside me, through my entire body, she fucking sets my skin on fire. We fall into a frenzy devouring each other's faces in a kiss that has more teeth gnashing than lips touching.

Sinking her body to mine, we slow our kiss to something sane and reasonable. She licks her swollen lips and pulls away, looking back at me alarmed. I grab her face and bring her lips back to mine. As hard as I am again, and as many times as we've done it tonight, the last thing on my mind is fucking.

It's *her*.

Where has she been all this time? It's her I'm thinking of. How she took me by complete surprise. How she upended my life. Her wit that makes my mind sharper, her dreams that are contagious, and the way she's got my fucking heart if I'm not careful.

Outside, the world is white. That gentle snow that fell earlier has turned into a whiteout.

I toss a hickory log on the fire, stoking it. Nothing burns hotter than hickory. The flames lap at my hands as I stir the fire. It needs oxygen to burn the way Erika wants it to burn—like in a Christmas movie.

A soft hand lands on mine as she rolls toward me, awakened from the crackle of the fire. Erika blinks up at me and smiles, her eyes shimmering from the flames.

"I must have dozed off." Her voice is low and raspy as she holds one of the thirty blankets laid out tight to her chest, covering her perfect tits.

"Look." I whisper and point out the living room window trying not to disturb the moment.

Her eyes lift to the white, heavenly powder that has become our view.

The expression she wears is illegible until I watch her lips purse together and come apart again in a tiny whisper, "Christmas."

She says it to the view from our fort of blankets in front of the fire. I grab a remote from my end table and hit power on my stereo. I hit several arrows forward, then press play.

Bing Crosby's *White Christmas* wafts into the living room. Gently, and much slower than I've ever seen her move, Erika pries her eyes from the white window to meet mine. "Kourt."

"Umm. Umm."

"You do love Christmas." She says it as a fact, not a question.

"Umm. Umm." I nod slowly, a partial smirk melting into a genuine smile as I slide under the blankets with her. Well past the point of exhaustion, our naked bodies mold together as she drifts to sleep in my arms to the music and the fire.

The heat of the fire almost blisters my face combined with the morning sun. Rolling away from the fireplace, I see heeled boots and black tights under a familiar maroon sweater dress. A purse and keys are gathered on the end table and several askew blankets have been folded neatly for me to put away.

Erika slides over to my side of the pallet. God, she's gorgeous looking down from above me. I'm betting we fucked and showered every ounce of make-up off her face, and I know I didn't finish shampooing her hair thoroughly, yet here she is smiling at me as beautiful as when I brought her here.

"Good morning, Kourt." She blinks down at me cool as a cucumber.

A grin saturates my face, and I shake my head in sheer marvel and disbelief as I pull her on top of me. She wrestles to sit up straddling me, and I grab her hands.

"I thought I made it clear the living room was a no clothing zone."

"You also promised me bacon and eggs, but I'm afraid your alarm clock didn't make it clear that it's after seven a.m."

"Wait, what? You're kidding?"

"You've got school, right?" She looks concerned, and it's very cute the way she waits for me to flip out and race to get dressed. She just wants to be right, and she is, only today's first period is my conference period since we don't have morning practice this last week. That, and something else just woke up.

"Oh my God, Kourt. You're going to be late, and I'm not going to be able to walk straight until Christmas." She protests but she still adjusts to my erection underneath her.

I'm naked under the blanket from last night, and I'm not leaving until she comes again. "We're not leaving here until I watch you come on my cock again." There. I said it out loud in case my hard cock beneath the crotch of her tights didn't make it clear enough. "Please. Now I want to watch." I slide the blanket down from covering my erection, so I can feel her directly on me.

"But I'm already dressed."

"Not a problem." Her fingers lace tightly through mine as I squeeze our hands together. She balances above me, baby blues staring into me, and I feel her getting wet through her tights. Letting go of her hands I bring mine down to her hips and drag her up and back down my shaft. The friction from the thin fabric of her tights making me harder as she sweeps back and forth along my cock. She's still looking at me in disbelief, until her breath gets shorter. I'm going to be chafed from this dry hump, but watching her on top of me like this is worth it.

Erika moans and throws her head back. She sucks in a deep breath and looks back down at me. Her eyes are wide as I dig my fingers into her ass cheeks through her clothes. "You're so big, Kourt."

"Use it. Come for me baby. Come on my cock."

The pink in her cheeks gets darker and she almost hums as she rides my shaft. A soft whimper spreads her sweet lips apart as she arches her back and comes. I work quickly, sinking my hand into the waistband of her tights, and palming her throbbing, wet pussy. Swiping as much as her arousal as I can, I stroke that hand up and down my pulsing cock about to explode myself.

Erika watches my face, my eyes fixed on hers, as she surprises me and brings those pink lips down to the tip of my cock. Wrapping them around my head she makes me come immediately. I release into her mouth and watch her swallow every drop.

Shit. Fuck. Damn.

"I suppose after that, you're going to tell me I have to drive you home?" I jump off the floor and reach around for clothes to dive into, scooping her into my arms the moment she turns her back to grab her things.

"Get dressed!" She slaps my naked ass, as I pivot away from her.

The sexiest woman alive just swallowed my load. Not because she wanted to impress me, not because she wanted to trap me into a relationship, and not because she's somebody's granddaughter trying to land the infamous widowed bachelor-basketball coach. Blitzen High is out of their mind if they don't think I'm showing up smelling like her.

To be fair, I can shower and change in the locker room before my first class, but right now, I'm wearing her on me.

"Wait... Is that a tattoo?" She tilts her head down to the back of me staring at my only tattoo.

"We've been naked all night and somehow I never saw that." She looks up at me oddly. "Number three," she mutters almost to herself.

"Surely you saw it on my Jersey. I've always been number three. It's my—"

"Lucky number," she says it for me.

"What?"

"Nothing. Actually, you'll have to drop me downtown. I had an errand to run before the game, so I met Ellis at town square, and we drove from there. I didn't let him pick me up from home."

"You didn't." I can't stop looking at her. An insane smile on my face.

"Are you blushing?" she asks, but she's the one with raspberry cheeks. If I'm blushing it's because she referred to her place as 'home,' not Josie's.

THIRTY

Too Early to Tell

My eyes blinking open to the crackle of that fireplace is a memory I cannot shake. The early morning sun turned a light bulb onto our space—yet the smell of cinnamon, and cedar still lingered, the fire, *him*. The smell of him was all over me. It still is—I drive away in my Bug from town square. It's quiet out this morning and no one seems to be up buzzing around.

My car cruelly takes it's time to heat up, but I'm not cold. I blow out a calming breath, so unnerved I want to shout at the top of my lungs. Wonder if the rated R version of Charles Dickon's *The*

Christmas Carol isn't Scrooge running through town shouting, 'Merry Christmas' and giving away turkeys to Tiny Tim because he just spent the night with Kourt McClain.

Okay, that's wrong, and got creepy somewhere in the middle. Also, it would be rated X, not R if it mimicked anything we did—any one of the times we did it.

What happened back there? To me? To him? To us?

Is there an *us* now?

Everyone in their right mind wonders what's next after great sex. Everyone except Archer, who dictates what's next.

But what happens after *that* kind of sex? The life changing, mind-blowing, nothing before this compares...

I'm driving home sore—can barely walk sore, and my core is still throbbing from riding him. I can't say what came over me in his arms, under him, on top of him, in the shower and even on the tiled bathroom floor, but it was a thirst impossible to quench.

The only uncomfortable moment of that night was waking up and getting dressed because I knew it had to end. The question is... what happens now?

I've got a Christmas festival to pull off and I don't exactly live here. What about after Christmas?

Maybe nothing.

Maybe nothing happens now, and I need to be a sane person and calm down. I need to take a moment to consider that although this may have been the greatest sex of my life, it could be the norm for Kourt.

He could simply be that great at it.

I also need to take into consideration the sheer amount of condoms that bachelor had, and all the places he had them stuffed and stored around his home for convenience. I would never safe sex-shame him, if that's even a thing, but it does let one know that he is—*active?*

Again, all of this could be the norm for him, and that doesn't make him a bad guy, or even an Archer. It would just mean it all felt a little different to him than it did for me.

My brows pinch together and my stomach sinks, but then it flips when I see his face above mine and feel his arms around me, replaying last night.

It scares me how much I trust Kourt. His eyes on my body giving away how much I turn him on. His hands on my skin the way no other has ever touched me... and what it does to me.

That's just it. I don't trust *myself* with Kourt. I'm not myself with him. I'm better. I have never responded to anyone this way.

My tape deck clicks as I turn up the road leading toward my street.

Oh, now you come alive. I'd just like to see you try it.

Soft music bellows its way into my Beetle as familiar strings pick up to a melody I recognize from my dream—No. It's from last night—*I'm Dreaming of a White Christmas* plays, and my heart beats like an arrhythmia in my stomach and through my head.

Not today mixtape.

I press every old button until the thing stops.

Helen. I need Helen.

Helen suspected a date, us being attracted and getting together, but this? Did she expect *this*?

Maybe Josie left instructions on what her great niece should do, should she stumble into the arms of Blitzen's acclaimed basketball coach and not want to leave them. All the while the holiday mix-tape in her vintage Bug seconds that emotion.

Helen takes a sip of her cold brew with her ungloved hand. The other black velvet glove is on the counter next to her keys. She's been pacing in my kitchen for the last twenty minutes and was parked in the driveway when I arrived.

"Helen?"

"Erika, I've learned not to jump to conclusions with you and my best friend. Obviously, after that display at last night's game, and with you appearing this morning in your sweater dress of shame, it's safe to assume that you did not sleep at home or Ellis' last night. Am I correct in assuming you and Kourt—"

"Like rabbits."

"Oh. My. God. This is worse than I thought."

"Much worse. I'm so sore, I can't stand up straight. He's so—"

"Don't. Stop. Uh-uh. No more." Helen throws her arms up in warning.

"I mean Archer used to say sex was just the combined experiences of two people trying to one up each other. Showing off what they learned from previous partners, as if that was the prerequisite to being a contender in bed."

"Wait. Was it not that?" Helen feigns confusion.

"You know, I have a friend you should meet." Now I'm the one pacing the kitchen.

"I'm kidding." Helen half-smiles. "Continue."

"And no. It wasn't like that with Kourt. I get that I don't have as much experience as Archer, and probably not as much as Kourt. But... he is the experience. It's all-consuming with him. My mind doesn't wander to what my body looks like in that position, or where to put my hands. It's just happening all at once and real from a million tiny sensations that burst—" I pause to look up at Helen who's now sitting on a bar stool with her elbows on the counter and her fists under her chin. She's chewed the top of her cold brew straw to pieces.

"Sorry. Too much?"

"Yes. Absolutely, but I'm used to your Great Aunt Josie."

"Ahh! Helen!"

"Gotcha. Now we both have a bad taste in our mouths." She hops off the stool and walks over to me. "Look. I just wanted validation that my hunch was correct. However, you seem very upset, and I must say, I'm not clear on what exactly the problem is."

"It could be me, Helen. I've had so little experience with great sex, and I've *never* had the physical and the emotional match up like this. It could be that it was the ultimate experience for me, and one of a number of experiences for your best friend."

"Are you trying to suggest that Kourt is good in bed and has this experience every time, regardless of who he's with?"

"Well... yeah, maybe."

"Okay, Erika. At risk of sounding jaded, or as if I have never experienced this incredible sex you speak of with anyone—it has been a while, mind you… since it was *that* good—but I say this to inform you, it's not like that all the time. At least not for the people who haven't gotten it right or landed on Mr. Right."

"Really?"

"Yes. Really."

"What about the condoms?"

"Oh, God! Tell me you used one."

"Well, more than one. Never mind. My point is, there are many at his house. A seemingly endless supply in—"

"In every corner of every drawer of every room?"

"Yes!"

"Darling." Helen sits me down on the stool she rose from. "Let me explain something to you about Kourt, and maybe men or bachelors in general. Especially his kind of a bachelor…"

"What's his kind?"

"Umm. Tall, handsome, hot body, basketball coach who can still play and works out, kind at heart under his cocky jackass-ery… Those elements alone make a single man a catch in most cases. In a small town where the population of women by far surpass that of men, it makes him a damn good catch. Add the fact that his wife died making him the youngest widower Blitzen has seen in three decades, and a reputation for being the un-gettable get—that makes him *the* catch. Not just in Blitzen, sweetheart. Women spanning at least five surrounding counties believe they are the one who can fix this man. I have friends that have come to visit from the city who—"

"Okay. I got it. So I am right about the condoms."

"No. The condoms are not to sleep with said women across Blitzen, five counties, and the greater Tri-state area. They are more control than protection. Yes... they literally serve as protection, such as in your case last night. But, for him as the most sought-after bachelor for miles, they represent control."

"I see. He's sending them a message, loud and clear," I interject. My voice sounds like Eeyore from Winnie the Pooh.

"Women have thrown themselves at him for the last three years. I watched a preacher's wife serve up her daughter at the funeral. He's like catnip in Blitzen. It's flattering as can be, but it also gets old super-fast. These women make it easy for Kourt to hide behind a no relationship rule or—"

"He has a no relationship rule?"

"Damn it. No. Not really, he doesn't. He does for them. For the ones he doesn't want. Some of them are suffocating. The condoms in every corner are his barrier in a different kind of way. He's letting them know he's not letting anyone, or anything, slip past him. I'm not telling you this so you think he's a bad guy. The takeaway is that he's a good one. And I really shouldn't be telling you anything. This is between you two. You have to know though, that he's never spent this much time with anyone—ever, Erika." Helen grabs her glove and keys and heads to the door. "Just don't break his heart. Life already did that once."

"Me?" *As if I'm the one with that power.*

Her cell pings.

"Duty calls."

THIRTY-ONE

Face to FaceTime

"We could have met for lunch. I've never known you to drive all the way home on your break." Helen sits on my couch fumbling through her work email searching for an urgent attachment while I shave.

"I thought I had a change of clothes at work, but I didn't, so I came home to shower."

"You didn't shower before work this morning? Dirty."

"I was in a hurry."

"Oh, I'm sure you were dribbling down to the last quarter if not overtime."

"Why? What'd she say?" I peek my head around the corner so I can see Helen.

"Good God, Kourt. Who owns this many blankets?"

"It gets colder this high up on the mountain." I towel my face and charge into the living room.

"Don't you have a heater?"

"I like blankets." My brow hikes as Helen looks up from her phone, clocking the fireplace and two pillows on the living room floor.

"Gross. Am I in it? Am I sitting in the sex den?" She jumps up and walks toward the window away from the living room.

"Oof! Not that chair! I wouldn't!" I stop her with an over-the-top hand gesture and a coy smile.

"You're disgusting. You have a bedroom."

My mind wanders to my bedroom and all I see is Erika in it. I spin from Helen and continue picking up blankets before I have to explain a hard on like we're back in junior high.

"Are you going to spill, or..."

"You were right. I'm sorry I'm a dick and fought you on it."

"I'd ask you to say it again, but it was almost painful to hear. And right about what exactly?"

I toss a couch pillow into its rightful spot and tilt my head, giving her a death glare.

"You can say her name you know. I'm sure you said it plenty last night."

I charge over to Helen with a throw pillow to beat her with.

"Okay, okay, okay. Uncle. God you're your giddy. I mean, I knew it had been a minute, but it hasn't been that long since you got laid."

I've never been laid like that.

"So what's going on?"

"Helen. It's insatiable. I can't get enough. I fucking *want* her. Like lose my mind level and I don't know how we kept it at bay so long and now it scares the hell out of me."

Helen puts her phone down and begins pacing the length of the window. "Okay. Woah. Woah. Just you two. Woah."

"You two? What did she say?"

"Again. Woah. Normally when two people get together to have sex who aren't sixteen, they wait. Wait for the other shoe to drop. Will the person call or text, does he live with his mother... you know. But this, I get that it's different—"

"You have no idea."

"Well tell me, Kourt. You got me up here on your mountain in the middle of a workday. Shoot."

I extend my hand leading her to sit at my kitchen island, and I run my fingers through my hair trying to find the words. "You know those incredibly happy in love people, who say things like, 'it's different when you find the one—you just know.' They make it seem like they know some secret and have a better life than the rest of us because *they* found *the one* or *their person*."

"Yeah..."

"Helen. I don't think even they have experienced what I have."

"Oh. Shit."

I shake my head and drop it into my hands. Helen pats my back and says it again, "Shit."

The look in Helen's eyes when she waves goodbye is the same knowing look she had at the funeral three years ago. She knew I had shut down that day, and would blame myself, just like she knows today I have no clue what I'm doing. But if it is serious enough for me to tell her—it's real and I've got it bad. Helen reads me like an open book no matter how closed off I get.

Did I jump the gun sharing that with her? No. She would've known the next time she saw Erika and me together. I have to be honest with my best friend because I might fucking need her.

I took a break last night from the holiday festivities and my personal pursuit. Not to be standoffish at all—but to rest. I figured her body needed it and so did mine. Christmas will be here before we all know it, and Erika has a lot on her plate. Helen said she and Georgia were dragging her to a committee that offered to volunteer, and then it was the trial night of the ice rink, to determine who and how to man the station.

It was a full night that didn't require my services.

Yeah, about that...

After my reveal to Helen, I want to be careful. I feel the need to make it clear to both of us. It's not just the sex for me. It's *her.*

Good luck with that. I can't think of her without wanting to touch her.

Erika and I hadn't really done the whole text thing yet, and I didn't call last night, again, to respect her time. Fuck if this isn't the opposite of every other situation I've been in. Forget three days before calling after a first date. I would leave those women stewing for three weeks with just a one word text response or two, before I finally called and asked them out again. Dick.

Now I'm the one stewing, hoping I didn't offend her or do something wrong by not calling or texting or showing up after the night we had together. When I pull up to town square after work, it's only around four, but the courthouse Christmas decorations are fully lit, and there are cars everywhere. June was right about the parking.

The poinsettia tree looks insane beside the ice rink. It's a tour de force that would rival the entrance to a five-star luxury hotel at Christmas. Erika has it lit from the bottom around the entire base.

"Hey Coach." A student calls from a small crowd of workers, and I wave back, nodding and mouthing hello to all who greet me as I get closer to the vendors.

"Thank you again, it's perfect." The voice that strains my dick against my zipper calls out to someone a few feet away. The young couple beside me waves goodbye to Erika, and her eyes shift to meet mine. We stay locked on each other for a moment.

My heart stalls. Then a smile raises her cheeks, and she takes a step toward me. I close the gap between us in four quick strides, then lift her into my arms.

Fuck it. I don't care what these assholes I love think. I only care what she thinks. And she's not mad at me, the way Quinn would've been for not calling. She respects the night we had and the night we needed apart.

Her face says it all. "Glad you could join us McShotty. Did you see June's tree?" She's smiling so brightly I want to take her right now. Happiness. It's contagious.

"It's the first thing I noticed. Hey, I have someone to introduce you to. Have all your vendors shown up?"

"Yes, but I haven't made it around to greet all of them yet. I was headed that way now."

"Good. I'll go with you, because one of them is my doing."

"I see. I'm intrigued. I have something to show you too."

"Should I be intrigued?"

"Regardless, I think you might have to put me down first." She clears her throat and smiles, dropping her eyes to the side of us to indicate we've drawn a crowd. I look around at half my town starring at us and instead of putting her down... "Ladies and gentlemen, Miss Erika Amherst." This time I spin her around before I let her go.

She laughs a wicked laugh. "Nice one. Way to play that one off. Subtle, yet effective."

"Anyone who doesn't see the effect we have is blind. Come with me." I reach my hand out for hers and take her to one of the booths setting up. "I want to introduce you to some very special people. They're the fruit cake booth I got you. They're famous around Kentucky and Tennessee, and I got them to agree to set up every night through Christmas."

Erika pauses her steps as she stares up at the massive banner boasting Kentucky Bourbon Fruitcake. "Wait. I thought we were done with the jokes and pranks since we…"

"You and I will never be done with that, not until I annihilate you in the sport."

"It doesn't involve a basketball, so I wouldn't get my hopes up—"

"And… this is not a joke nor a prank, only the very best cake you will ever put in your mouth. They could sell enough of these alone for our small commission to pay for the fire truck."

"Let me guess, they're not that great, because no fruit cake is, but she's some lovely old woman who saves babies, or you saved her cat from being stuck up a tree."

"Savage. You really don't like fruit cake."

"No one from this century does."

"You're wrong. The woman's wretched, she's a horrible person, and a ruthless negotiator. It's just incredible cake."

THIRTY-TWO

Fruit Cake Regifted

We arrive at the booth and the most angelic, kind older woman looks up at me. She and her staff unloading boxes of holiday-wrapped fruitcake are wearing Blitzen Volunteer Fire Department sweatshirts with the Famous Kentucky Bourbon Fruitcake logo stamped below it.

"Gotcha." Kourt whispers beside me.

My heart melts.

This is the kind of branding and advertising I'd do. I can't help but wonder if the fruit cake owner thought of that or Kourt did.

She looks as exhausted as any small business owner, but her eyes light up when she sees Kourt, and everything about her suggests she's honored to be at our Blitzen Old Fashioned Christmas.

"Erika Amherst, I presume?" The fruitcake lady extends her hand to me. "I'm Jan Edwards, and I know your Great Aunt Josephine. She's a huge fan of my fruitcake. Sends them across the US and internationally. Kourt might tell you, she kept me in business my first few years."

"It's incredible to meet you. I had no idea. There's so much of Blitzen I'm learning and discovering every day. I can't believe I didn't know about you." I glance around her tables at all the beautifully wrapped fruitcake and feel Kourt's warm hand on my back.

"Erika, Jan just got a contract for three major stores in Chicago, and a specialty chain in Nashville. She's been too busy to be seen around these parts." Kourt winks at Jan and she tosses her hand at him to hush. I'm realizing, as I see the massive logo on the industrial-size truck that her people are unloading from—she's much bigger than I think.

"Kourt told me about all you'd done here for Blitzen, and about you." Her eyes dip between us, and my pulse ignites.

Jesus, Mary, and Joseph. Standing next to the guy, I feel like I'm wearing the sex we had. Like people can see it or smell it on us. Butterflies sway in my lower belly, and I try not to smile too big or look caught.

"And that's what brings us here. Would you like to taste the fruitcake?"

How could I not after that? Ugh. I prepare for a mouth full of dry crumbs, chunky nuts, and scary, chewy, candied fruit as one of Jan's workers passes her a sample tray. Glutton for punishment, I dive in.

I stand corrected. It's—incredible.

"Oh, my God. That just gave me a better orgasm than you did that night."

Kourt kicks my shoe.

"What was that dear?"

"She said, 'It's so good, if she keeps eating this, her pants will get tight.'"

"Gotcha." I whisper to Kourt with my mouth full of *the* best cake I ever tasted.

The air feels and smells like Christmas and everyone in Blitzen is here, either working or walking around with their kids, pointing and smiling and taking holiday photos. Although I'm nervous about pulling this off for the masses... in these days leading up to Christmas, I can't help but feel I already have, especially as Kourt and I walk side by side through the brightly lit town square. Hot chocolate stands adorn every corner. They're smoking turkeys behind the ice rink, and it makes my stomach growl in the best way.

There's a crowd now where Kourt and I just left. They're all in line to get to the vendors, and a separate line waits outside the ice rink. It's really happening and walking beside Kourt, I feel the nostalgia of that place from when I was a kid. I won't ever have to search for it again. We just created it. It's all here in Blitzen.

"Erika." Kourt's voice is low, and it vibrates inside me. "This is magic. I knew you could do it, I just didn't know it would feel like this. You've pivoted an entire town on its axis, and I'm blown away." He turns to me, taking my hand in his as we walk through all the Christmas we helped make.

"Don't be blown away yet, we still have Walter's end coming up." A light chuckle resounds between us.

"The tree farm was packed last night, I heard."

"You heard right."

"I do owe you thanks, all of Blitzen does."

"You don't owe me anything, Kourt. You made sure this came true for me, not just the firetruck."

"I owe you more than you think, Erika." Kourt stops in front of me. His face is serious as he trails his fingers through mine. My body shivers at his touch and I realize my nerves aren't as much over the festival, Christmas in Blitzen, or my job and life back in Chicago. They're over him. It's been *him* this entire time. All of it. He has the ability to crush me in this very moment, and that is not what I had in mind when I signed up for a small-town Christmas via one eccentric great aunt.

"Kourt."

"I don't know what we're doing or where this'll go. This—you and me, Erika. This *feels*—" Kourt clears his throat and shakes his head, and I can't move or speak. I'm frozen. "You're leaving before long... aren't you?" He says it casually... forgiving.

Our gazes join for a long beat, and I can barely breathe.

"*Are* you leaving?" Now it's earnest. His honey green eyes sear the question through to my sole.

"Yes... I think." I look down and away from him. *Fuck. I don't know.*

"You think?"

"I mean, I wasn't fired, but they told me to take a leave during Christmas." My gaze lifts to meet his. He hasn't looked away from me. "I guess I had originally planned to go back before the New Year, dependent on..."

"Dependent on what?"

"Look, I didn't get fired, but my job's not certain."

"How do you mean?" His eyes chase my facial expressions and I've never seen him so invested. It makes me tremble down to my core, and I just want him to hold me. I just want to be back in front of that fireplace.

"As you would say, Kourt, I missed my shot." I'm so embarrassed. I haven't talked about this in depth with anyone but Archer, and not since I left, really.

"What does that mean?" He's voice is adamant. He's never asked me so many questions.

"It means, I went for a three-pointer and missed the whole damned backboard."

"Did you just try to basketball 'splain for me?" He looks away for a second and comes back with a tilted smile on his face.

Relief floods through my body like a warm river. He's smiling. We can talk about this, and I'm not under the gun the way I would be with the executives at the firm, and he's not crushing my heart. He's asking what I plan to do with it.

"I tried," I say with confidence. He squeezes my hand.

"Tell me about it. What happened?"

We start walking again. "It was a big pitch for a huge account—and when I got there, this snarky assistant had misspelled my name. *Erica with a C.* Then, the three main executives stood and one exited leaving only two in the room for the pitch. Three is my number. You know, odd numbers and all. Or maybe you don't. It's so stupid, Kourt, the way I think. I'm not far off from Aunt Josie over this stuff. And... I don't know... somehow it threw me. I let it. Why? I don't know. I'm an adult, and I'm fucking good at my job. But my pitch bit it... big time."

"Look at me, Erika." He forces my eyes to his.

"Nobody hits a hundred percent. You miss a shot—you can't be afraid to take another. If you are, you might as well turn in your uniform. You're done. If your bosses are worth a damn, they know that, too."

Since arriving in Blitzen, I've wondered if that's not the problem. Maybe they're not worth it.

"Sounds like you need to get back in that pitch room."

"Kourt—I—"

Music explodes behind us, as an alarm goes off on my phone. Right. The band.

"Is that a band?" He perks up—half changing the subject, and half curious. I'm still holding his hand, and he may not know it, but I refuse to let it go.

"Yeah. It's a cover band that volunteered to do three nights a week between carolers." I try to squash the pain in my voice and the tears threatening my eyes as the drums kick up, a solo trumpeter blows the intro and the lead singer belts, "It's the Most Wonderful Time of the Year."

We both smile as we walk past the crowd gathering to watch the cover band play. The song is so spirited one can't help but get happy, even though I'm not sure what was just determined about my fate with Kourt. The memory of my mixtape clicking on as I drove here today catches up with me and I snicker.

"What?"

"Nothing. Just. This song was playing in the car on my way here."

"Maybe because it is..." Kourt offers.

"What? The most wonderful time of the year?" I smile up at him, and I can't help but feel that because of him, it truly is.

"Didn't you have something to show me?"

"Yes. It's good news and bad news, but also a conundrum?"

"God knows we all love a good conundrum, especially at Christmas. Lead the way."

I punch his side laughing uncontrollably. If I stop, I might cry. *We're okay, right?*

It's okay that I don't know the answer. He doesn't have it either, yet. But he's still here, with me and willing to walk by my side. That's something new to me. In most cases, anything that can be a deal breaker... usually is.

Kourt stares at the large, empty sleigh, baffled. "Did somebody steal all the stuff?"

"No. Not at all. It worked, silly. That's the sad part. I guess a toy drive was needed as much as a food drive. Less than a quarter of the people with children on the food bank list have shown up and we're already out of toys."

"God. I didn't realize how much of Blitzen is living paycheck to paycheck. And what about the ones who don't get one at all."

"Yeah, well some of them have actually been here helping, I heard."

"You're kidding? Who?"

"I didn't ask. I thought it crucial to be discreet and not embarrass anyone. If people we gave to give back to the community or vice versa... that's what we're here for right?"

Kourt stares at the empty sleigh, deep in thought.

"It's also why what you did is so important. The food is the essential part. You did that. This is just figuring out how to make some young faces smile once their bellies are full."

Kourt grabs my shoulders and pulls me to him. He hugs me so tight I wish I could stay there all night. The smell of winter is on his coat collar, and his woodsy aftershave seeps off his neck as I drink his scent in.

He pulls away from me and forces a smile. "So, we just need more toys."

"Yes, but Fisher's gave all they can give. Blitzen donated what they could, and all other organizations are strapped with any proceeds or efforts going to the fire truck. It's not like we can just go buy more toys, not that many, anyway. Right now, June's having someone pull down the large decorative present boxes we didn't use. They're going to fill the sleigh with those for decoration, and when the kids come by to retrieve their toy, they'll get a pass for the ice rink and free skates rental. That's the best I could come up with for now."

"That's great. That's something."

"Well, they were supposed to get to skate for free, regardless."

"What about that group you and Helen went to with Georgia?"

"It's a ladies' quilting group. I mean, there are a lot of them, and they want to be a part of it, but—"

"They just want a booth to sell their quilts." Kourt's voice dips in disappointment for me.

"Pretty much. I did mention that we were running low on toys to see if we got a bite."

"Wait, don't they make twin size quilts for kid's beds? I know that's not an awesome toy and it's old fashioned, but—"

"This is an old-fashioned Christmas festival, and it's freaking cold in Blitzen. Who wouldn't want a new quilt for a bed spread to match their room, or have as their own Christmas throw for movie watching?"

"We made good use out of all my quilts and blankets—"

"Take it easy. This is for kids."

Kourt smiles deliciously then comes back to the topic at hand. "I'm just saying. Not a bad gift. But don't get ahead of yourself.

They won't have time to quilt them. There's no way, and we need that sleigh full, from now until Christmas."

"Are you kidding me? These ladies are hard core-quilters, with their own machines, and everything. You're right, they can't make a slew of twin size quilts overnight, but odds are if we ask, they've got plenty already made if they're willing to donate them. And what was that back there, McShotty... *'we need that sleigh full, from now until Christmas.'* Canned good Kourt is kind of hot when he takes a stance."

He leans down and bites my shoulder through my coat, and it doesn't matter that it's playful, my mind floods to when he did it in front of his fireplace, and heat pulls in my center.

A truck I don't recognize pulls up behind us, then turns and backs its tailgate up toward the empty sleigh. Bob slides out of the driver's seat and opens the tailgate.

"Bob?" Kourt walks up to greet him.

"Kourt, Erika. Good to see ya. Georgia said you all were running low on toys for the drive. Said you were about to run out."

"Actually, we did run out." I smile at Bob confirming.

"Well, I'm not sure these'll be of any use to you. I know they're not the trendy toys kids want, or what Fisher's donated. I don't have much of that in my store. Georgia convinced me to order these sort of hardware-themed toys years ago. The idea of having the kid version of what mom and dad were shopping for. Anyway, most of 'em never left the box, and they've been in the back collecting dust. I brought all of them I could find."

I move to the truck bed to peek at the few already-opened boxes. There are Radio Flyer Red wagons, little pink tool boxes and—

"No way!" Kourt pulls a long box off the truck. "Official vintage, Daisy Red Ryder BB guns still in the box? These are collector's additions, Bob."

Kourt is digging through boxes like a kid himself.

"The right kid might know it and want that. Anyway, Erika, I know the red wagons and pink tool boxes aren't remote control cars or Barbies, but if you need something to fill the-sleigh—"

"All this and a few of those quilts for kids and you've got a themed sleigh to fit your Old-Fashioned Christmas." Kourt smiles at me, and then at Bob. He's still marveling over a Red Rider BB gun I'm sure he'd like to possess himself.

I can't squash it. This is the third time in my Blitzen experience that this man has overwhelmed me. I race to Bob and throw my arms around his neck. Here goes the inappropriate hug again. That strange emotional connection I probably shouldn't broadcast in front of his former son-in-law, but I just can't help feeling a kinship toward Bob. This time Bob hugs me back tightly and there's a tear in his eye.

It's December, there is Christmas all around us, and the moment couldn't be more sentimental, or Christmas movie curated, until I pull away from Bob and see Kourt's face. It's not a bad face, just a face that noticed.

THIRTY-THREE

No Bacon No Eggs

As I walk Erika back to her Beetle, I can't help but think of the puzzle pieces the night has thrown at us. The ones that fit more perfect than I could imagine, and the few that don't seem like they belong in this box. She's parked way down from the events to give more parking to visitors, I'm sure. She thinks of everything.

Expectant blue eyes look up at me when her Beetle comes into view. *I know, sweetheart. I feel it too. The night is coming to an end.*

There is an amount of intimacy with her I can't say I've ever felt before. And the most terrifying part is, it's not just when we're fucking.

I knew when I met her, there was something about her.

I was immediately attracted, but spend any amount of time with her... if I'm honest, I knew by that damn meeting I was a goner. There was something different about her, and something different about the way she made me feel. The way she makes me care, in general. Not just about her, but about the things around me that used to be important to me. I'm seeing those things again in full color.

That doesn't mean it's right, though. For her, I mean. Blitzen's not her town. She's got so much unresolved back in Chicago. And I think she needs to resolve it, so she knows how valuable she is.

Then there's Blitzen.

I'm the one that chose to live in my hometown, in the town where tragedy struck and took something from me. My best friend is already putting herself out to be here for me, whether we both choose to admit it or not.

I could never ask that of anyone else.

Tonight, even after the talk we had that put some things out in the open, it didn't deter me. I wanted to follow her to the moon through a small-town fucking Christmas festival.

Then Bob. *Fuck.* Bob and Georgia. How much of a good sport can you ask two people to be? They embraced her the same as the town did, but not without cost. I can't imagine how it feels for them to watch us together and see a woman standing in their daughter's place. It's not like that at all, but that must be how it feels to them.

Only, Erika throws salt, sugar, then ignites the flame with alcohol as she runs up and hugs him. I'm watching Bob's emotional face, and all I can think is how much I want my dick in this woman.

How fucking selfish can I be?

I keep telling myself that Bob and Georgia took to Erika for who she is and no other reason, that even though it stings, she's of value to them as a person. Old ghosts don't fly around that. I know that's the truth, but it's hard not to have that haunting feeling that they're only embracing her, to be unselfish for me.

They want me to be happy as much as my own parents do. That's just something I could never choose at someone else's expense.

"Thank you for the fruitcake vendor, and the toy drive. Pretty eventful night."

"Thanks for the live band." We both force a laugh as my hand lands on top of hers, reaching for the driver's side door. We stay like that for a long moment. Erika standing inside her door holding onto it. Me standing outside it looking down at her with my hand covering hers. It's a position we both don't want to be in, nor do we have the willpower to leave.

I don't know how to do this—how to let something rest or breathe, when you want so badly to possess it in all the right ways.

I've never been in this position before, and I think I have to let her decide a few things for herself.

Erika's mouth parts as if she's about to say something. I wait, my eyes flickering to her plump pink lips, desperate to feel them, but she doesn't move them to speak. My eyes float back to hers and something changes in those baby blues. A determined streak I witnessed so many times on our truck rides. She shoots me a final glare, then slides in the car as quickly as she can, and shuts the door.

I watch in shock as she takes a deep breath, then musters a casual wave as if that's who we are now or that's what we've resorted to.

"Fuck." I hit the car as she drives off.

Did we just have our first mini-fight by default, or worse, did I take sex off the table entirely by trying to show her this was more, and now we both go home with nothing?

Nice work, McShotty.

THIRTY-FOUR

Breaking and Entering

"Woah." Archer looks at me startled as I come into view of my laptop. I guess I look that upset.

"What are you... uh... wear—well, it's colder in Kentucky. Hmm... you aren't dressed yet?"

"Dressed yet? Archer I've had a rough night and I'm going to go to bed right after this. I just changed into pajamas."

"That's not. No pajamas."

I look down at my vintage silk shorts that are very short, but he can't really see that far down. Oh. I guess Josie's matching camisole top is—*Oh*. Much more revealing than I thought.

"Get over it. You've seen your fair share of all this."

"Not all of yours."

"Well, you've never looked before, so…"

"There's definitely something different now."

"What?"

"Nothing. Listen, we have to talk about work. Not how much you appreciate my ice rink, not the vendor that didn't show up or the mean poinsettia lady that turned out to be your new best friend, or this crush you have on the football or basketball coach, but the Harmon case."

"Oh, Arch. I'm in hell."

"What? No, I thought you were in a Christmas snow globe. And since all is snowy and perfect there, could you please focus on work? I have something really important to tell you."

There's a loud pounding at the front door.

"Hang on. Someone's at the door."

"This late? What time is it?" Archer's voice fades behind me as I race to the front door.

My heart is pounding out of my chest with adrenaline that could move a mountain.

I know it's not Helen. She would've used her key.

I swing the door open and raise my eyes to Kourt's. He's standing in front of me in a sweatshirt with bacon in one hand and a carton of eggs in the other. His hair is a mess, and he doesn't even have a coat on.

"I promised you bacon and eggs, Erika."

I fly into his arms with my legs wrapping around him, my arms trapping his neck, and I let him figure out the bacon and eggs in his hands as I slam the door closed behind us and kiss him mercilessly. He drops the bacon and eggs on the entry table and turns my back to the door.

We groan into each other's mouths, and he's already hard against me. My heart is about to beat out of its cage. We're breathing so hard together as I pull back from him.

"Don't. Do. That. To. Me. Again," I yell.

"Never." He says into my neck as he lifts his eyes to mine. "Never again."

I jump down from his arms and storm into the living room, then back up to him. "I got in my car three times to go to you, but then I knew you'd be so mad if I drove that far up the mountain, and you—"

Kourt's mouth hits mine. He's on his knees on the floor in front of me, pulling me down and into him. His tongue chases mine, and I can feel how wet I am already, my silk shorts grinding against his cock.

I can't even catch my breath long enough to realize I'm wet for him and crying at the same time.

I'm so mad at him. "You can't just do that to me. If you change your mind or you don't want—"

"Change my mind? Are you fucking crazy?"

Kourt presses my entire upper body against his, and my legs close tightly around him. His chest is moving up and down as fast as mine is as he holds me tight, trying to calm us on Aunt Josie's living room floor.

"You either want me all the way or you don't want me at all. There's nothing in between when it comes to *this*." I cry out, sniffling my declaration into his ear.

"Trust me Erika with a K, there is nothing in between where you are concerned."

"Why did you let me drive away?"

"Because I'm a fucking idiot. I thought I was giving you space to decide, or softening my own blow when you leave—" With that word, his entire body stiffens, and he holds the back of my head and neck for me to look at him.

"Go anywhere you fucking want Erika—" Kourt raises his voice. "Go back to work at your firm in Chicago, go to New York or LA or back to the suburbs, just don't you ever fucking leave me."

I sink into him, my body going limp in his arms from relief. I don't know what brazen raw confidence has ignited in me, but I have no problem telling this man exactly what I want.

"Erika," he whispers softly in my ear, and I turn my face to him.

"Kourt." I say it firmly like a dare, and he smiles the biggest, devious smile known to man as I feel him swell beneath me.

The early morning sun pierces into Josie's kitchen as Kourt stands shirtless above a pan of sizzling bacon. I'm in his volunteer fire department sweatshirt he wore over here, and a pair of not-so-modest lace panties.

Trying not to sneeze from the pepper as I whisk the eggs, I reach across Kourt for the milk.

"I know what you're doing. You're determined to keep me from making good on my promise of breakfast." Kourt looks down at the lace that barely covers my ass.

"Says the man who declared his living room a clothing-free zone."

"I remember blankets being required. I do have a little tact."

"You're the one who ripped my vintage silk bottoms."

"I do love anything vintage. I'm sorry to see those go. I just had to get in there. Maybe one of those quilters can sew them back."

With the bacon sizzling, Kourt and I barely hear the door. Someone pounds again, or multiple people...

"Miss. Amherst? Open up!"

Kourt looks at me with wide eyes as the door pounds again and two cops plus the fire chief charge into Josie's living room. Wearing his sweatshirt, panties, and a spatula, I step behind a shirtless Kourt as the three men look back at the two of us, as shocked as we are.

Silence as the bacon crackles.

"Kourt, Erika?" The fire chief diverts his eyes.

"Chief, Danny, Travis?" Kourt holds my legs tight behind him.

"Ah, we got a call for a possible disturbance. A breaking and entering and assault was reported."

"Oh, my God, where? Do you guys need me? I didn't hear my phone."

"Ah, Kourt, the call came into the police station and dispatched to me for this address."

"Erika! Erika! Are they there? Are you okay?" My laptop screams from the coffee table, and I go to grab it on instinct until I feel Kourt's very large hand lock my bare thigh in place. *Right.*

"Just a second, Archer!" I scream toward the laptop.

"Who's Archer?" The cop with a name tag that says "Danny" asks.

"Travis, grab the sweatpants off the coffee table and the laptop, and don't fucking look in this kitchen," Kourt demands of his longtime friend.

"Ten four, Captain."

"He's not your captain when you're in that uniform," Danny barks with pointed eyes and a smirk.

"Or when I'm on a call or at the fire station and you're in your other uniform." Randy adds from his end.

"Yes, Chief," both Kourt and Travis answer in unison.

Travis tosses Kourt the sweatpants to hand me, and I slide them on behind him.

"Now, could somebody tell me what in blue blazes is going on here?"

Danny apparently has had enough. *Wait until they meet Archer.*

I smile at Travis as I slide the laptop from him and go to open my Zoom camera... only it's open—and not on mute.

"Erika! Thank God you're dressed and alive. I see they got you a sweatshirt."

"What are you talking about, Archer?"

"I saved your life. Last night... you went to answer the door, and you never came back to me. I almost dozed off, but then I heard loud dramatic talking, as if someone turned the TV up on a soap opera or late-night B movie. When I heard the first loud bang and your breathy cry, I realized what they had done. Someone got you to the door, broke in, turned the TV up so no one would hear your cries. But I heard them, Erika. Every last one of them, and I'm just so glad to see you alive and standing. Let me see your face, are you hurt? Is the perpetrator still there?"

Throats clear in unison in the background as Kourt steps into frame behind me.

"Let me guess, said perpetrator..." Archer looks up at Kourt. His jaw drops. "And this must be the basketball coach, I'm guessing by the height."

Archer's lips purse together, and he looks at me, fuming.

"Hello, Archer, I've heard a lot about you, buddy."

"You didn't get assaulted, Erika. You broke the cardinal rule and forgot to mute on what would appear to have been a very special occasion. I know. I sat through three rounds of it before I thought you died. So, there's that."

"You boys hungry?" I turn to see the fire chief behind us flipping the bacon.

Travis slides past Kourt and begins cracking more eggs in my bowl, and I let out a long sigh, as I zero in on my best friend with Kourt staring at him behind me.

"It's the least they can do. Where da' plates?" Danny, the police chief slides up to the bar and reaches for the silverware that Travis passes him.

"You don't have anything to say for yourself, Erika? I thought you were being murdered." My laptop reprimands me, and Kourt smiles into the frame, more entertained by Archer than I thought possible.

"Well, I absolutely was not being murdered." Kourt and I both smile into the camera. "If I had anything to say for myself, Archer, it would be, 'turnabout is fair play.'"

"Ohhh! No ma'am, I was never that—"

Kourt clears his throat into the camera, and Archer's jaw ticks.

"Whatever. If you had just listened to me last night instead of answering the door, you would know about the Harmon case, but don't mind me. Go on and have your Blitzen breakfast."

Kourt rises to step away, trying not to eavesdrop, but I catch him look at me on 'Harmon case.'

"They want you back, Erika. They made a mistake. I was tasked with groveling on their behalf."

"Then that's their second mistake, Arch. No one uses me or my best friend."

"Talk to me later, Erika. Don't let the dust settle. They're asking you back and talking promotions in the new year. Let it linger too long, and you know they're crooked enough to take your idea without you."

"Did you ever think we're better than working for people crooked enough to do that? You don't even need the money, Arch. What's your excuse?"

"Erika, wait!"

I shut the laptop and return to Kourt's side.

"Everything okay?" Kourt's hand on my back is soothing and the only comfort in the world I need at a time like this.

"I could ask you the same." I nod at Josie's kitchen, where two cops and the fire chief sit eating our bacon and eggs. My eyes drift to the empty plate with the grease-soaked, bacon crumbed paper towel the chief used to drain the meat that is no more, and I watch young Travis scoop the last helping of scrambled eggs.

I blink up at Kourt and he shrugs. "Guess bacon and eggs is a promise I haven't kept yet," he says, as he slides his hand down the sweatpants to cup my ass, unbeknown to anyone.

"I hold you to it, Kourt."

"Hey," he almost whispers in my ear. "I thought you said you and Archer never..."

"We did not. I was referring to a time he left his Zoom unmuted with one of his own lady friends."

"I'm not talking about that. I'm talking about the fact that he's in love with you."

"Kourt McClain."

Danny the cop winks at us from across the counter as he shoves the last bite of hickory smoked bacon in his mouth.

"All the grand gestures. The ice rink. Quote, 'saving your life.' You can't tell me the guy thought you were being assaulted."

"Kourt, Archer is a grand gesture. And that's as face value and insincere as me suggesting that of you and Helen." I try to keep my voice hushed while our guests are enthralled in a flattering conversation about Blitzen's Christmas festivities.

"Noted. But I didn't suggest you were a part of the equation. I said, *he's* in love with you."

THIRTY-FIVE

Winter Solstice

The winter solstice has finally arrived and so has Walter's big moment. The sun is low and setting beautifully, and the night has promised to be the longest one of the year. Walter set up a space for storytelling next to the feast offerings by the entrance of the cave.

Everything looks so surreal and ceremonious. I can hear the low prayers by the sweat lodge an allied tribe organized in the distance, to honor Walter and this occasion.

Every single official from the town meeting has offered their time and helped set up without me asking. The men came early and have stayed by Walter's side. My original idea of this magical night had me thinking I would be herding townsfolk up the mountain, begging them to participate.

They're here. All of Blitzen.

Tribes from surrounding counties who saw the ad in the Fisher's sales paper have joined us. Kourt and I brought Carol and G.W. Philipps up through the handicap ramp, or at least as far up as it goes up, and Georgia and Bob are bringing them home when they get too cold or tired.

I step back and look at the most beautiful mountain I've ever seen, surrounded by the most beautiful people. Judge Angelina Prichert catches my gaze and winks at me from where she ushers more people into the ceremony circle. She's wearing muted colors, to blend in, and no flashy hat or signature blazer tonight. Instead, I see an authentic Wampum Bear Necklace around her neck. June also came early. I should've known she and Walter go way back.

I peek over at Helen where I left her with her waitress friend, Dawnie from the dinner. They're watching Walter prepare the circle and I can't help the tears in my eyes. These are really good people. They're giving me more than I am them. It's overwhelming in the best possible way.

On contact, I sink into two arms wrapping tightly around me. I drink in Kourt's scent as I look up to meet his eyes.

"There you are. Hey... what's the matter?"

"Nothing. It's just—it's all so perfect. This is the best Christmas I've ever had."

"Come on now. It's not even Christmas yet. There's more to come."

"Even if it stops here, Kourt, I got way more than I hoped for."

Kourt turns me to him and pulls me close. "Hey, what's all this talk? The best is yet to come."

"Yeah, well, it's pretty great already."

Kourt doesn't scan the crowd or even hesitate. He drops his face to mine and coaxes my lips into a deep, reverent kiss that is so tender and sweet it makes my knees weak. I pull away first when my pulse is highjacked and I'm afraid I'm going to maul him in front of Walter's ceremony.

Kourt slams his tailgate shut when the last of the torches we had lighting the way down the steps for patrons are piled in. We wave at a smiling Walter as he drives away, and I can't help but feel as content as he looks.

"Come back up with me? I forgot something."

Kourt follows me dutifully, then begins looking around suspiciously as we hike back up the deserted mountain toward the cave. "Pretty dark to be headed back up here, don't you think?"

"I'm counting on it."

Kourt looks me over.

"Don't worry. I have a flashlight this time."

He freezes.

THIRTY-SIX

Caved

"**D**o you trust me?"

"In a cave? No."

Erika grabs my hand and runs us deep into the cave, with her industrial-sized flashlight lighting our way. The light stalls, illuminating the cave wall, and a solid, flat surface.

"Do you feel safe in this spot?" she asks, as if she's threatening to turn the flashlight off.

"Depends on what we'll be doing in said spot."

"That first night we were here—the way you left. You saved my life and ran away from me."

"You want a true confession?"

She nods.

"I think you know, if Walter hadn't shown when he did, I'm afraid of what I might've done—with your ass rubbing against my cock for so long."

She smiles. "I felt it."

"You'd have to have been paralyzed from the waist down *not* to have felt it. I was chicken. Saved by the fire call."

I pull her to me, and she pulls my coat off, then her own and begins laying them on the ground.

"Kourt, I was thinking we can finish what we started."

Her sweater goes next, then she lifts mine over my head. Erika clicks the flashlight off, and the world goes dark. Her hand presses to my chest and I breathe her in.

The smell and touch instantly magnify with no sight.

She rises up on her tip toes to reach me, and I grab and lift her, pulling her up to me before she can get there.

My mouth covering hers, as my tongue forces her to open for me in a kiss almost as furious as the one we shared on my bathroom floor. A whimper pulls from her lips and I all but growl into her tiny mouth when I feel her nipples peak against me.

"Erika," I pull her ear to my mouth, and nibble down to her neck then lick back up it.

"I don't have anything with me."

She sinks a little in my arms, just before she rises back up to meet my face.

"Oh... then I—"

Squeezing her tightly to me, my heart pounding at the warmth of her, I'm not sure what to say. I haven't slept with anyone without a condom since my marriage, but I can't bring that up. I say another truth, instead. "I get tested regularly and I'm clean."

"And I'm safe, and on the pill. I've only ever used protection with all partners. I've never... not used—I've been careful with everyone."

"Are you sure you want to do this then?"

Hot skin melts into mine and I feel her breath on my face moving to meet my ear. "I don't want to be careful with you Kourt. I want—you."

My mouth is back devouring hers, as I blindly guide us to where I remember the cave wall stands. Turning my body behind her, like I did that first night in the cave, I use the wall as leverage and slide us down.

She hits the floor and leans into my lap. Turning toward me she crawls up to my erection.

"What would you have done if Walter hadn't come that night?" she asks, moving closer to me. "Show me," she demands, in a whisper that meets my lips. Her tits resting on my chest and her stomach on my cock. My hands slide up her soft skin, tickling her ribcage as they move further to meet the lace of her bra.

Full tits burst at the seam of the under wire, and my large hands act on their impulse to release them.

Peeling the bra off her by practically bending the wire away from her body, my palms are met with hot, plush flesh and her erect nipples. I fucking roll them through my hands like putty as I groan into her cheek.

"*Hmm,*" her head drops to my neck as she mutters, "What would you let me do to you?"

Her hands move to unbutton my jeans, and I scoot up to adjust, allowing her to unzip and unleash my frighteningly hard cock. Erika rubs her thumb over my tip, tracing the pre-cum. Sliding to her knees, she perches above me and unzips her own jeans. My hands find her hips and slide them down her legs.

"But what about these?" She asks with a tempting smile I cannot see. "Would you have left them on me Kourt, or asked me to take them off?"

"Fuck." My finger traces below her waist, then down toward the center of the rim of her panties, as I guide my way to where I want to be. Hooking my finger into the crotch of her panties, I pull them down and slide a finger over her seam. "You're dripping wet."

"Show me," she whispers, still on her knees above me.

I sink a finger deep inside. Deep enough to make her moan so loud it echoes through the cave. Then I find her open mouth and press my wet finger to her tongue. My cock jerks at the breathy, almost inaudible sound she makes, and before I can stand it, I stick my finger back in her for a taste of my own.

"Come here," I demand.

My dick springs free as I pull my boxers and jeans down and reach to find hers where I left them rolled by her knees. "Take your panties off."

"Why?" Her voice is smokey and low. Quiet enough not to echo this time.

"You know why." In the pitch black, damp lace meets my hands as she gives them to me, and I almost spasm when she unexpectedly slides wet heat from her bare pussy up the length of me—pausing to leave her slit balancing on my tip.

"Is this what you wanted me to do to you that night?" She slides up a little, until I feel her tight entrance at the head of my pulsing cock. "Why?" she asks, as if unaffected.

"Erika," I say, my limbs heavy with lust and my mind soaring from the unknown. I can see nothing. I only feel her warm. Her tight, pussy hovering over my cock. She stays like that, positioned on my tip. Then I feel her fingers moving just above me and I can't see her face but in the silence of the cave—I hear her moan.

She trembles above me as her fingers rub her own clit, grazing the tip of my cock where she balances my cock next to her, like walking a tight rope. The feel of her hot, bare flesh touching mine in the freezing cave has me ready to spew uncontrollably.

"You're teasing me." My voice is like gravel. I can almost hear, feel or just sense her smiling as she works herself above me.

"You teased me that night." Her words come out breathy and there's nothing shy or vulnerable about them.

Fuck. She's touching herself for the first time in front of me and I can't see it. Oh, God, can I feel it, though. The silence of the cave adds to the torture when, in between the occasional drips in the background, I *hear* how wet she is for me. The slick wet sounds of her fingers touching everywhere I want to be, echo through my head. She's in complete control.

I am too, until I feel a gush of her arousal drip down my shaft, and I fucking lose my mind. My body takes over and I grab the little minx by her hips and push her down onto my cock.

A intense cry leaks through the cave as she screams out her next breath at being filled. This time, her voice echoes throughout the cave, and fuck if I don't get harder inside her at that sound. A sound I want her to make again.

Our echoes and the hard ground of the cave are forgotten as she catches her breath and begins to move with me inside her, and no barrier between us. Her hips roll into me slowly and I feel her back arch away from me as she pushes her body into mine with the new sensation of flesh on flesh.

We've gone from Christmas ornaments and sleigh rides to Winter Solstice—and the most intense fucking I've ever experienced.

"Why didn't you want me that night?" She slows her thrusts and drags her pussy back down my cock away from me. My hands find her hips. "I was scared. Not because I wanted you." My fingers separate and squeeze down to her ass cheeks. "I was scared of how much I needed you."

A ragged breath escapes her lips.

"And now?"

"I'm fucking terrified." My fingertips dig into her flesh and Erika slams back down onto my cock taking me as deep as she can and thrusting faster. Her arms find me and reach around my back, pressing her tightly to me while she fucks me senseless. Her body is shaking on top of mine, and I don't know how I've managed to go this long.

Her walls pulse as she cranes up to my ear. "Gotcha," she says, biting my ear tenderly and smiling into my neck as she continues to fuck my cock in the wild rhythm she ignited.

"Yes, Erika. You do." My dick twitches inside her, and her body quivers in my lap.

"Kourt!" she screams, echoing my name throughout the cave.

I can feel her throw her head back while her orgasm spasms around me, but I can't let her pull away from me. I grab the back of her head and neck and press her face into mine as tightly as our lower halves are fused together and, I come so hard inside her she gasps when she feels my release.

We stay here like this.

She's on top of me, straddling my lap, cradled into my chest and neck. I'm still inside her. And we breath together, listening to the silence of the cave, the occasional drip of water in the distance.

I'm unaware of the amount of time that passes before our once-steamy hot flesh turns clammy from the cold, and I feel her shiver in my arms. Only then do we wake from our stupor and attempt to pull away from what we just encountered together.

THIRTY-SEVEN

Your FATE or Mine

"I 'm nervous. You've never ridden with me before, I don't think." I flash a smile I can't control toward the very tall man sliding into my Beetle's passenger seat.

"Does getting hit by you count?"

Kourt motions out the window to where we parked his truck after driving in from the cave. "We can always get back in mine. The cab's still warm." He squirms to get comfortable while I fiddle with the heat to get her warmed up enough to pull out.

"Nope. I'm determined to see this one through. Hey, at least you can see if I've improved my stick shift skills."

"I can't speak for on the road, but the way you drive stick shift, especially in a cave, needs no improvement."

"Wow. That was—"

"True? Anyway, this is good. We can leave my truck suspiciously at town square overnight for once."

"Kourt! Oh my God. I never even thought of it that way. All this time... *All* of Blitzen?"

"Yup. Your car said it all. Guess they knew you were mine from the start."

Kourt looks around, fascinated, and fiddles with all the vintage bits in Josie's VW.

I, on the other hand, can't stop trembling inside from *'they knew you were mine from the start.'* I've actually been trembling since the cave. I meant it to be momentous, but I didn't know it would be historic, or apocalyptic—as in, there is no coming back from that kind of sex.

I've never been involved in any romantic relationship that didn't get stale or mundane by the third sexual encounter or so. I was beginning to think I was broken, or something was terribly wrong with me. Maybe Archer had me pegged wrong this entire time. Maybe I was more like the dude that got bored immediately after sleeping with someone.

Then there was Archer, separating himself from great sex and a potentially awesome match, just because he didn't want to get attached. His cynicism also led me to believe relationships end up that way. Eventually it fizzles out.

Now I know—nothing was wrong with me. I just hadn't found anyone good enough for me. I mean that as arrogant as it sounds.

There's something about knowing what you do to a person, and just how much you turn them on. It's a specificity far more powerful and sustainable than simply assuming someone loves and cares for you because you've been dating long enough for that to be the case.

I don't know what I did to get so lucky, but if actions truthfully speak louder than words, I already know all I need to know about how Kourt feels about me.

The tape deck clicks on, and I freeze on the steering wheel, waiting to see what will play before I drive off.

"Is that a cassette player?"

"Um hmm. You're going to get to hear my tape."

An intro of a piano chord plays, followed by a quick run of notes. I don't quite recognize it initially, but Kourt seems to. His eyes flash to mine and a half smile reaches his lips. The moment the first lyrics of that late seventies song by Kenny Loggins are sung, I recognize it immediately from my dream.

"Please celebrate me home," I mutter the main chorus.

Kourt dips his chin, then rises back up to meet my eyes. "You asked me once what my favorite Christmas song was, and I really do like most all of them, but if I had to choose—this would be my favorite. It's been my favorite since I was a kid and NBC did some "Home for the Holidays" campaign and played it before every commercial break." He smiles at the memory of it.

A tear stings my cheek, and I lift my hand to catch it.

"What is it?"

"Nothing. I just dreamed about this song, and now it's playing with you here in the car, and I guess, I do feel home." A stifled gulp leaves my throat and more tears fall.

"Erika," Kourt pushes loose hair behind my ears, and I try to laugh out of my tears.

"What did you say this tape was, again? A lot of people don't know or remember this song."

"It's my holiday mixtape. I got it at the flea market my first day in Blitzen. Funny enough—it was booth number three I bought it from."

I look up at Kourt to see if he picks up on that, not knowing if I should be reluctant to continue with my crazy talk. "And Josie's Bug happened to have a cassette deck. It felt kismet already. The first song it played was "It's beginning to Look a Lot like Christmas." It was playing when I hit you, and in the coffee shop you walked out of, and it sparked the idea for the Blitzen Old Fashioned Christmas."

Kourt's still smiling, but his eyebrows dent slightly in contemplation.

"It was a succession of songs after that. They all seemed to play at the right time, and they all seemed to lead me... well, to you. Even when I wasn't around the tape or driving in my Beetle. I think it was "Silver Bells" that played on my tape, then again that same night on the radio in your truck, when you and I drove through the courthouse lights and looked at the sleigh."

Kourt looks down and away for a moment, seemingly more perplexed as the music plays on.

"Was the booth you bought it from Hawkin's?"

"Yeah, I think so, Hawkin's Antiques. Anyway, apart from the music, you had that number three tattoo, and three is my number, and the whole Kourt with a K and Erika with a K thing—I can admit, Great Aunt Josie's eccentric, but even this got a little weird for me. I think the obvious signs scared me at first. But then so many more made me think it was my destiny to be here in Blitzen, and maybe my fate to bump into you. By the time you and I made it to your place, when track four—see, they all played out of order because the Beetle's tape deck has a mind of its own, or it's broken somehow, but when—"

"White Christmas. White Christmas is track four." Kourt's voice is low, bitter, and unrecognizable to me. The air in my Beetle stills and my heart plummets.

"Eject the tape, Erika."

His voice is like ice down my spine.

"My holiday mixtape?"

Kourt presses all the buttons frantically until the tape shoots out.

He stares at it, as if it's haunted, and slowly removes it from the cassette player. I watch him rub his thumb across the tape's label and the writing on it.

Chills course through my scalp and veins and I know something is terribly wrong.

"It must have been inside the tape recorder when I dropped that last box off to Mr. Hawthorn." Kourt says it almost to himself as he rubs his forehead.

"This isn't your tape Erika." He brings his eyes to meet mine. "It isn't your fate or your destiny. It's someone else's."

I can't breathe, and I don't know how I'm sitting upright. "Kourt, you're scaring me."

"This tape belonged to Angie. My wife. She made it for me when we were in college. We found a vintage shop that sold cassette players from the 80s. She took it back with her to school and made me a holiday tape of all my favorite classics and mailed it to my dorm. "Have Yourself A Merry Little Christmas" is on there. It was her favorite. That's why Bob got teary-eyed on you in the hardware store."

I swallow a gasp and try to breathe steadily, fighting the urge to vomit profuse apologies.

"She mailed it the first Christmas we were away from home and each other. When we were married, it was tradition for us to bust out that old tape player and the holiday mixtape to decorate the tree. That night, we had just gotten home and gotten the tree in the stand to decorate. It was unusually cold. The temperature just kept dropping. We were fighting."

I gasp as more tears stream down my face.

"We had been fighting a lot, over where to live. Blitzen suddenly wasn't enough for her. Maybe, it *was* me. Maybe I wasn't enough." His voice gets drier as he shrugs. "She got angry. Didn't want the tree or Christmas, just wanted out. That fucking tape I'd started when I set the tree up..."

His jaw clenches.

"It just kept playing... droning on and on in the background, like all was merry and bright. It felt like it was mocking us. Angie started yelling over it, then marched to the recorder, ejected it, and threw the tape at the empty tree. I just stood there. Depleted. She grabbed her coat and keys and slammed the door behind her. She was down the drive before I could stop her."

He blinks away the thought and shakes his head before facing me. "And the rest is a history you already know. So no, Erika, this tape is not your fate. It was mine."

The door shuts before I can take my next breath.

THIRTY-EIGHT

Side 2/Track 0

I don't recognize the address Helen texted me. It can't be her townhouse. Or maybe I just can't see straight with all the mascara staining my eyes.

I'm shaking so hard I can't press start on my navigator app. I just want to get there. I just want to be somewhere because I don't know what to do.

I have no memory of my drive toward this side of town into this strange neighborhood. I'm driving through a tear-stained grace of God or good fortune. Other than the street Blitzen Manor and Judge Prichard live on, I didn't know there were mansions in Blitzen.

The drive I'm prompted to turn into winds up to the largest mansion in the cul-de-sac, or is that still one house and it's own dead end?

This place is massive. It's a dark red brick mansion that looks to be at least three stories.

Parking my Bug, I race to the front entrance like a complete lunatic or some feral cat that just realized things might be better inside. My knock demands attention, and I don't care if I'm being rude. The door opens slowly, and I see a small white-haired woman who looks very much like Helen.

She's Korean and has Helen's trademark dainty build, delicate lips, and graceful chin. I'm so startled by the house and the stranger at the door who resembles Helen that I must have forgotten how crazy I look.

The older woman lets me in on instinct. She nods at me, smiling sympathetically, then looks me over, and pulls me further into the luxury home's living room.

A kitchen door slams, and I hear Helen yelling, "No, mother! I didn't forget. I said I'd handle it later." Helen takes a breath and appears in front of us.

She speaks several sentences in Korean to the woman who let me in, then I distinctively hear her say, *Kourt.* The woman turns to me and holds her arms out. She embraces me and squeezes me tightly.

"Erika, meet my grandmother. *Halmeoni,* this is Erika."

I hug her back with what little I have left in me, and she motions to Helen, pointing at my face. The older woman says something in Korean and walks to the kitchen.

"Sorry, she won't speak English to you, but she understands every word. She's going to cook you something, and she asked me to wipe your face for God's sake." Helen throws up her arm dismissively and rolls her eyes as she walks me to a sitting room.

"I'm so sorry I came to you like this. I didn't know where else to go or what to do. I thought you had a townhouse here and a place in Chicago."

"I do. Umm. My family just got back into town. They surprised me by coming home, here instead of the house in the city. They are, apparently, excited about a Blitzen Christmas."

"Awe." I begin crying inconsolably. "How come I don't know them yet?"

"Uh. That's my grandmother. She's Korean, and so is my dad. My mom's American, born and raised in Chicago, and please don't ask me anymore questions about the people making my holidays hell right now."

"Helen, are you rich?"

"Again, let's not waste time with conversations we can have at a later date. Let's start with why you have mascara streaming down your face and are at my family home that no one comes to but me or Kourt. And. I think I just got my answer."

"I'm horrible to intrude on you Helen. You belong to Kourt and maybe he needs you at a time like this, although I don't know what this is... I don't know anything anymore."

"Erika."

"The mixtape I bought at the flea market and guided my life by is Angie's."

"Oh, *shit.*"

"And to add insult to injury, I went on and on about how it was my fate or destiny to find the tape and meet Kourt. That each song was leading me to him like a sign."

Tears I didn't know I had left in me leak down my cheek. "I didn't know, Helen. I promise. How could I know that to him it was the worst possible reminder of that fatal night?"

"This is my fault Erika. Kourt called me on my way to the airport to get you. He mentioned he was going through old boxes and he was taking the last of Angie's stuff to Mr. Hawkins. That's what reminded me about the flea market. I remembered you loved Christmas, so I thought it was the perfect place to take you. How would I know that tape was in that box? Or that it would uncannily end up in your hands?"

"I don't think he knew it was in that box or inside the recorder either. Well... anyway, I guess I'm here because I don't know how to lose a love like this."

"Oh, my God. Did you say love..."

I look at Helen at the realization of what I just said, and I can't deny it.

"Shit." Helen gets up and paces around the room. "Now, wait a minute. The both of you. This is just a freak thing kind of hiccup. It's nobody's fault. Nobody did anything wrong to anybody—" Helen sits and grabs my hands. "I don't mean this callus Erika, but it's the same thing I told you when you found out about her... Angie's dead. This tape doesn't change that, nor does it change the fact that the tragedy happened three years ago. If you take away the tape, nothing has changed."

"Everything has changed. You should have seen his face."

"Oh, I've seen that face, alright."

"He'll never look at me the same way, and honestly... well, he left me there, Helen. And he promised he'd never do that again. I know it sounds silly, and the adult in me knows he had every right to step away and take the information in. He had every right to be upset by it, but it broke my heart. And that's something I can't handle from him. I haven't known him long. But I know he is the only person who has the ability to destroy me."

I stand with an odd resolve.

"Look, I better go. Get you back to your family, and he might be calling you. He might need you."

"Erika..."

"Erika, listen to me. You're going to get up, get dressed, hop a flight and I'll be there to pick you up from the red eye."

Archer doesn't sound too off with that plan.

"You're right. Blitzen has its Christmas fundraiser working out for the truck, I checked out Great Aunt Josie's spot, and I can just take myself home the same way I came here."

"That's right, Erika. Home to your best friend and Chicago, and don't forget your promotion—you'll be coming home to the

Harmon case. It's what you've pined for the last three years. Believe it or not—you have everything going for you."

"I have nothing going for me, Archer! This is the exact same position I was in when I sobbed on your tie and you passed me Josie's envelope. There, I was polka dots versus Ivy League. Here, I'm just some bored ad exec who forced Christmas on a small town and unhinged the widowed basketball coach's life."

"What did he say to you, Erika?"

"It doesn't matter, Archer. It's me. I'm the anomaly, I'm the mistake, or the fly in the ointment."

I look around my bedroom at Josie's. Somehow being downstairs didn't feel hidden enough. If there were chairs, and I knew the internet worked, I would truck to the attic. *And there it is:* There's no place far enough to hide from yourself.

"You are not the fly in the ointment back here at the firm. You're their prize pitch. Trust me. You need to read everything I sent over. They are desperate, to not only have you back to lead the account, but they want to promote you. I've been trying to tell you for days. Hell, they've put you above me on the account."

"Then that's another thing that shows their ignorance. Archer, it's too late. I don't want their second thoughts or to be sought after just because the results, data, or the client themselves finally made them see. Don't you get it? Someone else had to tell them. *They* didn't trust me. They didn't believe in me."

I drop my head and shake it back and forth. "Come to think of it, neither did you, and you're my biggest fan." I move to shut my laptop.

"Erika, wait."

THIRTY-NINE

4 Letter Words

"Woah. Look at that stubble you're growing there. I don't think I've seen you with a beard since—"

"Don't say it. There's been enough mention of her lately."

I drop my empty beer bottle on the coffee table and reach for another out of the pack beside me. Helen slams her keys on the bar and grabs something from my fridge.

"Kourt. You and I have always dealt in reality. I don't think two days before Christmas Eve is the time to stop. The reality is—nothing has changed. Nothing happened to change *anything*."

"No. Helen. The reality is, if Erika had gotten a fair crack at that pitch in the first place, she'd be living out her dream career job in Chicago, and I'd be coaching basketball and FaceTiming with my best friend, none the wiser."

"Oh, horse shit, Kourt. Erika *did* fail that pitch, or it failed her, and Josie had plans for her to be here. I know you find parts of my job silly, with the little estate details and people's quirky requests, but rest assured, Erika was going to make it to Blitzen by Josie's hand if I had to go get her myself. So be it the fickle finger of fate or of one Josephine Amherst—it was going to happen."

I chug my beer and pray Choi stops talking. I'm not even sure how she got in.

"I can't believe we're doing *what ifs*. We never do what ifs. What if Angie didn't take off that night, and you were still stuck in what ended up becoming a horrible marriage? And what if she eventually got so bored she did take Ellis up on his offer?"

"Helen!" I grit her name through my teeth, so I don't yell at my best friend.

"I'm sorry. I went too far."

"No. You don't get it, Helen. I went too far. I said things to Erika I can't come back from. Angie chose to get in that car and speed down the mountain, and I'll always blame myself, but I hope and pray a small part of me knows it *wasn't* my fault. I chose to let Erika down last night. That's on me. I just lost the best thing that's ever happened to me."

"What do you mean you lost? You two are so nuclear. Since she got here it's not a Christmas present, it's got to be a full-blown town Christmas fucking festival. It's not just a firetruck for the volunteer fire department, it's about property taxes that could destroy all of Blitzen. It's not an inconvenience to pick her up, it's the greatest thing that ever happened, that you can't be without, and this isn't even a fight that happened, but somehow it's the be-all end-all?"

"You don't understand. I love her. I love her so much, that I don't ever want to shut her out, and I fucking promised I would never do that."

"It's so new, Kourt. How would you have time to promise something like that?"

"That's just exactly what you don't understand. This isn't the moment where you're coming here telling me how good she is for me and 'get off the couch and shave.'"

My voice keeps getting louder. "She's too good for me! I let the anger and fear and fucked-up circumstances over that damn mixtape—over a couple of Christmas fucking songs— destroy what matters most to me in the world."

"Oh, my God, Kourt."

Helen plops down beside me with tears in her eyes.

"Okay, now don't you get all dramatic on me. I told you this already. What did you think I meant when I said that to you after the night we spent together?"

"I'm sorry, Kourt. Not all of us have had the phenomenon of that experience. Some of us just move home to help a best friend through a hard time, and neglect to notice they might be missing something big themselves."

Helen stiffens beside me.

"Goddamn it, Helen. I'm so sorry. I'm sorry I'm the shittiest friend alive. I'm sorry I haven't given back what you sacrificed for me, and that I never had this conversation with you in the first place. It should've also been about you when Angie died."

"It doesn't matter now. We're here. We made it this far."

"It does matter Helen, as much as anything else. I mean every word of it. And that's just the thing—I don't think I would have recognized how uneven our friendship is, if it hadn't been for her. She makes me see things differently. There's an entire world of possibility when you stop being complacent. She's that world. You've been trying to tell me that. To help me heal for three years, and I hid from all the good you tried to give. I'm sorry, Helen. I won't ever take advantage of your friendship again."

"Kourt. I don't know what to say."

"Say you'll let me do better, or I've lost the rest of what matters to me most in this world." I force her to make eye contact with me so she knows I mean it.

Helen flies off the couch and begins pacing in true Helen fashion. She came here thinking she'd get a sad stubborn sack, but I doubled, if not tripled down, and every bit of it is how I feel.

"Okay. Again, with the dramatics. But—Thank you, Kourt. It really means a lot what you just said. You... don't owe me an apology. You were that kind of friend to me when we were kids. You know you were. I was just returning the favor."

Helen spins on her toes and continues to pace. "As to your current love dilemma—since we're all saying that word out loud now. *Jesus.* Is this just because it's Christmas? Sorry. Don't answer that. You're serious for the first time in your life over something that matters to you, and that comment was pure jealousy. Moving forward, can you help me understand what was said better?"

I pull out another beer and hand one to Helen. She takes it. She's so desperate for alcohol at this point that even she'll consider carbonation.

"It wasn't just the tape. I think she has an opportunity back at the ad firm, and I know she needs to take it. It's not my business, so I couldn't really fish for too much. I just heard her buddy mention it on the Zoom."

"Archer?"

"Yeah. He seems to think she's got to come back for this. That they want her back. When she attributed our relationship to the tape, the fate and destiny and all the signs behind us meeting, I guess it scared me. Not in a crazy, eccentric fru-fru, Josephine Amherst way, but in a way that made me think she was relying on that to stay in Blitzen—or would rely on that to stay with me. And that song. My favorite. She was so emotional, she didn't even know what it meant to me."

Closing my eyes, I shake my head and take a deep breath. "I guess that scared me even more, because all that junk did feel real. Everything she was saying about the way we came together and experienced this. *Fuck.* I can't Helen." Our gazes catch and hold. "I don't want to talk about it anymore. I just don't want her missing the opportunity of a lifetime over track fucking four."

FORTY

Grand Gestures

If someone unexpected pounds on this door one more time, I think I'm diving off the mountain. There is a doorbell you know. At least, I think there is.

Ugh. I don't think I ever looked.

It would not be abnormal for Aunt Josie not to have a doorbell. I yawn as I swing the front door open.

"Okay, first, you're going to have to get dressed. Chop! chop! Let's get those perfect round tits of yours barricaded behind a bra, and how about some pants? Jeans are good, I know you own them."

Archer stands before me attached to a carry-on, with more luggage behind him, his eyes diverted from another one of Aunt Josie's vintage silk sleepwear sets I'm wearing.

"Apparently, she was a dish back in her day. And I find walking around *my* new home in these ensembles in minus whatever degrees outside, quite liberating. What are you doing here?"

"It doesn't matter what I'm doing here. What matters is that I am here, and I am not your gay bestie. I am your very heterosexual best friend who is not blind, so we will wear clothes in this house, Erika. Now, go get dressed while I unpack. Holy mother, look at this place."

"I know, right!" I call down from the loft as I remove my top and reach for a sweater.

"Doors. We're also doing doors, Erika. We will shut them when changing."

I practically slide down the spiral banister in my jeans and sweatshirt and peek behind Archer. He's staring into our Zoom through my laptop on the counter.

"Trying to see what happens when a tree falls and no one's there?"

"Yeah, actually, I've always been curious what it looks like when we go airplane mode."

"I can't believe you're here." I throw my arms around his neck.

"I can't believe I didn't come sooner." Archer clears his throat and moves away from me to his luggage. "So. Christmas!" He claps and rubs his hands together. "Blitzen and their firetruck and whatever we need to do to lock this place up for old Aunt Josie, and we're out of the snow globe, and back on the Harmon case."

Archer looks back at me to see if I'm on board. His sardonic charm fades to concern as my eyes water and I dive toward him.

"Oh, Archer. What am I going to do?" I hug my best friend tightly and try not to mess up his shirt. It probably cost more than his last-minute flight.

"You're going to pack your belongings, say goodbye to the locals, and get on a plane back to civilization with me." He says it in a low whisper in my ear, and I feel the foreign sensation of his hands tightening behind the small of my waist.

I guess the cocky bastard missed me more than I thought.

"This feels awful. It hurts. My stomach, my heart and soul. My brain hurts."

"Erika," he pulls my hands from behind his neck and steps away from me. "Is this—what is this about? Is this about the basketball coach?"

He sits on the edge of the couch, like he's got something to work out in his head.

I nod at him like a child who got caught doing something wrong. "Archer, I can't think or eat or sleep straight."

"Sleep straight?"

"You know what I mean." I sit beside him on the sectional.

"And here I thought we'd take in some local flare, maybe utilize the ice rental I sent, and be back before the office Christmas party."

"The office Christmas party's tonight."

"Like I said."

"Archer, I have obligations here. The way I see it, you came down to spend Christmas with me as originally planned. Don't you remember saying you would?"

"Fine. Let's backtrack and problem solve. It's what we do best. You're leaving Blitzen with me to be back for the Harmon account, like both our jobs depend on it—because they do. And in turn, hashtag, just because it's Christmas, I'm going to help you tie up your lose ends. Now, tell me what happened."

Archer's pacing in the living room like Helen does. I've never seen him so bothered. "Can you stop referring to it as mind blowing sex, or the best sex ever or the time you said he made you—"

"Sorry. You usually beg to know."

"Yeah, well. You usually don't have *that* much to report. I can see I've taught you well. Very well."

I shoot Archer the finger from the couch.

"There she is. Boy, I've missed you. So, getting back to that final night with the Ouija board Christmas music cassette tape—Hey... do you think it's the tape or is the Beetle possessed? Like it's got some less psycho, holiday version of a Stephen King's *Christine* car thing going on?"

"Is that a movie reference?"

"Not if you've never seen it." Archer dips his head defeated. "Sorry. Look, it's not like you broke up. Did you even have a fight? And were you two ever *really* together?"

I stare at Archer like a deer in the headlights. Or maybe I'm more of a raccoon caught digging through trash cans at this point. I'm grasping at straws to understand.

"He was stern with you, sure, but he was upset. And rightfully so. That's some heavy shit to unpack right here at the holidays. A couple of days before Christmas? That's an emotional peak for anybody. And it sounds like he wasn't as upset with you as he was the tape, or what you thought the tape meant, or what the universe made you think. I don't know, kid... from a male POV, he was mad at himself, not you."

"But, he left without saying goodbye or—"

"Did he call or text?"

"We don't really do the text thing yet, we just do—"

"Each other. Yeah. Got it. Loud and clear. Okay. Let's get to the bottom of this... You're not mad, just hurt, and disappointed?"

"Yes."

"And he might be mad, but from a female POV there's no fucking way he should be mad at you, as you did nothing wrong, and I've already assessed his end, so you two are in this weird limbo two days before Christmas waiting for someone to say something, or take off with me on a plane to go home to Chicago."

"Archer, no. But yes. I think that's it. At first, I felt there was no coming back from it, but that was because the emotion was so high over the wife element and the sad situation—"

"Do you... want to come back from it?" Archer's voice takes an earnest, inquisitive tone.

"I'm hurt deeply by his reaction. But I also don't see how he could have had a different one, under the circumstances. So, yes. If

I knew he wanted me, I don't see how I could not come back from it. Archer, what I mean is—I can't *not* come back from it. I can't *not* be with him."

I run my hands through my hair and leap off the couch. "Fuck, Archer. You're supposed to know what to do. What do you do when part of you wants to apologize, and the other part wants to run?"

"What would you be doing if there were no Kourt? Don't you have a Christmas festival to run? Isn't your best friend, who you've been dying to show around Blitzen, newly in town?"

My face lights up. "Actually, you and I aren't just downing hot chocolate and ice skating like teenagers, the town tree comes today. Decorating starts at one o'clock. We have to get it ready for the Christmas Eve tree lighting tomorrow night. I could really use your help."

"Let's start with a coffee, then head into town to see your Christmas festival."

Archer pauses and takes my hand. "Erika, people are like magnets. When one goes one way, the other follows, but when one does a complete flip, the other goes the opposite direction. It's the law of physics. I'm just saying, if someone turns and goes a different direction, you have no choice but to do the same. So, let's go to your Christmas festival. If he's there, he's there. He's not asking you to do or say anything. You do you."

FORTY-ONE

Signs

Walter calls me to come help with his twenty-five-foot tree. I say, "Yes," without hesitation. It's for her. It's for him. It's for the town. Exposing myself to town square and all the fucking festivities feels like Kryptonite without her.

But not knowing what she's thinking, or where she is, hurts just as much.

Putting one foot in front of the other to come what may is what has to be done.

All I want is for her to thrive in every way. If I've hurt her bad enough to send her straight back to Chicago to her ad agency, then that's what was supposed to happen.

If she's taking the opportunity to see her Christmas festival through, then she'll have her tree.

I'm sure Walter expects her here with me, but he's not nosey enough to ask.

We're trying to figure out if we can fit this sucker on his trailer without dragging the top of it, where it's thinner and could shed valuable branches. Or worse, break apart on our way in. The tree's every inch of twenty-five feet and the perfect shape.

"I left extra on the trunk thinking we might need it for balance, depending on the stand June wants us to use, but she's pretty even all the way around. I think we can go ahead and shave that extra off so we can haul her, without risking dragging the top."

"Let's do it." I hold the end up for Walter to slice the trunk.

He lifts his chain saw and gives it the smoothest shave imaginable. The man's got every tree trimming and pruning tool known to Christmas tree farms, and he uses this standard chain saw like an artist.

He could probably carve a ballet dancer's point shoe with that thing better than a shoemaker. His patience is unrelenting, and it's made him who he is.

We wrap the bottom back up so we can slide her back onto the trailer.

"Kourt, being sorry is poison. It's venom on the inside. The same as regret, guilt or hate. What's on your mind, son?"

"I'm not sure you have a sage antidote for this one, Walter. I don't think anybody would."

"Kourt, I didn't ask because I'm Cherokee. I can't read your fucking mind, son. I asked because I've known you since you were eight. You're only this quiet, with that look on you face, when something's troubling you, or you think you've done something wrong."

Walter offers me a cigarette.

I pass and light his for him. "Do you believe in signs, Walter?"

"Believe in them, or are you asking me if I think they exist?"

"The latter."

"Signs are everywhere, Kourt. In nature for all the animals, hell, at the car wash for people. Every turn we take in life has a different hill, lock, path, door, walkway, elevator, or waterfall. Each of those elements provide their own version of signs. Some of them are warnings that could save your life. Some of them are friendly reminders to stop and watch, enjoy, go the other direction, or do better next time. I don't think you're asking me if there are signs. I think you're asking me if it's okay to acknowledge them."

"Are you saying we go through life ignoring them?"

"Every second. We ignore them for selfish reasons, to stay on the path we want. Apathy or being complacent is so much easier than choosing to follow something that makes you do."

"Makes you do?"

"Yes, Kourt. You must always *do* something. It's the doing that counts, not the apathy."

I look at him like he just achieved world peace. "The doing."

"Your Erika asked me to open up my tree farm. Now all of Blitzen and surrounding counties have a beautiful live tree in their living room they experienced getting with their family. The fire department is that much closer to the firetruck. My people were heard by your people at the Calling of the Bears. And you and I are loading the biggest Christmas tree Blitzen has seen for a couple hundred smiling children and adults. It's the *doing*. Ignoring signs is fear, or worse. Apathy."

"Walter, I can't—"

"Do you love her?"

"Without a doubt."

"Then do something about it. The signs led you or her down a path. If you ignore them— you stop. It's not about believing in signs. It's recognizing them along the way. If you do nothing, you go nowhere."

Well, fuck me.

"That, and you're a fool if you fuck that up."

By one o'clock Walter and I have the tree set up, he's waving bye, and June and I are untangling the massive net lights. Once we get that thing draped across the tree, where we can reach an outlet, the hard part is done. It'll just be the fun of decorating the thing before tomorrow.

My heart thuds as I glance at the clock tower attached to the courthouse one more time. The hands seemed to have moved a little past one, and each minute passing makes me think she left. Or worse—she just didn't come.

A voice in the distance makes my pulse pick up. I'm behind the tree so I can't see her, but I see June's eyes light up when she does, and I maneuver as quickly as possible around the tree to put my eyes on her.

Shit. Dammit. Hell. *Fuck.*

What is that tool doing here? Erika's holding two hot chocolates while her Chicago buddy holds a turkey leg and a Christmas cookie, and the two of them look like they're about to go fucking caroling.

So—he flew down here then?

I gotta hand it to him. And according to Walter, he *did* something. I called it from the beginning. But he wouldn't be the person she thought he was if he didn't try, and I'm not worried. She's worth the friendly competition.

She's worth more than that.

I just have to remember, he's her friend. Her best friend. He's her Helen.

Keep telling yourself that, and you'll believe it.

My knuckles crack, I'm holding my fists so tight. Again, when this is over, and she's back in my arms, he'll still be the best friend. For her, I have to respect that.

"June, this is my best friend, Archer, from Chicago. He just flew down, and I thought we could put him to work."

"So nice to meet you, Archer. We'll take all the help we can get." June smiles up at him and he shakes her hand.

"He's the one who sent the skating rink," Erika announces.

"Well in that case, give me a hug, handsome!" June hugs the prick.

He's not a bad-looking guy, but I wouldn't throw around handsome. He's a walking GQ ad for the sole purpose of baiting women. He and Ellis should open up their own think tank.

"We can go pull all the boxes out—" Erika jumps right in.

"Kourt got them all a few minutes ago after he set up the tree," June explains boasting a smile, as I slide around the tree with a large ornament, and extend my hand.

"You must be Archer."

He looks me up and down before shaking my hand. I see his fucking jaw work when he notices I'm a lot taller.

"We should have a whole crew here before too long. Decorating's usually a favorite," June persists.

Blue eyes rise to meet mine and I realize, off June's words, I'm standing next to a bare Christmas tree with an ornament in hand.

The exact story I told her about Angie.

Erika's eyes water as she stares into mine—speechless. She's so hurt for me and worse—much worse—by me. I don't want her to ever feel that way. Not about her favorite part of the year, and what she's done here. And I don't want to ever hurt her like that again.

I extend the ornament in my hand to give it to her, as a pained smile invades my face.

Archer reaches out instead and swipes the big red diamond-shaped plastic between us. *Fucker.*

"And you must be the basketball coach. Heard you played a good game." Archer is as snarky and clever as they come.

Erika and I look over at him.

"The fundraiser, of course, with Jet Holloway. Nicely done."

"Thanks. It's ah, Kourt. Nice to meet you, man."

Before my eyes can find hers again, Helen trails the corner of the courthouse with a massive box. She marches up the steps in heels, and plops it down with the rest of the decorations.

"I'm so sorry in advance June. I know I've been little to no help, but mom made me bring these and just FYI, Rebbeca Choi is off her leash and out roaming the festivities with my grandmother. They're probably going to stop by to help decorate. I'm so sorry."

"Helen, I haven't seen your mother in ages. It'll be wonderful to catch up. You can tell her we have chairs back here, if your grandmother wants to sit and take a break."

"Thank you, June." Helen slides into our little circle in front of the tree, and it nearly kills me when I see her squeeze Erika's hand.

"Helen this is—" Erika nods toward Archer, but Helen's eyes are already locked on the guy. Even weirder, his are devouring her with a strange mix of alarm and excitement.

What the fuck?

Erika shifts uncomfortably.

June clears her throat. "Well, this is a peachy group, the four of ya. Either you slept together, one of you owes the others money, or two of you have a secret," June pipes in to state the obvious.

Apparently it's that there is an additional pink elephant in the group other than me and Erika.

"Nonsense. We just met." Helen chirps.

I'm with June. *Did they meet already? Because it looks like my best friend knows her best friend.*

I don't know this googly-eyed fuck, but I know Helen Choi.

"Oh, to be young again," June sighs and reaches for a box of large red bows.

A mic squeals, "Merry Christmas Blitzen!"

Mayor Harris calls out from the main stage. "Looks like our town tree decorating is well underway! And just a friendly reminder to get your tickets up front for tomorrow's Christmas Eve ceremony, when we'll light her up. Thank you all for your help and generosity!"

Car doors shut behind us and a slew of more people approach the tree.

Thank God—until, "McShotty! You owe me a date." My platinum blonde nightmare and food drive colleague ascends the courthouse steps.

"Nice work, buddy. Looks like you've got your Christmas dance card full." Archer says it loud enough for everyone's eyes to cut toward me.

I try to find Erika's.

"Erika?" A guy in a fitted Christmas sweater pokes his head around the corner, beaming.

Erika turns her attention to him. "Grinder Switch Coffee Press? Home of the Holiday Mountain Brew! I love your product and marketing." She beams back. "Are you setting up?"

"Yeah, actually, if I could pull you over about the slot we have. The guys just need to know the best way to face our ten-foot canopy, in case we end up with a line of people. Which way would you like our store front to face?"

"Oh, you'll absolutely have a line. Let's go take a look." And... she's off, leaving me with several pairs of eyes burning a hole through me, and I smell Kelsey's signature perfume far too close.

My head cranks slowly to the side to find her an inch away, staring up at me.

The only thing that could make this remotely better would be if all of Judge Angelina's hounds, pointers, and setters combined, were here. Barking. In unison. Racing to the tree to knock it down.

FORTY-TWO

Can't Walk Away

"**I** figured, Kourt. I'd have to be blind not to know." Kelsey's taking things better than I thought. "Can't blame a girl for confirming."

"I'm going to give you your money back."

"Kourt, I would *never*. It's for the firetruck."

"Then I owe you some lawn work."

Kelsey smiles graciously and shrugs.

An idea hits me. "Or, hey... what if I double the portion of the bet that covers the date, to send you and Trent out on the town?"

"Your assistant coach?"

"Yeah. It was basketball's contribution to the auction. He'd love to. I mean if—"

"Yeah, no—I mean, I would actually... really like that, too." Kelsey's smile grows slightly wider than the one she reserves for me.

Way to go Trent. Merry Christmas, buddy!

I slide away from Kelsey and the group of Blitzen faculty she's decorating with.

Helen and Archer are walking toward a booth together. They look deep in conversation. Odd. They're easily the same person, from what Erika tells me. I'm just curious what two strangers have to talk about.

Pulling my eyes from those two, I scan the grounds. Erika's nowhere in sight.

Fuck.

I know she's busy. It's the last day before Christmas Eve's town tree lighting—*Our Christmas*. It'll be our first Christmas together. My chest tightens at the thought of it.

But then, the possibility of not getting to be with her on Christmas... I stop in the middle of my town—the one she brought back to life, at the realization—the pain in my gut when I think of every Christmas after this one. Then I know what a part of me must've known since the day I met her. I don't ever want to spend Christmas without her.

It's dark out, and getting pretty late. Downtown's deserted when I pass through, heading to Erika's house. She's got to be home by now. We've been apart too long with no conversation, and this is an in-person one to have.

Pulling under her carport next to Helen's SUV, I spot Archer coming out to greet me.

This guy.

He buttons his coat and slides his hands into his pockets as he paces in front of the entrance, waiting for me.

"Couldn't stay away, huh?" His snark is as bitter as it is cold out.

"I could say the same thing to you." I prop my back on the front of the house beside him. Guess we're having a talk.

"How is she any different to you than the local yokels you date?"

"You know the answer to that, or you wouldn't be here."

"I came because of work. They were wrong and they want her back on the account."

"Didn't know what they had when they had it." I look him dead in the eye.

"They're taking her pitch. It's a massive career leap."

"That's not all you're here for."

Archer glares up at me, and for a second I see pain in his eyes. He's got it bad, or worse—he thinks he does.

"I've known Erika for four years. You've barely known her a month."

"And in four years what the fuck did you do about it? Make her feel like she wasn't good enough?"

Fuck this guy.

I step away from the wall, done with this conversation. He's not the one I want to talk to.

"She's everything, and you know it." Archer's voice slices through the cold air, and I consider whether I should leave it.

"Yeah, *I* do." I turn to face him. "That's the real difference between you and me, buddy." Staring down at him, my jaw ticks.

"She'll come back to Chicago with me, where she has a future. She sure as fuck doesn't belong here in Hicksville, USA. She belongs in a board room on the 30th floor in Chicago."

"Butt. Out."

"Wow. Impressive vocabulary," he hisses.

My eyes flare wide. "She's turned this town around in less than a month. Did you ever think it was her time in that pitch room, and it is now with me?"

Archer side-eyes me and blinks in thought. His hands leave his pockets and he scratches the back of his gelled hair and sneers. "Then why'd you leave her again?"

Because I had a fucking panic attack.

Couldn't breathe. Couldn't think for the ringing in my ears, the wicked memory washing over me. That tape. The one Angie threw at me the night she died—it had no place in my relationship with Erika.

"None of your fucking business, and I didn't leave her. I just had to catch my breath." I feel my pulse in my throat.

Is that what she thinks? That I left her?

"Right," he scoffs. "That, and you think you know her so well."

"I know how she makes me feel, and that's something you haven't come to terms with yet or didn't—until she left."

Archer's designer playboy image deflates, and I see a pissed-off, desperate man come at me.

Fuck. He's about to lose his shit.

Don't do it buddy. She's worth it, but you're not.

When this is all over, he'll be remembered as an overprotective best friend. I'll have mercy on him and not give him away. No need to add insult to injury and embarrass the guy, no matter how misguided his intentions are.

"And just how does she make you feel?" His face is three shades of red, and his temple is pulsing as he stops just short of being in my face.

I'm done being delicate. "Wouldn't you like to know."

Turning from him, I shake my head toward the door. If her best friend can't see it by now, I can't help him.

Or maybe that's the problem: He does.

As if I could say out loud how she makes me feel. As if I would fucking tell him.

Before her, my life was a succession of people who dread or fear the worst in life, me included. You take a problem and worry about the worst that could happen. Then in those rare moments of relief, when the something bad doesn't happen... most of us don't celebrate that good fortune. We go right back to stewing over the next problem. She's not like that. She's the relief. She's the moment when it all works out. And better than you anticipated... Erika is that all the time. I need that all the time. I want it. I *need* her.

He huffs out a loud breath behind me as I put my hand on the door.

"And just what do you think you're going to do? You're just going to walk in and get the girl?"

"I already have her. That's why you came. You're scared of losing her."

"Un-fucking believable. I know my best friend. If she needs anything right now, she needs space."

"Space my ass. Erika doesn't like it when I stay away from her for too long, and neither the fuck do I." I push through the front door with so much force it doesn't bother to close behind me.

A large, live Douglas fir stands in the corner where her silver tinsel tree used to be. My eyes shift to the loft, where the silver needles shine. A cabinet door closes in the kitchen and my eyes lock on Erika as she turns toward the living room with a tray of hot chocolates, a bowl of marshmallows and a spray can of whip cream.

She freezes.

Her hair is pulled up in a messy bun, showcasing her high cheek bones and beautiful neck, and her almost aqua eyes dance back at mine as our gazes catch and seem to cement in place.

A much longer beat than intended weighs down the room around us.

Finally, I move my mouth to speak. "You got a real tree."

"Yes." She nods without blinking or taking her eyes from mine.

"But how did you get it—" I lift my eyes to Helen as she crosses to the tree.

"There are pine needles covering every inch of my car's interior," she chimes in, the wound still very fresh.

"I'm sorry, Helen. I'm not the one who opened a window," Erika engages, almost robotically, her gaze still locked on mine.

"I'll buy you a new one." Archer's voice joins in as he closes the door behind me.

"Shut up, Archer." Helen barks as he moves toward the tree, where she lifts a string of wooden cranberries to untangle.

Erika and I stand frozen, ten feet apart while our best friends pretend not to know what's going on between us.

"I'm sorry," I whisper. Then clearing my throat, I speak loud enough for all to hear, "I can't explain it. I just... panicked. Guilt. Surprise."

My phone dings in my pocket and my eyes don't leave hers as it goes off again.

"I meant what I said that night. I just said it all wrong. The tape wasn't your fate, or destiny... it's mine. Mine to meet you. Fuck. I've fallen in love with you, Erika. I didn't think it could happen. To me."

Helen's phone dings in the background as I watch Erika swallow a shallow breath.

"I never felt this for Angie. Helen was right. We were just always together. Expected to be together. And maybe it's a sign, or fate like you said—but that tape brought you to me."

My emergency tone rings in my pocket as everyone's phones blow up with alerts.

"I know you have Chicago—"

"Kourt!" Helen tries to interrupt, but I don't let her.

"Just let me get this out!" I yell at Helen as I watch tears trickle down Erika's face.

"You think you love me?" she whispers.

"You know I do."

A loud thud interrupts everything as a travel trunk hits the entryway floor next to a pair of gold snakeskin pumps.

Our eyes trail up from the high heels to dark red hair and an even redder-lipped smile worn by one Josephine Amherst. Erika's great aunt's painted eyebrows lift in surprise as she surveys the situation.

"Oh my."

Helen ignores the front door and pushes her phone screen in my face, as my emergency line rings again and I answer. "Chief? What is it? I'm on my way."

My eyes shift back to her. "I have to go. There's a fire in Pikesville. All of Boonesborough County's been called in. It's the lumber mill." I pivot to head out.

"Be careful, Kourt." My best friend calls behind me.

"Yes, darling, do be careful." Josephine squeezes my hand as I pass, glancing back at a stunned Erika. Her eyes are wide and full of shock as I peel mine from her... and the front door closes behind me.

FORTY-THREE

Christmas Eve Eve

For a moment I can't breathe or move. My eyes shift to my exotic relation perched beneath her own doorway, and still nothing, as I blink up at Great Aunt Josie.

He said he's fallen in love with me.

Something stirs inside me, and I look around the room for shoes, my coat, keys—

A cool, boney hand attached to sharp, acrylic, mauve-colored fingernails squeezes gently into my forearm before I can take a step.

"Darling, is this any way to greet your presumed potentially dead great aunt?" She leans in and kisses my cheek.

"We figured you were still kicking due to the lack of paperwork, Helen's gag order, and your missing Range Rover." Archer tips his head in a nod toward my great aunt. He always did know how to speak Josephine Amherst.

He stares at me from across the room, and I feel the tension Kourt left in the air from the heat of his glare.

"Archer, darling. Come. Come." Aunt Josie throws her arms around his neck. "Whatever brought you to Blitzen?"

She's as coy as a cat as she glints her eyes my way then slaps Archer on the back of the head. "It took you long enough, my darling. Too long, I'm afraid. Did I just witness Kourt McClain declare his love to my great niece in my former living room?"

Aunt Josie turns her attention to Helen who is still reading her phone alerts.

"Helen. It's only been three days since we spoke, and the wheels have already fallen off." Josie sashays to Helen and, placing both hands on her cheeks, kisses her forehead. "Nice work."

Aunt Josie means it. She's not being facetious. The opposite game is her style.

Helen looks up from her phone to acknowledge Josie. "Trust me. It was all them. Those two are—"

"Made for each other." Aunt Josie claps her jeweled hands together and looks at me, her lashes high, and her eyes wide. "I knew you had it in you, duck. For some reason, you and I have never been able to participate unless it is a *great* love. I suppose we're rare that way. Or lazy. If it's not earth shattering—*why bother.*"

She smiles a crooked smile as Helen leaks out a small gasp behind us.

"How bad, Helen?" I don't recognize my voice as I demand answers, still ignoring Aunt Josie's antics. All I care about right now is the man who walked out that door.

"Erika," Helen turns her phone toward her, hiding the screen from me, and looks into my eyes with worry. "I know what you're thinking, but you can't get down there. The lumber mill is massive. It covers acres, and if these news reports are right—it's worse than you can imagine. You heard Kourt. They called in every fire department in the surrounding counties. There'll be a line for them to get through. We'll just be in the way driving down there."

"What are you even saying to me, Helen? You just told me that Kourt walked out of here to fight a fire that's worse than I can imagine."

"And why are you so upset about it?" Archer chimes in.

"Archer!" I can't even look at my best friend right now. He and Great Aunt Josie are about as warm and comforting as an iron gate.

"Aunt Josie." I run to her regardless. It's my last appeal, grabbing her boney, yet oddly strong arm. I shake my head. "Don't you know someone? Don't you know everybody? Can't you call, or—or get me to him? I have to be there. He has to know—that I—"

"That you what?" Archer's really pushing it tonight.

"Yes, darling. Use your words. You've always had an explicit vocabulary. I like to give our travels together credit. But I'm just an old woman reminiscing. Never mind you three. Chop. Chop. If you're hell bent on going after your hero, my little heroine, you're not going alone. And you sure as hell aren't taking the Beetle."

Aunt Josie makes a dramatic display of twirling solo to the door. Her gold wristlets jingle like Christmas bells as the charms clank together.

The woman looks like she robbed the store windows of Saks Fifth Avenue and an Arabian dancer back-to-back. "Come Helen, she must see this through. How I do love arriving in the nick of time."

None of us move.

We stare at her from our spots in the living room. She's bluffing. I know her. This is how she would say no to me as a kid. She pretends the world is your oyster, then makes you feel guilty for wanting to swallow it.

"It's too dangerous. For us and all the people trying to help." Helen serves it dryly, trying not to play into Josie's little scene. She must also know her all too well by now.

"Oh. Well, darlings, if Helen says we shouldn't, then we shan't. She's a smart woman that one." Aunt Josie tosses her coat back on the rack and ignores it when it doesn't catch but falls to the floor.

Archer runs behind her and hangs it up.

Sucker.

"In that case, we'll finish the tree and start from the very beginning. Oh, how we do seem to have so very much to catch up on. Where's the egg nogg?"

I glance over the three of them and I think I might crumble. Something sinks low in my gut. My pulse flipflops between heavy slow thuds and racing out of my veins. I've never felt this level of... *panic.*

"Erika, I think there's a box with icicles in the hall closet coming out of the loft." Aunt Josie all but demands and I trudge up the spiral staircase. "You should have seen the gold icicles on the tree in the lobby of the Four Season's Doha."

"Is that where you where?" I hear Archer below.

"No, darling. Not this time."

I roll my eyes as Aunt Josie's ambiguous answer fades in the background. She and I both love vintage icicles. Guess I adopted that from her. It's not a tree without that final touch. My heart thunders as I make it up the top step and land on the silver tinsel tree I moved up here to make room for the real tree. It's Kourt's tree. We had the same one, or strikingly similar as 1960's silver tensile style trees go.

"Helen," I yell down form the top step.

"Erika, it's only been five minutes. We made a rule. We're checking every twenty minutes."

My stomach swirls with warmth and butterflies when I think of standing by his tree and the glow of his fireplace just before he touched me in a way neither of us could come back from. I think I knew then that he loved me, but for him to say it out loud, tonight, in front of them... He means it.

Maybe the hurt of the mixtape was really embarrassment on my part.

I was humiliated that I thought it was mine when that couldn't have been further from the truth. It was just overwhelming in that moment. Here I've been fearing he walked away from me that night—when it might have been the one time I should have gone after him.

Now, I can't. I can't even tell him I love him back.

He was my everything before I mentioned that damned mixtape, and now he's walked away from me yet again. What if that's the takeaway or the real sign… that it wasn't my tape or destiny and this is the third time he's left me standing somewhere speechless.

"Hey." Archer stands behind me. I didn't even hear him come up the steps.

"I know this is bad timing, but the trouble is, it's never been the right time to bring it up. Can we talk about work?"

"Archer. I know all about it. They emailed me. Multiple times. There's a reason it's never the right time to talk about it. I don't think that job is right for me anymore."

"Right. Because of him. What? Are you going to hole up here in the Appalachian Mountains and make jam, or start an opioid addiction?"

"This has nothing to do with him, or Blitzen. It has everything to do with me."

"And what do you mean, they emailed you? Did they renege on the deal?"

"They doubled their offer."

Archer falls to his knees and fake begs. "Then what's the fucking problem?"

"Archer, I think you're missing one inherent point that must mean more to me than it does to you. *They didn't want me.* They didn't believe in me. They didn't *trust* that I could do the job."

"Erika, people don't always see things right away. Maybe they have to get used to it, or think about it a little longer, before it hits them over the head like a brick and they—" He turns away from me. "They fly out from Chicago to bring it back." He mumbles incoherently.

"What did you say?"

"I'm saying this happens all the time, especially to people's careers. You've got to work, right?"

"Yes, Arch. It does happen. But it happened to me one too many times, and I don't need them to work. Look at the two of us. You're talking about the longest running Zoom meeting of all time. I can work from home, from—"

"Here?"

"Well, yeah. If I want to."

"Do you think you might want to? Is that what this is about? Him?"

"No Archer. It's about the fact that I don't have to prove myself to them to be successful. I can apply for a job at a place that values what I bring to the table."

"What about me?"

"What about you, Archer? Do you really need the firm to know your worth? I know you don't need their money."

"Says the one who just got an email that most likely makes her my boss on the Harmon account."

"Archer, you've brought in more accounts than Sloan. We could open our own company. I'm just saying. I don't need to be with anybody that didn't want me in the first place."

"Icicles darlings... the Douglas fir is waiting!" Aunt Josie interrupts from below.

I pass Archer to grab icicles from the hall closet. "You coming?"

I look over my shoulder.

Archer's hands are stuffed in his pockets and he seems deep in thought. "Yeah."

He sounds defeated.

But he has to know, I gave my all to that firm. I have nothing left for them. I place a heavy foot down on the first step of the spiral staircase. Something hits me I can't quite place.

"Archer." I turn on the step to face his direction, my hand on the rail to head down. "Thank you."

"For what?" His hands stay in his pockets as he brings his face up inquisitively, to meet mine.

"For being here." I blink back at him and really look at him. "For knowing I needed you."

"You need me?"

"Always. You're my best friend."

Archer's face looks back at me, hopeful, and almost pained.

I smile up at him as I take the next step down. I've never been so grateful to him.

"Erika?"

I stop once more on the next step. "Yeah?"

The pause lasts longer than it should with additional silence from downstairs.

"Merry Christmas."

"Merry Christmas, Archer." My smile almost hurts my face. It's the biggest smile I've released since the night of the mixtape.

He'll never know how much it means to have him here with me in Blitzen to experience all of this. My emotions already heightened, I take to the curve of the staircase.

Helen's staring blankly at her phone as I reach the bottom. My heart plummets to my feet.

"Tell me,"

Helen shoves a local news feed in my face.

"It's not him, I promise. He's not one of the injured. I'm calling the chief's wife to prove it to you."

My alarm goes off, and I recognize my normal wake-up hour set for Christmas Eve and today's events. My stomach aches and growls and I squint when the sun shines through the living room window across the sectional where I apparently fell asleep.

How could I fall asleep?

Archer's snoring on the other end, and quite nearly a thousand text notifications fill my phone, from *Merry Christmas* to *Have you heard anything from Kourt?*

I blink my eyes open to clear the fog and zero in on one particular notification for a local news article.

Boonesborough County Lumber Mill fire is coming into containment this Christmas Eve morning with three firefighters in critical condition at Pikesville Regional. It's not known what fire departments the victims are from. Their identities have not been released. There is no word on just how much damage has been done to the lumber mill.

I fly off the couch like a psychopath who just heard Kourt's name listed among the three.

Calm down.

If it was one of our guys, the chief's wife would've called us by now.

I'm met with a fully dressed-to-the-nines Aunt Josie as my socks slide me into the kitchen. A drink holder of iced coffee sits sweating on the counter, and her stiletto nails crack a raw egg into her juice glass. She's wearing a full face of makeup.

Just as my worried mind tries to distract itself with some sarcastic thought about her waking up at four in the morning to shellac foundation on with a butter knife—her signature scent assaults my senses. I don't know exactly what kind it is, I just remember playing with the bottle when I was a little girl. Something with Caesar and pheromone in the title, and to my dismay, the decadent, overpowering scent of what gold should smell like consumes me.

Overwhelmed with emotion and the precious memories of my bold Great Aunt Josie in all her infamous glory, I lunge toward her and throw my arms around her.

"Oh, Aunt Josie—" My tears stain the collar of her blouse, and she doesn't flinch, but pulls me closer to her swan-like neck.

"*'Put your arms around me and hold me tight!'* It's what you used to say to me when you were a child. You all but demanded it when you'd beg to sleep with me and stay up late to watch old movies." Aunt Josie strokes the back of my hair. "Rapunzel was your very favorite fairy tale, and you must have made me read it a million times. It's still in your trunk, you know. The one we bought at the estate sale and had it refinished in fabrics from India."

I sniffle and try to stop from shaking, as the tears continue to fall. I haven't hugged her for this long since I was a child.

"You had such an imagination, my brave little doll. I could take you everywhere and you thrived, but I also watched you when we went nowhere. How inventive you were to play alone, this only child who came with her own source of built- in entertainment. I always felt you had something in you I didn't. I envied your ability to take flight or stay put, your laughter in rain or shine. I seek that my darling—that magic you possess."

She lifts me away from her. "There, there. No shame in tears. Anything worth anything at all has to be worth a tear or two."

"I've missed you so. Why did you bring me here?"

"Three things, duck. I'm more impressed by you than proud. That's saying a lot, because I've always been and couldn't be prouder of you. You have exceptional taste. I knew you'd turn heads in Blitzen, but to turn *that* one, as well as having that handsome Chicago head doing a double take? You are no longer my prodigy with men. You are my sensei."

She takes my face in her hands as she did Helen's last night. "That being said, I hope you learned the intended lesson: You, my beautiful great niece, are a big fish no matter the pond you swim in. I pray you won't forget that. I had an attic full of Christmas décor and the town had a storage busting at the seams with lights. They sat dormant for a decade or more, until my own flesh and blood came, saw, and *conjured*."

She raises her glass of raw egg to me in a toast and swallows.

I want to ask her everything.

Did she plan me and Kourt?

Is this still my house? Was it a gift or a loan?

Did Helen have something to do with it? What exactly is Helen's job description?

And... Where the hell has she been?

If I know my great aunt, I won't find out where she was until she wants me to.

Instead, I muster, "Have you heard anything?"

"Ah. You're just like your father in that regard. A one-track mind in matters of the heart. Not yet, but hopes are high."

"And the third thing?"

"Oh, yes. I bought caffeine, but you simply must shower and dress first. I love you darling, but you look dreadful. I can't have you greeting Blitzen's most eligible bachelor you snagged looking like that. Now, get dressed. It's Christmas! And wash your hair. He's the one who's been putting out fires. Not you."

FORTY-FOUR

A Blitzen Christmas

It truly is Christmas Eve in Blitzen. Finally. The holiday festivities we launched are moving full speed ahead, and I can't count the smiling faces on both children and adults. People started ice skating early this morning and every hour more vendors are arrive to set up.

This is the big day. The lighting of the town tree. Hopefully, a day they will all remember when they're home in front of their own trees tomorrow.

I'd be touched if I wasn't so sick at my stomach from worry.

I can't believe I fell asleep. Exhaustion must've set in.

Much worse, I can't believe I haven't heard from him.

The thoughts of not even receiving a text are triumphed over by the fact that he and I have never texted. It was always a call or in person. Yet, still, with every text notification I try to manifest: *It's me. I'm safe.*

Or at least a godforsaken thumbs up emoji by Kourt's name.

Going about my duties, I watch the clock tower like a hawk. One tedious hour after another. Morning becomes afternoon.

Still... no Kourt.

I grab my phone for the fifteenth time to search for Sharletta's number. As if I can't fathom I don't have the chief's wife's number saved in my phone. As if I think it will miraculously pop up and she'll text me: All is well with the Blitzen fire department.

The band plays enthusiastically behind me. It feels like *Jingle Bell Rock* and *Rocking around the Christmas Tree* are on a loop, even though I'm sure I've only heard them once. A crowd is gathered in front of the stage where the band plays, and the smell of hot apple cider drifts my way. The air is crisp, the sky blue—perfect Christmas weather.

I take a deep breath and the notes of cinnamon and clove lift my spirits enough to smile at the lovely friends I've made in town. Walking through the crowd— greeted by name, by one person after another, it occurs to me... I've made more friends in one month here in Blitzen than in four years in Chicago.

I'm so proud they're enjoying it all.

Keeping busy with idle tasks, I make my way toward the tree to store back-up extension cords under the tree skirt for tonight—the Christmas-colored extension cords.

My shoulders sink and I shake my head.

Kourt drove me to Fisher's that first time to get them.

That feels a lifetime ago now. Less than one month and that man changed my world.

Helen and Archer are headed toward me after helping a vendor set up for me.

She doesn't look frantic or upset, I clock, as I watch them walk my way. I keep hanging on to her words. *"I'm his emergency contact. If it's him, we would've been notified. He's not one of the three."*

A horn honks twice and the sirens pick up as Blitzen's fire truck pulls into the lot.

Everyone rushes to greet it. My breath catches.

The applause grows so loud as I look for his face but don't see it. Chief Johnson leaps from the old truck with the rest of the firefighters. Mayor Harris strides to the stage and silences the band as he ushers the chief onto the stage to take the mic.

His salt and pepper hair is almost completely black with soot, yet I've never seen the man smile so big. He races to the mic and waves.

"Ladies and gentlemen. All of you fine people of Blitzen, and wherever you hail from in Kentucky..." He stops the crowd with his declaration and out of breath puffs into the mic. "Merry Christmas, and please know, thanks to all of your efforts and support, we've saved the mill. There's a lot of repair, and some loss for Boonesborough County, but not all is lost."

The crowd roars.

"And Blitzen, thanks to these fine firefighters who saved lives and livelihoods—Thanks to you fine folks who rallied—"

A growing applause erupts near the parking area where the fire truck rolled in, as three men hop out of a familiar pickup truck.

Exactly... He's one of these three.

I wipe the tear that splashes down my cheek at the sight of Kourt walking toward town square. He's covered in soot, dressed in his bunker pants, suspenders, and a Blitzen Volunteer fire department T-shirt.

"And thanks to one Erika Amherst over here who gave us the means to persevere—Blitzen has gained! Let that be the last run of the old fire truck, as we've already raised more than enough to buy the new one!"

Chief yells into the mic, and people cheer back so loudly I hear nothing but white noise as I weave my way through the packed crowd toward Kourt.

I nearly crash into him as arms wrap tightly around my waist and bring me into the most glorious smell of smoke I've ever encountered.

"Erika." Kourt looks into my eyes as he holds me in place. I can't seem to catch my breath. I don't know whether to laugh, cry, or wrap my arms around him.

He hoists me higher, holding me. Tighter. He pulls me closer to him before I can give it a second thought, and I bury my face into his smoke and soot-coated neck. "You're here. You're really here."

I say it as if I'm awake and alert for the first time since he charged into my house with his declaration.

"Does this mean you think you love me too?" Kourt smiles like he's lassoed the moon.

I pull away from his neck to look at him. There's a pause as our eyes become submerged into each other's. The mic on stage squeals, and I'm taken out of the trance of Kourt, to peek back at the gawking stage and crowd below it.

Shaking my head at our audience, I lift my eyes back to meet his.

He raises a challenging eyebrow.

My brow arches to match his as my gaze fixes on him. "How do I know you won't walk away from me again?"

Kourt's eyes roam my face, wildly chasing the answer, as he lowers me to the ground.

A beat goes by, and I shrug with a coy grin, pivoting away from him. I take a step and a half toward the eavesdropping crowd when his voice fills the space between us.

"Marry me and find out."

I stop, frozen in my tracks.

The crowd around me is stunned as silent as I am. A gust of crisp wind blows a piece of hair by my face and I dip my head basking in the shock. *Guess he got me there.*

The clock tower chimes above town square, indicating the hour.

"You heard me. Marry me."

The clock chimes again as I turn to face him, my eyes bright with a hint of realization.

"It's three o clock, Kourt."

"Is that a yes?"

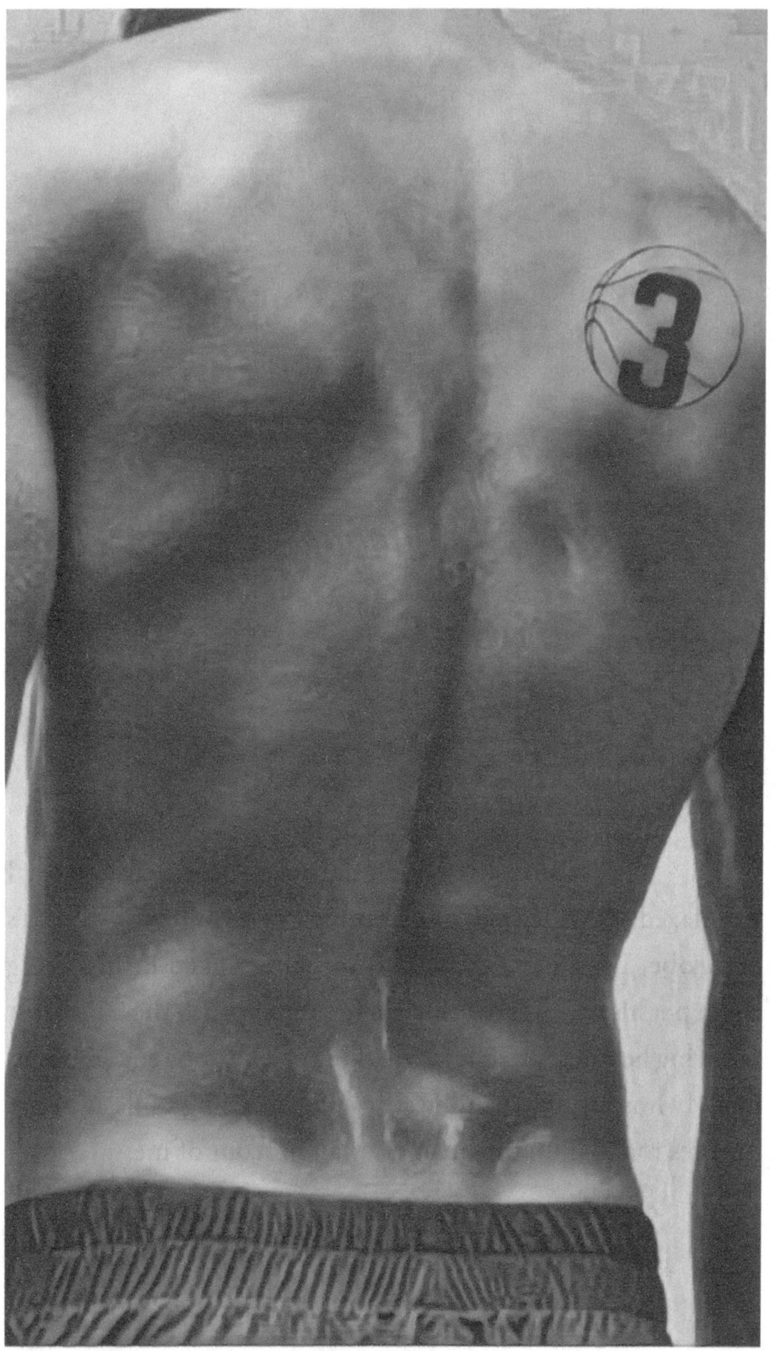

Epilogue

December 28th

Nestled on his couch across from the fireplace, I sit relaxed, cross legged, and propped on a pillow in Kourt's bathrobe. I'd think I'd be used to being naked in his living room per his rule, yet my skin tingles underneath the fabric just knowing he's nearby. The smell of him on his robe encompasses me. My nose crinkles, and I try to hide my rising smile as I keep my eyes focused on the business plan in front of me.

This is the first moment we've got to come up for air from all the Blitzen Christmas festivities, celebrating with Great Aunt Josie, and a shell-shocked Helen and Archer.

After fulfilling his promise to me of the infamous bacon and eggs breakfast we had yet to have until this morning, I sit across from Kourt, prepping my proposal for Archer.

The email suggesting I'll happily return to the Harmon account, only on my terms... remotely, and hired freelance for my special skills and contributions that will be sourced outside of Sloan and Swartz' jurisdiction, as I no longer work under them, went out to the firm earlier.

They may say no to my terms, but I'm okay with that outcome.

I've already garnered several of my own accounts to pitch Archer from Kentucky Bourbon Fruit Cake, Grinder's Switch Coffee, and Bob and Georgia don't know it yet, but a Blitzen-themed Old Fashioned Hardware Store toy line is about to be pitched to dawn its own spot in department stores every Christmas.

That should bring some residual income their way if we can brand them and I can initiate specific toy makers to sell under our umbrella. For a big enough retail spot in high traffic stores, it's a no brainer. I draw an arrow to a pitch graph listing the potential brands for the toy line then smile again at the thought of a little piece of our Blitzen Christmas on display across a few surrounding states.

My eyes trail up the tall specimen seated across from me. Kourt's sitting naked in a chair in front of the fire marking up his basketball game schedule for the new year. My teeth chew the inside of my cheek as I notice how handsome he looks in reading glasses.

This is the first time I've ever seen him so still, focused and studious. A foreign rhythm highjacks my pulse and something deep inside me feels more invested and more at home than I have ever felt before. This moment, this morning, is ours, with many more like it to come.

The fire crackles in the silence behind him, and Kourt's eyes rise from his coaching schedule to meet mine.

"What?" He smiles dubiously.

It's contagious and my cheeks nearly meet my ears before I hide my face with my knees.

"It's a yes, isn't it? That's what." Kourt rises and crosses over to me.

Good God, he's as hard as rock already. I love how attracted he is to me. How erect he gets just watching me smile or listening to me speak. He sinks to his knees in front of me and pulls my legs away from my face. His fingers trace lightly down the inner flesh of my leg from my knee to my thigh and back up again. The robe parts down the middle, as he focuses his hazel greens on my eyes. They speak of a thousand obscenities, pure love, and curiosity at the same time.

"I got you didn't I?" His voice is smooth and certain.

"Um-hmm." I nod with a sly confirming smile I make no attempt to hide.

"Don't think I won't make you say it, and loud and clear. But first we have to get dressed."

"And break your rule? So soon?"

"Um-hmm." He slowly puts my robe back together neatly. "I know there's a lot of things that could feel rushed about this, but

I want to make sure the things that matter, don't. I looked up your mom's holiday book club cruise from where she left out, and discovered they were returning today. They actually docked yesterday and stayed at a hotel for a book-signing and then all planned to fly back home from there."

I shake my head at Kourt in disbelief.

"So, I was able to get in touch with your mother at the hotel yesterday, and she agreed to let me fly her to Blitzen instead. I figured you two missed Christmas together... maybe the three of us could ring in the new year. At least, I would like that very much. I'd be honored to meet and get to spend some time with her. I thought maybe you'd want to show her what you did here in Blitzen. Get a little Christmas with her in before all the decorations come down. It's still Christmas in Blitzen until the first week of January. That's what your brochure says."

"Kourt." My eyes sting with tears as I try to find the words to thank him... to let him know I can't even fathom how thoughtful this is. How he remembered me telling him about her.

"I hope it's okay I reached out—"

I peel my robe apart and it falls from my shoulders as I rise to my knees on the couch, pulling Kourt to me. My mouth covers his and my tongue is not gentle as it demands his lips open to me. Inching to lay back, I drag him down on top of me.

"You're going to make me look bad if we're late picking her up," he mumbles as he fights to free his mouth from mine. He's making attempts to resist, but he's perfectly lined up to my entrance, his swollen cock nudging to be inside me.

"Baggage claim," I whisper in his ear. "She'll have a lot of luggage."

"So, what do you think?"

"It doesn't matter what I think, Erika... only how you feel." My mom looks me over and her eyes dance back at me. She hasn't stopped looking at me like this since Kourt dropped us at Josie's for some girl time. "That said—when's the wedding?" she asks without further hesitation.

"Mom?"

"You're absolutely glowing, Erika. At no point in Chicago or on a visit home from the city have I ever seen you lit up from head to toe like this."

"I haven't officially said yes yet."

I try to play coy before I clasp her hand and mask a squeal. "One year from today."

Excitement flashes in her eyes. "Christmas time seems quite appropriate for you two. That gives you a year to work out any kinks. And, by the way, I fell in love with him, too. From his first phone call tracking me down. He told me all about what my daughter's been up to in Blitzen."

She bounces a ponytail's worth of hair behind my shoulders and smooths it out as she looks me over again. "I can't say I'm surprised... just so proud and happy for you. Lucky. I feel lucky and grateful that you found such love. So glad you both recognized it."

"I couldn't have run from it if I tried."

"I'm more pleased than you know to be invited to share New Year's with you two."

That makes me smile, remembering how Kourt and I met. My life has been a whirlwind from the moment our eyes connected, and somehow, my mother just gets it.

Aunt Josie clears her throat.

"You too, Josie. I'm excited to spend time with you also," my mother placates.

Patting the sofa, Josie rolls her eyes. "Enough sentiment, you two ducks come talk with me. We have things to iron out." She lasers her focus on me. "Who's your Maid of Honor? Helen?"

I have to laugh. "No. Archer, of course."

Mom curves a brow, exchanging glances with Aunt Josie.

I give them a chin tilt. "He's my Man of Honor. Just as Helen is Kourt's Best Woman."

Josie sets her teacup on the table. Mom cooly slides a coaster underneath it.

"Speaking of ironing things out... those two? Have they come clean yet?"

I know exactly what she means, I just don't know what about. They spent Christmas Day as if we were all oblivious to their secret glances.

"What's this about Arch?" Mom leans closer, holding her teacup to the center for Aunt Josie to refresh her cup. The teapot is closest to Aunt Josie, after all.

In true Josephine fashion she misses the appropriate cue and plops two sugar cubes in mom's cup, knowing my mother has never taken sugar in her tea her entire life. I rush to answer, before Aunt Josie gets bored and stirs it for her with her stiletto acrylic pointer finger.

"I haven't pried it out of Archer yet, and Kourt says Helen's mum. But we agree—something is up between them. They've met before."

Josie lets out a shrill, vocal sigh the length of her leather-coated ballerina neck. "They've more than 'met' before, darling."

"Why do you say that?"

"Trust your Aunt Josie. You wait and see. There's more to that story."

CURIOUS
ABOUT

Helen & Archer?

their story...

Liberty Stowe

about the
AUTHOR

Liberty Stowe is a Contemporary Romance Author who hit the map with her debut Small Town Romance, *Steady Now.*

Still dancing at the Pink Pony Club or home, visiting... rocking on her grandparents' porch swing. With a heart split between the Piney Woods and the Hill Country, her mind often wanders to the footprints she left across West Texas and the nails left in the walls of all her Manhattan, Birmingham, and LA apartments. Love life: A Lana Del Ray song about Video games and Diet Mountain Dew, and a handmade spoon ring that could never truly be misplaced. If her books had a voice... Yola or Sierra Ferrell. And there's never enough time to throw the dog his ball as many rounds as he wants or to water all the flowers she'd like to grow. **TikTok/Instagram: @authorlibertystowe**